SECRETS
OF THE RIVER

BY

CAROLINE LUDOVICI

Copyright © 2014 by Caroline Ludovici

ISBN 978-1-4958-0346-8
ISBN 978-1-4958-0347-5 eBook

Published December 2014

INFINITY PUBLISHING
1094 New DeHaven Street, Suite 100
West Conshohocken, PA 19428-2713
Toll-free (877) BUY BOOK
Local Phone (610) 941-9999
Fax (610) 941-9959
Info@buybooksontheweb.com
www.buybooksontheweb.com

For Natasha and Alex

The Trebbia River, Italy
Spring 1945

The Decision

"Quickly! Quickly, Johann, hide in here! You'll be safe here, no one will find you down by the water's edge."

Still panting, and trying to catch his breath after scrambling down the hill, he bent down and peered into the weathered shelter that cut into the side of the steep riverbank. He hesitated before he entered, wondering if it really was safe. The doors had long gone, but their rusty hinges still dangled loosely from their posts. It smelled damp and musty inside.

"Johann, it's OK, go on! Just go in!"

He turned and glanced at her.

"Go on, go on, get in, quickly!" she insisted, almost pushing him. Her eyes darted up river, then behind her to check they hadn't been seen.

Taking a deep breath, he lowered his head and stepped into the boathouse. Something scuttled across the far end of the shelter and disappeared into the darkness.

Once inside, she relaxed a little.

"You'll be quite safe here, I used to play in here as a child with my brothers; it's all solid stone," she said, slapping the damp wall to prove it. "It used to be the old boathouse to the derelict castle on the hill above us. It hasn't been used in a hundred years or more."

"It will be fine," Johann said, flicking the cobwebs out of his hair. He looked around, still breathing through his mouth because of the acrid smell. "It is fine, Bea. Really, it will be a good place to hide. Thank you."

He forced a smile.

"The river can rise quite high when it rains," she continued, "but look, you'll be able to stay dry at the back; the little pebbles have formed a slope, see? It's a little higher towards the back wall."

He nodded. His head was still spinning at the thought of what he was doing. He could hardly think straight. He prayed no one had seen them. But only time would tell.

"Here, quickly, put these on," she was saying, opening his duffle bag that they had brought with them. "Give me your uniform. I'll take it back and bury it."

She spoke faster than usual, momentarily forgetting his Italian was far from fluent. But he managed to understand most of what she said, and he started to undo the buttons of his jacket as fast as he could.

"Burn it!" he said, ripping it off. "Don't bury my uniform, Bea, just burn it, or it could be found by the dogs."

His German accent was thick, and it reminded her to speak a little slower and clearer.

"I cannot burn it, Johann. It is far too dangerous. The smoke would draw attention, and there is always evidence left in the ashes after a fire has burnt out; The leather boots, the buttons, look; this hardware on the jacket... and then what about the helmet? It would look too suspicious if it was found half burnt." She sighed, looking at the helmet. "We should have left this at the house, I'll have to bury everything, it's the only way."

Johann looked at her then sat down heavily on a piece of driftwood. He detected the worry in her voice although he knew she was doing her best to sound confident and upbeat. What had he done, putting their lives at risk like this? He wondered if they would ever get away with it.

Since the shocking news of Hitler's suicide a couple of days previously, Johann's superior officers had received orders to evacuate the area immediately. The entire German army was retreating from Nazi occupied Europe; they were now heading home, fast. Johann's commanding officer, Heinrich Streuber, was no exception. He had wasted no time in packing up his belongings and then systematically helping himself to everything of value from the house that was removable, portable and able to fit in the car. This even included the silver cutlery service and many of the oil paintings that the Italian owners had tried unsuccessfully to hide in their basement before they had been forced to leave their home at the beginning of the occupation.

Johann had watched Streuber as he had calmly and methodically taken the paintings off the walls, carefully prised the canvasses from their heavy guilt frames and then rolled them between layers of newspaper. Johann couldn't help looking at his commanding officer in disgust when he realized what he was doing. For the first time, he saw Streuber for what he really was; a thief. He couldn't believe it. Any admiration or respect Johann had had for him over the past year or more, had disappeared in an instant.

"What are you looking at, Fuchs?" Streuber had demanded when he noticed Johann watching him pack away a large, heavy canvass scroll on the back window ledge of the car.

"Nothing, Herr Commandant, sir, I was wondering how I could assist you, sir," he lied.

Streuber stood up straight, stretched his back and thought for a moment.

"Well, since you have asked, Fuchs, that nauseating-looking 'Rococo' fresco on the ceiling in the dining room has always annoyed me, with its revoltingly chubby cherubs floating in the over-stylised clouds, and those ridiculously precocious Latin words of wisdom beneath it. It's so faded now anyway, the whole thing should all be re-plastered and repainted. So I'd like you, Fuchs, to help the returning Italian homeowners begin the restoration process for them. Bring the plastered ceiling down completely."

"Sir?" Johan wasn't sure if he had properly understood the order.

Streuber grinned to himself, continuing to hastily pack his booty into the back of the car. Two other officers, also stationed at the house, were packing their acquisitions tightly into the front and back seats from the other side. They smirked as they squeezed themselves into the tightly packed car.

"I will be leaving now, Fuchs," Streuber said, over his shoulder, "so your valuable contribution could be seen as a parting gesture, you might say; the compliments of the Third Reich!"

Johann noticed the smirk at the corner of Streuber's mouth. He hated him. He knew that he had been ordered to destroy the medieval ceiling, but he pretended he hadn't understood.

"…Sir?" he repeated, as he held the car door open for Streuber to get in.

"You heard me," he said dryly. "Get to it. It's an order."

Streuber squeezed into the back seat, arranging and pushing the bundles around him so he and his fellow back passenger could be more comfortable during the long journey home. They had, Johann noticed, even helped themselves to the ornate, sixteenth century gold chalice and candlesticks from the little private, family chapel that was tucked away on the edge of the property. There were large packages piled on the seat between the two of them, and even more bundles wrapped in blankets and sheets on the ledge behind them and at their feet. Johann couldn't believe it. He tried not to look shocked. Is this what the honourable German Army had been reduced to?

"I shall listen for the sound of your fire, Fuchs, it shall be a sweet melody to my ears as I drive off the property for the last time."

Johann gave a nod to indicate he had understood the order, and shut the car door for his commanding officer for the last time. He stood back on the steps of the house, and as the engine started up, Streuber rolled down the window.

"Now *GO* Fuchs! It is an order! Heil Hitler!"

Johann stood up straight and saluted his commanding officer, and with a crisp click of his heels, he turned and went up the steps and into the house as ordered.

Once out of sight in the hallway, he hesitated then, stopped. Through the open, double doors he could hear the dull, popping sound of the tires rolling over the gravel as the heavy, overloaded car rolled away. He peered through one of the little round windows beside the front door. The car circled the old, crumbling, fountain for the last time before it turned away from the house and slowly rolled away up the long driveway. Flanked on each side by ancient statues and poplar trees, the car seemed to quietly float away into the distance, in and out of the stripy shadows, running the gauntlet of gods, emperors and trees. At the top of the driveway, Johann watched as it stopped. The gates were opened, the driver hopped back in, and then it was gone.

And that was it. Silence.

Johann stood there, incredulous. He was alone. Just him, the crickets and the empty house. "That it," he had muttered to himself. "There're gone."

It was over. His war was over. As quickly, and as simply as that.

That had happened this morning, and by now, Johann surmised, Streuber and his fellow officers would be somewhere near the foothills of the Alps, and well on their way home to Germany. He felt resentful that he and Otto had been stranded at the house without so much as a second thought; left behind to find their own way home by whatever means they could. What a mess, he thought. Men were only men, beneath it all; regardless of the powerful uniform they happened to be wearing.

He wondered how far away his friend Otto had managed to get by now on foot. He hoped he had found a bicycle, which had been in his plan. But Johann knew that finding a bicycle until he could hitch a lift with other soldiers fleeing north, wouldn't necessarily guarantee a safe journey home; the towns were becoming dangerous, and the countryside and rural villages even worse. Word had it that British Special Units had been parachuting into Italy over the past few days to help the partisans, supplying them with guns and ammunition, which they were now using to pick off the departing Germans like flies. And worse still, the bulk of the American and British forces were only two days away to the south. Even if he had decided to leave with Otto this morning and they did eventually manage to reach Germany, Berlin, his hometown was now apparently surrounded and cut off. So heading for Berlin was not a wise option, anyway. Had he left with Otto, he wouldn't have known where to go.

Johann sighed. The more he thought of his situation, the more he realized he really didn't have a hope in hell. Leaving Italy was dangerous, but staying was just as bad. But he loved her, and he was ready to risk everything to be with her, as she was now doing for him.

"I do love you, Bea," he said, standing up so she could thread the string through the loops of his newly acquired trousers, "and I appreciate the terrible risk you are taking to hide me, and to be with me. I worry about what will happen to us both…"

"They are a size too large," she quickly interrupted, "but the string will help keep them up."

"You are risking your life, Bea. I can not believe you are doing all this for me."

Still, she ignored him.

"Bea!"

She stopped threading his make-do belt and looked at him. She thought for a moment before she spoke. She couldn't keep her guard up any longer, and spoke tenderly.

"Johann, listen; from the moment I first saw you, driving the officers through those gates, I knew you were not one of them. I knew you were different, you weren't like them..."

"Why? Because I was only nineteen and not yet as arrogant as the rest of them?" he half joked, not quite understanding what she had meant.

"No, Johann," she said seriously, "because on that first day, you looked me in the eye as an equal. You nodded at me, as a sign of gratitude and respect when I stepped aside for you off the driveway as you drove past. No German soldier acknowledges a local servant girl. Not like that, anyway. I knew there had to be good in there, somewhere behind those blue, foreign eyes. I knew you were not one of them. That's how I knew you were different, Johann."

He kissed her head, and held her close.

"You knew *then*?" he whispered. "Even I didn't know who I was then, Bea."

He stroked her beautiful long, wavy hair, and hugged her.

A series of shots rang out from the direction of the town further down the valley, and they both instinctively crouched down.

"It sounds like fireworks," she whispered, peeping outside the boathouse entrance.

"Don't be fooled. That was gunfire. Bea, you must be careful tonight. True, the partisans may be celebrating our withdrawal, but believe me, they are still out for blood. You cannot trust anyone with our secret, not even your mother, your brothers, anyone. You understand? I couldn't even tell Otto our secret! It kills me to have kept it from him, but I couldn't risk it."

He looked down and tried to swallow his guilt. He prayed his friend had made it on his own.

"Otto has been a good friend," he continued, "my only friend. I feel I have betrayed him by hiding my plans from him. But I had to. Our secret has to last a lifetime, Bea. It is far from over. It may never be over for us."

She stood up and snatched the duffle bag, shoving the rest of his uniform into it, tight lipped and refusing to listen to his pessimism. He grabbed her arm and made her stop and look at him.

"Listen to me Bea! Listen! It will *never* be over for us! Never! Each day we have to be careful. Look! A young girl seen even walking on her own back into town will look suspicious. They may even search you!"

She said nothing, and pulled her arm away.

"Bea, leave the uniform with me here. It will be safer, please."

He took the bag off her.

"If I cannot burn it, I will bury it here, under these pebbles at the back of the boathouse. You know they kill anyone who has been helping or collaborating with us, the resistance fighters are trigger-happy and suspicious of everyone. You know they shot four locals against the church wall in the next village only three nights ago."

"But the *Soldbuch*, and jacket, you cannot keep them with you..." she protested.

"I know, I know, not for long, but for now I can. Bea, listen to me! Not only are the resistance fighters cleaning Italy of Nazis and Fascists, but anyone remotely associated with them! That means *you*, Bea. In France, women are having their heads shaved by their own towns-folk, then paraded naked through the squares as punishment for befriending the soldiers. Some girls are even shot! Their own people do it to them, Bea. Their own people! You think they wouldn't do it here? Think again! Imagine if you were caught hiding me. It would be the end for both of us! You must leave everything here with me. Don't have anything on you associated with me at all. Just be careful, Bea, you *must* be careful, you promise?"

"I know, Johann, I will, I will, I promise…" she said.

"You must, Bea. Because in the shadows of every house and behind tree there are sharpshooters…" he was cut short in mid-sentence. Another round of distant gunfire sounded through the air. He sat down heavily again and rested his weary head in his hands. He shook his head in disbelief, in desperation. He knew that if they found him, her family and anyone else who knew would all pay the price.

"It will be fine, Johann! Stop worrying! No one suspects me. Look, I'll do as you say and leave the uniform and everything here with you." She massaged his tense shoulders. "And anyway, they think you Germans have all left the valley by now. There is nothing to suspect."

She kissed him on his forehead, and he sighed.

"Johann, listen. Just stay hidden here for a few weeks, keep your head down, and then when it is safe, my darling, you emerge as an Italian soldier with shellshock, unable to say or remember much, just looking for manual work. You'll see, we will be fine. It will all be over soon."

The noise of distant gunfire echoed down the valley again. It was hard to decipher whether it was in celebration or if it was hostile fire. He knew there was no turning back.

"When it's dark," she whispered, "find some reeds and branches to completely cover the entrance. They might come down the river, searching…"

"I know, I know," he interrupted. He checked for his pistol that he had tucked inside his shirt. "I will. Bea, you had better go before you are missed."

They crouched down at the entrance, scouring for any movement across the river.

"Here, I almost forgot," she said, taking a small tin from her pocket. "Use this. It's the boot polish for your hair. Cover your hair with it completely and leave it overnight. In the morning wash it out and your hair will be as dark as mine. I will try to get you a razor before your blonde beard starts to grow through. Did you leave your razor at the house?"

"Yes, in the bathroom adjoining my bedroom. Most of my things are still there. I thought I had better not bring them. They are all army issue items, which would be dangerous to have on me."

"OK, leave it to me. I will be back tomorrow at about the same time, with food and a blanket, and just a couple of toiletries."

"Thank you, Bea. It's better to leave the uniform here; even the helmet has a use. I can drink from it!"

He managed a smile, then looked down at his bare feet.

"Could you possibly bring me my socks tomorrow, too? I can't get my boots on without them."

"OK, I will try. The owners are back at the house already, but I will bring what I can without causing suspicion."

They quickly kissed, and held each other tight for a minute, and then Bea scrambled up the steep bank beside the boathouse, and was gone. Johann heard the dry undergrowth rustling on the slope behind him, and then there was silence.

He was alone. Now, he thought, he only had the sound of the lapping water for company, and the rat. Another burst of muffled gunfire rang through the still valley, but this time he hardly noticed it. He was thinking of Bea. Not a very honourable situation to be in, he sighed; at twenty years of age he had become a deserter, a traitor, and a fugitive in a foreign land. And in a few months, he would become a father.

THE FEAR

U nder the cover of nightfall, Johann felt it was safe
enough to emerge from the boathouse. He had
smothered his blonde hair with the boot polish, which
smelled pungent and disgusting, but at least, he thought, it
overpowered the smell of the rat urine in the boathouse. He
wondered how he was going to wash the boot polish out of
his hair in the morning without soap; water alone obviously
wasn't going to do it. His hands were covered in it, and the
more he tried to wash them, the more it just smudged over
them like a greasy paste. He wiped them off onto his jacket,
taking care not to dirty his new civilian trousers.

Cautiously, he ventured out of the shelter. Although the
fading light gave him more cover, he still took precautions
and crouched by the entrance first, checking the hill on the
opposite side of the river for any movement, any noise.
When he thought it safe enough, he came out and checked
the embankment directly behind him. He neither saw nor
heard anything in the semi-darkness, so he set out, following
the riverbank downstream. He kept to the cover of rocks on
the bank as best he could, looking for brush and branches
that he could use to camouflage the boathouse entrance with.

With the absence of the afternoon sun to warm him, it
was now getting quite chilly; much colder than he had ever
expected it would be. He was glad to still have his *toque*, or
balaclava, with him that he put round his neck like a scarf.
Although the winter snows had melted and most days were
sunny, this far north in Italy in springtime was still cold

11

when the sun disappeared behind the hills. He wondered how he was going to get through the cold nights in the boathouse. He didn't dare risk lighting a fire; the smoke would be seen for miles. The luxury of the warm house with its many fireplaces that he had kept so well stocked with firewood, was now a thing of the past.

After half an hour or so, Johann had gathered a good pile of brush for the boathouse camouflage, which would also help as a barrier between him and the cold night air. He started his way back towards the boathouse along the river's edge with his large bundle, but suddenly stopped dead in his tracks. What was that noise? He heard something!

Voices!

He froze, and his heart pounded. He held his breath, not daring to breathe.

It was definitely voices; men's voices! They were hushed, almost whispering. He crouched down low, holding the bundle of brush in front of him. He didn't dare move, and tried to determine which direction the voices were coming from. He listened hard, trying to stay calm and focussed, as he had been trained to do.

It came from upstream, he was sure of it. They were in a boat! He could now hear the slow rhythm of the oars dipping in and out of the water. But he still couldn't see much in the dark. Very gently, he put the bundle down, then, ran as quietly and as low to the ground as he could back to the safety of the boathouse. His mind was racing. He realized had left the duffle bag with his uniform and his *Soldbuch*, the I.D. booklet containing everything about him, exposed, lying somewhere near the back wall of the boathouse. The *Soldbuch* was his official twenty-four page personal history, which every German soldier kept with him at all times. He had to get it before anyone else did. It contained everything about him, including his photograph, his regiment, his signature, his pay to date, his uniform and even the weapons issued to him, and where he had fought. There was a page on his medical history and other pages showed his personal information, such as where he was born, his height, and his next of kin. He had to quickly hide it and his uniform, before he could hide himself.

He raced to the back of the boathouse as fast as he could in the dark, grabbed the duffle bag, then rummaged through it until he found the tan, leather-bound *Soldbuch.*

It was there, thank goodness. He relaxed a little and went to crouch just inside the entrance, waiting, hoping above all, for the boat to pass by.

As the boat drifted closer to the boathouse, he could hear the men whispering quite clearly. The voices were hushed, only speaking when they had to, and Johann wondered who on earth they could be at this time of night; Local fishermen, perhaps? He dismissed that idea almost immediately. It must be the local Italian partisans looking for Germans! His mind raced, as the voices drifted nearer. Then it suddenly dawned on Johann that he could understand the whispered voices. They weren't speaking Italian, they were speaking German!

He panicked. Confused and extremely worried, he broke out into a sweat, despite the cold air. Why were Germans coming down the river? And what on earth were they even doing in a rowing boat? Surely they should be heading north, back towards the Fatherland? He wracked his brains trying to think clearly. Perhaps these Germans were looking for him for desertion! Or perhaps the Italian resistance fighters had found out about him and Bea and had told some fleeing Germans that one of their own was hiding like a coward and they had to get him! Or maybe, the partisans had captured these Germans, and the Germans had made a deal for their lives. But why? They would have just shot them dead! No, he thought, these Germans coming down river had to be working alone. That's why they were whispering. They were hunting him down for desertion!

He felt sick. But why were they at liberty to look for him? They *must* have made a deal with the partisans. Perhaps it was Otto! Yes! Otto must have worked out that he was staying behind. Perhaps he got caught himself by the partisans and squealed to save his own life. Whatever had happened, Johann knew he would face the firing squad, if not from the Italians, then from his fellow Nazis for desertion.

Then an awful thought struck him; perhaps it wasn't Otto! Perhaps the partisans had found out about Bea, and were using her to catch him!

He felt desperate. Had the partisans interrogated her? Had they harmed her? Maybe even shot her? He had heard shots after Bea had left... surely her own brothers would have protected her?

Johann wanted to come out and face the people in the boat like a man. He needed to know.

But his instinct was to hide. He had to hide in case Bea hadn't been caught. If he gave himself up for nothing, that would be unimaginable.

He felt his way to the back wall of the boathouse and lay flat on his stomach. He waited and listened. He was distracted by a squeaking noise to his right; a rat scuttled over his foot. But the rats were hardly his concern now. The voices in the boat were getting nearer. He couldn't believe this was happening; they were approaching the boathouse! Of all the places to land along the river! Then a terrible thought came to him. He looked around the walls. If these men did come in looking for him, he was cornered!

Now he wished he had stayed outside where he would have had a better chance of escape.

Grabbing his helmet out of the duffle bag, he began to use it as a shovel. He shovelled as quietly as he could, so that hopefully he wouldn't be heard from outside. He scooped out a long, shallow trench alongside the back wall. When he thought he had made it deep enough, he quickly lay down in it and scooped back the pebbles over himself until he was completely covered up to his neck. He put a thin layer over his face and placed a small plank of wood over the area where his head was. He hoped he didn't have any part of him showing.

He lay on his side in his trench and listened. His breathing was loud and fast. He could hear his heartbeat pounding in his eardrum. He had to concentrate on taking long, slow breaths to calm down. They *must* have caught Bea, he thought, or how would they know where to come?

He could hear the men outside climbing out of the boat, and then heaving it onto the shore outside the entrance of his shelter. He couldn't believe they knew where to find him! He knew it was no fluke. He knew they had come for him. His time was up.

He quickly checked he was covered completely.

Then he remembered his gun! He had put it in the bag before he had gone looking for camouflage. "Oh no, the bag!" he almost cried out loud. In his haste he had stupidly left everything lying a few feet away from him! He stuck his arm out through the stones and reached as far as he could with his long fingers. He was just able to grab the open end and pull it towards him. But he cursed, as he had to sit up again in order to dig the bag into the hollow with him. He managed it, hugged it tight into his stomach, and quickly covered himself up again with his free arm. He listened, holding his breath and wondered if they had heard him. Luckily they were still outside and seemed to be discussing the weight of a box. They were deciding in loud whispers, which one of them was to walk backwards into the dark boathouse as they carried it. What were they carrying? Maybe they were going to blow him up with explosives!

He waited. Sweating and a little confused, trying to make sense of what was going on, he tried to focus on his breathing.

As far as he could tell, there seemed to be three men, all German. One of them was apparently called Heinrich. Could it be his commanding officer Heinrich Streuber? Surely not! He had already left the area at least eight hours previously. He wouldn't be looking for him - or would he? The more Johann thought about it, the faster his heart raced. He was stifling hot in his smelly trench, bursting to come out. It was all he could do to control his breathing. He concentrated, making himself calm down and think it through.

Streuber was an intellectual, an art historian and had been a lecturer in Berlin before the war. Johann had often heard him boasting to other officers over dinner, about how he had met Adolf Hitler personally in Vienna at the beginning of the war, and had apparently had a long conversation with the Fuhrer, discussing anything from the sculptures of August Rodin to the beauty of the architecture of Prague. So Streuber, Johann surmised, with his connections and intellect, would hardly be one to sink to such depths as to be sitting in a rickety, old rowing boat, risking his life surrounded by hills riddled with partisans, to be looking for his young orderly. After all, Johann reminded himself, it was Streuber who had fled the house deserting him, not the other way around!

Then to his utter panic, he realized the three men had come into the boathouse. He listened carefully. He heard the loud crunch of the stones under their feet come to a stop.

"What is that foul smell?" one of them asked. "Can you smell that pungent odour? It almost smells like boot polish! It didn't smell like this in here the other day when I came and checked the place out."

"*Boot* polish? Don't be ridiculous. It smells more like rat urine, if you ask me," another voice answered.

"Come on, let's get on with it," an irritated, third man hissed. "We can't waste any more time. Getting here was excruciatingly slow going. We need to get out of the area tonight before the back roads are blocked completely. We have already lost a precious day."

Johann could hear them back outside unloading the boat. They made several trips from the boat to inside boathouse entrance.

"Having to leave all this behind, kills me," the same voice continued in a hushed tone. "Had I foreseen the disastrous turn of events unfolding over the past couple of days, I would have had everything sent to Berlin months ago. This is just ridiculous."

Johan's heart thumped. He was now certain. He knew that voice without a doubt; it was Heinrich Streuber. There was no question about it; the irritated voice was unmistakable.

"But Heinrich, you can't blame yourself for not knowing what was to come. Hindsight is a wonderful thing. Even the Fuhrer's own collectors themselves couldn't have known this was going to happen. I am sure they are all in shock, just as we are."

"The whole thing was still unbelievable; Hitler's cowardly suicide in his bunker, the retreat of the greatest army, the enemy pushing north, it's a complete nightmare."

"But what do you think will become of the Fuhrer's vast collection of art for his Museum in Linz? It would be unimaginable if the treasures are lost to the enemy," one of them said.

"Have no fear there, Franz, the *SS* will be hiding everything underground as we speak, if they haven't already. The Alps are riddled with passages and mines perfect for the job. The SS are no fools. The British and Americans will not be getting their hands on our treasures, don't you worry."

"Just let them try!" Franz uttered under his breath.

"Gentlemen, please, the Fuhrer's art is hardly our concern now," Heinrich said. "We have to take care of our own interests. Whether the Dutch, French or Italian acquisitions have been safely hidden from the enemy is irrelevant. Keeping this little collection secure until we can get back to Italy at a later date is what we must concentrate on now. The longer we stand around talking aimlessly, the more dangerous our position becomes. Franz, lead the way, I want to get this lot hidden and myself home in one piece, preferably this century. Come on, let's move!"

The crunch of stones under foot as the men walked towards Johann's flimsily covered hideout was almost unbearable. With one side of his face pressed to the ground, the noise of their steps was amplified in his ear, making the anticipation of being caught at any minute torturous. His clothes were drenched in sweat and he screwed his eyes shut, waiting for the pathetic little scrap of wood covering his head to be kicked off, exposing his ridiculous hiding place. He felt like a coward, and his mind was telling him to stand up and face the consequences like a man. But he still couldn't move. He just couldn't bring himself to do it. He thought of Bea, and their unborn baby growing up without a father. If he stood up he would surely be shot. This situation was even worse than he had first imagined; not only did he know what these men were doing, but he now knew where they were hiding their plunder! As if being discovered as a deserter wasn't bad enough; he now knew the secret hiding place for their stolen stash. It was all over.

He couldn't do it. He couldn't stand up.

He instead waited for his fate like a coward, knowing his little trench at the back of this dank, old boathouse was going to be his final resting place. He prayed that Bea and the baby would survive this ordeal, and that Bea wouldn't be the one to find his body. He prayed for his unborn child, and his mother back in Germany, if indeed, she was still alive.

"You are sure everything will be secure here, Kristoff?" Franz asked.

"If this cesspit is anything to go by, I seriously have my doubts," Heinrich said. "It's not damp up there in the castle, I trust, as it is down here, Kristoff? I don't want the paintings damaged in any way, you understand? They are worth a fortune…"

"Absolutely not. You may rest assured. Firstly, the castle is completely safe. It is derelict, on private land, and in fact quite dangerous to trespassers. Therefore it is most suitable for our purpose. There are vault-like chambers beneath the castle that are perfect for our needs, and the inner chambers are completely dry. No locals go near the castle at all. I might add, that in any other great country, such as Germany or Austria, the castle would have been renovated and made beautiful once again, but not here. It has been left untouched and crumbling since Napoleon came through this way."

"Good. What about access?" Heinrich quizzed him. "Derelict or not, the castle must still have its main access from the road up there, no?"

"Not any more, the main access is not only impassable, but completely untraceable, having become completely overgrown to almost jungle-like density. But from these boathouse steps, through here, you see, behind this small door, the ruin is still accessible, but I must warn you both, it is quite a climb. We must watch our step in the dark."

"Good," Heinrich said. "The climb will also be a deterrent to others. The worst case scenario is that it may take up to a year before we are able to come back to collect all our acquisitions; who knows how long the British will stay on in Italy after the war or how long it will be before we are able to return. So this castle has to be absolutely secure."

"I assure you, it is very difficult to reach from the land and this is really the only access to the castle from the river," Franz said, kicking at the shingle under foot. "We can block this door with this stuff before we leave." He kicked the pebbles close to Johan's head, "…just as an extra precaution, we can jam the door with it."

Heinrich felt a little more relaxed now that he knew the storage place was secure.

"You know," he continued in a lighter tone, "I have a buyer already interested in these chalices. Perhaps my wife will get her lakeside home after all!" he said, laughing to himself. "And I can tell you, gentlemen, one of these paintings alone that I wrapped up, could be as valuable as that 'Madonna and Child' brought back from Paris last year for the Fuhrer. I bet even the Fuhrer himself would give me an offer for two of these, at least!" He laughed, but then remembered the Fuhrer was dead, and he frowned. How quickly things had changed.

"After this week's events, I wouldn't bet on anything," Kristoff said dryly.

"We are still strong. Germany will always survive, you'll see. It is not over yet," Heinrich added.

One of the men stepped back onto Johann's arm, which only had a thin layer of stones covering it. He stood there, with his full weight pressing down through the pebbles, almost breaking it. The pain was excruciating, and the stones cut into his flesh. It took Johann all his might not to yell out and pull his arm away.

He heard a thud, thumping on wood, like a shoulder against a door, then finally the weight was released off his arm and the foot moved. He heard the men lifting the box, balancing other objects on top of it, shuffling around to fit through the door, then walking up some steps on the other side of the door. Their voices became fainter and fainter until it was completely quiet again.

Johann waited a few minutes until he was one hundred per cent sure they were far enough up the steps and out of earshot, then he slowly sat up and brushed the stones and dirt off himself. His arm was limp and bruised, but he was grateful it was not broken and he gently rubbed it until he felt the circulation coming back.

THE OPPORTUNITY

C rouching behind a rock a few yards from the boathouse, Johann waited for Streuber and the other two men to return back from the castle on the hill above him. The thought had crossed his mind of hiding further up river, away from the boathouse, but he had decided against it; he knew the hills were dotted with the trigger-happy partisans. It just wasn't worth the risk. He even thought of jamming the door at the back of the boathouse, and taking off in their rowing boat, leaving Streuber stranded as he had done to him. But where would he go that was safer than the boat shelter? Also, they would then know that someone knew what they were up to, and would be after him, for sure. The boathouse was invisible from the hills above, and barely noticeable from the river. He had to stick it out here, he thought. It was the best place to be for now. He couldn't go anywhere, and certainly not without Bea.

He desperately needed to dispose of his *Soldbuch*, though. It was a liability having it with him. If he had any chance of a starting afresh with Bea, he needed to leave no trace of himself for anyone to ever find out who he was. He had to get rid of his identification booklet. If anyone should find his uniform, it would be suspicious, but he wouldn't necessarily be linked to it; a discarded soldier's uniform could belong to any thousands of German soldiers who had occupied and fought in Italy. But having his *Soldbuch* found, without a body to go with it, would create suspicion and would probably provoke a manhunt. The partisans would have a field day. So if burning it was too dangerous because of the smoke, and burying was out of the question because of sniffer dogs or high tides bringing it back to the surface, his only option was to get it as far away from him as he could.

He had a plan. It was risky and he had to act fast.

He listened at the door to the steps. He could hear no one coming down just yet. He knew they would be back soon though, as there were still more stolen property to be carried up which they had left by the inside entrance of the boathouse. He crept out and carefully checked the hill behind him. Although he couldn't see the steps leading up to the castle because of the undergrowth, he couldn't hear any voices or footsteps. He placed the little leather *Soldbuch* carefully in the inside pocket of his uniform jacket, then went over to the rowing boat. He leant over it, folded his jacket up as small as he could make it, and then tucked it under a coiled up rope in the stern, completely hiding it. Should the jacket and *Soldbuch* ever be found by the Italians, hopefully they would presume the soldier had escaped downstream and abandoned the boat. In the unlikely event that Streuber should find it, it would hopefully be too late. Once Streuber had escaped down river, he wouldn't bother coming back for Johann. Streuber would be well on his way home. And should Streuber ever return after the war to collect his plunder, he would hopefully find his treasure intact, exactly where he had left it, no questions asked. Johann knew he could never have anything to do with the stolen property. He could never risk letting anyone know that he knew about it, or where it was hidden, as the risk of blowing his own German identity was too great. He would have to forget what he saw or heard. He had his baby and his love to think of.

The moon had come out and seemed extremely white, glowing like a light bulb onto the black river. It shimmered and danced on the still surface, playing games with the night, creating shadows and putting Johann in more danger as he leant over the boat to re-check that the rope was still completely covering the jacket.

Convinced he had hidden it well, he ran back to his hiding place beside the rock outside the boathouse, and waited. He knelt down low, crouching over to stay hidden, and praying that the officers would finish their task quickly and be on their way again. He wanted them out of his life forever.

The sound of a loud splash jolted him with a start and he realized he must have drifted off to sleep. He found he was leaning against the rock, and his head could have easily nodded into view as he slept. But luckily he hadn't been seen or heard. Peeping out from behind his rock he saw, under the moonlit sky, that the three men were already back in the rowing boat and had pushed off onto the river. They seemed to be struggling to reach an oar that had rolled overboard in their haste to get going. After a few minutes of unsteady manoeuvring and cursing each other in loud whispers, they finally managed to get the oar back on board. Then there was silence.

To Johann's surprise, they didn't row, they didn't whisper, they didn't dare make a sound.

Johann watched them slowly drift past him, their dark, still silhouettes crouched down low, motionless. The splash of the oar falling overboard had obviously worried them, and they clearly feared that someone in the dark hills overlooking the river might have heard them.

Johann understood their fear, but he felt indifferent to their fate. He owed them little respect or concern. They were behaving like common thieves, and he hardly cared what happened to them. It hurt him, deep down, that he had been abandoned at the house to fend for himself without any arrangements for his leaving or prior warning. He had been a loyal soldier and faithful orderly to Streuber. He had been proud as any other young man to have served in the German army for his beloved country. But now things were different, as Streuber had illustrated by his actions; it was every man for himself. The sooner they disappeared from his life, Johann thought, the better.

He watched the boat slowly and silently drift towards the bend in the river, where it disappeared out of sight. They were gone.

"Goodbye, Streuber," he whispered. "I never want to see you, or hear your name again."

He felt relief that they were gone. He could relax. He stood up to stretch his legs. He had his hideout to himself again. He thought about bedding down for the night, but decided he'd better first go back for the camouflage he had left a few yards away. As he walked along the water's edge, he felt a pang of emotion at the thought of his *Soldbuch* floating away. It was his identity, his life, and it was gone. He was no longer a German soldier. Those proud days as a teenager, training in the 'Hitler Youth' program were now a memory that he would do better to forget. This was new life, he was a new person. He sighed. He had to try and wipe it all from his mind. This was his clean break, a new beginning. He had to think differently, now. He had to become someone else. He was no longer Johann Fuchs.

Suddenly, he was startled by voices calling out from the hills around him. They were so clear they could have been a couple of hundred yards away from him.

His heart pounded.

"Identify yourselves!" they called out in Italian. "Identify yourselves! Who are you?"

Johann flew to the rock, diving to the ground so fast he hit his chin on the stones. His eyes, wide with fear, his heart pounding, he wondered who had seen him from the hills above.

There was silence. His heart was about to explode.

Were they calling down to him? They had said, "Identify yourselves," he thought, which meant that they had perhaps seen more than one person. He hoped so, anyway.

He didn't move. He waited.

The voices called out again, this time in English and then German, and Johann surmised they were coming from the hills behind him just around the bend to his right. Again, in Italian, they called out. He was now sure that they were calling down to Heinrich Streuber and his two comrades in the boat.

Johann heard nothing for a while, he hardly breathed, waiting. There was no response at all from the boat. He could see the reflection of flashlights over the water's surface from around the bend in the river, but nothing else in the blackness. As far as he could tell, Heinrich and the other two still had not responded.

A sudden burst of shots echoed around the valley. It was deafening to his ears.

It stopped. Johann heard yells and shouts from the boat. The firing started up again, and this time it didn't stop. Above the gunfire he could hear splashing in the water, shouting, and complete mayhem only yards away from him.

"Don't shoot! Ve are Ingleesh... do not..." The plea was cut short in mid sentence by a rapid spray of gunfire.

And then there was a hush. A deadly hush. The firing had stopped, the shouting from the boat had also stopped. Johann listened, his heart throbbing. All he could hear was the agitated water, which now seemed eager to reach him on the shoreline; small, choppy waves lapped at the water's edge a little faster and stronger than before. He dared not move. The silence was sickening.

Then quite suddenly the silence was broken, this time by shouts of joy.

"Viva Ita-lia! Viva Ita-lia! Vi-va Ita-lia!"

The loud cheers rung out in the hills around him. The partisans celebrated from the darkness, firing erratically into the air, their singing and chanting echoing down the river and across the valley.

The boat continued to drift downriver, slowly and silently, and with it the last trace of Johann Fuchs.

PRESENT DAY

Heinrich walked quickly through Malpensa Airport's arrival's area towards his two brothers, who had been waiting some time for his delayed flight from Munich to arrive. He greeted them quickly with a handshake and without any apology for having kept them waiting. He had always been abrupt, even as a young man, so they hardly expected anything else from him.

"Lets get going," he said, after grabbing his bag off the conveyor belt. "The sooner we sort this out, the better. I don't really want to be here any more than I have to. Already, I have a buyer in Munich waiting for my return. He's as anxious to see what there is here, as I am. I trust that you two have got the ball rolling in the valley and know where we're going. I don't have time to mess about."

The two brothers glanced at each other, remembering why they hadn't seen Heinrich for over a year.

"We've done quite a lot of preparation, actually, Heinrich," Friedrich offered, almost defensively. "But it's not as cut-and-dry as you'd expect. We've pretty much narrowed it down to a two-mile stretch of river. I think once we all sit down and systematically go over the letter, we'll be able to piece it together with the map. We have some other leads too, which we can discuss on our way to the hotel."

"Yes, and we've also found a place where we can rent a boat," Walter added. "So we can conduct our search from the river, rather than being restricted to land, which would, we have found out, be extremely difficult. It's pretty rural, to say the least."

"A boat?" Heinrich questioned with a grimace.

"Yes, we need a boat; you really can't see much from the hills for the trees and undergrowth. You'll see what I mean when we get there. It is quite undeveloped; just a few little villages dotted here and there, nestled in the hills. Roads are really few and far between."

Heinrich sighed. Boats were really not his thing. Never had been.

"Well, shall we get going? You've rented a car for me too, I hope, so we aren't joined at the hip, and I hope we're in a decent hotel, at least."

"Yes. And Heinrich, just relax a little, please!"

* * * * *

CHAPTER ONE

" A lex, do you feel a bit kind of nervous, too?" Natasha asked.

Her brother was sitting in the front seat, watching the narrow road ahead gradually wind its way up into the hills. He turned round and looked at his sister. He shrugged.

"Nervous? No, why would I be? I love the windy roads, don't you? It's great sitting in the front. It's cool."

"No, *you dork*, I meant, because we're getting closer."

"You're the dork! There's nothing to be worried about, silly!" Alex laughed.

She sighed and stared out of her side window.

She was definitely feeling apprehensive. She wasn't expecting to feel like this, but she was. She had been really looking forward to seeing her mother, who had been working the last couple of months on a new archaeological dig in Pisa. But the problem was that there had been a change of plan and now they weren't going down to Pisa just yet. They had been invited to stay with Gabriella and Lorenzo in their home in the hills outside Piacenza for a couple of weeks. The new plan was that the four of them would all go on to Pisa together to meet up with their parents at the dig. Natasha wished she could have just told the driver to keep on going, instead of turning off the motorway towards Lorenzo and Gabriella's home.

But that wasn't really the crux of problem. She was actually looking forward to seeing Gabriella and Lorenzo again; they had been through a lot together last Easter, during their stay at the desert dig, and had become quite close under the very dangerous circumstances. So that wasn't the problem. Nor was it the relationship between her mother and Gabriella and Lorenzo's father that bothered her. Not any more, anyway. Natasha would have been the first to admit that she'd hated Marcello when she first found out about it. But she had now managed to accept Marcello. She even liked him, kind of. So Natasha just couldn't pinpoint what it was that was causing her stomach to churn. It was just the whole thing. The circumstances surrounding this entire trip, she thought, were just all a bit weird.

She groaned inwardly.

Alex turned around again and looked at her.

"What's up 'Tash, tell me! What's wrong?" He sounded genuinely concerned.

"I'm OK. I just don't like being a guest in someone else's house, I suppose. It's all going to be a bit, you know, stiff and formal."

"Come on, it's fun! I like being a guest. And they're really rich! I bet we have someone to make our beds for us and lay our clothes out like they do in films!"

"Oh God, Alex, grow up."

Julia, their mother was now engaged to Marcello. He had suggested that before they all got together in Pisa, the four teens should first 'get to know each other' again by spending time together in the house.

"All this 'getting to know each other' is ridiculous," Natasha mumbled, "has he completely forgotten that we all 'got to know each other' pretty well already, in that dark cave with our hands tied behind our backs?"

The problem was, she thought, the four of them weren't exactly going to be on their own at the villa. They were going to be under the tough scrutiny of Lorenzo and Gabriella's cantankerous old grandmother, the Contessa, who lived with them. She was apparently a bit of a dragon.

"Alex, you do remember Gabriella saying that her grandmother ran their home with an iron fist, don't you? It's not going to be much of a holiday at all. The whole thing is just awful, having to be polite, having to engage in intellectual conversation over dinner, and trying to make a good impression so as not to let Mummy down. I wish I'd stayed in London with Dad now."

"You're nuts, Natasha; this is going to be fun."

She sighed heavily, and as the car climbed up into the hills of the lush, Trebbia Valley, Natasha knew there was no turning back, ever. Everything she knew and was comfortable with seemed to be drifting further and further away. This was the turning point, the sealing of the deal. Her mother was still going ahead with the marriage; it was like the beginning of... she wasn't sure what.

Looking at the road ahead, she tried to focus of something else. They were approaching the town that Gabriella had described to her. Natasha examined it objectively from a distance, as an artist might before he sat down to paint it. The thick, ancient walls with their sun-bleached, weathered crenulations looked more like the fortifications of an old castle than the walls of a hillside town. Shimmering in the sun, they seemed to naturally cling to the hillside, almost giving the impression that they had grown from the earth itself and were a part of the landscape. That was the thing about Italy, she thought, it was all so old and natural looking. Really, you had to be an adult to appreciate it, or in the right mood for it, at least.

But she wasn't.

"I think this might be their little town," Alex was saying, jolting Natasha back to the present. "We're probably getting quite close to their home now."

"I know. You don't have to remind me."

"Come on Natasha! We're on holiday, for goodness sake. Cheer up! And we're going see Mum in a few days, so snap out of it."

"I know, but it's this first part that I'm not looking forward to. Don't you remember Gabriella telling us how strict her grandmother was?"

"No."

"Well I do. Don't you remember she was telling us how their grandmother had practically brought them up since their father was away so much? And when he came home even *he* was on his best behaviour?"

"Oh come on, she was only joking, 'Tash. Get over it."

They entered the town, driving under the old archway and portcullis with its heavy, spiked iron prongs designed to keep intruders out. They weaved at a snail's pace through the tight, cobble-stoned streets. They passed the central piazza, where the old men sat in the shade of the trees playing chess, and young mothers stood chatting as their children chased each other around the fountain. As always in Italian towns and villages, there was the large, oversized memorial statue of a soldier, standing central and proud in honour of all the young men who had lost their lives during the last two wars. A group of tidy-looking teenagers sat on the steps beneath the statue talking loudly and eating ice cream.

"I wish we could stop here for an ice cream," Natasha said. "Alex, do you want to try and ask him if we can stop for a bit?"

"I would, but we'd better not; they're probably waiting for us at the house. Our flight was late in, remember?"

She remembered, but stopping would have delayed their arrival a little longer.

The cafés and trattorias around the square were buzzing with families with children, which reminded Natasha of previous holidays they'd had in Italy with her parents. She wished things could have stayed the same. But things didn't, things just kept moving forward.

The car eventually took a bumpy right fork out of town, and emerged on the other side of the hill. Only a knee-high, stone wall separated them from the deep valley that dropped away down to the Trebbia River, which glittered like a shiny snake in the sunshine below.

Alex tried to find out from the driver about a castle he had spotted on one of the hills further up the valley, but neither Alex nor the driver really understood what the other was saying.

The driver, who apparently lived at the house too, had introduced himself as Piero when he had collected them from the airport in Milan. He seemed very friendly, and had shaken hands enthusiastically with a big smile, which had made Natasha feel less apprehensive about getting into a car with a complete stranger. He was probably in his early fifties, had a kind face and thick, straight, greying hair, that was layered longer than a man of his age in England might have had; that was, Natasha thought, unless he was an old rock star, or an actor. He occasionally ran his fingers through his hair, looking in the mirror as he did so. He wore a wedding ring on his finger, and although he didn't speak English, he seemed to have a friendly air about him when Alex tried asking him about the old castle he'd seen on the hill.

"No, no," Piero said, shaking his finger at it. "*E qui! La casa di Lorenzo e qui avanti!*"

He pointed up the road, smiling.

"Oh, OK. Whatever you say," Alex said, not really understanding a word.

"I think he thought you presumed the castle was their home, Alex," Natasha said, with a giggle.

"*Ancora due minuti, e siamo arrivati! Due minuti!*" Piero said, and held up two fingers to make sure the children understood.

"Oh, I get it! *Due minuti!*" Alex repeated happily, having at least understood what that last bit meant. Piero pointed up to the left side of the road, through a long gap in the trees.

"Montesonnellino," he said, and Alex nodded back blankly. Piero rested his cheek on his hand as if he was indicating he was tired.

"*Montesonnellino*," he repeated, "*E il nome; la villa, la casa di Lorenzo e Gabriella. Montesonnellino!*"

He pointed through the trees on the left.

And then Alex saw what Piero was talking about. His eyes widened in disbelief.

"'Tash, did you see that house? I think I just caught a glimpse of it behind the railings! It's massive! Wow," he said, " look at those the gates!"

"Oh no," was all Natasha could groan. Her stomach ached in anticipation. "Here we go."

CHAPTER TWO

P iero slowed down and clicked the button on the visor above the windscreen. The massive, black, wrought iron gates slowly opened forward to let the car through.

"*Siamo arrivati!*" he said. "*Benvenuti a Montesonnellino!*"

Gabriella had told Natasha a little about her home when they had met last Easter. Whether Gabriella was being modest, or, due to her innocence, had simply been unaware of her fortunate situation, the home she had spoken about hardly matched what Alex and Natasha saw beyond the gates.

They slowly drove down a long, gravelled driveway lined with tall poplar trees and weathered, marble statues. Three quarters of the way down the driveway was a large fountain with mythical creatures dramatically rising from the centre with water spewing from their mouths. Natasha did remember Gabriella mentioning something about her having fountains in her garden, but she had never imagined they would be quite on this scale. The driveway split in two around the circular fountain, and beyond it, standing pale and sun-bleached, was the large, handsome, terracotta villa that had been in Gabriella and Lorenzo's family for generations.

Piero pulled the car up to the wide, stone steps at the front door and came to a stop. Before Alex and Natasha could even open their doors, a Great Dane came bounding from the house towards the car. It barked excitedly, wagging its stump of a tail and jumping up at the car windows. It dribbled and slobbered on the glass, making them think twice about getting out.

"*Basta*, Darius, *basta!*" Piero half shouted and half laughed at the dog. He indicated to Natasha and Alex that it was perfectly safe to get out. The dog calmed down after being stroked and told in Italian that he was a good boy, then, he waited patiently for Piero while he carried the luggage from the car. He then trotted up the steps with him, and into the house.

"Natasha, Alex, at last! We have been waiting all day!"

It was Gabriella. She came running out of the house with her arms outstretched.

"I am so excited you are here!"

She skipped down the steps, grinning from ear to ear, her black curls bouncing on her shoulders.

"It is so, so, so good to see you!" she said.

The girls hugged each other warmly.

"Natasha! Look at you! Your hair is so pretty now!"

Gabriella stood back and looked at her. For a second, Natasha felt a pang of fear go through her as she was reminded of the circumstances in which her long hair had been cut off, last Easter.

"Thanks, Gabriella, it's great to see you. And you're not looking so bad yourself!"

She really wanted to tell Gabriella how her face was looking so much better from when they had last seen each other, and she could see that she wasn't limping anymore, but Natasha decided she wouldn't drag all those horrible memories back.

"It really is good to see you, Gabriella," she said with a grin. "It's been quite a while!"

"I know, I know! You too. Now that you are here at last, we will have such fun!"

Gabriella went to kiss Alex on each cheek.

"It's so great to see you, Alex. Welcome to Italy!" she said, and she meant it. She had missed them both.

"Thanks. But what a whopping great house you have here, you're so lucky. It's more like a palace than a villa!"

Gabriella shrugged with a grin. "Well, it's very homely inside. Come, I will show you. You must treat it as your own, now."

"Where's Lorenzo? Isn't he around?" Alex asked.

"Yes, yes! He will be here. His tennis coach will be leaving soon. Lorenzo is so anxious to see you. He has been waiting and looking forward to this time for weeks! He has something he wants to show you, Alex. Anyway, come with me and meet my grandmother. She is waiting for you on the *portico* with refreshments, or I should say, the veranda?"

"Whatever! It's all good to me," Alex said happily.

Natasha took a deep breath, and let Alex follow Gabriella up the steps first and into the wide, cool hallway. It seemed gloomy after the bright sunlight outside, but their eyes soon adjusted with the help of the two little round windows each side of the doors.

"I think Piero was trying to tell us what 'Monte-sonne-llino' meant," Alex said. "Well I think he was, anyway."

"Oh, I suppose it could be translated as, 'little sleepy mountain' or 'dozy little mountain', something like that. It is the name of the villa."

"Oh! Now I see what he was doing now with his hand resting on his face. I thought he was just tired, or something."

They walked past several large oil paintings hanging on the walls, of family ancestors mostly dressed in clothing of the sixteenth or seventeenth-century. There was also an Admiral or sea Captain in his Navy uniform, looking very handsome and proud, with a sword at his side and a fleet of ships in the background behind him.

"Who's that?" Alex asked.

"That one is Alessandro, he was the General of the Fleet of Galleys. I think we were fighting the Turks at the time," she said with a guilty smile and a shrug, "whenever that was."

In the centre of the high ceiling was a fresco of two interlocking coats of arms. It was very faded and pale, but Alex could make out an anchor in one of the quadrants, which he presumed had to do with the admiral on the wall. It had a 'lion passant,' which, he had learnt recently in French class meant a lion lying at ease, as opposed to a 'lion rampant', a raging one, snarling with its sharp claws showing. A wide, stone stairway swooped off to a curve to the right, and Alex wondered how many boys over the centuries had slid down the polished bannister, coming to an abrupt, prickly stop against the carved pineapple at the bottom.

"This is my favourite painting," Gabriella was saying to Natasha, "she was the young girl for whom this house was built. It was a wedding gift from her father. She was only a year older than you are, Natasha, when she married, about sixteen, at the most. Can you imagine? And her husband was only a year older than her."

"How did they know what to do?" Alex wondered out loud. "I mean," he quickly clarified the question, "I wouldn't know how to run a house or know how to be a husband. That's pretty major, isn't it, being married in your early teens?"

"It is true, yes, but in those days people did marry very young. I suppose the life expectancy was shorter, so it made sense. It was an arranged marriage, of course, between the two families, probably agreed upon when they were babies. But I imagine they had supervision and advice after their wedding day from many people on both sides of the family. I don't think they would have been left on their own to cope with the running of a large house such as this. I am sure it was full of people to help them."

"Actually, I think I remember you mentioning her," Natasha said. "Didn't you say her family home was on one of the hills nearby?"

"Yes, it is visible from one side of the garden. It is practically a ruin now, though, over grown and derelict. I can point it out to you when we go outside. It is easy to see, it looks like a small castle with a tall tower on one side of it. Her mother probably climbed it every day to wave to her daughter. But it's really only a short distance away, so I am sure her mother was here often."

"Yeah, I think we saw it on the drive up here," Alex said. "It looks cool!"

They walked through the hall, passing two or three rooms to the left and right, and Natasha tried to peep through the doors that were ajar as she walked by. Gabriella led them into a large, comfortable-looking sitting room. It looked well used, with a large fireplace, three large sofas, a couple of armchairs and magazines and books lying on side tables.

"This is our family room. We have games and cards, and chess over there. Do you like to play, Natasha?" Gabriella asked.

"*I* do," Alex said, eager to fit in, "but Natasha doesn't, really."

"Alex! How can you say that?" she said, thumping him on the back. "You're the one who's addicted to video games, not me!"

"Whatever," he said, shrugging happily.

Across the back wall there were three sets of tall, French doors that opened out onto the veranda. They followed Gabriella through the first set.

Covering the veranda, which ran across the whole length of the house, was a vaulted ceiling supported a by long line of stone columns, leaving the vista open to the formal gardens beyond. Between each column stood a sturdy, white, marble urn overflowing with pink and white geraniums and ferns. A frail, old man in a straw, floppy hat holding a watering can was at the far end by the last of the urns. He had left a little puddle on the tiles at the base of each one, showing where he had been.

Then Natasha saw half way along the veranda, sitting in one of three oversized sofas, Gabriella's grandmother, the Contessa Amelia Bonamici-Milanese. She was reading a newspaper and hadn't yet seen the children approaching. Natasha was able to have a good look at her before she glanced up from her paper. She was a rather thin woman, but looked fit and healthy for her age and well 'groomed,' Natasha thought, to use her mother's awful expression. Because of this, it was hard for Natasha to gage the Contessa's age. Natasha could tell, even at a first glance, that she had probably been attractive in her youth. She had good posture, and even managed to look elegant even while doing something as mundane as reading the paper. Her thick, streaked, grey hair, not quite shoulder length, curled under like an inverted wave around her neck.

"They are here, Grandmother!" Gabriella called to her excitedly. "They are here!"

As Natasha and Alex approached the Contessa, she put her newspaper down on the coffee table in front of her.

"Ah, so you have arrived at last," she said. She uncrossed her long legs and took her reading glasses off to have a good look at her young guests.

"My goodness, you both look so pale! Don't they have *any* sun at all in England?"

She studied Natasha.

"Well, thankfully, your complexion is something we can easily rectify. More importantly," she added, turning to Alex, "I see you both have good bone structure, and that is an encouraging start. There is really nothing we could have done about that."

She patted the cushions each side of her on the sofa without taking her eyes of the new arrivals.

"Come and sit down and tell me a little about yourselves. There is some catching up to do if I am to be your step-grandmother."

Her Italian accent was only just noticeable, as she spoke English fluently, distinctly and with ease. She offered her hand to both the children to shake, and Alex did a quick half bow, as Lorenzo had done to him when they had first met at the desert camp. Alex remembered thinking how cool it had looked, and was now glad of the chance of making a good impression on Lorenzo's grandmother. It seemed to work, as she acknowledged it with a slight nod. Natasha was aware that she could have done a little curtsey, but she didn't. A handshake was plenty. She wasn't going to grovel, she thought.

Before leaving London for her new job in Pisa, Julia, Natasha and Alex's mother, had reminded her children that while they were in Italy they should make a special effort with their manners. Traditional values were still a part of everyday life in Italy, she explained, even more so than in England, and she reminded Alex that first impressions were the ones that stuck.

"As a young man, Alex, you should always stand until you are invited to sit, stand up when a lady enters the room and remember to address adults by their full name or title."

She had told him to look people in the eye, and to talk clearly, and was to never offer his hand to an adult to shake before they first offered theirs to him.

"Why? I thought that would be polite," he said.

"No, it would actually be quite a rude faux pas. You see, a younger person, or a child of any age, should always wait for the adult to offer their hand first."

"Why?"

"Well, there's a protocol one must follow; you offering your hand to an adult would imply that you were the superior. You should always wait for the adult to offer theirs first. There are similar rules for adults to follow too," she explained.

"Like what?"

"Well, a lady always offers her hand to a gentleman to shake first; the man should never take her hand before she has offered hers. But of course they always do, the rule is hardly even known these days. Men just barge ahead like bulls in china shops, shaking women's hands whenever they feel like it, regardless of protocol!"

"Why shouldn't a man offer his hand first? That's just old fashioned, Mummy," Natasha said.

"Well, it's not really, Natasha. Think about it, a man wanting to shake my hand first, puts me in the awkward position of having to shake it. It's almost forcing a lady to hold a stranger's hand whether she wants to, or not. Believe me, Natasha, there may be a time when you don't want to shake a strangers hand, and you should have that choice. Traditionally, the man should wait to be offered a lady's hand. It should be our choice, not theirs."

"Now that makes total sense," Natasha said, "I like that rule."

So with these useful tips of etiquette fresh in their minds, Alex and Natasha sat down each side of the Contessa on the sofa, smiling politely but not quite sure what to say. Alex, remembering the Contessa's comment about his bone structure, leant on the arm of the sofa and very casually brought his hand to his face and surreptitiously examined his cheekbones. Unfortunately he was still none the wiser as to what she had meant, so he made a mental note to look up 'good bone structure' on the Internet when he got home.

"Gabriella, *dar*-ling," the Contessa was saying, "could you be so kind as to pour your friends, or should I say, your stepbrother and stepsister-to-be, some lemon juice?"

Gabriella giggled and jumped up happily from her seat and poured them each a glass of juice. She scooped a spoonful of crushed ice from a silver bucket into each glass with a little silver ladle.

They thanked her politely and took a sip. Natasha remembered the last person she had drank a glass of freshly squeezed juice with. Only that time it had been offered in a jam jar. She looked into the glass, so wishing Yanni was there. Her heart ached for him. Her thoughts were sharply brought back to the present by the Contessa turning to her and addressing her directly.

"I hear from my son, Natasha, that you have a secret yearning to do archaeology, too. I admire a young person who knows what she likes from an early age. It is quite admirable. And might I add that I understand that you recovered remarkably well from those unfortunate events that befell you in the desert. My son believes you all did very well to come out of the ordeal without mental scarring. And I must say, I agree with him. You see, in life it never pays to hold grudges. Remember; when something is over, it is over. Such as the war, for example. It is so much healthier for the mind."

Natasha nodded politely with a smile and looked into her glass. She felt the Contessa's eyes on her, but she couldn't immediately think of anything intelligent to say, about the war, whichever one she was referring to, about their horrible ordeal in the desert, or about anything else. She was about to say something nice about the juice, then changed her mind as she thought it would probably sound stupid. Her face turned red, her mind raced. She felt the Contessa's eyes watching her, waiting.

After what felt like an eternity, the Contessa smiled politely, then turned to Alex on her right, and looked him up and down.

"And you, Alex, have you any thoughts for your future? Are you a diligent student like my grandson, Lorenzo? How old are you, my boy, about thirteen?"

"Yes I am," he said, then quickly added, "Contessa." He looked her directly in the eye and smiled as his mother has told him to. "I like computers and would like to do something along the lines..."

"Computers! Oh, my Goodness!" she interrupted. "Don't talk to me about computers!"

She shook her head and waved her hand in the air as if to dismiss the subject, her bracelets jingling as she did so. "I am *totally* addicted to 'eBay'. I have bought the most wonderful and the most *useless* things. Is it not true, Gabriella? A week does not go by without the little postal van tooting his way up the hill to deliver a parcel of some kind or another that I'd won weeks before and *totally* forgotten about. And e-mail! Is it not the most wonderful invention? How did we ever live without it! And do you know, Alex, I am writing my autobiography for the future generations of the family, which, I suppose, will now include you. I believe this is the duty and obligation of everyone over eighty years of age, from every walk of life, to write their memoir. It may seem boring and dull now, but one day it will be most interesting, if not fascinating reading. What I wouldn't do to read my grandparents' memoirs had they written them. It is a duty, and I do believe that most strongly. You see, it is a personal recording of history. And this, Alex," she added as she tapped him on the knee with her folded glasses, "I am doing all on my little laptop computer. So my dear boy, study well, and I am sure you will go very far with your computers. And now, you see; now you have made me give away my age..."

They smiled politely.

"Now, Gabriella, I'm sure your two guests will want to change out of their travelling clothes and have some lunch. I have arranged for Maria to have it ready for you down at the pool house."

The Contessa picked up her newspaper again, and put her reading glasses back on the end of her nose.

"So drink up both of you," she said without looking up, "Gabriella can show you to your rooms. I will see you all for dinner tonight at seven o'clock."

CHAPTER THREE

G abriella led Natasha and Alex up the wide balustraded stairway to the second floor. At the landing she turned to the left, and they followed her through an archway into an ante-room, past a stone fireplace with logs neatly waiting in the hearth for winter, and two comfortable armchairs placed at an angle at each side of it.

"Well that wasn't as bad as I thought it would be," Alex said, reflecting on meeting Gabriella's grandmother, "I think she is actually quite nice, really, Gabriella."

"Oh, my grandmother? She is nice! You can ask her anything and she will know the answer. But she has eyes at the back of her head. She also knows when something is happening even before it has happened!"

"Wow, really?" Alex's eyes lit up. "You mean she's psychic?"

"No, Alex, it means she's clever, you dork!" Natasha said, and thumped his shoulder, "or sneaky," she added quietly out of Gabriella's earshot.

Gabriella pushed open the first pair of double doors at the far end of the anteroom.

"This is your bedroom, Natasha, and Alex, yours is the one next door. Lorenzo and my rooms are to the right of the stairs; it is almost a mirror image of this side. My grandmother's apartments are in the middle section between us. You will get used to it very quickly. Ah *bene*," she said, seeing luggage in the room, "your things have been brought up. Good old Giovanni."

She stepped aside and let Natasha enter the room first, and Alex had a quick peep, then disappeared next door to check out his room.

"It's a lovely bedroom," Natasha said.

The walls were a washed-out soft pink with a green fresco border of delicate faded leaves cascading from the ceiling in the four corners of the room. She walked over and touched the carved oak figurines in the headboard then climbed up on to the high bed and sank at least eight inches into it.

"It's rather opulent, Gabriella."

"It's not really opulent, Natasha, it's just… well; Italian."

Gabriella took a long run and leaped onto the bed, landing with a bounce the right way round beside Natasha.

"Years of practice!" she said, laughing at Natasha's stunned expression.

It was OK here, Natasha thought, as long as she wouldn't have too much contact with the Contessa. She could tell how pleased Gabriella was at having them to stay; Natasha remembered that it was a new chapter in Gabriella's life, as well as her own. She just wished the Contessa wasn't there.

They kicked off their shoes and Natasha began to slowly unwind. They lay back on the bed talking and catching up on their lives since they were together three months previously.

"You know there is a big party planned to celebrate our parent's engagement," Gabriella informed her.

"Oh, no, I didn't know. You mean here, at the house? While we're staying with you?"

"Of course at the house!" Gabriella laughed. "It is for my father and your mother! Of course while you are staying here! We are all family now!"

"Oh, so who's coming?"

"Everyone and anyone! It is so that your mother can meet our friends and family, and for them to see my father's new bride. It will be an evening to remember. Did you bring anything suitable to wear?"

"No, I didn't. We didn't know anything about it."

"Good, so we shall have to find something for you in Pisa!"

Gabriella told Natasha that there was to be a small orchestra, and the ballroom was going to be opened for the first time in years.

"I have never known a party here," she admitted. "There are going to be marquees on the lawn, and wonderful decorations. They have started to prepare for it already at the side of the house. It is going to be a beautiful event Natasha. Magical! There is even someone coming from England to do the beautiful lighting in the garden. It is the talk of Milan, you know!"

Natasha smiled at Gabriella for a moment, and then looked down.

"You know, Gabriella, I'll be honest with you. When I first met you, I did think you were a bit... well," she hesitated, wanting to say 'irritating' but didn't, "...spoiled. But you've shown, even just now by the way you are talking about your father's and my mother's engagement, that you are the most unselfish person I've ever met. And I must admit you sort of put me to shame."

Gabriella looked at her, a little shocked.

"Remember, Gabriella, when they first told us about their engagement?" Natasha continued.

Gabriella nodded. "Yes, I do. We were all together in that hot, hot tent. We all thought we had been asked to meet there because we were in big trouble! I remember it well!"

"Yes. But my point is, well, it took me a while to come to terms with it. You see, to be perfectly honest, I resented your father," she paused, feeling ashamed, "...and you just welcomed my mother, and me, and Alex..."

She turned away, unable to look at Gabriella.

Gabriella was quiet for a moment.

"But Natasha," she said, "understand this; you don't realise how miserable my father was. You know, he could hardly stay in this house for more than a day as the memories hurt him so much. Yes, it is true, I was... I *am* happy for him, and for your mother too. But I was also happy for Lorenzo, who suffered very much when my father was absent for weeks and months at a time. And also for me, too, you understand. It was very horrible, first losing our dear mother, and then, when our father was never here, it was as if we had lost him, also. I resented his being away, just as Lorenzo did. So yes, I am happy for Father, and for us. This way, we get our father back, and we gain much more, besides."

They sat in silence for a minute. Then Gabriella nudged Natasha in the ribs.

"So you see, Natasha," she said, "I am also a little selfish!"

Natasha nodded. "OK, good. That makes me feel better."

CHAPTER FOUR

A lex was busy checking out his room next door. It was as large as Natasha's, he was pleased to note, but it had two single beds instead of a double. Because the shutters were almost closed, and the tall, double, indoor windows shut, the room was dark and smelled of mothballs. But it was still cool, he thought. He could see a sofa, an armchair and a large mahogany writing desk, well stocked with stationery. On closer inspection, the writing paper had a faint watercolour print of the villa printed at the top of each page. He had seen stationery like that once before in an old hotel room in Corfu they had stayed at with their father, but having it on one's home stationary, he thought, was pretty nice. He would use it to write to his father, just to give him an idea of what the house was like, he thought. Before they had left London, his father had told Alex that he wanted all the gory details about Marcello's house, so this writing paper would be perfect.

Looking around the room, Alex couldn't help noticing the unusual wall decor. It was hard to miss, really; a classical fresco of a landscape was painted directly onto the walls around the whole room. There were trees, rolling hills and crumbling, overgrown ruins. There was a temple or abbey on the wall between the two windows, and on the large wall behind the beds, there was a scene with a couple of shepherds in old fashioned tunics, resting on some fallen pillars with their sheep grazing around them. Alex wondered if this had been Marcello's room when he was a child, and the scenes of ruins had sparked his interest in archaeology. It was certainly faded enough to have been here when he was a child; the plaster was even peeling off in places.

Alex thought how weird it was that this was going to be his second home, or third, he corrected himself. Whichever order he categorized them in, it would certainly need some getting used to. But he decided it wasn't such a bad thing, only different. The only bore about the whole set-up here, he thought, was having to wash and change every evening for dinner. Looking at his two holdalls that had been placed at the foot of his bed, he wondered if he had brought enough clothes to last a week, let alone the whole summer.

He opened the heavy door on the wall facing his bed. This, it turned out, was his bathroom. It seemed very old-fashioned. The high ceiling created a sort of echoy, hollow feel to the room. There was a very worn, cast iron bath in the centre, supported by black, clawed feet. The bath looked so deep, Alex calculated that if he sat in it when it was full, the water would probably come up to his neck. The squeaky-looking brass taps looked like they had been there for a hundred years. There was an upright wooden chair beside the bath with two stiff, neatly ironed bath towels folded over the back of it.

"Well I suppose you and I are going to become well acquainted over the next few days," he muttered, feeling the side of the cold bath. "But then again," he thought, touching the stiff, rough towels, "…maybe not."

He looked at the mirror over the warn basin and could hardly see his reflection. The old, speckled glass had faint greyish-brown spots seeping from the reverse side of it, as if it had some terrible disease. He was reminded of something his mother had once told him after returning from one of her weekend antique hunts. She had bought a mirror for her dressing table, and when he had grimaced at the 'age spots' on the glass, she explained that they were actually a good thing in antique mirrors. Personally, he thought the whole idea of collecting antiques was pretty weird. He couldn't understand anyone wanting to have dead strangers' furniture in their homes. Glancing at the old mirror again in the bathroom, he wondered if Natasha would let him use her bathroom. He really didn't like his much at all. He had to devise a little plan so he could wangle it. Perhaps he could tell her that he had forgotten to pack his toothpaste, then, he would *have* to use her bathroom!

Satisfied with his little plan, he went back into his bedroom. He pulled open the first set of tall, inner windows then pushed the heavy outer shutters as far as they would go, loudly banging the outside walls of the house.

"Whoops! Sorry, Your Highness!" he joked to himself.

He gingerly leaned out over the windowsill to see if he had damaged anything and saw a few pieces of the faded pink plaster on the path and flowerbeds below.

"Oh dear, sorry, Ma'am," he muttered.

He took in the view and breathed in the fresh air. The sun poured into his room and the hot air smelled sweet. He closed his eyes. He was happy to be in Italy. He loved the hot, peacefulness of the Italian countryside; the high-pitched sound of the crickets, the dry leaves of the shrubs and plants rustling in the hint of a breeze. It reminded him of how far he had travelled today. The view from his window looked out to the side of the villa, and he could just see the white sparkles of the pool through the trees in the distance.

"Fantastic!" he said to himself. To the right, through the trees, he could make out patches of the red clay of the tennis court. He tried to see if Lorenzo was still having his lesson, but he couldn't see any movement on the court or hear the thwack of tennis balls.

"ALEX! CIAO!" Lorenzo's voice startled him from behind.

"Oh Lorenzo! You made me jump! You're here! I was just looking to see if I could spot you on the court through the trees! Hello!"

"Welcome to Italy! Welcome to my home! I am *so* sorry, Alex, I was not allowed to cancel my tennis lesson, but I did try, believe me. And I had to make up an extra hour because of the storms last week. It has been crazy weather!"

"No problem, it's great to see you!"

The boys shook hands and slapped each other on the shoulders with affection. Lorenzo, in his tennis whites looked particularly tanned, making Alex feel as pale as a sheet. Lorenzo's voice was deeper than when they had last seen each other, and his hair was longer, too. It was wavier and beginning to curl over his ears and around his neck. It made Alex feel very school-boyish with his 'short, back and sides' hair cut.

"How was your trip over here? Uneventful I hope, unlike the last one!" Lorenzo joked.

"Definitely. We didn't even get held up at gun-point, once!"

"Oh dear, how boring. I will have to arrange something!" Lorenzo laughed. "So is your room OK, Alex?" Lorenzo checked the thick mattress on his bed for him. "A little better than that thin camp bed, no?"

"I'd say a whole lot better! It's great Lorenzo, thanks. The room is perfect."

"This used to be my father's, when he was a boy."

"I thought it might have been, looking at the walls..."

"I know, and look in here," he lifted the lid of a trunk that was behind the door, "there are his toy trains and cars, and look, maps, and his boyhood secret plans! All his childhood memories are in here. He was apparently an avid explorer and archaeologist even at ten, according to my grandmother. She kept everything."

He closed the trunk.

"So you think you will be OK with this room?"

"Oh, yes fine. But won't your father want his room when he comes back from Pisa with my mother?"

"No, no, don't worry about that, it's all yours. He has the whole top floor. He has an office up there too. He doesn't use this room any more. He hasn't slept in here for decades. It's yours, Alex."

"Oh, I see." Alex looked a little worried.

"What is it?"

"When you mentioned your father's mother keeping everything... I mean your grandmother... I mean the Contessa, it just reminded me... well, I just hope I've brought enough clothes for all this changing you do in the evenings. Do you think I'll get the chance to have my clothes washed while I'm here?"

"*Ma*, Alex!" Lorenzo smiled kindly and put an arm around his shoulder, "we are not at the desert camp now! Don't concern yourself about anything! You are on holiday and will be very well taken care of. Maria, Piero's wife, sees to all of that kind of thing. You will be fine. Please, let's talk about something other than laundry! Come on, find some shorts, get out of those hot, English clothes and let's go downstairs. There is something I've been waiting to show you."

CHAPTER FIVE

L orenzo pushed open the double doors and stood aside to let Alex enter the room first. "This is the library, Alex."

"Impressive," he said, and walked in. Wall to wall glass fronted cabinets covered every inch of wall space, all crammed with leather-bound books from floor to ceiling.

"Wow! How cool is that! You've even got one of those ladders that wiz around the room on little casters. I didn't think people had them in their homes."

Lorenzo shrugged, a little embarrassed.

"That's not why I brought you in here. Look closer. There is something I think you will find very interesting."

Two well-worn, leather sofas faced each other in the middle of the room, with a long, narrow table behind each of them. Beside the table lamps, there was the Italian daily newspaper, an English newspaper, magazines and a tray housing a few pairs of reading glasses and pencils. On the floor, a deep, red Persian rug bound the furniture together like an island. An impressive room, Alex thought, but he wondered why Lorenzo would be so keen to show it to him. He certainly didn't intend to do any reading on holiday, that was for sure. He looked at Lorenzo, who stood grinning at him, obviously waiting for some kind of reaction.

Alex was a little puzzled.

"What, is it a test of some kind?"

Lorenzo gave him a shrug.

"Keep looking!" he said.

Alex scoured the room for a clue.

"What am I looking for?"

"OK, I'll give you a hint. Something small and plentiful."

"Small and plentiful?"

That wasn't much help. The books were plentiful, but not particularly small.

"Come on, tell me! I give up, Lorenzo, tell me!" he said, walking round the room for a third time. "What is it?"

"OK, I'll give you another hint. Look at the handles on the cabinets."

Alex walked over to the nearest wall of cabinets to have a look. He stopped dead in his tracks when he recognized the symbol carved onto the round knob.

"A swastika!"

"Yes. On every handle."

"But why, Lorenzo? Why swastikas? That's pretty creepy."

"The house was occupied by German officers during the war, and they left their mark."

Alex walked around the room and checked every set of knobs. Lorenzo was right; they had left their mark, all right. Every single mahogany handle was beautifully engraved with a swastika. There must have been at least twenty pairs of them.

"Why didn't your family have them removed after the war? It must be a horrible reminder every time anyone comes in here to grab a book. Why would anyone want to keep these swastikas on the handles?"

"I think for exactly that reason, Alex, as a reminder, so we never forget. If they had been removed, I, for one, would never have felt the significance of the occupation. And I, then would have been unable to show you. Seeing them so close, and being able to touch them like this, has shaken you in such a way that just telling you about it, would never have had the same impact. It is part of the house's history. It cannot be erased. And I suppose it shouldn't be."

Alex thought of his bath upstairs. He wondered if some German officer had sat in it with the water almost up to *his* neck. He wondered who and looked into that same shaving mirror. He wasn't sure how he felt about it. It was more than a little creepy.

"Come, Alex," Lorenzo said, leading him out of the library. "There's something else I want to show you."

"There's more?" Alex wasn't sure if he wanted to see more.

Lorenzo took Alex into another room across the main hallway, where a long mahogany table had ten high-backed chairs tucked in around it. It was obviously the dining room, Alex thought. The arched ceiling, with the wide, curved supporting beams reminded him of a cathedral. Between the beams were painted chubby cherubs, floating amongst the clouds. The cherubs were holding long scrolls, showing curly, Latin writing. Alex tried to read some of the script, thinking there might be a clue hidden there, but he couldn't understand much at all, not because it was old and faded, but because he didn't know the vocabulary. Now he wished he had opted for Latin at school. It would have been cool to be able to read it.

One section of the fresco nearest the fireplace, he noticed, was almost blackened from years of smoke escaping from the chimneybreast.

"Is that what you wanted to show me, the old chimneybreast? Or the scrolls up there in the cherubs hands?"

Lorenzo shook his head.

"Neither. You're so, so cold. Keep looking."

Alex examined the fireplace mantle. It was at least five feet high, and very deep. The grate in the hearth was large enough to burn a couple of tree stumps the size of car wheels. Impressive? Yes, but again, he wondered what he was supposed to be looking for. There wasn't even a knob in the room, except for the two door handles, and he had already checked those for swastikas, none to report there. He checked the chairs to see if there was anything carved on them, but saw nothing really interesting, they just had a swan on the fabric and some leaves carved up the legs. He searched the polished wooden floor for clues. Nothing.

Lorenzo had that grin on his face again, enjoying Alex's confusion.

"I give up. Come on, give me a hint then," Alex said at last.

"Look up at the ceiling again."

Lorenzo pointed to the far end of the room.

"I thought you would be interested, Alex. Remember when we were planning our escape from the cave you told Gabriella and me about Colditz?"

"Yes, I do. But what am I looking at in here? I can't see any swasti...." he stopped.

Looking up at the far end of the room, he saw what Lorenzo was talking about.

"Lorenzo," he said slowly, hardly believing his eyes, "those aren't... *bullet* holes, are they?"

"Semi-automatic rifle, I believe."

Alex didn't say a word. It sent a chill down his spine. He was almost afraid to speak. He looked at the holes sprayed in the wall on the far side of the room. They went in an arc from halfway up the wall to the ceiling, over the door to the kitchen and then down the other side. Alex didn't know how he had missed them when he had come in; it was so obvious now that he was looking at it.

"I thought it was just the plaster falling off... I didn't really look..."

He didn't like it. Although the Nazis had left over sixty years ago, it felt as if they could be back any minute.

"My grandmother told us that the Germans did this when they had to leave the house in a hurry. The allies had landed to the south of Rome on the beaches, you see, at Anzio, thousands and thousands of them, and they were gradually fighting their way up the country, pushing the Germans north. It took many months and they suffered terribly during the long, winter months."

"Who, the allies?"

"Yes, of course Alex! The Germans, too. There was terrific fighting around Rome and throughout the surrounding countryside and villages. Thousands of young men died; British, Polish, American, Indian, Moroccan and New Zealanders..."

"Really?"

"Yes, it took many months of battles to push the Germans back. Have you not heard of Montecassino? The countryside is full of cemeteries of young men, not much older than us, who were killed so far from home. My father says that Italian soil has soaked up more foreign blood than it will ever produce in wine."

"Lorenzo, that's horrible."

"I know, and believe me, Alex, we have a lot of vineyards in Italy. We should not forget, ever. During the last war the Italian resistance fighters were very active in this area, it was a nightmare for the Nazis, as it is so hilly around here. There was a lot of underground partisan activity. Especially here in these hills and valleys."

"Really? That's cool!"

"Yes, it was. I like to think that if I had been alive then, I would have joined them, too. Most people think of France whenever resistance fighting is mentioned, but here in Italy it was very active, also. The partisans played a large role in expelling the enemy. We also suffered greatly because of it."

"I didn't know that, sorry."

"You know, Alex, for every German soldier that we Italians killed, they rounded up ten of us Italian guys to be shot in retaliation."

"*Ten*?"

"Yes. Ten. Ten for one. If the Germans couldn't find ten men to take, they took boys to make up the numbers."

"You're kidding."

"I'm not. And listen to this; should a German officer be killed, not just a regular soldier, but an officer, it meant one hundred Italian males were rounded up and shot."

"A hundred! A hundred lives for one officer? That's insane!" Alex was horrified.

"Yes. Not many people know that. They, the partisans, had to find ingenious ways to hide our male population. Trap doors, underground bunkers…"

"Oh God, Lorenzo, I can't imagine how horrible it must have been. I didn't know about the raids on ordinary civilians. They didn't teach us that when we did the war at school. It's not mentioned in any history books we have."

Alex focused back on the spray of bullets on the wall.

"But why would the Germans do this to your home?"

Lorenzo shrugged. "This is nothing, really. They destroyed a lot of things in the country, in retaliation, you know, at the end of the war. Some things much more precious than our dining room wall. Ask my father; he feels physically ill if you mention it."

"Like what? What do you mean?"

"Well, for a start, him being an archaeologist, I think the burning of the two incredible, ancient Roman pleasure barges, that for over two thousand years had rested at the bottom of Lake Nemi, is still very bad for him to think about. This mindless destruction was the worst thing for him."

"What, you mean there were real ancient Roman barges, on a lake?"

"Yes, at the bottom of the lake, just outside Rome. They were built for the Emperor Caligula. Caligula used to hold his lavish, extravagant parties there in the hot summer months, as it was cooler there, out of the city, and of course, very private. He would escape the oppressive heat of Rome and go to his two barges on the lake with hundreds of guests. They were really enormous floating palaces, opulent beyond imagination."

"Incredible! I've heard about Caligula. There was a film on him that my mother didn't let me see."

"Well, how can I put it, Caligula wasn't one of the best Emperors that Rome ever had. However, my father said that these two barges he had built were luxurious beyond imagination, even to our present day standards. They had hot and cold running water in the private marble bathrooms and Jacuzzis with gold taps. My father actually has trouble talking about their destruction, as it hurts him so much."

"So the Nazis destroyed them?"

"Yes. It was a travesty. Mussolini had spent several years and a small fortune carefully raising them from the depths of Lake Nemi. His engineers used an ingenious way to drain the lake, so as not to damage them. There was a museum built on the shore to house them and to restore them and their precious contents. The world had seen nothing like these barges before. And they were in such good condition. They were the only two in existence, even in Roman times."

"So what happened?"

"Well, upon their departure, the Germans simply burned the museum and the barges as they went through the area. It was a loss to the whole world, not just to Italy. It was terrible. All the research, the artefacts, the documentation in progress; all burned to ashes. And the fact that there were no other boats ever built like them, makes it all the more devastating."

Lorenzo prodded at the dry logs in the hearth with a fire-iron.

"Wow," Alex said. "That really sucks."

"Yes. It hurt our national pride; it was a pointless destruction. The Germans also stripped us of our other treasures; they stole priceless artwork and furniture, emptying hundreds of stately homes, art galleries and museums."

"I didn't realize that."

"Well," he sighed, "on the bright side, thankfully the Nazis, on the whole, loved and appreciated art. Which is lucky really, if you think of what they could have done had they not. Hitler was a great collector, you see. His commissioned art collectors were well organized and systematic the way they stole it; he had historians and art dealers working for him in all the occupied countries to fulfil his dream of having the world's best collection in his new museum in Austria. He felt it was his right to have the best paintings in his possession. And then, of course, there were those under him, who plundered and stole just for themselves; the opportunists, officers and soldiers who just helped themselves, mainly stealing for their own pleasure, or as security, something to live on after the war. Many of our paintings were taken from this house, and things from our chapel."

"Really? That's horrible!" Alex said. He also thought it amazing that Lorenzo had his own chapel, but didn't probe him on that point.

"I shouldn't take it personally," Lorenzo continued, "but I do. When I am older, I'd like to investigate the theft of our family paintings and personal items."

"Well, why not start now? Why wait?"

"Where would I start? Anyway, it's 'small fry' as you say, no? Compared to everything else that was stolen. Our family 'treasures' are really not that important compared to the other things they took from Italy."

"So what? 'Small fry' or not, they were still your family's things. We were burgled a couple of times in London; It's horrible. But I can't imagine them doing it openly, as if it was their right. Weird."

Alex and Lorenzo were quiet for a moment.

"Lorenzo, I wonder where all the art went after the Nazis had lost the war? I mean the big stuff they took from galleries and art museums. Where is it all now?"

"It is still being recovered. Auction houses are always on the lookout for missing paintings. To their credit, much has been recovered in the last fifty years and even recently, like the one by Klimt, a couple of years ago."

Alex nodded knowingly, but he really didn't know what Lorenzo meant; he hadn't heard of Klimt.

"So much of Italy's heritage is still missing, Alex. Some paintings were recovered in mines and tunnels deep in the mountains in northern Italy, only a couple of hours from here. But most of the hoard will be hanging in very respectable galleries, and, I should think, in private homes of the rich and famous all over the world. Without proof of origin or original ownership, no one can do very much about it."

"What about the art stolen from your house? Do you think you'll ever get that back?"

"No, it's gone. They left the family portraits, but took the rest. I suppose there was not a market in anonymous faces. My grandmother has promised to document the paintings that were taken. I hope she does it soon; I worry, in case her memory fades one day. But she is not one to be pushed."

"It would make me so furious to have been openly robbed," Alex said. He looked up at the bullet-sprayed wall again.

"Luckily he missed the fresco; he mostly got the top section of the wall and the edge of the ceiling where there's only sky."

Lorenzo looked up at the arc of bullets.

"You know, you're right, Alex. I hadn't looked at it that way. The detailed paintings on the ceiling and over the doorframe are almost untouched. It has miraculously escaped the majority of the bullet spray."

"Miraculously?" Alex shook his head. "Na; I think this guy had a conscience. Or maybe he was just a bad shot."

Lorenzo examined the pattern of the spray. "A bad shot, I doubt. The conscience theory sounds better. Come on, let's go. I'll show you the river."

"You know Lorenzo," Alex said as they closed the double doors behind them, "I think your English has improved a lot since Easter."

"Actually, I feel very comfortable talking in English now. It flows easier."

"They say when you start to dream in another language, you've really mastered it."

"Ah, then I will never know," Lorenzo said.

"Why?"

"When I wake up, I can never remember my dreams!"

CHAPTER SIX

"Gabriella, can I tell you a secret?" Natasha asked quietly.

Gabriella sat up on her sunbed and looked at her. They were lying by the pool, flicking through the magazines that Natasha had bought at the airport.

"Of course," Gabriella said. "You have a secret? Tell me yours first and then I will tell you mine."

"Well," Natasha started, "promise you won't repeat it to *anyone*?"

"I promise! What is it?"

"Well, you remember Yanni, at the dig last Easter…"

"Of course I remember him! The hero who saved me from dying a terrible death in the heat of the desert! How will I ever forget him! He is the kindest person in the world…"

"Well, yes, I know, Gabriella. But I sort of *really* like him. I was going to tell you before, but I thought you might say something. You wont, will you? I just can't stop thinking about him."

"No! You like him? After all this time? You haven't seen him since then, have you?"

"No," Natasha said with an embarrassed smile.

"You mean you really like him *that* way? I had no idea. Did you let him know? Did he like you back?"

"I don't know," she shrugged. "But he did give me lots of attention at the dig, and he saw that I had problems with …" she hesitated. She had to be careful, as it was Yanni who had helped her accept the fact that her mother was going to marry Gabriella's father.

"... with the engagement and stuff, and he sort of talked me through it."

"That is so nice of him! But do you think he liked you too?"

"He did touch my hand once, and he pulled my plait a couple of times before it was... you know, cut off, and he did tell me my hair looked nice once it had been cut properly afterwards. Actually, he said it made me look older. Do you think that means anything?"

"I don't know. He is a bit old for you isn't he? He must be at least nineteen or twenty."

"Twenty. But I really, really need to find out if he is in Pisa with your father. Will you help me? How can we find out if he is there? I can't wait to see him; my heart misses a beat when I think of him! I'll die, Gabriella, if we get to Pisa and he isn't there. I counted the days until I came to Italy, hoping to see him. How can we find out if he is here?"

"Natasha! You are crazy! But we can ask my grandmother. Perhaps she will know."

"No, No! Not *directly*! We'll have to do it in a roundabout way, I don't want her to know anything!"

"OK, we can ask about my father's excavation, and who's there. We'll do it tonight. At dinner."

"OK!"

They high-fived each other.

"Now Natasha, shall I tell you mine?"

"Your what?"

"My secret!"

"Your secret?" Natasha couldn't imagine Gabriella having a secret at all. "Oh, yes sorry, of course, I forgot," she said.

"Well, it is hard to say, because I don't really know for sure..." Gabriella stopped, and almost changed her mind.

"What, Gabriella, tell me!"

"It is about my grandmother."

"Your *grandmother*? What?" Natasha was intrigued. "What kind of secret could there possibly be about your grandmother?"

"You cannot tell *anyone*, not even Alex or Lorenzo."

"I won't! What is it Gabriella?"

"I... I... I think she is..."

What, a witch? Natasha wanted to say.

"Come on Gabriella, I told you mine," she prompted her.

"I think my grandmother and Giovanni, our old gardener, are..."

"Are..." Natasha tried to help her spit it out.

"You know; close."

"*Close*?"

Gabriella nodded, unable to look Natasha in the eye.

"You mean like, as in, *close,* close?"

Gabriella said nothing; she just looked down.

Natasha burst out laughing. She had to sit up so that she didn't choke.

"Gabriella that's the funniest thing I've heard in years! You've got be joking!"

Gabriella wasn't amused at Natasha's reaction. She looked hurt.

Natasha tried to control herself and look serious. She apologized for laughing, but it was still hard not to smile at the thought of it. She frowned as she composed herself. She tried to look as serious as she could.

"I'm sorry, Gabriella, but the gardener?" she asked. "You mean the one who we saw watering the plants on the veranda?"

"Yes, Maria's father," Gabriella mumbled.

"But Gabriella! He *has* to be at least a hundred years old! And your grandmother is no spring chicken either! It's not even worth thinking about! And to tell you the truth, having just met her, I think she would probably set her goals a little higher than falling for the ancient gardener, don't you?"

She tried hard not to laugh again. He would certainly have to be a desperate man to want the Contessa, she thought.

Gabriella looked Natasha in the eye. She hadn't smiled.

"I saw them," she said softly, looking down. "I was walking to our family chapel last Monday, as I sometimes do, with fresh flowers, and I saw them, beside the chapel wall."

"Saw them... what? You mean... like, kissing?" Natasha was horrified, and the smile disappeared from her face. She couldn't believe it.

"Well, not exactly, but they were standing next to each other, very close, and my grandmother was... she was..."

"What?"

"I think she was rubbing his back, or something. She had her arm around him."

Natasha sat back. She grimaced showing her utter revulsion.

"No way! That's disgusting!"

Gabriella lowered her eyes again as if she carried her grandmother's shame on her shoulders. Natasha looked at her and thought for a minute. This was serious. A dark, dark secret in the illustrious Bonamici-Milanese dynasty? But she knew it was silly. Gabriella must have been mistaken.

"Look, Gabriella. Let's not jump to any conclusions here. It could be very innocent. And it could have been two totally different people."

Gabriella shook her head. "No, it was definitely them."

Natasha thought again. "Well, so what if she hugged the old gardener? It doesn't have to mean anything more than what it was; a back-rub and a hug. Perhaps she had been working him too hard. Perhaps he just... needed a back-rub! Perhaps he was sore; He is very old, after all."

"Natasha! They were hiding beside the chapel!"

"Oh."

"You see? It is a grave secret I have to bear forever."

"Look Gabriella, we'll keep an eye on the situation. I'm sure it will all turn out to be nothing. Maybe it was poor light and it was, in fact, Giovanni's wife you saw and not your grandmother."

"I hope not, his wife has been dead for decades."

"Oh."

"Natasha! She is my *grandmother*! Please, promise you won't mention it to the boys, they would never understand!"

"OK, promise. Though I'm really not sure I understand, myself."

CHAPTER SEVEN

"That is the Trebbia River," Lorenzo announced to Alex with pride, pointing to the glittering river below them. The boys had left the manicured gardens of the villa behind and had walked with Darius, bounding happily beside them, to the unkempt, overgrown edge of the property, where the land began to slope away towards the river.

"And down there, unfortunately, is where the Romans suffered the most terrible and humiliating defeat in two hundred and eighteen B.C."

"Really? Down *there*?" Alex grinned at Lorenzo, not quite sure if he was joking or not. But Lorenzo was perfectly serious.

"Yes, down there, exactly. We were under attack from Hannibal of Carthage. You know about him, don't you? He is famous for marching with his elephants all the way from Spain to invade Italy by crossing over the Alps."

"Well I kind of remember learning about Hannibal and his elephants, but that's about all I remember, really. I didn't know he was from Carthage. We do the Romans briefly at school the same term that we do the Vikings and Boadicea. But we don't really go into much detail of individual battles. Well, not that I can remember, anyway," he admitted.

"Well, as you can imagine, I know quite a lot about this battle, with this river on my doorstep," Lorenzo said. "And we 'do' the Romans in school in detail!"

"That makes sense. So, what happened here then, with Hannibal?"

"Well, Hannibal and his brother Mago, had marched his thirty-seven elephants, his infantry of over ninety thousand men, and all the equipment that went with such a massive army, from Spain, to… well, here."

The boys looked down again at the winding river, which was almost mirror-like in the sunlight.

"That's incredible!" Alex said.

"It is! What happened down there was to become known as the Battle of Trebbia. It's where we Italians tried to stop him advancing on to Rome."

"And did you?"

"Well, not exactly."

"Oh."

"I know. It wasn't good."

"I'm sorry. Maybe the Romans were in shock, finding out he had done the impossible by coming over the mountains," Alex suggested. "It's hard enough to come down with skis on; I can't imagine what it would be like to come down with an army and the elephants. Imagine how the Romans must have reacted when they heard about it! They must have been incredulous!" Alex was pleased to get the word in, had learned it only a couple of days previously.

"Perhaps," Lorenzo said with a smile. "They knew of his enormous army advancing like a machine. It moved at an unbelievable pace. They tried to catch up with him before he reached the raging Rhone River in Germany, thinking it would be a major obstacle for him. But the Romans arrived three days too late; Hannibal had already crossed the river and had moved on."

"Wow. How did he cross the river?"

"He had chopped down trees and made rafts strong enough to carry the elephants and his whole army across. The man hardly stopped for breath. He was a machine!"

"I like the sound of Hannibal. He had guts."

"You wouldn't if you were Italian. Even the hostile tribes he encountered along the way didn't stop him; he still managed to move quickly, keeping our generals at his heels. He always seemed a step ahead."

"Cool! How did he manage that?"

"Well, he used scouts to run ahead to gather information about the terrain he was about to pass through. This saved a lot of time, so he always knew of the shortest and easiest route to take."

"Like a sort of reconnaissance?" Alex asked.

"Yes, exactly. And of course, once he knew about the terrain ahead, he could plan his next attack. He showed respect for the customs and beliefs of the people whose territory he needed to march through, so he could win them over to his side without having to fight them. Therefore, his army always swelled, rather than shrank."

"That's clever!"

"Wait a minute, who's side are you on, Alex?" Lorenzo pretended to be offended and thump him on the arm.

"Ha! Not sure yet, keep going!"

"Well, he crossed over the Alps during the winter, I think the Romans expected Hannibal to wait until spring, when it would have been much easier."

"Wow, I bet his men really respected him, to follow him into the unknown like that."

"Yes, or to have the promise of all the riches of Rome waiting for them when they reached their goal."

"True." Alex knew from first-hand experience that some people would do anything for money; being held for ransom in a dark cave was still very clear in his mind.

"But why did he come all the way from Spain? Wouldn't it have been easier to have just sailed directly from Carthage in North Africa to Rome? That's just a quick hop across the sea!"

"Hannibal wasn't in Carthage, he was already colonizing Spain."

"Oh." Alex was confused.

"Spain was a massive stronghold of the Carthaginians, you see. His people were the famous Phoenicians, the greatest seafarers who had colonized most of the Mediterranean coastline for generations. The Greeks and Romans had both become tired of the Carthaginian sea supremacy; for years they had been at war with Carthage, and tremendous sea battles had taken place to try to put and end to it. You can imagine it, with the hundreds of oarsmen below decks heaving at the long, heavy oars..."

"Yeah, just like the movies!"

"Yes, but it was real. Eventually, though, after years of fighting, Hannibal's father, a great general, lost control of Sicily, which was the most important colony, being right in the centre of the Mediterranean, you see. So when they lost Sicily, they went west and took Spain, to build up a mighty stronghold there."

"Oh, I see. So that's where Hannibal was..."

"Yes, Hannibal was in charge there. And don't forget, Alex, attacking the Italian coastline directly would have been difficult, as it was heavily guarded. A sea invasion would have been far too obvious; no surprise to anyone, least of all the Romans."

"So I suppose Spain was far enough away to the west, and the Romans couldn't see what was brewing there."

"Exactly, from Spain, Hannibal could launch this massive campaign; organizing, planning and recruiting the one hundred thousand men he needed, from all around the Mediterranean. It was an enormous endeavour which took time."

"Wow!"

"Not only that, he had an eleven thousand-strong cavalry, and all the cumbersome machines of war that were needed, from battering-rams to giant catapults. He had thirty-nine elephants trained exclusively for battle, and I suppose they pulled the cumbersome equipment too. You can imagine what a major operation it must have been." Lorenzo said.

"Enormous. Quite frightening really, I wouldn't want to see him coming my way. I just imagined it was him with a few men and the elephants. I had no idea it was such a massive army."

"It was; nothing stopped him, rivers, valleys, not even the Alps. There is a famous quote of his that I really like, which he used before he started crossing the Alps; 'We will either find a way, or make one,' and I think it says it all about him in a nutshell, don't you?"

Alex nodded. He thought about the enormous undertaking, and what it would have entailed, and how driven Hannibal must have been.

"What happened to the elephants?" he asked.

"Elephants?" Lorenzo shrugged. "Many of them died in the treacherous icy conditions on the mountains. He lost hundreds of men too. By the time they came down and into the valleys on the Italian side, they were starved and in terrible condition. But they had done it."

"Wow. So how did they keep going?"

"With his rallying speeches, his encouragement, and enthusiasm, Hannibal got his army to its feet again."

"It must have been terrible. Just imagine; hungry, weak, their feet would have slipped, been cut open and suffered from frostbite in the ice and snow. Poor animals."

"Animals? I thought you were talking about the men!"

Alex laughed. "But you'd think he'd have waited for the snow to melt. But I suppose had he waited for spring, your lot would have been waiting for him!"

"Exactly. That's why the whole expedition became so famous. He did the unthinkable."

"So what happened down there on the river? You still haven't told me."

Lorenzo sighed, and looked down the valley.

"Down there, Alex, on the banks of the icy waters, is where this Battle of Trebbia took place. I think Hannibal killed fifteen to twenty thousand Romans."

"Really? Fifteen thousand men died, down there? You mean actually... down there?" Alex starred back at the tranquil, glistening river.

It was hard for him to take in. He tried to picture the scene with fifteen thousand horrifically wounded, dying men writhing in the river and on the banks below him. He imagined the colour of the icy water.

"But that's horrific, Lorenzo. That's...." Alex shook his head in disbelief, "that's a lot of blood and bodies. Even one thousand men lying there would be a lot, but fifteen thousand? I've never been so close to such a horrible scene before. It feels kind of weird."

"Many of the Romans drowned in the river of course," Lorenzo continued. "Hannibal lost comparatively few of his own men, and most of those he lost were Gauls, his latest recruits from his march through southern Germany. I think we Italians killed the last of the elephants here. I don't think he had any left after the Battle of Trebbia. Some historians say one survived, but we don't really know for sure."

Alex was quiet while he took it all in.

"Well at least you put them out of their misery. Poor animals," he eventually said.

"What? Poor *animals*? What about our men being hacked and sliced to death down there! You English are strange the way you put animals before people!"

Lorenzo was joking, but there was a hint of seriousness in his tone, too.

"Well, I suppose I'm a bit of a conscientious objector in this case, Lorenzo, being neither Italian nor Carthaginian. I can't take anyone's side, except the innocent. And the innocent in this battle were the elephants and horses, without a doubt."

"Oh come *on* Alex," Lorenzo said, sarcastically. "He was invading *our* country! Were we Italians not the innocent?"

"OK, I understand Hannibal was the aggressor, true, but the Romans had certainly done their share of invading and plundering too. All roads did lead to Rome, Lorenzo, and that's because you Romans had built them. You guys were already taking half the world!"

"That's good! *Very* good, Alex!" Lorenzo chuckled, enjoying the banter. "Especially coming from an Englishman! Let's not forget your British Empire!"

"OK, OK, point taken! I suppose every nation has had its day of plundering some time or another, including mine. But I still think the elephants got a raw deal, though."

He stared down at the river again. He still couldn't get his head around the fact that over fifteen thousand men had died down there in the glistening waters.

"Why do you think the Romans lost so many men Lorenzo? I thought the Romans were great fighters, if not the greatest." Alex asked.

"Well, they were, but it was still the early days of Rome. Italy was not completely united. Hannibal, being Hannibal, took advantage of this. The tribes in the Northern Provinces had nothing to do with Rome and were actually a headache for them. However, the Roman commander Sempronius fell into a trap, you see. He was very eager for a battle, and Hannibal knew it. Until then, Hannibal had called all the shots first by carefully selecting the ground in which to fight to his advantage. Sempronius, not realizing this, fell for it completely."

"How?"

"Well, it was winter, and very cold. Sempronius had already tried to stop Hannibal twice, and failed. As I already mentioned, Alex, the Romans were always at his heels, always one step behind him; it was humiliating for the Romans."

"Yeah, I can see how that would have been embarrassing."

"And frustrating. But Hannibal's plan here at Trebbia was very clever, he took all this into account. Almost playing a mind game, he knew Sempronius would be seething inside. So Hannibal sent his younger brother Mago with a light Numidian infantry and cavalry to hide along the riverbank in the marshes overnight, just down there, do you see? Down there, to the left; it is still marshy, even today."

"Numidians? Who were they?" Alex asked.

"They were the great horsemen from Africa, you've heard of them haven't you, Alex? They were actually the greatest horsemen on the planet, the Numidians."

"Oh, yeah, yeah!" Alex said, nodding confidently.

"So they laid their horses flat on their sides, and hid low throughout the night in the reeds and waited to give the Romans their early morning call."

"So the Romans had no idea they were there? How many Romans were there?"

"Thousands. They were camped all along that side of the riverbank, over there. At dawn, a few of Hannibal's infantry sneaked into their camps and woke them up by taunting them, shaking their tents and making a loud noise."

"I should think they must have leapt out of their skins!" Alex said.

"Well, Hannibal knew they would immediately jump into action and come out to fight. He planned it, knowing they would be half dressed, in the freezing cold and without having eaten breakfast. He had it all worked out, you see. The cold, sleepy Romans chased what they thought was a small number of Numidians back across the river. But what they didn't know was they were chasing them towards Hannibal's well-fed, warm, dry army in waiting."

"Oh my God, what happened?"

"Remember the Numidians lying low with their horses in the reeds?"

"Yes..."

"Well, they got up and attacked the Romans from behind, chasing them further into the hands of Hannibal's awaiting cavalry, towards that flat plain over there."

Lorenzo pointed to a meadow further down to the left of the river.

"Wow, that's clever. But how did he know the Romans would come out and fight?"

"Of course they would fight! They wouldn't just roll over in their beds and go back to sleep! They couldn't say, 'oh, do you mind waiting a moment before we fight, we haven't had breakfast yet and we need to get dressed', they did exactly what Hannibal imagined they would do! They jumped into action.

"But what has not having breakfast got to do with it? Couldn't they fight properly without it? The Romans were tough. Come on, Lorenzo, this is an army you're talking about, not a girl-scout camping trip."

"Yes, but remember, Alex," Lorenzo said, grinning at the thought of a girl-scout camping trip, "it is December; snow on the ground, and it's freezing. Alex, you need food in your belly to fight a hand-to-hand battle. Even just carrying he weight of one of those swords, alone, is energy sapping. Have you ever held one or lifted one?"

"Nope."

"I assure you they are very heavy. Having to fight continuously, one on one, eye to eye, face to face, until you kill or you are killed yourself, and then to turn immediately to the left, to the right, to the next one..." Lorenzo acted it out, turning, slashing, and ducking, "... beside you, behind you, in front of you. You have to fight to the death again, and again, swinging that sword, then to the next, and the next, one after the other, watching your back, guarding your flank, left and right, keeping your balance in the slippery mud and snow, swinging and clashing this heavy sword! It's not something you could do for long if you are wet, cold and hungry," he said, panting.

"Wow, OK, I get it. You did that pretty well, Lorenzo!"

"Believe me, a full stomach helps you keep warm and gives you energy. Battles lasted for hours, if you were lucky enough to survive that long. It was physically exhausting. And Hannibal knew this, of course. That is why he planned it to the last detail, shaking the Romans from their beds in the early hours."

Alex looked down the valley again.

"Unbelievable," he muttered. "And I suppose Hannibal's army had eaten breakfast..."

"Oh yes, and they had prepared for battle. They had rubbed themselves down with olive oil as protection against the cold, too," he said.

"That's cunning. That is so well planned, I must admit." Alex said.

"I know. But there's more; Imagine running into the elephants, which were like armoured tanks. Most men had never seen such animals before. Just imagine the horror of seeing those coming towards you dressed in armour and with soldiers on their backs! Terrifying! What a way to die! There was also the cavalry of a thousand horses, who cut the rest of them to pieces along the river."

"Oh my God, that's horrific. I'm amazed there was anyone left to tell the tale."

"I know. I don't think there were many Roman soldiers left alive. The rest of Hannibal's infantry, who had been hiding down there in the marshes over night, easily finished them off."

"Oh Lorenzo, that's enough. It's too awful."

Alex was quiet for a while. He stood looking down at the river, imagining the horror and bloodshed that had taken place below. It was almost beyond comprehension.

A lone canoeist in a white t-shirt and baseball cap paddled into view, and Alex wondered if he had any idea of what had happened in those crisp, pristine waters beneath him, just over two thousand, two hundred years before.

"It's funny,' Alex said after a while, "unless you are actually told of something that happened at a particular place in the past, you wouldn't have any idea about it. I mean, looking at the river now, there is absolutely no clue of the death, pain and carnage that took place here. You could go for a lovely summer swim and picnic down there, right at that exact spot, and never know anything horrific had ever happened there at all."

"Remember the cabinet doors in the library?" Lorenzo asked him.

"I do," he said. He thought for a minute. "And I now understand why they've all been left there. Had your family removed them, there would be no trace of the German occupation in your home, right?"

Lorenzo nodded. "Right."

They watched the canoeist paddle out of sight round the curve in the river.

"It's just so weird," Alex said, quietly. "I mean, what is time, space? Those are the same rocks, the same bend in the river, but it's like it never happened…"

"Alex, you are becoming quite the philosopher!" Lorenzo joked, slapping him affectionately on the back.

"Lorenzo, there must be stuff buried down there, I mean from the battle, mustn't there?"

"Actually, my father spent many hours as boy down there on the banks of the river and in those meadows over there, looking for artefacts, but I don't think he found much. And you are right about the swimming and picnic," he added, "we can rent a couple of canoes while you're here."

"That would be cool! But you'll have to show us what to do, I don't think we've ever been in a canoe before."

"No problem. We could make a day of it. We used to do it often, with my… when my mother…"

Alex nodded. He got it.

Lorenzo walked a few steps ahead and called down the bank to Darius, who was exploring at the water's edge.

"Did you get him in the end?" Alex asked, catching up with Lorenzo.

Lorenzo tuned and looked at him blankly.

"Who?"

"Hannibal! Did the Romans get him in the end?"

"Oh, yes! We won the Punic wars. Thank goodness, or Europe would be a very different place today."

"Would it?"

"Yes. Well, I may sound biased, being an Italian, but I suppose the end of the mighty Carthaginian Empire left the gates of Europe open for us to conquer. The Romans were able to go forth and civilize the rest of the barbaric world!"

Alex grabbed Lorenzo and they wrestled playfully, pretending to push each other down the hill.

"Darius! Help!" Lorenzo called, and the dog immediately started bounding up the bank towards them. As boys waited for him, they noticed something dark and limp hanging from his mouth.

"Oh no, what has he found this time?" Lorenzo said in disgust. "The last time I took him on a walk, Alex, he had caught a rabbit! It was still half alive. I had to put it out of its misery, it was terrible."

"Oh, I hope it's not a rabbit, I don't think I could face that."

They waited until at last Darius had reached the top of the bank, panting, with his latest prized possession hanging from his mouth.

"What is it? Drop it, boy," Lorenzo said, pointing at the ground in front of him. The Great Dane obediently dropped the object at his feet. He stood there, proudly wagging his stumpy tail.

"What on earth...?" Alex looked at the slimy-looking thing and groaned in disgust. "It looks like a boot, Lorenzo!

It's a disgusting, mouldy, knee-high boot. Look! It's filthy and coming apart at the seams. It's really nasty."

"Well, it's better than a half-dead rabbit," Lorenzo said. "*Vieni*, Darius! You can have it for a day or so. You will soon tire of it. *Andiamo*! Come on, Darius, let's go home."

Darius picked up the boot and ran ahead towards the gardens with his smelly, rotting, newfound toy flapping between his jaws.

Alex turned to take one last look at the river.

"Alex, come on, you can't stay there all day! Come back and have some lunch. The girls are probably wondering where we are."

"But Hannibal could have stood right here, looking down at the Romans camped on the banks of the river! It makes me just want to stand here and take it all in."

"If you think like that Alex while you are in Italy, you will never move again! Come on!"

CHAPTER EIGHT

I t was late afternoon and the four were sitting around the pool. They had finished lunch, swam and sunbathed, and Natasha and Alex were already beginning to tan a little. Alex had told Natasha about Hannibal's amazing story and the battle that had taken place on the banks of the river below the property, which had fascinated her. She was looking forward to going down to see the river herself.

They were both beginning to feel relaxed again in Gabriella and Lorenzo's company, and the conversation around the pool had become a little more personal. The subject of their parent's engagement was on all of their minds, but it hadn't been mentioned, as yet.

"I wish my father were as lenient as yours," Lorenzo said. He was perched on the end of Gabriella's sunbed, adjusting the strap of his underwater goggles. He had realized, after listening to Alex and Natasha talking about their lives in London, how much freedom they both seemed to have compared to him.

"We are accounted for every single hour of the day," he continued. "Either by my grandmother's watchful eye, or by the fact that everywhere we go, Piero is waiting for us in the car. It is like being stalked by the KGB! And even my father, from wherever he is in the world, is always keeping an eye on me, always expecting me to do the right thing. I find it very difficult at times. I sometimes feel as if I am being strangled. My grandmother reports back to my father even if I break wind!"

Alex laughed.

Natasha smiled and looked at Lorenzo; he didn't seem to be joking.

"But Lorenzo," Gabriella said quietly, "I think you may see a change in Father now. I think Papa's control over you was a sort of defence, or a front. It was the only thing he could do from a distance to show his presence in your life. I mean, he can't show his love in his absence, but he can show his control. It is a kind of love, Lorenzo; you could try to see it in a positive way. But I think he will be more relaxed now, he has been spending much more time here with us, hasn't he?"

Lorenzo nodded.

"We first saw the changes in him in Medinabad, at Easter, remember?" his sister continued, "when your mother was with him, Natasha. Our father is much, much happier. He is a changed man. He will be home more often now, you will see Lorenzo, and you will have more privileges and more freedom. He is at least here in Italy these days, not half way around the world any more, and he comes home to see us several times a month on weekends. He is trying, Lorenzo."

Lorenzo nodded without looking up at his sister, and Gabriella turned to Natasha.

"Our father has been too upset to even spend time here at the house, you see, after our mother died. It hurt him to stay here, and we… well, Lorenzo especially, took his absence personally. But my grandmother told him that he shouldn't, and she explained that Father was still suffering inside, very badly, from the heavy loss. She told us that the memories in the house were too much for him to bear. That is why he was away so much."

"And what about *us*?" Lorenzo suddenly burst out. He stood up and tossed the goggles into the pool.

"Does Father not think the memories are too much for *us* also? I see her everywhere, I hear her everywhere. I can even smell her in her room, in her empty closet; is it not too much for us? Does he think we do not feel it too? Does he honestly think that we are not suffering?"

Without waiting for an answer he quickly walked around to the deep end of the pool. He knelt down with his back to them and fiddled with the little bucket-shaped filter in the ground beside the pool's edge.

There was an awkward silence.

Natasha, sitting on the edge of shallow the end, had been drawing on the hot paving stones with her wet finger that she periodically dipped into the pool. Now she stared down at her watery art, watching evaporate in the sun. She dared not look over at Lorenzo. She felt awkward and didn't quite know what to say. She wanted to comfort him, but she didn't know him well enough, and even if she had, she wouldn't have known how to go about it. It was obvious that he was still very upset about his mother's death and his father's lack of involvement in his life. She felt very conscious that her own mother would be replacing their mother, in a way, and she felt sorry for Lorenzo, almost guilty. She realized how kind he was for not showing any resentment towards her or Alex, which, she thought, would have been well within his rights to be, since he was suffering so much inside.

She glanced over at him. He was still squatting down with his back to them, fiddling with the filter. Natasha now realized that her own sadness over her parents' divorce was nothing compared to the pain Lorenzo and Gabriella had been going through over the loss of their mother. If she had resented Marcello, she couldn't imagine how Lorenzo must have hated her mother coming into the picture. It hit her like a ton of bricks.

Natasha eventually broke the silence.

"I'm so sorry about your mother," she said softly to Gabriella, but loud enough for Lorenzo to hear. "I can't imagine how hard it must be, Gabriella. I am very sorry for your loss. You are both very brave. I don't know how else to say it, but I am just so, so sorry."

She felt terrible, and fought back the tears herself.

"Thank you, Natasha." Gabriella said, wiping her eyes with a finger under her sunglasses. "I suppose it has made us grow up a little faster. Life is very different now. Very different. But our grandmother has tried to be like a mother to us. Hasn't she, Lorenzo?" she asked, calling over to brother at the other end of the pool.

Lorenzo shrugged his shoulders. He still hadn't turned around. Natasha watched him as he again, tapped the little plastic filter out onto the grass and put it back into the hole in the ground.

"Gabriella, do you think your grandmother likes our mother?" Alex asked, unaware that the question could have been insensitive. "You can be honest, we won't be hurt."

Gabriella hesitated, then, gave a little sigh before she answered. She answered as honestly as she could.

"I think Alex, that she is glad to see her son happy again. But, in honesty, she probably would prefer an Italian wife for him. I know she has tried on several occasions with dinner parties and inviting beautiful ladies to come to stay for weekends."

"Really?" Natasha asked. "Like she would try to pick someone for him?"

"Oh, Yes! One was an Italian Princess, Natasha, but Papa was never very interested..." she called over to her brother, "... was he, Lorenzo?"

He stood up, and came back into the fold. He sat down next to Natasha at the edge of the pool and dangled his feet in the water, as she was. As he sat down, he looked her in the eye and held his gaze for an extra second, his dark, moist eyes letting her know that he had been upset. His stare was broken by a shy smile, as if he was letting her in on his secret, or, Natasha wondered if he was forgiving her somehow, for her mother. She felt he was letting her know it was all right. She felt he was confiding in her, and Natasha wanted to hug him. She felt a sort of closeness towards him she hadn't felt before. They sat next to each other, gently swirling the water around with their feet, their arms touching, and neither of them pulling away.

"My grandmother knows that your mother loves our father," Gabriella was saying to Alex, "and she knows that coming into our family will not be easy for her. She is very courageous in a way, joining the family as a second wife, and my grandmother understands this. She mentioned it once to us, remember, Lorenzo?"

He nodded, and with a sudden flick of his foot, he splashed a dragonfly that had landed on the water's surface.

"She sees that Father is laughing again," Gabriella continued. "That is enough for her. Grandmother told me so."

The four children sat in silence for a while. Natasha couldn't think of anything to say. It was awkward.

Alex stood up.

"I think I'm getting a bit burnt," he announced. "Come on Lorenzo, get in the water, man! Lets clear the air."

Alex dove into the pool, completely splashing everyone and causing loud shrieks of protests from the girls. He swam under water to the deep end of the pool, loving the cold, sharp, tingling sensation over his overheated back. He surfaced between two inflatable chairs that had been bobbing around the deep end, tempting him since the conversation had become a bit tricky. As he awkwardly struggled to pull himself up onto the first inflatable, something caught his eye behind the bushes beyond the diving board. Something definitely moved. He settled himself into the squeaky, slippery chair and lay back with his arms behind his head on the backrest and pretended to close his eyes, really keeping them slightly open so he could watch the bush through his wet eyelashes.

There was a definitely someone standing there watching them! He could just make out a blue shirt and a foot through the foliage. He put a hand in the water to casually paddle his chair closer to the edge of the deep end to get a better look. Suddenly, his wrist was grabbed from below the surface and he was pulled under, flipping the chair into the air and landing upside down. Lorenzo immediately surfaced grinning from ear to ear and grabbed the inflatable and pulled himself into it.

"Lorenzo!" Alex laughed when he came up for air, "Lorenzo, we're being watched!"

He swam to the edge and pointed to the bushes.

"There, behind you to the left; I think there's someone standing in the bushes, watching us."

Lorenzo rolled off the chair, went under water and surfaced beside Alex at the pool's edge. He flicked his hair off his face, and laughed.

"Alex, the last time you saw 'something', you got me up in the middle of the night in my pyjamas, remember?"

"Yes, I do, and I was right! *Re-mem-ber*?" Alex replied.

Lorenzo pulled himself out of the pool, and went straight towards the bushes in question.

"I hate to tell you Alex, but there is no one here. Does that not sound the slightest bit familiar?" he chuckled.

"Oh no, here we go again!" Alex got out and checked the bushes for himself. Lorenzo was right, there was no one there.

"I suppose you're going to tell me I dreamed it! Blue shirt and brown shoes? Did I dream up those little details, too?"

"Alex," Gabriella called from the shallow end, "that would probably be Giovanni. I hate to say it, but being a gardener, he spends much of his life behind bushes!"

CHAPTER NINE

"*B* ona sera," the Contessa announced as she walked into the dining room.

It was just after seven in the evening, and the four teens had showered, changed and had come down to the dining room for dinner. They politely stood behind their chairs.

"Please sit. I'm sorry I am a little late," The Contessa said as she walked round to her place at the head of the table, "between the emails, eBay and a little research here and there, time just flies."

Lorenzo pulled her chair out for her, and she sat down. He helped her slide it in again.

"So, Lorenzo," she said, unfolding her napkin, "you have shown your guests all the interesting things to see around the house, I hope?"

Alex instinctively glanced up at the machine-gun spray in the plaster at the end of the room. He wished he hadn't been reminded of Nazi officers again, it was bad enough having to take a shower in that spooky bathroom of his, upstairs. He might have got away with not having one, but the smell of the chlorine in his hair would have given him away. But he was happy in the thought that he had probably broken the world record for having the fastest shower in the history of mankind.

"Yes, Alex saw the swastikas in the library, and I even showed him the river," Lorenzo informed her. "I took him over there before lunch and showed him where Hannibal had attacked our army."

The Contessa nodded in approval. She put her napkin neatly on her lap and then poured herself some iced water from the jug next to her glass.

"And what did Alex think of our valley and its history?"

"Fantastic!" Alex answered enthusiastically, "...Contessa," he quickly added. "I think it's pretty amazing to have had a battle like that so close to your home! I could have stayed up there all day, just imagining what it must have been like."

"Well, do. I have a copy of Livy's account of the whole battle in the library if you would care to borrow it. Take it over there and read it with the vista in front of you."

"Thank you, I'd like to," he said, then quickly added, "...Contessa."

He settled in his chair and thought how he was going to enjoy his stay here. He liked the Contessa; he thought she was actually quite friendly. He wasn't sure who Livy was, but it didn't really matter. It was probably one of her intelligent, old friends, he thought. He glanced up at Natasha who was looking at him with daggers in her eyes, but he didn't care.

"Natasha, are you looking forward to going to Pisa next week?" The Contessa asked, making her jump.

"Your mother telephoned this afternoon," she continued, "I think you were all down by the pool when she called. I must get that phone connection for the pool-house working. Oh, and she said she would call you tonight, at around nine. Lorenzo, please pour our guests some *spumante*. We make our own wine here, of course, it's our own label; you must both try it. It is sweet, but not too sweet."

"No thank you." Natasha said politely, and thanks, she thought, for bothering to tell us about the call. Had she known her mother had phoned she would have called her back. But Natasha thought she had better make an effort to be polite to the Contessa, for her mother's sake, since she knew her efforts to impress the Contessa this morning hadn't gone too well. She decided to not worry about saying the wrong thing; she would just be herself and talk freely.

She took a quick sip of water.

"I can't wait to see my mother, we haven't seen her for a couple of months. And I am really looking forward to seeing the Pisan excavation, too."

"Indeed? Is that so, Natasha?" The Contessa said, watching her.

"Yes, I was reading about what they've found so far on Marcello's website..." she hesitated, "I mean, I mean, the Professor's website..." she started to change colour, but she continued, felling confident in the fact that at last she could talk to the Contessa about something interesting.

"Before we came out here, I was reading up on what they're doing, it's quite fascinating. It's amazing that the ships are in such good condition. The silt and moisture has preserved them so well, and a lot of perishable organic stuff like rope, and leather and even some woven baskets still on the Etruscan ships, I think, are still intact. There is even wine and oil in one of the holds, in those odd shaped clay containers..." she forgot what they were called, and tried to remember.

The Contessa nodded and knew exactly what she meant.

"Amphorae," she said, in a matter-of-fact tone.

"Oh, yes, amphorae," Natasha repeated, gathering her composure. "I can't believe that had they not needed a new terminal for the little railway station, all these ships would have been hidden underground forever! It makes you wonder what else is still under the city that will never be brought to the surface."

"Indeed," the Contessa agreed, examining her closely.

"Yes!" Gabriella agreed enthusiastically, "and under any city for that matter! You are right Natasha! Natasha knows all about the excavation, Grandmother. Isn't she clever?"

The Contessa ignored her granddaughter.

"Well, I don't know about that," Natasha quickly said to Gabriella, "but I am looking forward to spending time at the site, and watching the excavation. My mother told me that..."

"My dear child," the Contessa interrupted with almost a snigger, "I hardly think there is space in the confined area for spectators. It is totally sealed off from the general public, with pumps and machines, pipes and wires everywhere. The mud is inches deep. The last thing my son needs is further hindrance. So, I rather think you would be in the way, don't you?"

It was like a kick in the stomach. She felt dismissed like a child. She felt crushed. It was her main reason for coming to Italy; to see her mother and the excavation she was working on. She had read all there was to read about the sunken ships on Marcello's blog, which her mother wrote for him, and she had taken an interest in the dig since she had found out she was coming to Italy. She had even told her teachers that she would do a presentation on it when she went back to school in September. Now she had been dismissed like a stupid child. The Contessa's tone had been very condescending, and Natasha hated her for it. If it hadn't been for the hate she felt for the woman, she would have cried.

"Natasha!" Lorenzo laughed, distracting her, and trying to make light of his grandmother's cutting comment, "you know more about the site than we do! You are even as enthusiastic about it as my father is! I am sure he we will show us all around. Grandmother, you don't realize, Father wants us all to show an interest in his work."

He glanced at his grandmother to see if she had realized he was crossing her. She seemed not to have noticed, and was serving herself vegetables from a tray that Maria was holding for her. They started discussing a phone message that Maria had taken. The Contessa seemed totally oblivious to Lorenzo's stand, or to the fact that she had hurt Natasha. Natasha grinned at Lorenzo, appreciating what he had done for her. She hoped the Contessa would choke on a piece of asparagus.

Lorenzo dipped his fingers into his glass of water, and without his grandmother seeing, flicked it at Natasha. She flinched, then, silently mouthed him to stop it. She wiped the drops off her forehead and cheek with her finger and looked over at the Contessa to check that she hadn't noticed.

"Lorenzo," the Contessa said from the end of the table while helping herself to a healthy portion of the veal and lemon, "perhaps you could pour Natasha some more water, since you think she needs cooling down so much."

She then poured herself a glass of wine and took a sip. Natasha could see Gabriella giggling behind her napkin at her brother who had been caught red-handed.

"To continue on the subject of the excavation, Natasha," the Contessa said, "compared to the excavation you saw in Medinabad, this one is quite different. Very few unskilled workers, I might add. These types were just not needed."

The wrist did a dismissive flick.

"...Here, at the Pisa site, there are many more scientists and restorers. I understand from my son that this is much more technical, and as a result extremely slow-going compared to the excavation in the desert. It is also, I might add, the most unsavoury, dirty, and muddy environment in which I have known my son work to date. The further they excavate, the wetter the site becomes; so very frustrating for my son. Not only is it frustrating, but extremely expensive, of course. I believe he is having to use pumps to extract the filthy water around the clock. It is really archaeology at its most unglamorous."

She made a subtle grimace to show her distaste, shaking her head at the thought of it, and took another sip of wine.

"All those years at university, to be working all day, up to his neck in mud!" Lorenzo joked.

The Contessa immediately put her glass down and looked at her grandson.

Lorenzo flushed as he realized he had really done it now.

"You may make flippant comments and snigger at your father, Lorenzo," she said sternly, "but you would do well to remember that your father is one of the most highly respected archaeologists in the world. He would..."

"I am sorry, Grandmother," Lorenzo interrupted quickly, "I was not really laughing at..."

"Your father's hectic schedule," she continued, ignoring Lorenzo's attempt to quell the situation, "between writing reports, lecturing across America and Europe, and being up to his 'neck' in mud, as you so finely put it, is how he keeps you and Gabriella in the extravagant lifestyle to which you are accustomed. May I suggest that you remember your father 'up to his neck in mud' next week when you are having your one hundred-and-twenty Euro private tennis lesson."

"Forgive me, Grandmother, I really did not think..."

"No, Lorenzo, you did not. Perhaps you would like to leave the table, so that you can. Good evening Lorenzo."

There was an agonizing silence. Natasha stared at her lap not daring to move.

"Of course, Grandmother," Lorenzo eventually said, placing his napkin on the table beside his plate. He rose from his chair.

"Excuse me," he said quietly to Natasha and Alex. "Good evening," he said to his grandmother, and left the room.

Silence.

No one dared breathe. Maria made a hasty retreat back into the kitchen.

Natasha looked wide-eyed over at Alex. He looked down at his plate.

The Contessa broke the awkward silence.

"Gabriella, do you remember Signor Muretti?" she asked in a lighter tone, as if nothing had happened.

"Yes, I do, Grandmother. He was very kind to me at the camp in Medinabad after I ..."

"Well, Signor Muretti will be getting a break from the oppressive heat in the desert. He is returning to Italy to attend the engagement party. I understand he is bringing his wife and daughter, whom I do not believe we know. Oh, that reminds me, another three confirmed guests. *Maria...?*" she called over the children's heads towards the kitchen and rang the little bell on the table.

Maria immediately came back into the dining room and stood next to the Contessa. She was instructed to add three more confirmed guests to the list, which was apparently growing longer by the day. Natasha and Alex had a chance to glance at one another and show their discomfort with exaggerated facial expressions. They both looked across the table at Gabriella, hoping she could do something to get them out of the room. But Gabriella smiled at them both reassuringly.

Natasha sighed. What an awful holiday this is turning out to be. And this certainly wasn't the best time to fish around to find out if Yanni was in Pisa, either. She looked at the Contessa reading the party guest list. Gabriella had obviously seen someone else hugging the old gardener, she thought. No one in their right mind would go near this woman if they didn't have to.

They were in for a long evening.

Chapter Ten

N atasha woke early the following morning and lay in bed trying to go back to sleep again. But she couldn't; her mind was racing. She wanted to leave for Pisa straight away to be with her mother. She didn't think she could last another day in the same house as the Contessa, let alone another week. She thought about Lorenzo and felt so sorry for him. She didn't understand how he could put up with the Contessa beating him down, as she did. Gabriella definitely seemed to be the favourite grandchild, and Lorenzo took it like a Saint without even taking it out on his sister, as most siblings would, she thought.

She sighed and rolled over. She looked at the clock on the bedside table. It was only five forty-five. She got out of bed and pushed the outside shutters open. She hated waking up to artificial darkness; she would much rather watch the sun rise through the windows. She took a long, deep breath of the early morning air.

"That's better," she said.

In the garden below, to the right of the window, she saw Darius sniffing around the plants, and she wondered if Maria or Piero were up already. She crept out to the anteroom outside her bedroom and peeped into Alex's room. He was sound asleep. She went in, anyway.

"Alex, wake up," she whispered.

He groaned and turned over.

"I'm bored and I want to go outside. Want to come and take Darius for a walk with me?"

Nothing.

"Fine. I'll go on my own, then."

She waited a moment for a reaction. Still nothing. She sighed and went back to her room and sat on her bed. She wished she could text her best friend back home, but her cell phone had been dead since she had arrived in Italy, and she didn't have a European adaptor to charge it; her English one didn't fit in the socket.

She got dressed, then tiptoed across the landing, quietly passing the door to the Contessa's apartments, and then on to Gabriella's room further down the hallway. She quietly opened the door, and peeped in. But with the shutters closed it was pitch black, so she didn't even bother going in. She crept down stairs, hoping that perhaps she would find Maria in the kitchen for company. But there was no one around. The kitchen door on to the veranda was open, so she went outside. She walked around the house to see if she could find Darius, and sure enough, he found her. Whispering, she greeted him warmly, and asked him if he wanted to go for a walk.

"Come on, take me to the chapel, come on boy, are you coming? *Vieni!*" she said

It was a lovely clear morning, and though the air was still cool and a little misty, there was the promise of another hot day ahead. Perfect for a little meander, she thought.

Setting off along the manicured brick path towards the swimming pool, she walked through the rose garden, and then she veered to a path off to the right towards the direction of the chapel. Darius trotted on ahead, sniffing the ground and marking almost every other plant along the way, then coming back to her, enjoying her company a for few yards, before going on ahead again to explore more early morning scents.

The family chapel was smaller than she had expected it to be. Its old, weathered wooden double doors were almost as wide as the stone building itself. She thought she'd better not open the doors without permission, so she looked around outside the chapel, instead. There were only a dozen or so graves in the graveyard, and unlike English gravestones, Natasha was surprised to see a black and white photograph of the deceased person embossed into the marble slab above the inscription. It was a bit eerie seeing the dead person's image; she felt it made it all the more personal and sad. She slowly walked around the graves, looking deep into the faces in the pictures, wondering if she might find Gabriella and Lorenzo's mother. The first two graves were of men, one old with a large white moustache, wearing a strange-looking woollen hat. The other gravestone depicted a much younger man dressed in military uniform, who must have died at war, she thought. There were two women each side of the men; one old and the other quite young with beautiful black eyes that stared back at Natasha. She looked at the name. It couldn't have been Gabriella's mother, she thought, this lady was called Beatrice Dafiume, who had died in nineteen fifty-eight at the age of thirty-one, it said. Lying next to Beatrice Dafiume was a very small grave, with no photograph or name, just a date, and Natasha presumed that the young child buried there must have been hers.

What a cruel world it was, she thought. She wondered who they might have been. Beatrice must have been connected to the house somehow, or why else would she have been buried with her child in the family chapel? Then Natasha remembered what Gabriella had told her about Giovanni's wife, and she wondered if this might be her. She didn't know for sure, but if that were so, this little grave next to Beatrice would be for Giovanni's baby, which would make it Maria's brother or sister.

Natasha looked again at the date on lady's grave; Beatrice had died July the first, and the baby a few weeks before her, in June. It was early July now, that would make sense! Perhaps this really was Giovanni's wife and child, from years ago, and he had been thinking about them, grieving, when Gabriella had seen him here with the Contessa. Perhaps the Contessa had been comforting Giovanni, and Gabriella had thought it had looked like something else! She could hardly imagine the Contessa comforting anyone, but if she gave her the benefit of the doubt, she felt that this was probably what Gabriella had seen.

She felt confident that she had solved Gabriella's dilemma, but why Gabriella hadn't worked that one out for herself, Natasha didn't understand. Before she started back towards the house to tell her the great news, she walked around the side of the chapel for one last look for Gabriella's mother's grave. She stopped. She heard something behind her. She froze then, slowly turned round.

The low, morning sun shone in her eyes, but she could see, standing on the path, with the sun silhouetting his dark figure, a man who must have been watching her for a while. He didn't move. He just looked at her for a long, uncomfortable moment. He then touched his straw hat with a nod.

"*'Giorno,*" he mumbled, starring down at her.

"*Buongiorno,*" she replied. It was Giovanni. She slowly backed away from him, turned and quickly ran, cutting through the bushes towards the house.

CHAPTER ELEVEN

"**A**lex, Are you awake yet?"

"No. Go away," he groaned.

Natasha crept across his room and opened his shutters, letting the morning sun flood in. She then plonked herself heavily on his bed and waited for him to open his eyes.

"Alex, I don't think I can do this," she whispered, shaking his leg. She shook it again when she got no response.

"Alex, wake *up*! I said, I don't think I can *do* this!"

He opened his eyes and squinted at her.

"You can't do what, 'Tash?"

"Shh! Not so loud! I can't stay here much longer," she whispered. "I can't do this; The Contessa, the creepy gardener... it's a horrible holiday! I want to go and see Mummy in Pisa!"

He slowly sat up. He glanced over at the door, then indicated to her to shut it. She tiptoed over and closed it as quietly as she could, checking that no one was listening outside.

"Did you see Lorenzo last night? After... you know, dinner?" he asked.

"No. I was too scared to come out of my room in case I saw The Bat again. I don't know where Lorenzo went. Did you see him?"

He shook his head. "He wasn't in his room when I peeped in before I came to bed. You don't think he's run away, do you, 'Tash?"

"Well, if he hasn't, he should have! But he'd better not go anywhere without me; I want to escape too!"

"Don't be so dramatic."

"Melodramatic," she corrected him. "Well, I hate it here," she said. "That weird gardener creeps me out, the Contessa is a real cow; I couldn't even talk to Mummy properly last night, with the stupid phone out there in the hallway where everyone can eavesdrop in on the conversation. It's just Medieval! The old rat-bag probably keeps the phone in the hall just so that we can't complain about her to anyone, or plan an escape out of here."

Alex threw himself back into his pillow.

"Oh go back to bed, Natasha, for goodness' sake. And make up your mind; She can't be a bat, a rat and a cow!"

"Yes she can. Well, all I can say is, thank God Mummy called during dessert, or we could have been sitting at the dinner table all night without any excuse to leave! I need to tell Mummy stuff. I wanted to ask her if we could to go to Pisa right now. We can't stay here another day!"

"Speak for yourself, 'Tash, it's not all bad, you know. It's just meal times that we have to suffer, that's all!"

"*Suffer*? We're supposed to be on holiday Alex!" She thumped him on the leg in frustration.

"Ow, that hurt!" He kicked her off his bed.

There was a quiet knock at the door.

"May I come in?" the voice asked.

It was Lorenzo, in his dressing gown. They invited him in and he sat on the other bed.

"Lorenzo, are you OK?" Natasha asked. She was glad to see him and genuinely concerned.

"Yes, thank you, and I am so sorry to have put you both through that episode last night, I am, truly sorry. My grandmother was right to have disciplined me. I was ungracious about my father's work, but it was not intentional, it is not how I feel towards him, at all. My grandmother misunderstands me; she thinks I am still bitter for his being away so much. But in honesty, I'm not. Not anymore. I just didn't think."

"Hey, Lorenzo, it's OK, it's over," Alex said. "Forget it. We don't think you did anything wrong. You don't have to apologise to us. So anyway, what shall we do today? Shall we go out somewhere?"

Lorenzo smiled at him. "Thank you," he said. I am glad you two are here. Truly glad. Well," he said, in a happier tone, "should we rent some canoes? It is a perfect day for the river."

"Great, let's do it!" Alex said. We could check out the part of the river where Hannibal's battle was. Perhaps we'll find something interesting."

"Well, we could certainly try." Lorenzo said, kindly. He had been to that section of the river himself a dozen times searching when he was younger, as had thousands of other opportunists. But he was happy to let Alex have a go, too.

"Do you have a metal detector we could use, Lorenzo?"

"No!" he laughed. "And Alex, I wouldn't be allowed one, even if I had begged for one!"

Alex was surprised.

"Why on earth not? Especially living here in Italy. You could find all sorts of old, cool things."

"My father says it is cheating. Too many people are robbing the earth already with metal detectors, and nothing is learnt or recorded from their findings. He says they usually keep the artefacts without reporting them, so history is basically lost forever. You've seen how they work so carefully and meticulously on my father's excavations, they record absolutely everything and anything, even which layer of earth and the depth an artefact comes from."

"Yes, of course, it's my mother's job too, don't forget!" Alex said. "We watched how they did it last Easter, at Queen Sorrea's dig, remember?"

"Of course, but when something is dug up using a metal detector, neither the metal detector owners know what they have found when they tug it out of the earth, nor do the experts know, as they simply don't hear about it. My father says metal detectors are for idiots who don't even realize what it is they have found. Most times interesting artefacts are tossed aside as unimportant, when they could in fact be a vital piece of history. Father calls it *plundering the earth like a bull in a china shop.*"

"O-K..." Alex rolled his eyes. "Sorry I mentioned it."

"But there is nothing to stop us looking for artefacts with the naked eye," Lorenzo offered.

"Well, naked eye it is, then," Alex said, jumping out of bed.

"OK, great! I shall find Maria so she can make us a picnic lunch. That way we can have the whole day out without having to come home when we're hungry. See you downstairs in an hour?"

"Shame we can't ask her to make a picnic dinner too," Natasha said, after he had left.

"Cheer up, Natasha, our holiday starts today. You'll see."

"Maybe," she admitted. She headed for the door, "Oh, and before I forget, Alex," she said in an off-hand tone, "I think I left half my bathroom stuff at home, you know, my toothpaste and things. So do you mind if I use your bathroom instead of mine, while I'm here, you know, to make it easier?"

He grinned at his sister. "Sure, be my guest!"

CHAPTER TWELVE

Heinrich jumped out of the boat first and held it steady for Walter and Friedrich, who were tightly holding everything they needed for the expedition; camera, binoculars and detailed maps of the valley. Once on terra firma, they stretched their limbs and surveyed the little marshy island.

"This must be it. From the brief description in the letter, it cannot be anywhere else," Friedrich said hopefully. "This must be the spot!"

"Well, Friedrich, either it is or it isn't," Heinrich said, sounding a little irritated. "Let's get the letter. Let's open the map out and have a look then, shall we?"

It wasn't even eleven o'clock and already the sun was giving Heinrich a headache. Even in his youth he had hated the so-called 'outdoor life', so being on a wild goose-chase now at his age was already beginning to take its toll. He was annoyed at Friedrich for having him fly out to Italy prematurely, especially since it was Friedrich who had initially received the letter, so he felt that Friedrich should have done all the time-consuming research before calling him to come down to Italy. All Heinrich wanted was to find the paintings and whatever else was stashed with them, then, get them out of the country as quickly as possible. The paintings could easily be sold to private investors, such as the one already waiting for him back home. What was left over, they could sell at auction. But none of that was going to happen while they dithered aimlessly about on the river.

Heinrich turned to his brothers.

"Look, I believed from our phone conversation that we would have found the cache within a day of arriving here. You both implied that the location wasn't going to be hard to pinpoint, at all. I am far too busy and really don't have time to waste like this. This is just ridiculous, standing on a lump of mud in the middle of a river. There is nothing here."

He started to walk away from his brothers, but stopped after a couple of steps as his shoes began to sink a little. Friedrich caught up with him and pulled him over to a dryer spot.

"When I read the letter to you over the phone last week in Germany, the clues seemed quite straightforward, Heinrich," Friedrich explained. "Firstly, an abandoned, empty rowing boat could only mean one thing; that the art had been already stashed. Secondly, since the bodies were found downstream, this would indicate that the art was somewhere upstream, right? And thirdly, it is not our bloody fault it is not turning out to be so easy to find!"

The three brothers were exasperated with the whole thing. Heinrich's intentions for a quick recovery of the cache to then back to his cool, air-conditioned gallery in Germany were proving to be wishful thinking. He didn't know what was worse; is incompetent brothers or the insects attacking his neck.

Friedrich opened up the detailed tourist map of, 'The Province Of Piacenza And The Trebbia Valley'. He laid it on the ground at their feet. He then fished in his inside blazer pocket for the letter again. It was addressed to, *The Surviving Family of the Late Herr Commandant, Heinrich Streuber.*

He opened it and turned to the second page.

"Look. It says here," he read, "*the boat was found abandoned at the head of the first island before the river split into its many tributaries, between Statto,*" he pointed at the map, "over here, *and the town of Roveleto*, which is here. So, this has to be it. This is the island where they hid it!"

Heinrich took a few steps away and closely examined the little muddy island. He could see nothing on it that would induce anyone to hide anything of value there at all. It was flat, marshy, and obviously prone to flooding in heavy rains. Burying anything on the low island would be pointless. There were no buildings, no rock formations to speak of, just overgrown weeds and reeds, just as the islands were further down river; flat and unremarkable.

"They didn't land here," Heinrich said at last, standing with his back to them.

"But Heinrich, it says…"

Walter was about to read a section of the letter again, but he was cut short.

"I said, if you'd let me finish, they did not *land* here. I think the boat stopped here; it probably ran aground. I think they were already dead. I think our grandfather's body and the two others with him just floated on down the river for a mile or so before they were finally washed up on the bank."

His two brothers were silent for a couple of minutes.

Friedrich lit a cigarette.

"You have a good point," he said, "it was springtime and the river was probably higher than it is now, with the snow-melt."

"Show me on the map again…" Walter said. He took the map from his brother. "Where were the bodies found, exactly?"

"About here, I believe." Friedrich pointed to a spot on the map a little further down river. "Though it is vague from this confession, this man Otto, says in this paragraph, that he dropped them off north of Statto, I'd say about here; it's probably that dirt track marked by the dotted line. In fact, isn't that where we rented this boat from? How ironic!"

Heinrich took the map to check for himself.

"Interesting. Perhaps we can make some inquiries there," Walter suggested.

"Definitely," Heinrich said. "We'll question the boy at the boatyard upon our return. Read the letter again, Friedrich, one more time."

Friedrich began to read the most relevant section of the letter slowly and precisely, so they wouldn't miss any clues.

"… one of them knew of a place to get a boat. After dropping them off I was to drive to a point south of Roveleto and to wait for them there, which I did. It was while waiting for them at this designated place that I heard the shots ring out over the river. I shamefully admit that I then did something that I deeply regret. I drove off in fear for my own life. I presumed they had all been shot by the partisans, so I did not see any point in hanging around. It was dangerous to stay and find out. I did not know if they had already hidden their acquisitions or not. That was far from my mind. But I later found out that they must have done so already…"

"Coward!" Heinrich spat out, "no wonder we lost the war with pathetic soldiers like that."

"He was only eighteen or nineteen, Heinrich. Would you have done any different at that age? And if he thought they were dead there was really no need to risk his own life in finding out. He had to get out."

"If it had been my duty, I would have checked."

"Well, then you would have been a fool..." his brother snapped, "and dead."

"Oh, please," Walter interjected, "you have not seen each other for over a year and already you are fighting as if you were thirteen years old again. For heaven's sake, Heinrich, at least the old man has confessed to abandoning his superiors, it must have been on his conscience his whole life."

"And for good reason. Lucky for him he has died, or I would have seen to him myself for abandoning my grandfather. What else does he have the nerve to admit? He probably stole the hoard himself!"

"No, I don't believe he did. Listen, he says; '...*they must have already hidden it because the boat was apparently found empty and there was no mention of paintings, or anything else by anyone.*'

Heinrich shook his head and walked towards the boat.

"Look, Heinrich, I know this isn't as easy as we thought it would be," Walter reasoned, "but we are so close, we just have to think this through."

"You think; I'm going back to the hotel. I've had it for today."

Walter was beginning to wish his brother would go just back to Germany, instead. It just didn't work, the three of them together, never had. But he tried to keep the peace. When they were apart, all they did when they spoke on the phone was talk of bonding and becoming one, strong, brotherly team. Once together they became competitive and the whole idea was seemed ridiculous. Words of bonding flowed easily over the phone, but it only took a couple of hours before they were almost back to their boyhood fights again.

"Let's concentrate with the task at hand and recap," Walter tried. "So the soldier, Otto, is picked up on the road, presumably by our grandfather, Heinrich, and the other two officers, having already turned back on themselves as the main road to Piacenza is too dangerous to proceed any further with the stolen art in their possession, right? It would have been dangerous even without the hoard, as far as I can make out from this."

"Right," Friedrich agreed.

"Good. This much we understand. So this young soldier, Otto, who was on foot, is picked up and told to drive back towards the river so that they can carry out their plan B, which they had obviously prepared for, in case there was a problem getting out of the area. It was riddled with partisans. Right Heinrich?"

"Right," Heinrich agreed.

"So this Otto was ordered to drop them off at a boatyard, around here. He helps them load up a boat, and is then instructed to pick them up further down river, presumably after they had hidden their valuables."

"Exactly. Otto then drives the car around the hills, to a point further down river to wait for them, but he instead abandons them like a coward when he hears shots."

"We know all that, then what happened, Friedrich?"

Friedrich skimmed down to a later section of the letter.

"He goes on; '*I am afraid they are dead. But was not sure until the following day, after I had abandoned the car. (Keeping it would have drawn too much attention to me). I am on foot once again, taking the back roads, heading north. I eventually get a ride with four German soldiers I did not know, who ask me, out of the blue, if I knew anything about the bodies found in the river the previous night, apparently shot by freedom fighters. Alarmed, I said I didn't, and they informed me that the men had been German, probably high ranking officers, judging by their age, who were trying to escape by boat. They were dressed as Italian peasants. I asked how they knew they were German, and they told me jokingly that their boots were apparently of the highest quality, and stuffed with more cash than any Italian peasant would see in a lifetime. The word was, that they had been shot by the Italian partisans. A Soldbuch was also found on the boat. That was the real give-away, though. I was shocked to hear that the Soldbuch found in the boat was that of a regular soldier called Johann Fuchs, who was my close friend. This upset, and also perplexed me greatly. His Soldbuch and jacket were apparently tucked in the stern. Johann was, like myself, serving under Heinrich Streuber at the house on the hill for almost eighteen months, but his body was not found in the river; the picture in the Soldbuch obviously didn't match any of those men found in the river, so they knew he wasn't amongst the dead. I only hope he made it home, though after many years of unsuccessfully*

trying to contact him or members of his family after the war,
I have to presume he did not make it. Why his Soldbuch was
in the boat is a mystery to me; I can only presume he met up
with Steuber somewhere along the river. I certainly did not
bring him to the river in the car with us. Of course I knew
nothing of my friend's Soldbuch in the boat until I was in the
car with these other soldiers, on my way to Milan and it was
not in my power to go back looking for him. Had I known
about it earlier, I would have. I was asked by the soldiers if I
knew the soldier in the Soldbuch; Fuchs, or the other dead
Germans found on the river, and I of course had to deny all
knowledge of anything. They told me that they themselves
had taken the initiative to raid the nearby villages that night,
as there was no one in command anymore giving orders.
This raid was, of course, the taking of three hundred local
males in retaliation for those officer's deaths. The villagers
were rounded up by the fountain in the main square...'

Friedrich stopped reading and looked at his brothers.

"So he wasn't feeling any remorse about abandoning our grandfather, his commanding officer. He was only feeling guilty for not checking into the whereabouts of this soldier-friend of his, Fuchs. Unbelievable!"

"Grandfather was *dead*, Heinrich! At least the old man had the decency to write and let us know about it! And don't pretend to be sentimental; we didn't even know our grandfather. Had this old man not written to us, we wouldn't have a hope of finding the paintings, nor would we even know what had happened to him in Italy. And at least he has confirmed for us what mother always told us; that there is a cache waiting for us somewhere along this river. I am shocked though, at the soldiers rounding up three hundred Italians to be shot in retaliation for our father's death, aren't you?"

"Why? War is war. That was then. The Italians knew the rules. But why this Otto didn't think of writing years ago, I'll never understand," Heinrich said.

"Because it is the confession of a dying man, Heinrich, surely you understand that! And he was afraid of the consequences. He was as involved in the art disappearing as our grandfather and the other two officers were, whether he wanted to be or not, at least in the eyes of the law. Surely you can understand that!

Heinrich shook his head. He'd had enough.

"Look, are we going to find these paintings or not. I can't see the point of standing here on this muddy island for another minute. We have learnt absolutely nothing here."

"What we have learnt, Heinrich, is that the paintings are not hidden here or beyond this point. Which means we must look upstream," Friedrich said.

"No. *You* look upstream. Take me back to my car. I'm going to find out who this Johann Fuchs was, and I'm going to find the boatyard owner. You two can go up and down this stretch of river until you're blue in the face. I can't waste any more time. Take me back to my car and I'll see you later at the hotel. Come on, get in the boat, I've had enough. I'm going to leave you two to your river cruise."

They climbed back into the boat, and Heinrich sat in the stern, grabbed the outboard handle and revved up the engine. They took off up river back towards the rental office, wasting no time. Heinrich wanted his inheritance, and he was going to get it.

CHAPTER THIRTEEN

I t was a beautiful, clear morning, and the river looked crisp, calm and inviting. The four teens had been dropped off by Piero at the boatyard rental office on the banks of the river, only a couple of miles downstream from Montesonnellino. It was a small, secluded boatyard, in a clearing shaded by trees at the bottom of an unpaved dirt track. A large, old shed, which doubled as an office, supported the yellow and red rental canoes and kayaks that were neatly stacked against it. While Lorenzo and Gabriella pointed out to Natasha the two-man canoes they had booked for the day, Alex wandered over to the river's edge and looked at the speedboats bobbing in the water by the jetty. He wished they could take out one of those instead.

"How much a day to take one of these out?" Alex asked a young man who had come out of the office to meet them.

"Day? Non, ees by hour. But also you must have eighteen years and more, and licence for boat, so sorry," he replied, making an apologetic gesture with his arms.

"Shame, want to bend the rules?" he asked, jokingly.

"Please, you come to have important directions for safety?" the young man asked, encouraging him to come back towards the canoes. He pointed to the two canoes he had pulled out for them near the jetty.

"We must make important safety for you now," he said.

"OK." Alex reluctantly went back to rejoin the others. He knew how to swim, he thought, this was all a bit of an overkill.

They were each given a life jacket, and Natasha and Alex were shown the basics on how to paddle and steer the canoe, in very broken English. Their instructor, Lorenzo noticed, was paying particular attention to Natasha.

"*Sprechen sie Deutch,* Signora?" he asked her, when the paddling lesson was over.

He offered to help her tie her life jacket. He bent over her to reach for the dangling chords, and seemed to be in no hurry untangling them. As he leant over her shoulder, Natasha could feel the warmth of his breath on her neck. She instinctively pulled away, feeling uncomfortable, and looked around for Lorenzo.

"*Permesso, Signora?* Is OK that I am doing this?" he quickly asked.

"I can do it myself, thanks," she retorted, feeling a bit stupid for letting him get so close. He looked about twenty and, as were most Italian young men, he was very handsome. But that was no excuse for getting so close, Natasha thought.

"You speak Germany or Ingleesh?"

"I'm English," she said. "You know that, you just demonstrated to us how to use the canoes in English," she snapped.

"Ahh! You are Ingleesh! All Ingeeish girls are very beautiful! I am thinking you are maybe Germany, because many Germany tourist coming here in the summer, and I non speak Germany good. So I say safety in Ingleesh, every time, for all nationalities. Today also before you coming here, Germany people come, I say safety in Ingleesh, but they non listen! I am thinking the man coming before, is your father maybe, no?"

"Oh, err... no, my father is not here. I don't know what man you mean. I don't know what you're talking about."

"Ah, *non importa. Io,* my name is Aldo. And your name, *come ti chiama?*"

He rested one hand on his chest and the other he offered openly towards Natasha, in an almost theatrical manner. She hesitated, as his hand was poised for her to shake. She wasn't sure if she wanted to shake it. Now she understood what her mother had meant about not having to shake hands with someone she might not want to. Lorenzo immediately stepped in between them, asking Aldo if he could check his life jacket for him. He suggested that Natasha got into the front of the first canoe and waited for him.

"Good business you have here on the river with these boats," Alex offered as he walked past them, carrying the other canoe with Gabriella, "are they all yours, Aldo?"

"Boats? My father and before my father-father. Long time before me," he replied, using his hand to wave back the years.

"Good business?" Alex asked.

"Ah, yes, good business in summer. River is good, many people coming for to swim, for to take out canoe. You know to swim, non?" he quickly checked, remembering his duty and responsibilities. "And if you falling in river, you must always the feets first, like so, to non bang onto rocks, non? Is important! Always the feets to be first!"

He checked that both Natasha and Alex understood. He had forgotten to mention that during the safety demonstration.

"Yes, yes, we can all swim, thanks," Natasha said impatiently. "And if we get chucked in the river and get swept away we'll definitely drown feet first, got it! Thanks! Come on, let's get going."

"So why do tourists come here, Aldo?" Alex asked, "to look for artefacts from Hannibal's battle? You know, fighting … Hannibal?" he did a quick sword fighting display to demonstrate his question.

"Come *on* Alex," Natasha called from the canoe, "get the canoe in the water and get in with Gabriella. Let's get going, we can't stay here all day!"

"They coming here for to look at river, the mountains, but *Annibale*, I think, non. You looking for things of *Annibale*?" Aldo asked him.

"Well yes, actually, I am. I'd like to find a spearhead or something. I really like old stuff. It's pretty interesting. I heard all about the battle here with Hannibal and the Romans. It's just incredible!"

"Yes, incredible and interesting, also." Aldo agreed, "I like also, very much old things. I have very interesting thing. You want, I show you?"

"OK, yes! Cool! What is it?"

Aldo seemed pleased that Alex was interested.

"Please wait," he said happily. "I return. *Aspeta un momento.*"

"Come *on* Alex, let's get going!" Natasha called again.

"OK, just wait a second. He's got something he wants to show me. He's gone to get it."

Lorenzo grinned at Alex. "I think you've made a friend, Alex."

Alex shrugged happily, and they watched Aldo run through the gauntlet of stacked canoes and into his office. He came running out again a minute later with an old biscuit tin.

"Please, to look!" he said catching his breath. "This is of my father-father. Of many years before."

He indicated for Lorenzo and Alex to sit down on the jetty with him. Lorenzo sighed, then complied, squatting next to Alex. Aldo dusted off the lid of the little tin, then put it down gently in front of them on the deck.

Natasha reluctantly climbed out of the canoe and she and Gabriella wandered over out of curiosity, to see what he had in his little treasure box. He beckoned them to sit down on the jetty beside him. He carefully opened the tin.

Lying on top of an old, leather passport-sized booklet, were two small bundles, wrapped in several layers of discoloured tissue paper. Aldo carefully took out and unwrapped the smaller of the two, first. It was a very small, brown coin, about the size of a five pence piece. He carefully put it on the palm of his hand to show his intrigued audience. He looked up at Alex for a reaction.

"This is of *Annibale!*" he announced proudly.

"Wow, from Hannable's battle, here at Trebbia? Aldo, that's so cool! That's amazing!" Alex was astonished.

They all examined the coin in turn, and Aldo turned it over a couple of times so they could see it properly on both sides. Gabriella and Lorenzo were being more polite than interested, as old coins and artefacts were hardly a novelty to them, having a celebrated archaeologist for a father. But they looked none the less.

On one side of the coin was the profile of a woman facing to the left, wearing earrings, and a high, elaborate hairstyle. And when Aldo turned the coin over, it showed the distinct shape of a tiny horse.

"Are you sure it is from Hannibal's time?" Natasha asked. She was fascinated, and asked him if she could hold it. Aldo gently placed it in her palm, taking the opportunity to hold her hand as he did so. She pulled away, ignoring the contact.

"Yes, it is," Lorenzo confirmed under his breath. He'd seen coins like that before in the museum in Piacenza and Rome.

"Where did your grandfather find it? And how do you know its age?" Natasha asked Aldo. He explained in Italian what he knew about it, and Lorenzo translated back into English for Natasha and Alex, trying not to sound too bored.

"He says, according to his grandfather, that it was found on the edge of the field that I pointed out to you yesterday, Alex, by the banks of the river where the battle took place, remember? By those reeds."

Alex nodded with enthusiasm.

"And the coin is bronze," Lorenzo continued. "The lady is Tanit, the Phoenician Goddess. Her hair is tied up with corn, which symbolises her role as earth mother and Goddess of fertility. The Carthaginians worshiped her, as she was the lover of their chief God, Baal Ammon."

"Aldo just said all that? In one sentence?" Natasha asked.

"Not exactly," Lorenzo said dryly. "He just said where his grandfather had found it. I filled in the rest for you."

"That's so cool! Let me feel it?" Alex asked.

Natasha placed it in her brother's hand.

"What's that other thing he's got in the tin, wrapped up in tissue?" she asked, trying to see without touching. Lorenzo asked him in Italian, pointing to the other object wrapped up in the crispy tissue paper.

Aldo carefully opened the second bundle and proudly took out the precious object. Alex's eyes widened when he realised what it was.

"Wow, Aldo, that's absolutely fantastic!" he said.

Aldo took Natasha's hand and placed in her palm a very rusty, pointed spearhead.

"He probably owns a metal detector." Lorenzo mumbled under his breath.

The spearhead was a little longer than the length of Natasha's outstretched palm, and shaped almost like a long, smooth leaf, with a thin, pointed, finger length protrusion at the base, which would have originally been imbedded into the wooden shaft.

"That's just fantastic!" Alex repeated. "Did your grandfather find this on the battlefield too? Do you think it was once inside a dead, Roman soldier?"

"Alex! That's horrible! How could you think of such a thing?" Natasha almost dropped it in disgust.

"I'm only wondering. Perhaps the grandfather found a skeleton near it, like Queen Sorrea, remember? There was an arrow stuck in her; it's not so far fetched. Can you ask him, Lorenzo?"

Lorenzo reluctantly translated the question into Italian.

"He says he does not know if it was ever in a body. He says there were no bones nearby when it was found."

"Good." Natasha said under her breath.

"Signor Aldo?" A voice called from beside the office. A family who had arrived to take a boat out on the river had apparently been waiting for him. Aldo looked a little disappointed, and apologised that he had to go. He carefully wrapped the spearhead and coin back into the tissue paper, but as he folded the tissue around the spearhead, Natasha noticed a light tan, worn and weathered passport-sized booklet lying at the base of in the tin. But what drew her particular attention to it was the design that was embossed on the cover. She starred at it, not quite knowing what to think of it. It was a black silhouette of an eagle with its wings splayed open, its head turned to the left, and it was carrying in its talons a large circular wreath. Inside the wreath, as clear as anything, was a big, black swastika.

She stared at it for a moment, as Alex chatted with Aldo. Under the swastika, there was a long, German word, beginning *personalaus...* or something. She couldn't quite read all of the word upside down. But under that long word, she could clearly read the word **SOLDBUCH** written in large, clear letters.

She glanced at the others to see if they had noticed it, but they hadn't. Alex was still going on about the spearhead, and Lorenzo and Gabriella had already got up to go and were re-adjusting their lifejackets. She was about to ask Aldo what it was, but he put the two artefacts back on top of it, and then the lid back on the tin, and had already stood up to go, so nothing was mentioned.

Alex thanked Aldo for showing them his treasures. As Natasha climbed into the front of Lorenzo's canoe, her mind was still on the little book with the eagle and swastika. She wondered about Aldo's grandfather, and she looked back at him as he walked towards his office to greet his other clients. Unfortunately for her, at that moment Aldo turned round to look at her, saw her looking at him, and gave her a big smile and a wink. She was mortified, and quickly looked away.

"I saw that look you gave him," Lorenzo said, as he pushed off from the jetty.

"What look? You saw nothing, Lorenzo. Stop being a jerk."

Chapter Fourteen

"**K**eep your strokes even Natasha, or we will be going in circles all day!"

"I'm doing my best, Lorenzo, it's all very well for you sitting in the back having a free ride, you're supposed to be helping, you know! You've done nothing the last hour except give out instructions! How come you're so grumpy anyway?"

"Grumpy? Who says I am grumpy?" he said, grinning.

She dipped her paddle into the water and splashed him, wetting his shirt.

"Did that wipe the smile off your face, oh brother-to-be?" she giggled.

"Not as much as this will for you!"

He splashed her repeatedly with his paddle until the canoe started rocking side to side and Natasha didn't know whether to cry with laughter or with fear of capsizing.

"Stop it! I'm absolutely soaked! I can't believe you did that!"

He leant forward and said quietly, "I saw you looking at Aldo. Do you like him, Natasha?"

"No, of course not! Why, would you have a problem if I did?"

He splashed her again.

"It is not my business."

"Too right, it's not!"

"But if I am going to be your brother and your protector, I should know who you like!"

"Err, I don't think so!"

She dug her paddle in the water again and completely drenched him.

"Hey you two," Alex called from his canoe. "Shall we stop and have a break? Look, there's a perfect little beach over there where we can pull the canoes onto the shore. Then I can have a wander and look for artefacts along the bank."

"Great! Land! I can dry off!" Natasha said, splashing Lorenzo one last time.

They paddled over to the bank and unloaded the canoes. They laid their towels down on the shore to dry off in the sun.

"Peace?" Natasha offered Lorenzo, as they sat down.

"Peace," he said, and they 'high-fived' each other.

"Thank goodness," Gabriella said. "I wouldn't like you to splash the food."

She organized the picnic, laying it out neatly on the rug, and Alex wandered off to scour the pebbly shore for anything interesting he could find, taking a ham *panino* with him.

"I love this prosciutto," Natasha said to Gabriella after her first bite. "To me, it *is* Italy; the crusty bread, the cheese. I even love the sparkling orange juice and its distinctly bumpy shaped bottle. I don't think we even get that in England."

"And the boys? You love the Italian boys too?" Lorenzo asked, watching her closely.

"No. They're just like the Italian potato chips; too greasy."

"Well," Gabriella giggled, "I agree! At least this is a good prosciutto sandwich. We are lucky to have Maria. She always takes good care of us. True, Lorenzo?"

He nodded in agreement, unable to talk with his mouth full.

"So, tell me; about Maria," Alex asked as he came over, already bored with searching the riverbank for artefacts, "so she's married to Piero, right? And they live in that side bit of the house next to the kitchen?"

"Yes," Lorenzo said, "it is a largish wing of the house, actually. Her father is the gardener, Giovanni. They all live there."

"Oh, I didn't realize that. The creepy old man who lurks in the bushes, that's her father?"

"Alex, that's not very nice," Natasha said. "But I must admit he does seem a bit weird. He seems to appear from nowhere. He's definitely very sneaky."

"Too right he is! I forgot to tell you!" Alex said. "Wait 'till you hear this! When I got up this morning, after you both left my room, I heard someone walking on that path beneath my window... when I looked out, there he was, standing directly under my window starring up at me!"

"Really? You kept that quiet!" Natasha said.

"Perhaps you had been snoring," Gabriella suggested, "and he came to see what the noise was!"

"Or he's really an axe murderer planning his way into your room!" Natasha hissed.

Alex threw a pebble at his sister. "Well thanks for that, I'll sleep well tonight!"

"Actually, it is neither of these things," Lorenzo said seriously. "He has been with my family for over sixty years, I believe. There is nothing sinister about him at all, other than he chooses not to talk too much. He is just old, and quiet, and he takes good care of the house and my grandmother. In fact, my grandmother speaks very highly of him, and trusts him, and I believe she would be lost without him."

Natasha glanced at Gabriella, and they gave each other a knowing smile.

"I'm sure she would," Natasha said under her breath.

"Perhaps he's got a secret!" Alex suggested. "You know; a past! And he's mooning around making sure we don't find out about it!"

"Oh, please, Alex," Lorenzo said. "You two are funny the way you imagine things. He is an old man who prefers to keep to himself. There is nothing more to say about him. He is just part of the house. He was probably looking up at the house thinking about a job that has to be done."

"True," Alex said, remembering the patch of stucco he had knocked off the wall with the shutter.

"But isn't that in itself odd, Lorenzo? Think about it. The fact that he's been here forever and you don't know anything about him?" Natasha asked.

"Well, we know his daughter, Maria, she is lovely, almost part of the family. And we know that Giovanni's wife, her mother, died many years ago. And we know that he is a gardener, and without him things wouldn't be the same. What more should we know?" Lorenzo asked, and bit into his *panino*. They sat in silence for a minute, eating.

"Was his wife Beatrice?" Natasha asked.

"Yes! I think it was." Gabriella said. "How did you know?"

"I went for a walk early this morning. I hope you don't mind; I couldn't sleep. Darius and I went to the chapel together. I saw her grave and noticed that it was about this time of year when she died. And there was a little grave for a baby next to hers. Was that theirs too? If so, he might be in mourning…"

Gabriella looked at Natasha, and understood what she meant.

"Ah, I see," she nodded knowingly. "That explains everything." She smiled at Natasha with relief. "You see there is nothing strange about him after all, or about his conduct…"

"Well, maybe not, but I'll tell you all something that is *definitely* a bit odd," Natasha offered, "well *I* think it's strange, anyway."

"Tell us! What is it?" Gabriella asked.

Natasha put her *panino* down so she could concentrate.

"You know when we were looking at Aldo's coin and spearhead this morning?"

"Of course. How can we forget," Lorenzo said, "*Aldo, Aldo, Aldo...*" he cried in a girly voice.

"Lorenzo, *basta*! It is enough!" His sister nudged him to stop.

"Well," Natasha continued, ignoring Lorenzo, "there was something else in the tin that he didn't show us."

"Like what?" Alex asked. "*I* didn't see anything else."

Gabriella agreed with him. "No, Natasha, there was nothing else in the tin, nothing of interest to us, anyway. There was only an old book."

"It's the book I am talking about, Gabriella. Didn't you see what was on its front cover?"

"No."

"I can't believe how unobservant you all are! It was staring you all in the face!"

"Well tell us, Miss Know-It-All, what was on the front of this book, then?" Alex asked.

"It was a real, Nazi swastika, and some German words printed under it."

"You're *joking*!" Alex said.

"No, I'm not. I told you it was a bit strange, and it is, isn't it?"

Natasha was unsure of the significance of it, and glanced at Lorenzo for a reaction.

He looked perplexed. This was interesting. Much more so than the common ancient artefacts, he thought. This was the kind of history he liked.

"Did you see what the writing said?" he asked.

"I think it said *Soldbook*, or *Soldbuck*, something like that, with a capital S. It looked sort of worn and old. Do you know what that word means, Lorenzo? You do German at school."

Lorenzo shook his head. He didn't know, but he looked worried.

"But it had a swastika on it? Are you sure, Natasha?"

"Yup, sure. A big black one, with an eagle gripping the swastika in its talons. There was another really long word too, under the swastika. Something starting with '*personal*... somethingsomething, all one word, too long to read upside down, anyway."

"That makes sense; German words do tend to grow. If you could remember any more I could try to translate it." Lorenzo offered. "It's probably one of the personal identity books that German soldiers had to always carry with them. I remember reading about it. It was a good system; full of information."

"I can't remember anything else about it. I only saw it very quickly when he was wrapping up the coin and spearhead to put back in the tin. I wished I had asked him. I wish you lot had seen it."

"So Aldo's grandfather was a German soldier then," Alex said.

"We do not know that for sure," Lorenzo said. "Let us not jump to conclusions. I presumed the grandfather was Italian; he could have just come across the booklet as he did the coin and the spearhead. What is obvious, though, is that the grandfather was a small-time collector of interesting artefacts."

"Or he could have just been a murderer. He could have killed the owner of the booklet," Alex suggested, "and taken it off his stiff, dead body! Perhaps he was one of those partisan fighters during the war."

"Alex! Do you have to?" Natasha protested.

Lorenzo shrugged. "Perhaps, it is possible, but we cannot accuse anyone of murder, Alex, any more than we can presume the grandfather was a German soldier. Hundreds of German soldiers died in Italy during the war. Their possessions must be littering the fields from here to the Alps. He had ancient artefacts too, remember."

"Yes, but we could try to find some answers, we could ask Aldo some indirect questions, perhaps." Natasha suggested.

"Remind me, why is it our business?" Gabriella asked. "We just can not go around asking people what their family members did during the war, or if they killed anyone. People are still very sensitive about the war. It is still very recent for us here in Italy, in a way. The scars can be found everywhere. And why would Aldo tell us?"

"You're right, Gabriella," Natasha said. "Look at that film, *The Sound of Music*, for example, the most famous musical of all time, translated or dubbed into so many different languages around the world, but almost completely unknown in Austria or Germany. Why? Because..."

"Because it is so painfully stupid, boring, and annoying," her brother butted in.

"No, Alex, you *dork*, because it is still too sensitive a subject, *dork*! It's too close to home!"

"Or they had better sense and just couldn't sit through it," Alex retorted. He looked at Lorenzo. "Believe me, Lorenzo, you wouldn't be able to sit through it..."

"Shut up, Alex, I'm only saying that we can't go around questioning people's past," Natasha said. "The war is still a very sensitive subject. And by the way, you've obviously forgotten, Alex, you're the one who always wanted to be Kurt when we dressed up as the children from the film. Remember your lederhosen Dad brought back from a trip to Innsbruck? And your green felt hat with the feather? Lorenzo, he slept in them!"

"Bollocks! I never!" Alex protested. "Don't listen to a word she says, Lorenzo!"

"OK, OK you two, enough!" Lorenzo said. "Lets get back to the subject of the booklet. We can't go around prying. It's just not our place. And if there was something to hide, do you really think Aldo would tell us?"

They thought about it. He had a point.

"Well, on second thoughts, he might tell *you*, Natasha," Lorenzo said after a while. "You two seem to be getting along particularly well."

"No we certainly were not! And I really don't want to have a one-on-one conversation with Aldo, anyway. You boys can do it. Keep me out of it."

"Me too," Gabriella agreed. "And I bet he knows nothing about it, anyway."

"I think we should ask your grandmother what it is, though," Alex said. "She lived through the war, she might have some idea what the booklet, whatever it's called."

"OK, but why don't we ask Aldo some indirect questions while we're waiting for Piero to pick us up." Lorenzo suggested. "And if we get nowhere with him, then we can approach my grandmother."

"Rather you than me," Natasha mumbled under her breath. "I think I'd rather watch *The Sound of Music*."

CHAPTER FIFTEEN

Lying back on her towel between Lorenzo and Gabriella, Natasha listened to the soothing, gentle lapping of the water at her feet. Feeling the warm sun on her face, she finally felt she was able to relax for the first time since she had arrived in Italy. That distinct aroma of Gabriella's sun cream, for a moment, gave her a flashback of hot, summer holidays with her parents before they split up. She let out a long sigh. Life was weird, she thought. This was OK, though. It was cool. She was happy with the way things were going now.

She drifted in and out of sleep, half listening to the conversation around her. She liked the thought of having Lorenzo and Gabriella as stepsiblings. They were all getting along well and she imagined her life expanding with the Italian connection. Pretty soon, she would probably be splitting her life between three homes, and it wasn't really such a bad thing at all.

"Look, it's that family we saw earlier at Aldo's boatyard," Gabriella was saying to Alex. Natasha half opened her eyes and saw the canoes drift past.

"Wave!" Gabriella said, as she herself waved furiously at them.

"No!" Alex said indignantly. "I'm not waving. It's weird how people wave at each other just because they're in a boat. You wouldn't dream of waving if they passed you in a car."

Lorenzo laughed at the thought. "Very true!" he agreed.

"You're just an old grump, Alex," Natasha mumbled from under her cap.

"No I'm not. You girls are just weird. Hey, Lorenzo, want to show me some canoeing tips? I'd like to learn how to turn it around on the spot, like you do. Feel like going back in for a bit?"

"OK, but first I need to show you the basic biomechanics of the paddle stroke, Alex," Lorenzo offered as he stood up. "To get the most out of your stroke, you have to do it right from the start. And like all things, there is a wrong way and a right way. Your posture, your arms, the angle of the paddle as it enters the water, the depth you immerse it before pulling it through the water..."

"Oh please, Lorenzo, I wish I'd never asked!" Alex laughed.

He turned back to Gabriella. "His middle name isn't Anal, is it, by any chance?"

"No, it's Antonio," Gabriella replied honestly.

Natasha giggled under her cap. She would have to teach Gabriella about sarcasm, she thought. But not now.

The girls sunbathed, leaving the boys to their paddling lessons on the river.

Natasha wasn't sure how much time had passed before Gabriella woke her with a nudge.

"Listen! I can hear a motorboat," Gabriella said, sitting up. "It's coming from downriver. The boys had better pay attention, the river is a little narrow here."

"That'll wipe the smiles off their faces!" Natasha joked. "They'll have to hold on for dear life when it goes past."

The girls could now see the boat coming into view. It had already passed the family they had waved to earlier, making them rock and sway violently from side to side. And it was fast approaching Alex and Lorenzo, who hadn't yet heard the engine over their laughing, splashing and going round in circles in their canoes. But from the shore, it was obvious that the boat was travelling at quite a speed. Natasha stood up.

"Look at the wake behind it, it's going much too fast!" She shaded her eyes and walked into the water for a better view. "It doesn't seem to be slowing down at all."

"Natasha, you are right. They have to slow down… they will have to cut the engine…"

Natasha was now standing up to her knees in the river. She started desperately waving her arms at the boat to slow it down. Then she called and waved at Alex and Lorenzo to try to get them to come in to shore. Alex noticed her waving and cracked up laughing.

"You can't get me to wave that easily!" he called to her.

"ALEX! THERE'S A BOAT!" she yelled back, waving more frantically at him and pointing downstream.

"LORENZO! GET TO THE EDGE!" Gabriella shouted.

"They've got to cut the engine before it's too late! It may not have seen the canoes!" Natasha said.

In horror, the girls watched the boat speed towards their brothers, and no amount of shouting at the boat or waving their arms would stop it. Within a couple of seconds, the boat had driven between Alex and Lorenzo's canoes, swerving so violently that it caused their canoes to capsize, immediately throwing both Alex and Lorenzo into the cold river. The speeding boat's passengers hadn't even turned back to look at the mayhem they had caused.

Natasha yelled for her brother, but he had completely disappeared beneath the choppy water. First to appear above the surface was Lorenzo, but there was still no sign of Alex. Natasha panicked. Lorenzo was coughing, but managed to swim to his canoe, grab it, then, give the girls the thumbs-up to let them know he was OK. He looked around for Alex, but couldn't see him. He called for him, then to the girls.

"Where's Alex?"

Natasha was screaming his name. His canoe was slowly drifting downriver but he wasn't anywhere to be seen. Lorenzo started swimming as fast as he could towards where he thought the canoe had capsized, and dove under water. He surfaced, took a deep breath and dove again. He popped up again; nothing. He gasped for air and went under again. Then Alex's head appeared a few yards from him, downriver. The girls screamed his name and pointed for Lorenzo to go after him. Natasha could see blood on his forehead, and she ran along the water's edge to get closer to him, then, dove into the water. She swam with all her might out to her brother, oblivious to the river's icy temperature. At last she reached him. Although dazed and bleeding, he was able to grab her shoulder. He swallowed some water and coughed, gasping for air at the same time.

"Alex, kick! Kick, come on, kick!" Natasha splattered.

He looked at her, confused.

"Alex, help me. Kick! Move your legs!" she pleaded.

He didn't seem to move, he just grasped onto her shoulders tight.

"Lorenzo, help me!" she called out.

Before she could call for him again, Lorenzo was there. He turned Alex around then began to swim him ashore, safely and efficiently, using the sidestroke. Lorenzo got him to the water's edge and gently sat him down on a towel.

Alex was still a little dazed.

"Lie back, Alex. I need to look at your head. Lie down," Lorenzo said.

He did as he was told and looked up at Lorenzo.

"Say something, Alex," Natasha pleaded.

"I'm OK. I'm OK, guys, I'm OK," he said at last. "Really, I'm OK, now."

"But Alex, you're bleeding! Your forehead!" Natasha said, almost crying. She turned away. She hated the sight of blood.

Lorenzo applied pressure on his forehead with a towel. "It's not as bad as it looks. The blood makes it appear worse," he said, examining the wound. "It isn't too deep. We can stop the bleeding. Just lie still, Alex, and relax. I think you are a little concussed.

He willingly lay down for a few minutes, and the colour returned to his cheeks.

"I'll be OK. Thanks for coming out to me, Lorenzo. I feel a lot better now. I don't know what I hit my head on. I think my life jacked came off somehow over my head when I was chucked overboard."

"Unbelievable!" Lorenzo said, as he ripped open a Band-Aid from his First Aid kit. He applied it to Alex's forehead. "Absolutely thoughtless! *Idioti*! I am so sorry this happened, Alex. I should have been more aware of the situation."

"Na, you couldn't have seen what was coming any more than I could, Lorenzo."

"Perhaps, but I should have. I am truly sorry."

"Hey, I'm fine. I was feeling a bit dizzy, but I think I'm fine now. It was kind of crazy, wasn't it? Those guys in the boat were in a hurry!" Alex said, sitting up.

"Yes. It was very odd behaviour. We will have to find out what was going on."

Natasha and Gabriella walked down stream to rescue the paddles and canoe.

"Alex could have drowned…" Natasha said. "He could have drowned…"

Gabriella comforted her. "I think it would take more than that," she said kindly. "He didn't drown, and he is OK." She hugged her sister-to-be. "You were so brave, Natasha. You rescued him!"

CHAPTER SIXTEEN

By late afternoon, Aldo's jetty was slowly but surely coming into view. Aldo was sitting crossed legged on the edge, smoking a cigarette, waiting. He jumped up when he saw the two canoes heading back towards him.

"You had good time?" Aldo asked Natasha, as he helped her on to the jetty. "You were so, so long time!"

"Well, there was a sort of accident, Aldo. It was a bit dangerous, really. We were all a bit shaken, and we couldn't head back here straight away. Alex needed to rest."

"Accident? Oh *Dio*! You are OK?" He touched Natasha's arm with concern.

"It's not me, it's Alex," she said, pulling her arm away, "my brother. He cut his forehead. He could have drowned. He was a bit concussed, I think. It was horrible."

"Yes, I don't usually stick these on my forehead for fun, you know," Alex said.

Lorenzo related the whole incident in Italian, and Aldo soon got a clear picture of what had taken place.

"The boat who make accident, is this one?" Aldo asked. He walked to the other side of the jetty and pointed to one of three boats that were tied up along side it.

"Yup, that's it," Alex said dryly. "The one with the blue hull. That's the one. So the jerks rented it from here!"

Aldo nodded. "They are Germany mens who I asking you before, if one is your father. You remember I ask you, Natasha? They return here, after renting boat, and asking many, many questions, of my father and of my father-father.

Why?" he shrugged his shoulders at his own question. "Why after river excursion them wanting information of my family?"

He shrugged again and managed to look annoyed and worried at the same time. "Why they asking many questions of me? What is? Why drive boat fast like crazy people, to make accident so?"

"That's weird" Natasha said.

Aldo lit another cigarette, took a big drag and offered the packet around.

All politely declined, except Alex.

"Thanks, I'll have one," he said, reaching for the packet.

"Alex, don't you dare!" Natasha protested, pulling his arm back.

"Lorenzo," she said, refocusing, "can you ask Aldo in Italian about those men. What were they asking about his grandfather? It's a bit strange isn't it, since we were going to do the same?"

"I know," he said. "I was thinking exactly that, myself."

"Yeah, ask him," Alex said, it's not just a *bit* strange, it's kind of *really* strange. And I've got a bloody dent in my head to prove it!"

Lorenzo asked Aldo in Italian what exactly these men wanted to know from him. Aldo and Lorenzo spoke in Italian for some time, Aldo becoming more upset as he spoke and using his arms to show his annoyance. Lorenzo eventually turned to Natasha and Alex and translated Aldo's emotional account.

"Those men wanted to know how long Aldo had been here, on the river, and if it was a family business. Aldo told them that his grandfather had been a boat-builder. Apparently this used to be his boatyard, and his grandfather's fathers' before that. One of the men was quite persistent with his questions and seemed agitated when Aldo didn't give him the answers he needed. He asked him if his grandfather were still alive, and Aldo told them that he wasn't, and so they then wanted to know about his father. Aldo told him his father was not their business. This is when two of the men left in their car, but the older one stayed and probed Aldo further."

"What did he want to know?" Alex asked.

Lorenzo spoke with Aldo in Italian again then, translated.

"He apparently asked Aldo if he, his father or his grandfather had ever found anything of historical interest or value along the river that they hadn't reported. Aldo said he immediately felt guilty and thought of the coin and the spearhead that he had shown us, but he didn't tell the German about it, in case it was something he should have declared, and they would report him. Aldo didn't know who the German gentleman was and obviously didn't want to get into trouble. Although the man said to Aldo that he was a reporter for a German history magazine, he didn't seem convincing as he was too abrupt, and Aldo wondered if he could have been some sort of government a tax collector, checking up on antique objects. So Aldo didn't want to show him anything he had..."

Aldo interrupted Lorenzo and added something else for him to translate.

"And anyway," Lorenzo continued, "Aldo says he felt that he wasn't obligated to tell them anything. He knows nothing about them. They even paid for the rental in cash, which was unusual for tourists, so there is not even a credit card name."

"Quite right," Natasha said. "He's not obliged to tell them anything. Sounds fishy to me. They're definitely up to something, and driving that boat so dangerously was very odd behaviour."

Aldo interrupted Lorenzo again.

"Aldo asks us if we think he had been right not to show his artefacts to them."

"You didn't have to do anything!" Natasha said. "Nobody has the right to be rude and question you."

She felt a bit sorry for him. He was definitely worried about the whole incident and had no backup, with his father being away. She looked at Lorenzo to translate her support for him, but he didn't. Gabriella stepped in and translated for her, and Aldo seemed to calm down a little. Gabriella told Aldo that her father was an archaeologist and that he used to walk along the river looking for artefacts as a young man, so he shouldn't worry about having those things in his possession. She asked Aldo if he would like to report the men to the police, especially since their conduct in the boat was irresponsible and so dangerous.

Aldo shrugged. He really didn't want any trouble, especially since his father had left him in charge in his absence. Reporting anything to the police would only be confirming to his father that he couldn't be left in charge without trouble.

"Two of these mens say they return tomorrow. They take boat again. Tomorrow we see what happen. If is no problem, so, no police." Aldo seemed happy with his conclusion, and invited his four new friends into his little office. He spoke to Lorenzo and Gabriella for some time in Italian, and Natasha and Alex tried hard to get the gist of what he was saying. He asked Lorenzo to translate again into English.

Lorenzo hesitated.

"Come on, Lorenzo, what?" Natasha asked impatiently. "What did he say?"

"He asks that we take his grandfather's box home with us for safe keeping," Gabriella explained. "He trusts us and because my father is an archaeologist, he thinks his grandfather' treasures will be safe with us, just until these German tourists have gone home. He is worried that they are after his coin and spearhead."

"Oh, Aldo," Natasha said, "are you sure we should take them?"

"Yes, *certo!*" Aldo confirmed. "More better for now. Please. I non like trouble come here for these things. German mens say they return, and maybe they asking if I have something from river... So, I say non! I have nothing from river! Is true!"

He stood on his desk and lifted the tin down from the top shelf on the wall.

"We will take good care of your grandfather's box," Natasha offered.

"Shall we ask him about the book in there too?" Alex asked the others quietly. "Now would be a good time."

"Yes Lorenzo, go on; ask him." Natasha prompted him.

Aldo handed the tin to Natasha, and Lorenzo asked him about the booklet with the swastika on the cover.

"Ah yes, book is of my father-father, also."

"Your father-father, I mean your grandfather, was he German, Aldo?" Natasha asked.

"*Ma, non!*" Aldo laughed. "He *partizano*! He find this book in boat, many years before..." Aldo continued in Italian, and then waited while Lorenzo translated.

"Sometime towards the end of the war, his grandfather apparently had a rowing boat stolen from the yard. When he and his friends found the boat further downstream the following day, the boat was empty, but for this booklet found in the boat, tucked inside a German uniform jacket. Aldo's grandfather told him that three bodies, full of holes, presumed to be from the boat, were recovered from the river around the same time..."

Natasha put her hand over her mouth. She stepped away from the tin.

"Get a grip, Natasha, this river has seen a lot worse than that, believe me!" Alex said.

"Shut up!" She elbowed him, and Lorenzo continued the translation.

"...The men were found a little further downriver from the boat. They had been shot, but after their recovery, there was apparently some confusion whether this book belonged to any of those men at all."

"Why?" Alex asked.

Lorenzo asked Aldo.

"He says the three bodies found were all apparently a lot older-looking than the soldier in the picture. But their identities were never known. The men were not in uniform, in fact, Aldo says the men were dressed like farmworkers. Their clothes were worn and scruffy."

"Well why did they presume that they weren't farm workers then?" Alex asked.

"When they were dragged to the shore, they were found to have soft, clean, manicured hands and fingers, unlike any local farm labourer would have had, and all three were closely shaven, their hair was neat and cut very short."

"You mean after they were shot, they checked over the bodies? Lorenzo, that's just revolting! How could they?" Natasha was horrified.

"Wow!" Alex said. "It's like a mystery or something!"

Gabriella had walked away. It was more than she could handle.

"It is." Lorenzo continued. "But listen to this, Alex, more importantly, and this is what really gave them away; Aldo said they were all wearing standard German issue boots, with a lot of paper money hidden inside them. Aldo's grandfather and his friends thought they were probably high-ranking German soldiers; probably officers. But it was always a mystery to his grandfather why the men were on the river; it would have been more sensible for them to have travelled north by road with the rest of the German army, instead of rowing towards Piacenza, dressed in disguise, as they were. It did not make any sense. "

Aldo spoke again, then, waited patiently for Lorenzo to continue in English.

"He says that his grandfather kept the booklet as a memento, since it was his boat that had been stolen. He kept it in this box all his life, and then passed it on to Aldo, with the spearhead and coin."

Aldo frowned. "I not like this book. Only I like very much, these," he explained, pointing to the ancient artefacts. "I am eleven years age when my grandfather give me these. I love very much."

"Wow, what a story!" Alex said. "Who shot the men in the boat? Can you ask him?"

Lorenzo put the question to Aldo, and he took a long drag of his cigarette. He then shrugged and said something to Lorenzo a little dismissively.

"Aldo says it is not important."

Natasha thought how the beautiful Trebbia River now looked nasty and uninviting. There was death all around. This horrible story about the booklet was really more than she wanted to know. She had visions of the three men floating down the river with their short hair and their black boots stuffed with money, and the image wouldn't go away. She was now reluctant to even take the tin with the identity booklet, let alone hold it in her hands to look at it.

"Tell Aldo we should only take the two ancient artefacts for safe keeping, until his father returned. He should keep the swastika booklet here. I don't think we should have anything to do with it."

"OK," Lorenzo said. Lorenzo translated into Italian.

"Well, he says he would like to keep everything together in his grandfather's box, so they do not get lost. He does not have many mementos of his grandfather, and believes it would be safer for us to hold on to them all together, just until those inquisitive Germans have gone. That's fine by me," Lorenzo said.

Alex agreed. "We'll take good care of everything until Aldo feels safe and asks for them back. Does Aldo know where you live, Lorenzo, for when he does want the tin back?"

Natasha glared at her brother.

"Yes, I told him," Lorenzo said. "I told Aldo he could come to the house anytime and collect the box when the three tourists, or whatever they are, had gone."

"We'd better go," Gabriella said. "Look, Piero is waiting in the car over there with the engine running. Who knows how long he has been waiting."

"See what I mean, about not being free?" Lorenzo said quietly to Natasha.

"Kind of," she said. "But don't complain about having a chauffeur to anyone else, you might not get too much sympathy."

They said goodbye to Aldo and shook hands, and he kissed the girls on their cheeks. Lorenzo told Aldo he'd be welcome to come over and use the pool anytime. Aldo seemed happy to have made new friends.

As Piero drove them up the lane, no one had noticed a car parked a in the shade of a copse of trees. When Piero had driven away, a man got out of the car and walked down towards Aldo's office.

CHAPTER SEVENTEEN

"Good morning, Contessa," Alex said politely, as he and Natasha passed her on the stairs. Natasha looked at the Contessa and managed to force a smile for her mother's sake. But it wasn't easy.

"Good morning, children. Did you enjoy your day on the river yesterday? You both look like you have caught the sun, thank goodness. What on earth have you done to your forehead, Alex?"

"He cut his head yester…" Natasha was unable to finish her sentence before the Contessa interrupted.

"Well, Alex, I hope you won't be wearing that thing over it on the night of the party," she said, looking at the dressing. "Anyway, I have left this morning's paper out on the veranda so that you can look at it after breakfast; there is an article about my son, which you would do well to read. Gabriella or Lorenzo will translate it for you."

"Oh, thank you Contessa," Alex said in a revoltingly sucking-up tone. "And no, I wont have anything on my forehead the night of the party, don't worry. Maria looked at it last night and said it will heal quickly enough."

Natasha glanced at him wondering how he could be so slimy. But as difficult as it was, Natasha thought she had better make an effort to be engaging, for her mother's sake. She quickly thought of something to say to the Contessa.

"Will you be joining us for breakfast, Contessa?" she asked angelically, hoping she had already had her breakfast.

"I cannot just now, Natasha, I have an appointment with someone this morning who wants to interview me about the history of the house. Oh…" she said, sighing, "there is always *something*; never a moment's peace. I believe he is doing some kind of historical research for a German magazine of some kind."

She flicked her hand in her dismissive manner and continued up the stairs. Natasha and Alex heard her close her apartment doors behind her.

"OK, let's *eat!*" Alex jumped down the bottom four stairs and headed out to the veranda.

Lorenzo and Gabriella were already at the breakfast table, and had helped themselves to the buffet on the sideboard against the wall. They were tucking into melon and ham.

"Good morning, you two!" Gabriella said. "Did you sleep well? It is late! Did you sleep in?" she laughed.

"Well I woke up in the night, worrying about floating, dead bodies on the river and then I must have fallen asleep again, because I slept until eight," Natasha said. "How about you two?"

"No, not me. There was much to think about," Gabriella said.

"Well, I slept fine," Alex said. "I thought I might have got a headache or something, but I was fine. I think I can take this off too," he said, removing the dressing on his forehead. It's only a cut."

"I know you slept well, Alex, I could hear you through the wall." Natasha said.

"Liar!" he retorted. He cheerfully sat himself down next to Lorenzo, who passed him the orange juice.

"Drink some of that, it's good for wound healing," he said.

"Lorenzo, where did you put the tin?" Alex asked.

"It is in my room. But I think I might put it in your room, in my father's old trunk, if you don't mind. It will be safer and wouldn't be at all out of place there, is that OK?"

Alex shrugged. "Fine. Did you have a look at the German soldier's identity-thingy after we got home last night?"

Lorenzo shook his head. "No, I was too tired," he said. "I thought I'd rather we were all together to examine it."

"Well let's have a look at it after breakfast, then. I was hoping we would've had a moment to see it last night, but after we'd finished supper and spoken to our mother on the phone, I was so wacked I fell asleep on top my bed."

There was a yelp from the end of the veranda by the kitchen door. Maria had almost been knocked over by Darius running past her at full speed. He was carrying in his mouth the filthy, old boot he had found down by the river.

"Darius!" Gabriella called as he shot past the table and down the steps. "You crazy dog! Poor Maria! Darius is lucky he did not get hot coffee spilt over him! What has he in his mouth?"

"He found it down by the river when Lorenzo and I took him for a walk," Alex said. "I wouldn't touch it if I were you, it's pretty disgusting. It's a mouldy old boot."

The girls groaned in disgust.

"Don't worry, we have no intention of going near it!" Gabriella said.

Darius had jumped off the veranda, ran down the path, and had disappeared behind a well-manicured hedge. They laughed, as they could just see his hindquarters and the stump of his tail wagging as he barked excitedly at something behind the hedge.

Suddenly, they saw the rotting, old boot flying through the air over the hedge, away from the house. Darius watched it, tracked its trajectory, and happily bounded after it.

Maria giggled as she watched the spectacle.

"What on earth…?" Natasha mumbled.

"My father is going crazy with the dog!" Maria laughed. "Darius likes very much my father and wants to play all the time with this boot. Always Darius brings back the boot for my father! Nobody else, not even my husband, Piero, who loves Darius! Only my father! I see my father hide the old boot many, times, and Darius find it again, and again, and again, and carry the boot back to my father! He is so crazy, this dog!"

They giggled, and as they did, sure enough, Darius came running back to the old gardener with the recovered boot flapping between his jaws. He placed it at Giovanni's feet, and wagged his tail. Giovanni, who was trimming the hedge, did not seem amused at all; his thin face didn't show any expression of any kind. He slowly bent down, picked up the boot and calmly walked off around the side of the house and out of view, with Darius trotting beside him waiting for him to throw it again.

"You like coffee, Alex?" Maria asked.

He didn't really, but he saw that both Gabriella and Lorenzo were drinking *caffè latte*.

"Yes please, a little. Do you have sugar and enough milk?"

"Sugar is here on the table, and the hot milk… ah, is empty, I get more for you, one moment, please," she said. "And Natasha? You like *caffè latte* also?"

"No thank you, the orange juice is fine, Maria. Thank you."

Maria placed the jug of freshly squeezed orange juice close to Natasha's glass for her to help herself. "Please!" she offered, with a swoop of her hand the assortment of bread rolls, sticky apricot pastries, cheese, ham and fruit that was on the sideboard behind them.

"Please, to eat!" She then left to get the milk for Alex's coffee, and Natasha and Alex got up and helped themselves to the buffet.

"Well, I don't know about you, but I have been thinking all night about the soldier's little book," Gabriella said.

"Me too," Natasha said. "It's horrible. I wish I'd never seen it in the first place."

"Why?" Lorenzo asked. I think we have to look at it. How can we not? It is interesting and a part of our history."

"Well I don't want to see it," Natasha announced. "It's the identification papers of a shot man who floated down the river right where we were canoeing yesterday. It could have blood smeared on the pages or something; the whole thing is horrible, and I don't want to even think about it. Can't we just have a normal holiday for once?"

"You mean a boring one. Everyone has those," Alex said. "Well, I have to agree with Lorenzo, I wouldn't mind having a look at this old soldbook, if that's how you say it. It is a bit gruesome, I admit, but it's interesting; kind of fascinating, really."

"Well you can count me out, I don't want to see it," Natasha announced.

"You almost pronounced it properly, Alex," Gabriella offered, referring to his question. "It is *sold-buch*, with a soft *h* on the end. But although I don't like it either, I think we should perhaps look at it, whether it is a pleasant task or not, Natasha."

"Why?" Natasha was surprised at Gabriella. She looked at her, wondering what on earth would have induced this interest in the horrible thing.

"Well, I have been thinking about this, and I think it is odd that the Germans were questioning Aldo about his artefacts. You don't think they were looking for something else instead, like the *Soldbuch* perhaps?"

There was a crash as Maria approached the table. She had dropped the jug of hot milk on the floor and it smashed into pieces, splashing Alex's legs. She stood there looking stunned with her eyes wide open.

"Maria, *va bene*? Are you all right?" Lorenzo asked, jumping up to help her.

"*Si, Si, mi scusi,* I do not feel… sorry Alex, I get more milk…" she quickly went back into the kitchen, and the four children looked at each other.

"Don't worry, Maria," he called after her. "I'm happy with the orange juice…"

"Did we say something to upset her? She looked like she'd seen a ghost!" Natasha whispered.

"I don't know, but whatever it was, I've got hot milk all over my legs!" Alex said.

"Here," Natasha said passing him her napkin. "Let's finish breakfast and get out of Maria's way. Can we take the newspaper with us down to the pool, Gabriella? Your grandmother said there was an article in there about your father. I'd much rather read about the dig than talk about this dead soldier's booklet-thingie, wouldn't you?"

"Oh yes," Gabriella said. "Much nicer. I think it is about the latest ship he has found. My grandmother was just telling me about it before you came down. It is deeper and older than the other ships, and it's lying on its side, but it still has many things on board, just like the others you read about before, but this one is even better. I will translate it for you."

CHAPTER EIGHTEEN

"Signor, please follow me." Maria said in Italian to the well-dressed gentleman at the door. She couldn't imagine why anyone would travel all the way from Germany to see the Contessa, but according to her mistress, this is what he had done.

"The Contessa will see you in the drawing room, this way, please."

"Thank you."

His Italian accent was thick and Maria watched him as closely as he eyed the portraits on the walls in the hallway. Why the Contessa had to talk to anyone this morning was a mystery to her. They had enough on their plate with the preparations for the engagement party without the added strain of entertaining prying strangers. She opened the double doors to the drawing room and let the gentleman enter the room. The Contessa was already waiting and stood up from her chair and walked over to meet him.

"Good morning, Herr…?"

"Hoffmann," he lied.

"Herr Hoffmann. Please take a seat," she said in Italian, then added in German, "shall we continue in German, or is your Italian proficient enough?"

She offered him her hand and after he had shaken it, she offered him the armchair beside the unlit fireplace.

"German would be easier for me, Contessa, thank you. Or English, if you prefer, but my Italian, I'm afraid, is very basic."

"So, what is it, Herr Hoffmann," she said in German, "that fascinates you so much about my house that you would want to write an article on it?"

He looked her in the eye; her German was fluent, even cutting. He realized by her composed demeanour that perhaps she was not going to be such an easy pushover as he had hoped.

"Your German is excellent, Contessa, you put me to shame."

"Do I indeed?" She looked at him. "I had a good teacher. Now, why are you here? Please remind me."

He felt uncomfortable. Why, he wasn't sure. But he was now almost sure this was the house where his grandfather had been stationed. He could feel it. His brother's inquiries in town had proved most useful. The house also fitted the description from the letters his grandfather had written to his grandmother. Even the chair he now sat in, felt right. He just knew his grandfather had sat in it, in this exact spot, by the fire, and he knew it was here in this house that he would find some clue to the whereabouts of his grandfather's missing artwork. But even more extraordinary, and quite an unexpected coincidence, was that the teenager's car that his brothers had followed back from the river, had brought them right up to the gates of this very house that he had intended investigating!

It was all falling into place. But what 'it' was, he hadn't quite worked out yet.

He felt the Contessa's eyes watching his every move. He quickly decided that his best strategy to extract any relevant information was to be as direct and to the point as he could be, without giving too much away. By offering just enough, he would earn the old woman's trust, and he would then be rewarded with some kind of information that he could use to put this wild goose-chase to an end.

He put a concerned expression on his face and chose his words carefully before he spoke.

"Why am I here?" he repeated with fake a laugh. "It is a delicate and rather sensitive matter, Contessa," he said, starting his scam. "I believe, when we, or I should say, the *occupying Germans,* as we were during the war, were in this region, this house was used by officers as a headquarters for the whole Trebbia-Piacenza region."

She nodded slowly, and waited for him to continue.

"And," he said, still treading carefully, reading the nod as confirmation that he was on the right track, "I propose to write a series of articles on the artwork and treasures that are still missing that the unfortunate, expelled families, such as yourselves, perhaps, might have lost. I believe that we Germans, with the atrocities of the war far behind us, in a united Europe such as it now is, should be seen setting things right, finding these plundered treasures. We should be leading the way by returning them to their rightful owners once and for all. Of course, much is being done within the art world to obtain the whereabouts of the important museum pieces, such as the missing Rembrandts, the Picassos, the Degas... but my quest is to find the more obscure pieces, such as family paintings and portraits, or pieces taken from local chapels and local village churches. I want the world to see that it is Germany who is at the forefront of the research and investigations..."

It was such a good speech, he almost believed it himself, and the thought did almost cross his mind that if he hadn't ulterior motives, he might actually follow up on this brilliant idea.

He waited for the Contessa's response, but it didn't seem to have stirred her, she just looked at him. So he continued.

"Any publicity for the cause is good publicity, Contessa. *Someone* somewhere must know something. It will get people thinking, looking and inquiring, if nothing else. Most, if not all prominent homes in Italy suffered the same fate during the occupation, as you and your family no doubt did. Personal treasures from beautiful homes such as yours were stolen up and down the country. I would think that this one, especially, has some stories to tell, has it not, Contessa? Stories you might tell your grandchildren perhaps, of the terrible… loss?"

He waited for her to respond. He thought he had laid the trap well. Information would soon be forthcoming. Anything would help; even whether or not all her family's paintings had been recovered, he thought, that would be a start!

The Contessa took her time in answering. She broke out into a smile.

"And why would you think that, Herr... Hoffmann?"

She picked up a little silver bell on the round table beside her, and shook it.

"Would you care for a spot of English tea? I find it clears the mind quite well."

She called for Maria, and the double doors immediately opened and Maria came into the room.

"We will have some tea, Maria, thank you."

Maria nodded, gave Herr Hofmann a sly look, and left the room.

The Contessa then returned her attention to her guest, who was still waiting patiently for a reply.

"Where were we? Ah, yes. You know, Herr Hoffman, I must say it is quite extraordinary."

"That I am starting this crusade?" he interjected, "for the recovery of stolen art, Contessa? I would think that…"

"No," she interrupted him with a smile, "it is quite extraordinary that you are not the first to make inquiries recently about the house. Only a few days ago a couple of tourists in town were asking about my home and its history. Also Germans, I believe. A strange coincidence, do you not think, Herr… Hoffmann?"

It took him by surprise, but he tried not to let her know.

"Very," he said as sincerely as he could. How news travels in these incestuous villages, he thought. Is there anything this woman doesn't know? He hoped his brothers had not been so stupid as to give their names when they were making their inquiries around the town.

"...But I believe these tourists were called 'Streuber', according to the hotel proprietor," she offered with a smile. "So, Herr... *Hoffmann*, they are obviously no connection to yourself or your noble quest..."

She smiled with her mouth, but her eyes penetrated.

"So, let us recap to your quest," she continued. "As I understand it, you have come all this way from Munich to try to recover and return the family valuables that were taken from my house by your native officers, and with no promise of reward for yourself? How kind! I would say that was very..." she looked for a word as if she was plucking it from the air, "...commendable!"

She was toying with him. He could feel it. If she knew of his brothers' inquiries in the village, and even their names, she would probably know he was booked into the same hotel and under the same name as them too! He felt a fool already. Then his heart missed a beat... she just mentioned that he had come from Munich, had he told her that? He couldn't remember. Even the hotel didn't know that! So she was testing him! Perhaps she had checked him out already and knew he was an art dealer! It was he who was supposed to be in control of the meeting, not her! He wasn't used to being made a fool of, and he wished he could leave quickly without losing face. He shuffled in his chair. He had to keep his calm.

"Well, my reward would be in helping to put things right, Contessa, through my articles, and the good they eventually would lead to. One painting that finds its way back to the walls of its original home would be worth a million in itself. As you know, there is much still hidden and unaccounted for in this region."

"Indeed." She looked at him with a fixed smile. "As there is all over Europe. This is news to no one. If I didn't have such an *un*suspicious mind, I would think there was perhaps an ulterior motive behind your article. Few people do things for nothing, Herr Hoffmann. On the contrary, they do things for profit. It is a world where survival of the fittest still rules; Every man for himself. It's how the world turns, I'm afraid. But you say you are different, Herr Hoffmann, I must say, I find it rather refreshing."

He was dumfounded by her bluntness, but more still by her insight. He threw back his head and forced a laugh. This is not how the interview was supposed to go. He had to keep his cool.

"Call it a love of the arts, or call it correcting the misjudgements of our forefathers. I am merely here to help. And to do this, I need your assistance. You see, what I am asking, Contessa, is if you have any recollection, or stories that might be interesting for my articles. Who knows, something might jog someone's mind somewhere, and give me or the authorities a lead, even to the whereabouts of your missing paintings."

"Did I say there were missing paintings?" she asked him.

He hesitated. He really couldn't now remember what she had said and what she hadn't, he was so stressed. She really hadn't told him anything. He felt on the defensive, but he had to stay calm.

"Well, come now Contessa, I suspect there are. A great house like this could not have got away without some manner of theft, if theft was the order of the day."

"I was a young girl at the time, and my memory does not serve me well, I am afraid I cannot be of assistance to you."

Liar, he thought. There's nothing wrong with her memory. She means she won't be of assistance. What is she hiding?

"My dear Contessa," he said, "how terrible it must have been for you and your family, to have your house taken from you during the war. I know how horrible that must have been. The occupation, the…"

"With respect, Herr Hoffmann, you know nothing. You have absolutely no idea. I am sorry I cannot help you. Now, if you will forgive me, I have some important business to take care of."

She got up from her chair. She had had enough of the charade. She rang the bell for Maria to cancel the tea.

The fruitless, humiliating meeting was over, and Heinrich Streuber was actually glad of it.

CHAPTER NINETEEN

A lex had initially told Lorenzo that he could play tennis, and he honestly believed he could; after all, he had hit a ball around a court hundreds of times since he was eight, or so. He even belonged to a really nice, leafy tennis club only a stone's throw from his home in London. He sometimes played a game or two with his friends after school, and at weekends, or knocked up against the practice wall while waiting for his mother to collect him from the club after swim practice. So he thought he had a decent game, but now, after about five embarrassing minutes on the court with Lorenzo, Alex realised there was probably more to it than just hitting the ball over the net, trying to keep it between the white lines.

"Alex! I thought you said you could play!" Lorenzo laughed from the opposite side of the court as he watched him for the fifth time reaching for a ball, and either hitting it out or catching it on the frame of his racket.

"I know! I thought I could too! How come your balls are bouncing so high after they hit the ground? They take off like bullets! I can hardly get my racket on them! I think I have it, then before I can swing, it's too late!"

"It's a little thing called topspin, Alex. I hate to tell you, but it's pretty basic tennis."

Alex stood there, looking at him. He was hot, sweaty and confused.

"But I can hit the ball in England, honestly I can, Lorenzo. I play with my friends! Perhaps it's the altitude here, or something."

Lorenzo laughed. "That is a good excuse, I'll remember that one! Alex, look, come over to my side of the court and I'll show you how to hold the racket for the forehand. There is a technique, you know, a correct way and several wrong ways to it. When you know this you will then be able to hit properly, very hard, and keep the ball in the court, and even be able to play around with the height and depth of the ball, too. But first, we must take a little time to learn the basics!"

"I *know* how to hold the bloody *racket*, Lorenzo!"

Alex was now insulted. He was annoyed with himself as much as he was with Lorenzo for getting into this embarrassing situation.

"Well, I am sorry, but it is obvious that you don't. You are using almost a volley grip for a groundstroke. Come over here, Alex, I will show you something. The grip is the first thing I must show you, then, you need to learn the footwork. Although the ball is round, you have to almost imagine that there are different sides, or edges to it. You never just hit it, anywhere; you have choices, for the different types of spin. Especially when you serve."

"Do I?" Alex said despondently. He knew there was no getting out of it. It was sounding far too complicated already.

"You see the power of the swing is mostly through the legs. By moving into the ball, and by getting under it like this… low to high…" Lorenzo demonstrated in slow motion by turning sideways, bending his knees, stepping towards the ball with his outside foot. "…and hitting it from underneath the ball, lifting it up and over, finishing your swing with the racket high over your left shoulder, like this, with your chest facing the net. …"

"You have got to be joking, Lorenzo! All that, to hit a bloody ball? Tell me you're joking!"

"...No, I'm not joking. This creates the type of spin that will keep your ball easily clearing the net and still landing in the opposite court, no matter how hard you hit it. It is what makes the ball bounce high. You need this spin to keep the ball deep, to keep your opponent back, or he'll be all over the net and you will be finished. It is good for sharp angles too..."

"Oh Lorenzo, it's all a bit technical isn't it? I mean, can't I just hit the ball any way I want to?"

"Of course you can, but you will look a fool, and you cannot call it tennis. Come, copy me, turn sideways to the net as if on a surfboard and swing your racket like this... I'll give you a topspin forehand before you know it."

And so with the evening sun casting long shadows across the red, dusty court, Alex was given his first proper tennis lesson. He was extremely glad the girls had gone for a walk and were not around to witness the humiliating scene.

Having swam and sunbathed enough for the day, Gabriella offered to take Natasha to see the horses at the paddock at the far end of the property. Natasha followed Gabriella along the narrow path that cut through a yellow meadow. As her palms stroked the tall grasses at her side, she was reminded of when Yanni took her hand to help her jump off a little wall by the mosaic he was excavating. She wished she could find out if he were in Pisa with Marcello and her mother; she would do anything to see him again. She wished she could find out if he was there at the dig.

This could be a nice holiday, she thought, if she knew she would be seeing Yanni at some point. But aside from missing him, there did seem to be a dark cloud hanging over the place. All the weird stories surrounding the house were putting a bit of a dampener on things. She decided to approach Gabriella on the subject.

"This is a really beautiful area, Gabriella, with the hills and the river cutting through the valleys and stuff, and the castles and medieval towns dotted all around, it's really cool... I don't think anyone has such a cool home as you do. I mean, look! How many people in the world have a neglected Repunzel-like castle on a nearby hill; it's amazing. I understand why artists come on painting holidays here, I really do, and why serious canoeists spend days on the river. It's all so beautiful..."

She thought before she continued. "But Gabriella, doesn't it upset you, or at least make you feel uncomfortable sometimes, living here, with all the things that have happened here in the past? I mean like the Nazis in your house and the thousands of Roman soldiers killed in the river only a stone's throw away from your bedroom? I don't think I'd ever want to go near that river again."

"You can't think about it like that. Life goes on, Natasha. Anywhere you go in the world there will be a story to tell. People have lived and died everywhere. It is just whether we know about it or not. Do you think there are not stories about your river, the Thames? You said you live close to the river. It must have horrible stories too! And your house is old, it must have a story to tell too; good and bad, you just don't know it!"

Natasha shrugged. "Maybe. I suppose you're right about the Thames, too. In the Middle Ages, they used to dunk nagging housewives in the filthy river, or much worse, weigh down old ladies who were accused of witchcraft, with stones. They were then thrown into the river to see if they would sink or float."

"Ah, I see, if they floated, they were innocent?" Gabriella presumed.

"No. They were guilty."

"Oh, but if they sank..."

"Yup, they drowned."

"So you see," Gabriella said, "every river has some nasty story to tell. And I bet there are worse things that happened in that river too. There are also happy things that take place on my river. But happy stories don't make it into history books, do they?"

"Tell me a happy story about your river, then," Natasha said.

Gabriella thought for a moment.

"Well, you know, people are always having picnics and kissing down there on the little beaches. That is very happy!"

Natasha laughed. "You're right, if you focus on the bad things, I suppose that's all you'll see."

"Yes and now I will show you a truly beautiful thing. You will see what makes me happy!"

Gabriella's pace quickened as they neared the paddock. She cupped her hands around her mouth and called her horse in a high-pitched tone.

Artamis was at the far end of the large paddock, grazing under a cluster of trees with three other horses. They looked up when they heard Gabriella's voice, then, they steadily made their way across the field over to the girls. Natasha, who could ride well and loved horses, climbed up onto the gate for a better view of them.

Artamis was a beautiful speckled chestnut, and he led the way.

"He is pleased to see us, look at his tail. Artamis!" Gabriella called. "*Vieni quoi!*"

He came over, moving its head repeatedly up and down as if nodding 'hello' to Gabriella. He stood close to her, snorting and loving the contact as she adoringly stroked his face and main.

"He's beautiful," Natasha said. "You are so lucky to have your own horse. I would do anything to have my own, Gabriella."

"I am fortunate, I know. But you told me you ride in London, no?"

"Yes, but it's not the same. I don't have my own horse. I ride on Sunday mornings in Richmond Park, which isn't too far from my mother's house. But we never really have the chance to get emotionally close to any particular horse. Every week I seem to be given a different horse to ride and as soon as we are back at the stables, we have to muck them out. It's a form of slave labour. So I don't even get to spend time with the horse I had ridden that day; there certainly isn't much bonding with them."

"That is a shame, Natasha. Artamis is my closest friend. He knows all my secrets."

She hugged his neck, whispering in his ear in Italian.

Natasha watched in silence as the horse nudged Gabriella's shoulder with affection. But she felt sorry for Gabriella; she had a beautiful home, clothes, lifestyle, everything a girl could wish for, but it didn't make up for the loss of her mother. Natasha wondered if she had been in the same position, if she could have coped as well as Gabriella was, especially without holding any resentment or a grudge towards someone coming in to replace her mother, as her own mother was doing.

"Gabriella, do you know what the plan is, I mean, do you know if my mother is going to live here, in Italy? Has it been discussed at all?"

"No, nothing has been said to me. I am not sure what will happen, but when they are married, I suppose she will come here more often when my father is here, it stands to reason, no? Perhaps she will live here. That means you and Alex will move here, too!"

Natasha hoped not; she didn't relish the prospect of living with the Contessa. She wondered if this is what the holiday was all about; seeing if she and Alex liked living at the house. But then she remembered that Gabriella and Lorenzo lived and went to school in Milan during the school term. She felt relieved.

"I'm not sure what's going to happen either, Gabriella. We all have to go to school, don't we? Nothing has been mentioned to Alex or me about any future plans. Maybe we will just come here in the holidays, and carry on as usual."

It was all a bit of a mess, as far as Natasha could tell.

"Maybe Lorenzo and I will be coming to London to stay with you, who knows?"

"Maybe, but our house is so tiny compared to yours, it's a London terraced house. It only has three bedrooms, well four, I suppose, if you count my mother's office."

"Oh. That is a small house. Maybe they will buy a new one so we could all fit in together? That would be nice, no?"

Natasha smiled.

"Come, stroke him. He likes you! Do you know, Natasha," Gabriella said, "last year, I used to come out here to sleep at night. No one knew I came, not even Lorenzo. I would creep out of the house when everyone was asleep. It was very strange, Natasha, because sometimes when I came, I found there was a blanket neatly laid on a soft bed of straw in the corner, waiting for me."

"Really? Who put it there?"

Gabriella shrugged. "I really don't know. How could I find out? It was a little difficult, as I couldn't ask anybody as that would let them know that I was coming to sleep here. I didn't want my grandmother to find out, or she would forbid me for sure."

"Don't you think it was your grandmother then, who put out the blanket?"

Gabriella shook her head.

"Definitely not. I don't think she would approve of anyone sleeping with animals, do you? And she never ventures beyond the rose garden, anyway."

"Oh. Well, perhaps it was Maria, then."

"I do not think it was her either; at first I thought it may have been her, but she asked one morning why I had brought half a field into my bedroom. Some hay had dropped off my clothes onto the bathroom floor, you see. She suggested I use a bag to feed the horses instead of carrying the hay in my arms. So she had no idea I had been sleeping outside, she just presumed I had been feeding the horses. And if it had been Piero, he would have surely told his wife. They would both have known. And Giovanni just does his own thing, he takes no notice of anything."

Artamis sniffed Natasha's hair.

"He thinks it is straw Natasha, be careful!"

She smiled, still thinking of Gabriella coming out here in the dark alone.

"You know you can always talk to me, Gabriella. I will never replace Artamis, but my room's a lot closer than this field is."

Gabriella thanked her.

"Recently, Natasha, I am better. It helps when Papa is home more often. And soon perhaps, your mother will be here too, and you two, we will be like a family."

Natasha nodded.

Suddenly, they were distracted. A dog started barking from behind the shrubs and bushes to their left. Artamis bolted to the far end of the field.

"What is Darius doing all the way out here?" Gabriella asked. "He doesn't usually come this far from the house without one of us with him. I can't see him. Can you, Natasha?" Gabriella climbed the fence and strained her neck in the direction of the barking.

Natasha stood up and balanced herself on the upper rungs of the gate looking beyond the left side of the field, but she still couldn't see Darius.

"No, I can't see him. I think he must be somewhere beyond that clump of trees and bushes over there. Shall we go and see what all the commotion is?"

They jumped down and followed the barking. She was about to call Darius as they approached the bushes, but Natasha quickly stopped her. She put her finger to her mouth.

"Shh… wait," she whispered.

They squatted down and listened.

"It sounds like someone is digging in the earth with a spade. Shh... Get down low. Listen!"

They gingerly peered through a small gap in the bush. There was definitely someone digging, not far away, on the other side of it.

"It must be Giovanni," Gabriella whispered.

"How do you know?"

"He digs a lot. And there is no one else!"

"But what's he doing out here?"

"I think he is digging a hole. Maybe he's planting a tree," she whispered.

"Out here? Very fishy," Natasha said under her breath.

"What does it mean? What is *fishy*?"

"Strange, you know; odd. Why do you think he's digging a hole for a tree out here so far from the house? This isn't part of the garden."

Gabriella shrugged.

"I think he's burying something!" Natasha said, straining to see through the leaves.

"No! But what?"

Darius started barking again and they squatted as low to the ground as they could. He then started barking at the bush they were hiding.

"*Hau ab! Bloedes viech!*" Giovanni's voice shouted at the dog. "**Darius, *hau ab*!**"

The girls looked at each other and their mouths dropped open.

"That's German," Gabriella whispered. "I am confused! Giovanni just told Darius to be quiet... in German!"

CHAPTER TWENTY

G abriella and Natasha belted up the steps of the veranda and into the back of the house. They were desperate to find their brothers. Giovanni talking in German when he thought he was a lone was just too odd. But as they neared the drawing room, they hesitated at the French doors. Lorenzo and Alex were sitting in there with the Contessa.

"Oh no, what do we do?" Natasha whispered.

"Ah, here you are, girls," the Contessa called to them through the open doors. "Please come in and sit down. You are just in time. I have something to tell you."

They looked at each other, then sat down on the sofa opposite the boys, wondering what was coming next.

"Gabriella, darling..." her grandmother started, then hesitated, looking at her clothes, "my dear child, you are filthy! In fact both of you... could you stand for a moment, and not sit on the sofas. Thank you."

She waited while the girls stood up again, sparing the sofas.

"I was just telling Lorenzo and Alex," she continued, "that it has been arranged for you all to leave for Pisa this evening."

"Tonight? But why grandmother?"

"Oh let's see," the Contessa hesitated for a second, "there have been some problems with the company handling the arrangements for the engagement party," she said in an off hand way, "they are hopelessly behind schedule. The marquees should all be up by now and ready to decorate and the outside dance floor already laid and finished, and they are not, so this week is going to be very busy and the house full of staff milling around. I am afraid you four will be very much in the way. So I think it better if you leave tonight. I was just about to tell the boys that you can all go upstairs and pack your bags. Piero will leave in about an hour."

"*Ma* grandmother, can we not leave in the morning?" Lorenzo protested. "We have not even had our supper and ..."

"Lorenzo, did you not hear what I said?"

"Yes, I did, grandmother, forgive me, but could you just explain why we have to leave tonight? What is the urgency? I mean, tonight or tomorrow morning, it makes no diff..."

"Yes, of course, Lorenzo," his grandmother interrupted. "I will explain: You are leaving tonight, because I told Piero to take you tonight." She looked at him in the eye. "So if you would like to eat, I suggest you go to the kitchen and ask Maria to make you all something now. You may all go upstairs and pack your bags. You will be leaving within the hour."

Natasha and Alex looked at each other and smiled.

"Your father is expecting you in Pisa at around nine. Well, I do hope you enjoy your stay in Pisa. It is such an interesting city," the Contessa said in a happier tone, as if there was nothing unusual about the whole conversation, "and you will be pleased to learn that the tower is open to the general public once again. I believe it was closed the last time you were there, Gabriella. Though I understand there may still be those enormous, ugly weights around the base of it. But better that than no *campanile* at all."

She rose from her chair.

"Well, do enjoy your stay, I will see you all in a week or so, when you return for the party. Now you will have to excuse me, I have some nagging paperwork to attend to."

She walked over to Gabriella, bent forward just enough to avoid physical contact with her dirty clothes, and Gabriella kissed her on each cheek.

"Good night grandmother," Gabriella said.

"Goodbye. And children, please try not to keep Piero waiting."

Chapter Twenty-One

A very loud, giant mosquito, with enormous black wings, was hovering outside Natasha's bedroom window. The buzz became louder and louder and was about to fly into her room and attack her. But before Natasha completely woke up and opened her eyes, she thankfully realized it wasn't a giant mosquito nightmare, only the noise of a Vespa outside the hotel in the street below. She lay there, relieved that the dream was over before the mosquito had got her. With her eyes still closed, she listened to the morning sounds of the busy city outside, enjoying every moment of it. The distant honking of cars, the vespas and Italian voices were, for Natasha, as much a part of Italy as the sound of crickets in the hushed, dry countryside, the splash of someone jumping into a swimming pool or the smell of suntan lotion.

Even with her eyes still closed, Natasha could tell by the brightness through her eyelids and the warmth at the end of her bed, that the sun was already streaming through the open windows. She turned over and snuggled into her pillow. The cotton sheets felt luxuriously crisp and she could smell the furniture polish on the wooden headboard. She was happy; she was in Pisa and with her mother again.

She went over the previous evening in her mind. It had been fun; they had arrived late, and had met up with her mother and Marcello in the lobby of The Grand Hotel. It was a lovely reunion, and her mother looked happier than Natasha had seen her look in a very long time. They had eaten at a wonderful, rustic restaurant down a little side alley around the corner from the hotel, which Marcello said was Pisa's best-kept secret. She believed him; the entrance was an old, weathered door with peeling paint, without a knob, knocker or a sign. After Marcello knocked on the door, they had been warmly greeted by the proprietor, who led them down a flight of old, stone stairs into a vaulted dining room with beautiful faded frescos on the ceiling. One side of the restaurant opened out onto a lush walled courtyard, with vines, urns and statues, and there was a small fountain on the far wall that trickled water from the mouth of a terracotta goddess. It was like a secret garden, and all Natasha had wanted was for Yanni to appear. But he didn't.

She had watched Marcello that night over dinner, and she could tell that he really loved her mother. It was the first time she had not felt resentful towards him. She thought they fitted well together; they certainly seemed very happy. She couldn't remember her mother ever laughing and being as relaxed in her father's company, as she was in Marcello's. In all the years of her growing up when her parents had been together, she couldn't even remember her mother and father holding hands, not once. Now it seemed her mother couldn't let go of Marcello. Well, she thought. It can't be such a bad thing.

The phone on the bedside table rang. She ignored it, hoping Gabriella would wake up and answer it. But she didn't, it kept ringing until Natasha had to open her eyes. To her surprise, Gabriella wasn't in her bed, or even in the room. She must have got up early to be with her father. Natasha stretched over to stop the relentless noise, and picked up the heavy, old-fashioned receiver.

"*Buongiorno* Natasha!"

It was Marcello, calling from the lobby. He asked her in Italian if she were coming down for breakfast.

"OK, I'll be down in a minute, Marcello," she replied, feeling pleased with herself for understanding the gist of what he'd said. "Is my mother downstairs too?"

"Of course! We are all waiting for you. Gabriella also. She wants to know if you like it?"

"Like what?"

"Did you not open your gift, Natasha?"

"No, I didn't see it! What gift?"

He laughed. "Look down at the, how do you say, the feet of the bed!"

She glanced at the bottom of her bed. A large white shopping bag lay at the end of it.

"Marcello, I see it! I'll be down in two seconds!"

CHAPTER TWENTY-TWO

"**D**on't you love it Natasha?" Julia asked her after she had settled down at the breakfast table. "Marcello and I bought them for you last week. I couldn't wait for you to have it. Gabriella has one too."

"I do, I do. You're very generous, Marcello, thank you, I love it!" She put her new Louis Vuitton bag over her shoulder, feeling the leather. She thought she'd better not mention the pointless slaughtering of innocent animals it took to make it. There was no point; they were dead anyway, so she may as well enjoy it.

"It is my pleasure," Marcello said. "Now you are old enough to carry it off. I thought this one would suit your colouring. Gabriella has a dark one."

Gabriella was sitting next to her father with her arm around his neck, beaming from ear to ear. She had her new Prada bag on her shoulder. It seemed everyone was happy. Even Lorenzo and Alex were preoccupied with their new iPads. Natasha secretly would have preferred one of those, but kept it to herself.

"So, this morning, I suggest you four go exploring around Pisa," Marcello said, "and do all the main sights, as I have a long meeting after breakfast with the city planners. Then later this afternoon I will be free to show you some amazing things that we are uncovering at the excavation site. You will be fascinated, Natasha, there is much to take in. One of the ships has revealed something quite moving. But we shall save it all until you are there to see it. Oh, and I have made arrangements for a personal guide to show you around today... ah, speak of the devil, here he is! He has arrived safely I see, on his little, red Vespa."

Marcello stood up from his chair to greet the guide, and Lorenzo followed suit.

Natasha turned round and to her utter shock saw Yanni walking through the door of the restaurant, heading towards their table.

She could hardly control her surprise. She was stunned.

He looked so tall, tanned and with those distinctive curls, he was more like a Greek God than an archaeology student. She couldn't believe it! He was here, walking towards her! She had checked her email every day since last Easter for a message from him saying if he was going to Pisa with Marcello, but she had never heard anything. And here he was in the flesh! She just couldn't believe it; her dreams had come true.

She did her best not to blush, but despite her efforts, she felt the uncomfortable burning sensation rising up towards her neck as he approached the table. She picked up her cup for something to do, for somewhere else to look, and to hide her stress, but she had to put it down again as it trembled too much and she feared she might spill the chocolate or worse, drop the cup.

"Yanni," her mother greeted him. "Good morning! Come and join us! Do sit down!"

"Hello, hello," he smiled, greeting everyone around the table. He grabbed a chair from the next table and pulled up between Alex and Natasha. He was handed cup and he poured himself a black coffee. He stretched for the sugar, brushing Natasha's arm with his forearm, and she nearly died. He was here, she kept thinking, sitting next to me!

It was a tight squeeze and she felt his knee against her leg.

"Sorry," he said, glancing down, pulling away a little and smiling at her. He tried to move his chair a little further towards Alex.

"No problem," she managed to say nonchalantly. She was trying not to faint, as touching his knee was as good as an embrace. Was he really here, or was it a dream?

"So, how have you all been?" he asked the four of them. "It is good to see you! And Gabriella, I hope you have not been escaping down too many cliff-faces, saving the world from disaster since I last saw you! Ha!"

They laughed, and as Gabriella answered him, Natasha was inwardly begging for him to speak to her, not Gabriella.

He then turned directly to Natasha and took her by surprise.

"And how is school? You know, Natasha, in September I start my degree in London. I changed my course. Remember, we spoke about it? I really am to do archaeology. I have abandoned the business studies and economics. So you will have to show me your hometown, now that I am coming. I will be totally at your disposal!"

She nearly choked.

"That's great," she said, trying to control her breathing. She wondered if it were obvious to everyone that she was nearly having a cardiac arrest. She could feel her face throbbing, and finally she couldn't take the stress anymore of looking like a beetroot in front of everyone, so when Yanni turned to talk to Alex, she got up to leave the table for the ladies room. Her legs felt like jelly as she tried to walk as coolly as she could across the dining room.

Once there, in the sanctuary of the ladies room, she could think, she could breathe. She leant over the wash-hand basin, took a deep breath and looked in the mirror. She was distraught to see how red she was; she could have cried! She ran the cold tap and desperately splashed water on her face and neck, trying to cool herself down.

"Natasha, are you all right, darling?"

She looked up, shocked to see her mother standing next to her.

"Oh yes, Mummy, I just swallowed my hot chocolate too fast, that's all, I was going to cough and splutter at the table but managed to control it until I reached the ladies room..."

She faked a cough and cleared her throat a few times to prove the point.

Her mother smiled at her.

"He's a good looking young man, isn't he?" her mother said, kindly.

"Who?" Natasha asked, feigning indifference.

"Come on," Julia smiled, "dry your face."

She handed Natasha a paper towel.

"Let's go and finish breakfast," she said warmly.

"Oh Mummy, I think I'll stay here for a while, if that's all right..."

Julia put her arms around her daughter, and held her tight.

"You're growing up so fast I don't know whether to laugh or cry," she whispered. "I'm so proud of you. And I'm so glad I won't have to be away from you for any length of time again. I've missed you terribly, Natasha."

"Me too," she said. She felt ashamed she had been so transparent, but was glad her mother had come to her rescue. "I missed you a lot, Mummy."

"I know, I'm Sorry. But we will be spending a lot more time together from now on. Things are working out for all of us, I think. I wont have to leave you so much."

She hugged Natasha again.

"Come on, we can't stay in here all day," she said kindly. "Ready?"

"OK." Natasha said, and took a deep breath. "Ready."

CHAPTER TWENTY-THREE

"Alex, go slowly!" Yanni called. "You will become dizzy and then disappear over the edge!"

"I'm fine!" he called back. "See you at the top, mate!"

He disappeared around the bend.

Natasha and Gabriella had taken the assent of the tower very slowly, staying close to the centre wall. Gabriella had done it plenty of times before, but this was Natasha's first time, and she wasn't particularly enjoying the experience. She felt as though a magnet was pulling her to the outside edge, especially on the side that tilted so much. To make things worse, there was no railing at all, just the intermittent white marble columns every few feet going round and round. She didn't like it at all.

"I wouldn't do this on a wet day, you could slip right off," she said to Gabriella. There was genuine worry in her tone.

"Let me take your arm," Lorenzo offered, who had waited for the girls to catch up with him.

"I'm OK, thanks Lorenzo, Gabriella might need you, though."

"Yes, of course," he said, and he went to guide his sister.

"People have, I am sure," Yanni said, coming up behind them, continuing the conversation where they had left off.

"What?" Natasha stopped, pretending she didn't know what he was talking about. Yanni offered her his arm.

"Gone over the edge. Some have even jumped! I read it in a guide book."

"Yanni, that's horrible!" Natasha said. She took his arm. It felt strong and muscly.

"Yes, horrible, but true. Think about it. The tower was finished in 1370. Imagine what could have happened here since then! I am sure many people have gone over. You know, at one time, people could only come up here in three's, as it was thought it might deter pairs of lovers from jumping off the edge."

"That's crazy!"

"Who knows? Lovers have been known to do crazy things, no?"

He smiled at her. She was in heaven. She was alone with Yanni, on the Tower of Pisa, holding his arm and they were talking about lovers. She just wished she didn't feel so dizzy; it was more the thought of the tower collapsing than anything. In fact, she really wanted to go down. She didn't need to go to the top. But she pressed on, mainly because she was holding onto Yanni.

They eventually made it to the very top of the bell tower, or *Campanile*, as Lorenzo and the rest of Italy called it. But Alex wasn't satisfied with that. He and Lorenzo went up a flight of tiny steps right to the top of the leaning tower, a narrow walkway above the bells, which was really just a circular, narrow ledge.

"Hey you guys, come up here! It's amazing! You feel like a bird!" the boys called over the inner railing to Gabriella and Natasha, who were on the bell level below.

They reluctantly followed Yanni to the top level. There was a railing on both sides of the narrow ledge, which was still not nearly enough for Natasha. She felt the exaggerated tilt of the tower pulling her to the outer edge more than ever, and she wanted to go down.

"Alex, it's horrible! I feel the tower is going to topple over, I feel like it's pulling me over the edge."

"So go down, scaredy-cat!"

They walked around the narrow walkway, gazing down at the green grass of the *Campo Dei Miracoli* with all the ant-sized tourists covering it. And across the terracotta rooftops they could see far beyond the edge of town to the countryside. To the West was a bird's-eye view of the vast, white *Duomo*, the Cathedral of Santa Maria Maggiore and its cemetery. Other than that, Alex noted, there wasn't much at all to see. He thought it was all a bit disappointing really.

"OK, lets go down then," Natasha suggested. "You're right, Alex, it's a bit unexciting up here."

But it wasn't easy to get to the steps. Unfortunately, there were other tourists with them on the upper ledge, including a bunch of noisy Italian children whose teacher was having trouble keeping them together, making it difficult for others to move around. There were also three men on the opposite side, with a pair of binoculars, giving the teacher and the children filthy looks as they tried to squeeze between them and the railings.

Alex wandered round to the north side of the rim in order to get away from the children and Yanni joined him.

"Great bird's-eye view up here," Alex said. "But I would make sure I had thick curtains if I lived in one of those houses down there. I wouldn't want anyone looking through my windows with binoculars!"

He nudged Yanni to look at the three men a few feet away from them.

"Pisa is all a bit modern-looking from up here, isn't it? Not what I expected at all," Natasha said. "It's not like most ancient Italian old cities, is it?"

She walked past Alex to stand next to Yanni and squeezed the railing tight. "I think I expected Pisa to be more like Florence, or something."

"Well, there is a good reason for that," Yanni said. "During the war, Pisa was bombed extensively by the allies; this is why it is so modern-looking. Those buildings have only been there since the war. And did you know that this poor, old Tower of Pisa itself was very nearly detonated and blown up by the Americans?"

"Really? Why?"

"The Germans were up here shooting down at them. It was a perfect observation point. Look, from up here, you can see anything coming from every direction. It was a headache for the Americans, who were having trouble advancing into Pisa. They realized it was because of the tower. See, it is relatively flat countryside beyond the city, and the tower was doing the allies no favours at all."

"Wow. Imagine the soldiers who stood right here, where we are now, Alex said. "You can see for miles! Perfect for missile launching. Perhaps the Germans felt safe up here as the Allies wouldn't dare blow up such an historical building."

"The Americans were hardly concerned with that!" Yanni retorted. "They probably didn't know or care what it was; their lives were at risk, and one old tower probably looked like any other to them. Its eight hundred year history was irrelevant, especially when they were target practice. I read that the tower was only saved by chance."

"Really?" Lorenzo asked. "I didn't know that."

"Yes it was about to be blown. Eisenhower had given permission to blow up any historical building if it saved an American soldier's life. Those Nazis have a lot to answer for, thinking they could take over Europe." Yanni said bitterly.

"It is in bad taste to talk about the war in public. And you shouldn't inflict your opinions or influence young minds," one of the men interrupted as he approached them. "You should really keep your slanted opinions to yourself."

Yanni turned and saw a well-dressed man standing to his left, who had obviously been listening in on his conversation.

"One should teach the youth of today to be open-minded. To see all sides of the equation," he continued.

"You, above all people, should be more aware that this is still a sensitive subject."

Yanni looked at the man.

"Excuse me?" He couldn't believe he had been interrupted by the rude stranger.

"I think you heard me," the man answered, his German accent now noticeable. "You know what I am talking about. You sound like a Pole, are you not?"

Alex's eyes widened. He saw Yanni's back stiffen. He thought there was going to be a punch-up.

"Is everything all right, Yanni?" Lorenzo asked, walking over to Yanni as backup. He eyed the other two men who were also approaching from the other side of the narrow walkway.

"My nationality is my own business," Yanni said to the man, starring at him. "And as far as I remember, there is a thing called 'free speech' in Europe. I can say what I like to who ever I like. Come, Alex, Lorenzo, girls, it is OK... let's go."

He then turned to walk away.

"I thought as much," the man called after him. "Walk away ..."

Yanni stopped, turned around and walked back towards him.

"Excuse me, but do you have a problem?"

One of the other men stepped in.

"Please, excuse us. There is no problem," he said to Yanni. "Heinrich, come. Leave it, there is nothing here for us, let's go."

CHAPTER TWENTY-FOUR

"Just imagine, we would never have known about these ships lying for centuries under this little railway station, had it been for a much needed updated waiting room," Marcello said joyfully to his four visitors. "It's incredible, really, don't you think? They might have been buried forever."

Wearing hardhats and rubber boots, Natasha, Gabriella, Lorenzo and Alex stood at the edge of a large pit overlooking one of the partially excavated ancient, wooden ships, where Marcello proudly stood, in his trousers tucked into his muddy boots. Planks of wood had been placed on the mounds of earth surrounding the ship, providing a walkway. These raised banks had been created by the tons of earth removed from the pit, and the whole excavation site was wet, slippery and rather confined, especially compared to the last dig they had got to know so well in the dry, sandy desert.

Natasha and Alex were surprised at the difference between the two digs. This one seemed such a messy environment compared to the cleanliness of the open desert. Besides that, running around the whole perimeter of the muddy excavation site was a temporary steel retaining wall that had been erected to keep the excavation safe, "And to keep the rest of the world out," Marcello explained.

The enclosure seemed crowded to the four onlookers, for, as the Contessa had mentioned, there were many more archaeologists and scientists working on this site than the one in the desert. This one was a bustle of activity. Everyone

within the area confines was wearing tough boots and
hardhats, and with the noise of the water-pumps chugging
into action every few minutes to drain the bottom of the pits
where the ancient ships lay, it felt more like a construction
site than an archaeological site. Much to Gabriella's dismay
they seemed to be getting muddy just by watching, and she
made a point of standing a few feet away from Alex, who
had already slipped on the planks and was completely dirty
and wet down one side.

But Natasha wasn't worrying too much about that;
While Marcello was explaining about the site, and about the
first ship, she had a watchful eye out for Yanni. But she
couldn't see him anywhere, either excavating the ships, or
around the perimeter of the site as she had hoped to.

"Different?" Marcello asked her, grinning.

She nodded. "Yes, very."

Marcello walked them round the side of the first ship to
give them a closer look from a different angle.

"It's so cool!" Alex said.

"It is indeed. Who would have believed that I would be
doing this, up to my neck in mud and dirt, with all *my*
training and experience?" Marcello asked laughing, looking
up at Lorenzo through the corner of his eye. Lorenzo looked
at him, shocked. He flushed, realizing his grandmother must
have reported back to his father about the incident around the
dining table, and what he had said. But before Lorenzo could
think of an answer, or an explanation, his father had run up
the slope and was slapping him on the back, laughing. He put
his arm around his son's shoulders.

"Certainly not I! But, my boy, it is so much fun! Come,
I will show you all something else. Lorenzo, be careful,
don't slip, my boy."

He walked them around to a section behind a low,
metal barrier where sheets of plywood covered a large crater
in the ground. Marcello asked the boys to step down and

help him slide one of the large sheets back that covered the crater, so he could expose what lay beneath.

"Do you know where we are now? We are standing in one of the harbours of ancient '*Pisae*'. There were two harbours, you see, the second is over there. Both harbours were well sheltered and both, we believe, were used simultaneously. *Pisae* was an important naval asset to the Romans during the second Punic War. It was a hub of activity."

Alex felt happy that he actually knew what Marcello was talking about. The Punic wars, he now knew, thanks to his walk down to the end of his garden with Lorenzo when he had first arrived at his home, were the wars that his hero Hannibal, and his father before him, had fought to control Sicily and the Mediterranean with the objective of taking Rome. Alex couldn't believe the ships that he was looking at could have been the exact ones that had set out to get Hannibal.

"That's incredible. That would be the Roman General Sempronius, right? The one who was chasing Hannibal?" he asked Marcello.

"Absolutely! Among others, Alex, Hannibal had many Romans after him. He was a big problem for us Romans!"

Marcello could see his daughter's eyes glazing over with boredom, so he quickly got to the point.

"This ship here, is B2," he said, pointing at a large wooden hump in the ground. "I have a strong suspicion that this ship probably sailed from Carthage before it capsized here and sank in the harbour."

"Is it a battle ship?" Alex asked.

"No, actually it's not a man-of-war, I think it was a merchant ship. This is the first of the ships that we found with much of its contents still intact. After examining the contents, it confirmed for me why I do not believe these ships were sunk intentionally, as some people think."

"Why don't you think they was sunk on purpose?" Natasha asked. "I read about them before we came out here. They're all lying on top of each other at different angles and depths. They must have been sunk intentionally, maybe to stop other enemy ships coming into the harbour, to make a barrier during wartime. Wouldn't that make sense?"

"Yes, this is one theory. But, you see Natasha, most opinionated people haven't seen this..." Marcello walked around the hull. "The cargo inside this one, for example, is far too precious to be lost intentionally. They would have emptied the ship first, don't you think, to save the precious cargo, before sinking it intentionally?"

"Good point," Natasha said.

"What kind of precious cargo?" Alex asked, his eyes lighting up.

"Well this particular ship was transporting live animals, including horses, probably to be sold at auction. There are goats, too, and even a ram. In another section down there, there was a female lioness."

"Wow!" Alex said. "Cool!"

"So you see, live animals, especially exotic ones such as those, were not something anyone would want to intentionally go down with a ship."

"How terrible Papa! So the horses died?" Gabriella asked.

Marcello made a sad face at her and nodded.

"That's terrible. But what would they want with a lioness in Pisa?" Natasha asked.

"I believe it was destined for the arena, unfortunately. It would have been a very, very expensive commodity to lose. It would have drawn the crowds and packed the arena seats. So you see, the ship sinking with these animals on board, I believe for certain, would have been a major catastrophe."

"I see your point," Natasha said. "A disaster for many I'm sure. Least of all the poor animals!"

"Yes, I am sorry. Archaeology always has a sad story to tell."

Looking at the muddy hull of the ship, it was hard to make out anything distinctive that they could recognise. Exposed wooden planks that must have been a floor or a deck, stretched for about twenty-five feet, and there were other beams running over the top of it. Amongst the planks, were indistinguishable partially excavated artefacts, labelled, and flagged and to the children, quite unrecognisable. Leaning against each other towards the far section of the hull Natasha noticed groups of amphorae, most of which were half excavated from their protective, muddy cushion, and most of them were still in one piece. She realised this must have been the ship she had read about in the paper. She asked Marcello what had been inside the amphorae.

"Wine, in the large ones, and olive oil in the others," he said.

"So just with this precious cargo alone, even without the exotic animals on board, that would prove that the ship sank by mistake, wouldn't it?" she asked. "No merchant would want to lose all that wine and olive oil intentionally. And even if the amphorae were empty, he wouldn't want to lose dozens of them for no reason. They cost money, even in those days, I'm sure."

"My point exactly, Natasha." He smiled at her. He could see her mother in her.

"Can we go and see another ship?" Alex asked.

"You can see as many as you like. Some you cannot, of course, as they are still lying under others. There is actually another ship, about six feet below this one, at right angles on it's side, but we have to finish excavating this one first, then move it before we can even peep at the one beneath it."

"So you actually move them, Father?" Lorenzo asked.

"Oh, yes. We build a fibreglass shell around them to protect them during transportation. We are building a wonderful museum to house them, just as we did for the obsidian mask and Queen Sorrea. Some ships over there are already in the preservation stages. We can watch the process if you like, your mother is working on one of these today. She can explain to you how it is done."

There was a quiet groan from Gabriella. She had had enough already and was itching to go shopping and show Natasha Pisa. She watched Alex and Lorenzo drag the cover back over the exposed section of the ship, and then reluctantly followed her father and the others along the slippery planks to the next ship.

"Shall we leave, Natasha? Have you had enough by now?" she whispered.

"Not just yet. We've only just got here, Gabriella. Do you mind? It's not every day that I get to see something like this! It's actually very interesting."

Gabriella sighed, as Natasha quickened her pace to catch up with Marcello.

"So why do some experts still feel the ships were sunk intentionally? If they read your reports, they would know they weren't." Natasha asked him.

"Good question Natasha, I think it is because it is still quite baffling, even to the experts, why so many ships were lost in such a small area, you see. It has also been suggested that the vessels were sunk to help create the riverbanks, as well as the theory we already mentioned, that they were sunk to stop an invading enemy from coming up the river from the sea. These are good ideas, and had the ships been empty I would have probably agreed. Also, I have to tell you another reason why I can dismiss this intentional sinking theory altogether. You see, there are not only the remains of animals and expensive cargo on board some of these ships," he hesitated before he added, "...there are people, too."

He looked at Natasha, remembering their conversation last Easter at the tomb of the warrior queen. He had confided in Natasha about his heart-felt emotions when excavating human remains. She gave him a quick glance, but quickly diverted her eyes again when she saw he had remembered too.

"People inside the ships? Wow! Have they still got their skin and hair and stuff?" Alex was asking.

"Please Alex, no! Do you have to?" Gabriella said. She had really had enough.

Marcello walked them along the planks towards another giant lump in the mud.

"I will show you, I will, all in good time," he said with a grin. "Be careful you don't slip. As you can see, we are continuously extracting the water with pumps, and in other areas, like over there, where we are adding water to preserve the vessels. It is a very complicated excavation. The nicest thing about Queen Sorrea," he chuckled, "is that she was clean! O Dio, give me back the beautiful desert of Mesopotamia! I miss my Queen Sorrea!"

"And I miss your chief helper," Natasha muttered to herself.

Marcello walked on ahead, laughing to himself and scratching the back of his neck at the thought of the complications they had overcome over the last couple of months.

"Where are all the volunteers?" Natasha called to him nonchalantly.

"This excavation site is different; there were no volunteers. No, the people working here are all qualified professionals and experts from many various fields... well all except one, Yanni is an exception."

While Marcello went on to explain how geologists had spent weeks examining the way the silt had flowed and settled around the sunken vessels, and other scientists examined the excavated cargo to determine where it had come from or where it was going, Natasha heard none of it. She scoured every muddy vessel hump and man in a hardhat, looking for Yanni.

"...By examining the cargo, they could even determine the time of year each sinking had occurred; even the tiniest piece of grain could give compelling information," Marcello explained. "Oceanographers are researching Mediterranean currents to determine the routes the individual ships had taken, which also might give some clue as to why the ships had all sunk so close together, and over such a vast timespan, ranging from between two hundred BC and five hundred AD."

"So what information do they expect to find, Father?" Lorenzo asked.

"The general consensus from the scientists, archaeologists and historians is that all the vessels had probably been caught up in extremely strong currents, or they had simply overturned whilst in the docks loading and unloading their cargoes during raging storms, which had caused tremendous flash-flooding. It must have happened often."

"So how many ships are there? Have you found all of them?" Alex asked.

"About twenty something?" Lorenzo offered.

"Actually, amazingly, we are now up to thirty. It is hard to tell if there are any more, as each boat is at a different depth. The youngest, or shall we say, most recently sunk ship, is obviously nearer the surface, while the oldest vessels are the deepest and hardest to excavate. Twelve ships have been completely excavated, catalogued, cleaned and preserved so far. But the progress is extremely slow."

"So where did the river go? How come it's not still here?" Alex asked.

"Good question! It seems that every time there was a major flood, over the hundreds of years, the course of the river changed, and the city just had to adapt itself around it. So today there is no longer a port at the river's edge in Pisa. As you probably noticed from the top of the tower, that Pisa is very much an inland city, nowhere near the sea. It is fantastic really that we found these ships, because Pisa itself is now a relatively modern city, due to the heavy bombing during the war. Much of old Pisa was destroyed. These ships are lucky to have survived, as were the old buildings in the *Campo dei Miracoli.*"

"Yeah, that reminds me," Alex said. "We came across a weird man when we were up the leaning Tower."

"Oh yes?" Marcello said. "What was weird about him?"

"He wanted to pick a fight with Yanni."

"No! A fight? With Yanni? I can't believe that. About what?"

"I'm not sure. I think it was about the war."

"The war? What do you mean 'the war'? Which war?" He glanced at Lorenzo for conformation.

"The last one, I think, " Alex said. "He was talking about free speech and stuff."

"Well, Yanni was explaining to us about the bombing here in Pisa, during the war, and this man just butted in. He wanted to argue," Natasha added.

Marcello frowned, but said nothing.

"What Father?" Lorenzo asked, trying to read him.

"This morning, Yanni called me early to say he needed a day off. Perhaps I have over worked him. He didn't fight, did he?"

"No, he was cool." Alex said. He and Lorenzo filled Marcello in on what had happened at the top of the tower. Natasha flushed, and had turned away. No wonder she hadn't seen him all morning. Now she knew why; he wasn't even here! She felt crushed. How could he not be here, when she were here?

Chapter Twenty-Five

"This is one is a beauty, boys," Marcello said, looking lovingly at a large, wet, wooden mound that was resting at an angle on its side. "It is a man-of-war. Almost fifty feet long and twenty feet wide, with a very shallow hull, which enables it to navigate extremely shallow waters where others would run aground. It is very well preserved, too. As you can see, it looks like a ship almost ready to take to the high seas again."

Gabriella wondered if she were looking at the right ship, and then gradually sided close to Natasha.

"Cant we creep away and go shopping, now?" she whispered.

"Yes, OK, I'm ready to go." Natasha whispered back. She felt a little grumpy. She had seen enough of the ancient ships for one day. Especially now that she knew Yanni wasn't there.

"It's fantastic! What's that stuff all over the far end of it?" Alex was asking.

"That is the fibreglass. We coat them with it to create a tough shell, so it holds its shape and is strong enough to let us work inside it."

"Oh, right, I've seen palaeontologists on TV doing a similar thing with dinosaur bones."

"Exactly!"

Marcello squatted down to the level of the ship and touched it, almost affectionately.

"This ship is also special, as it has given us many coins, oil lamps, ropes, cups, ceramics, and leather sandals, amongst other items belonging to soldiers and sailors. And the anchor is one of the best preserved of all of them so far. This, of course, is because of the lack of oxygen in the silt around it."

"Why does oxygen destroy things?" Lorenzo asked. "I thought it gave life, Father."

"You are right," Marcello said, climbing back out of the little crater. "The oxygen enables the bacteria to live, but it is this that also rots away our precious finds. So technically speaking, the oxygen does not destroy; it enables other bacterial organisms to live and do the destroying. Oh yes," he added, "this ship is also special because it has a graffito carved into one of the planks. Amazing! The only other place I have seen one like this is in Pompeii."

"A graffito?" Alex questioned him.

"You know, Alex; writing on the wall," Lorenzo offered. "You've seen that surely, in London, on bus shelters, underground stations…?

"Oh, but we call it 'graffiti' in England."

"Well, graffiti is plural, like spaghetti, gelati… 'Graffito' is only one," Lorenzo explained. Here, on the ship, there is only one writing, so it is graffito. If there were two writings, it would be graffiti."

Marcello stood grinning at his son, nodding his head in agreement.

"Cool, I didn't know that!" Alex said. "Un gelato; due gelati, Un cappuccino; due cappuccini!"

"Exactly, Alex. You're a quick learner. From a heavy topspin forehand, to Italian grammar all in a couple of days! Whatever next?" Lorenzo joked.

"So what does it say?" Natasha asked, forgetting her annoyance over Yanni for a minute.

"It is someone's initials. Probably a sailor's," Marcello said. He looked over to another section of the site to his right. "Shall we find your mother? She has been waiting for you to see the boat she's working on."

They followed him a couple of yards to where six people were working on another ship. One of them was Julia. They were covering the whole ship in clear plastic film, then, applying squares of fibreglass cloth over the plastic, until it was about five inches thick.

"Hello my darlings!" Julia said, looking up from her messy job.

"Hi Mum, that looks fun," Alex said. "Wish I could help."

"Well it's a bit tricky, darling; it's a bit like creating a plaster cast on a broken limb. Only it's quite a big one, really," she wiped her hair from her eyes with the back of her gloved hand. "Keeping it secure and protected is paramount, especially when we move it to the museum. There's a liquid resin to be painted over the top of this, to hold it all together... it's not easy, or much fun really."

"Is this a man-of-war, too?" Alex asked.

"No, this one is a small cargo ship. It dates from about two hundred and forty BC. But it went down very quickly," Marcello explained.

"How can you tell it sank so fast?"

Marcello and Julia glanced at each other. Marcello sighed, and she nodded to him, as if giving him permission to speak.

"Well, it... it unfortunately... well, it contains a sailor, you see. And his dog," Marcello said reluctantly.

"You mean... they're still..." Natasha grimaced.

Marcello nodded. "Yes. I mean exactly that. They are below here. The sailor is quite a tall man, and his teeth are very worn down in the front. Because of this, we believe he was probably a rope-maker."

The four children absorbed the information in silence.

"But how does that tell you the ship went down quickly?" Alex persisted.

Again, Marcello hesitated before answering.

"Alex, we know this, by the position in which they were found." Marcello said. "Unfortunately, the way they died, and the way they have remained trapped in the silt throughout the centuries, tells us this very clearly. If it will not upset you, I will tell you."

Alex shrugged as if he could take anything. Lorenzo knew what was coming; he had heard it from his grandmother. Marcello glanced at the girls.

"Well, you see," he continued, "the sailor and his dog were hit by a beam that swung from behind, which was caused by the sudden listing of the ship..." He showed the angle with his arms.

"As the ship violently tilted, the heavy cargo rolled and..." he hesitated, "well, let's just say they were trapped. I am very sorry to say that hey were first crushed and then drowned. It was not an instant death."

"Oh my God!" Natasha was shocked; that wasn't what she had expected at all.

"But how can you tell?" Alex persisted. "How do you know it wasn't an instant death?"

Marcello was reluctant to continue, but he did. He spoke quietly, really not enjoying having to go into the details.

"The sailor, trapped as he was, had one of his arms outstretched as far as he could, trying to release his dog from under the beam... but I am afraid he could not. They died together. It was not a very pleasant task uncovering them." He glanced at Natasha. "I'm sorry."

Natasha looked at him and walked away. She couldn't bear it. She and Gabriella quietly told Julia they'd meet back at the hotel later.

They made their way back to the site office and took off their boots.

CHAPTER TWENTY-SIX

A fter leaving the excavation, the girls gladly took to the streets of Pisa for some retail therapy.

"Let's think of something completely different," Gabriella said, taking Natasha by the arm. "No more talk of dead bodies, or anything horrible. Let's do Pisa!"

Natasha already had the go-ahead from her mother to find an evening dress for the party and Pisa was not short of boutiques and designer shops to choose from; The shops on *Della Loggia, Borgo* Street and *Corso Italia* were wonderful to explore, and it was fun for the girls to be on their own and free. It was novelty for Gabriella, who seldom had the chance to shop unsupervised with friends, as Natasha did in London. When she did shop for new clothes, it was with her grandmother who had to first approve the clothes. Natasha realized that Gabriella's whole wardrobe was basically chosen by the Contessa, and Gabriella had very little say in what she wore at all.

Seeing the restricted life Gabriella led, Natasha was beginning to understand her more. She realized how judgemental she had been when she had first met her last Easter. She remembered thinking how prissy she had looked at the desert dig, with her flowery blouses and childish bows in her hair. But Natasha now realized it wasn't really her fault; she was always under the strict control of the Contessa. In fact, Gabriella was really as normal as the next fourteen-year-old. She just couldn't express it as freely.

Natasha found a dress that she liked almost immediately; Gabriella and said it flowed beautifully when she turned, and it had a low neckline, but without being too promiscuous or distasteful. The price tag was reasonable, just under the limit that Julia had set her. She didn't really want to go looking in another shop for the sake of it, so she put it on hold for her mother to pick up later, as planned.

"I'm sure Yanni will be unable to resist dancing with you all night when he sees you in that dress," Gabriella said.

"Lets hope! I daren't think of it, in case it's like jinxing the evening!"

Despite the anticipation of the upcoming engagement party, inwardly Natasha was feeling a little deflated; Yanni's decision to take the afternoon off had annoyed her. She couldn't understand why Yanni hadn't been at the excavation site when he knew they all were going to be there. She had really hoped he could have shown her around the site himself. She was also feeling down about something else too; she worried about the poor, tall sailor with worn-out teeth who had died here so long ago trying to save his dog. Not only was she upset for them and how they had died but, she was also upset with herself. She thought she had made up her mind to be an archaeologist. She thought it was her passion to dig up the past and put the lost pieces of history together. But now, upon her first visit to the fantastic excavation that she had been looking forward to visiting for so long, and experiencing only a tiny portion of what the job would entail, she had stupidly 'bottled out' after hearing the first unpleasant story the excavation had revealed. Pathetic! She now wondered if she had the stomach for archaeology at all, and it really bothered her.

She suggested to Gabriella they find a place to have a drink and ice cream somewhere. That would make her feel better, she thought. She could think about something else.

They found a café down a side street away from the hoards of tourists who gathered around the bell tower, and grabbed the last empty table outside so they could relax and watch the people walk by, which seemed to be an Italian past time. Natasha began to unwind again. But as they waited to be served, she did a double take. From the corner of her eye, she thought she recognised one of the men from the tower walk past. When she saw him, he quickly turned his head away. She told Gabriella to quickly turn round and look, but she was too slow; by the time she had turned around, the man had gone.

"Relax, Natasha, enjoy your holiday," Gabriella pleaded. "He is a tourist like us, he has every right to be in the street. As long as he doesn't come over and tell us what we can or can't talk about, I don't care."

"I just got the feeling he was watching us, that's all."

"Forget him. There are plenty of ladies here for him to watch if he wants to! Let's eat something. He's probably just embarrassed being associated with the man who was so rude to Yanni."

"Yeah, the idiot!" Natasha said, then, changed the subject to something more important. "Gabriella, talking of Yanni, where do you think he was today? I mean, what could be so important that he had to have the whole day off? It's kind of annoying. Why wouldn't he be at work this afternoon at the dig?"

"I don't know. I hadn't noticed he wasn't there. Maybe he is tired. Do you still like him as much as you thought you did, now that you've seen him again?"

Natasha shrugged. She did, but she was hurt. She hadn't really seen him enough to know.

"I doubt he would be too tired to come to work," she said. "He seemed fine when we went with him up the Leaning Tower. I was just hoping to talk to him, you know, about his coming to London, and his mother, and stuff."

"His mother? Why would you want to talk about his mother?"

"Well, when we were in Medinabad, Yanni and I went for a walk, and he told me a story. It wasn't a very nice story, really. Apparently his brothers were so protective towards their mother after their father died, that they actually chased a suitor away, an old friend of their father's, so that she couldn't see him anymore. They were jealous, you see. They ruined her life in a way. He never came back to see their mother again after they confronted him."

Gabriella listened, but was a little confused as to why Natasha would be told such a personal story by Yanni, when they hardly knew each other.

"Then, of course, the brothers themselves one by one, including Yanni, basically abandoned their mother and the farm as soon as they were old enough," Natasha continued. "That's nasty, don't you think? I think that's really, really selfish, to stop her having a new husband and then to leave her alone on the farm..." she said, trying to get Gabriella to agree.

"Well yes, I suppose it is," Gabriella said, still a little surprised at Natasha's interest in Yanni's family. It was also a little close to home for her too, which Natasha hadn't realized. But what Natasha failed to mention to Gabriella, was that when Yanni had told her the story, it was to show Natasha how wrong Yanni and his brothers had been to have done that. Yanni had noticed Natasha acting selfishly and a little immaturely towards her mother over her relationship with Marcello at the desert dig. The talk he had with her was a sort of lesson to her, or subtle advice on how not to make the same mistake that he had. But that part of the story she couldn't divulge to Gabriella.

"I just can't believe how anyone could interfere in someone's life like that!" Natasha exclaimed. "I am dumfounded. The poor mother... it's quite obnoxious."

"Natasha," Gabriella said, trying to catch her eye, "Yanni is..."

"What...? Inconsiderate? I know!" she cut Gabriella off. "To even think that he and his brothers had the right to determine who the mother could talk to..."

"Natasha... he is..."

"What?"

"Girls!" A voice said from behind Natasha. "I have been looking everywhere for you!"

Natasha turned around and nearly choked. Yanni was standing right behind her. He looked around for an empty chair that he could pull up. Natasha wanted to die. Her face turned colour of beetroot and she wished the earth would swallow her up.

"May I join you? We need to talk."

He didn't smile.

Natasha panicked inside. Had he heard everything she'd just said? Worst of all, she didn't really mean it. Now he seemed angry. Oh God, she thought, she would have to apologise and try to explain! She took a gulp of Coke to buy time while she thought how she was going to do it.

"Of course, Yanni, please sit with us," Gabriella was saying.

Natasha couldn't look at him. From the corner of her eye she saw him tuck his dark blond, curly hair behind his ears as he pulled in his chair and settled in next to her. She flushed at his being so close, but at the same time she knew she had blown it. She had run him down, twisted things around, and he had heard everything. It was only because she really liked him, and was upset he hadn't been at the dig, but how could she explain that? Now, the stress of the whole thing was making her sweat. She dreaded what was coming next.

"I wanted to find you," he said. "I just went to the site and when I saw that you two weren't there, I was concerned. Your mother told me you were shopping."

"Why are you concerned about us shopping?" Gabriella asked, almost laughing.

"I didn't want you to be approached by anyone while you were out on your own together. I really need to talk to the four of you, but when I heard you two had left the site, I came to find you. Has anyone spoken to you?"

"Wait, what do you mean?" Natasha was confused. She wasn't expecting this.

"Have any men approached you this morning?" he asked. "I mean, since we went to the Leaning Tower."

His tone was serious. Natasha was surprised by his question.

"Unfortunately none, but several have looked!" Gabriella replied with a giggle, not quite understanding the seriousness of his question.

Yanni ignored the flippancy. "Gabriella. Please listen," he continued. He leant in closer in earnest. "Have you been spoken to, or questioned by anyone?"

Both girls shook their heads.

"No, why?" Natasha asked.

He thought for a moment. He looked down and picked his words carefully before he replied.

"Alex and Lorenzo must hear this, I want to talk to all of you four before I approach your parents. But I must be sure before I worry them."

"*Ma* what is it, Yanni? Worry them about what?" Gabriella asked impatiently.

He pulled his chair in closer still and leant over the table so they could both hear his lowered voice.

"At lunchtime today," he said quietly, pausing as he checked the tables to his left and right, "I was eating at my usual place, at a corner table by the window of Toni's Trattoria... I like it there, it is not too expensive and it is always busy and noisy, you know..."

"And," Natasha said, wishing she had been there with him, "go on..."

"Well there were large windows behind me which were wide open. Although I could not see the people sitting at the tables outside, the other side of window, you know, because of the wall and the flowers, I could certainly hear them. Not that I listened, but I was so close, and so some words I heard coming from the people sitting there made me pick up my ears."

"Words like what?" Natasha asked.

He looked at Gabriella.

"Montesonnellino."

"*What?*" Gabriella shrieked. "That is the name of my home!"

"Well yes, I know this, Gabriella. Marcello told me about your home and its history. This is why I was surprised. So I listened. They were talking in German, but it was not clear to me if they said they had been to Montesonnellino, or that they wanted to go there. Unfortunately my German is not so good. But I think I understood they were looking for something. What exactly they were looking for, I could not understand. But I think they also mentioned the Contessa, your grandmother."

Gabriella shrieked, then checked herself.

"Listen, Gabriella," Yanni said, "I couldn't properly understand. They spoke of the river, I think, but I could not be sure of in what context. It was hard to understand, and I was in shock as well."

"How would anyone know about Gabriella's house? And why would they want to? What is it to them? Why?" Natasha was almost challenging him. It seemed unbelievable.

"Exactly! I don't know, Natasha! But of course then I listened very hard, and moved my chair a little closer to the window and leant back, so I could hear everything. It was then that I realised it was the three men from the Leaning Tower! The same men who had wanted to provoke me this morning, remember?"

"No!" Gabriella gasped. "It cannot be true! They cannot know where I live! That is crazy! But who are they? But..." Gabriella's voice quivered. She was on the verge of tears.

"Wait, Gabriella," Yanni said. "I was as shocked as you are, and when I realised who they were and that we had already come across them, I knew it could not be a coincidence, and I had not made a mistake trying to translate what they were saying. They were definitely talking about your home. No mistake."

"No!" Gabriella tried not to cry.

"What did you say to them? Did you question them?" Natasha asked.

"I was going to go to their table and confront them, but then I thought it better if I were to follow them instead. It would be more beneficial to find out where they were staying, no? Confronting them would have been fruitless. So I quickly paid for my meal and followed them back to their hotel. Now I know where they are staying."

Gabriella was doing her best not to cry. She felt sick with fear.

"Perhaps they had been up the Leaning Tower this morning for one reason; to follow us. And that confrontation with me had some purpose," Yanni said. "Perhaps they had planned the contact."

"Or maybe it was the other way round; because of the confrontation, they looked into who we were afterwards," Natasha suggested.

"Oh, Natasha how could they find out who we were; don't make it worse!" Gabriella pleaded.

"I don't know," Yanni said. "But whichever way round it is, I do not like it. This is why I came to find you. The boys were safe within the excavation compound, but you weren't out here on your own."

"That is kind of you, Yanni. But why would they want to know about us?" Gabriella asked. The thought of strangers wanting to know where she lived was very frightening.

"What do they want with us? Why would they even want to know who we were, or the name of Gabriella's house, so far from Pisa? What would it be it to them?" Natasha asked.

Yanni shook his head. He really didn't know the answer.

"Would they be looking for my father perhaps?" Gabriella wondered. She looked at Yanni for some form of reassurance. The ordeal in Medinabad had come flooding back to the three of them.

"Perhaps my father has unearthed something these men want. Just like last time!"

"No. I too thought about this. I do not think so. We have not found anything so precious here on this dig, or as valuable as the queen's mask. No, this excavation here in Pisa is of a different nature. It is more like a time capsule, there are not 'treasures' to speak of that anyone would want to steal. No. This dig has more historical value than monetary value. Somehow I do not believe they are interested in your father, or his work here. They mentioned 'the four teenagers', not your father."

"What? They mentioned us?" Natasha was horrified. "You kept that quiet! What did they say about us?"

He shrugged. "They didn't mention names, but it seemed to me when they said they knew the four 'teenagers' from the river, I presumed it might be you four. But what this means, I really don't know. If indeed it was 'river' they had said. I was really hoping you and the boys would have a better idea about what these men wanted."

Natasha's colour had changed. The healthy, embarrassed beetroot colour had long gone, now she was as white as the tablecloth.

"I wonder," Natasha said quietly, "you don't think, Gabriella..." Then she stopped. "No," she said to herself, thinking better of it.

"What?" Yanni asked. "You must tell me everything. It is important. Tell me anything, Natasha; these men mentioned the four of you as if they had seen you before the tower incident. I think they are maybe looking for something you have."

"But what? We have nothing! Our bags are expensive…" Gabriella put her new bag on the table to show Yanni her new present from her father, "but you can get these all over Italy! We have nothing!"

"Well, from the way they were talking, I understood that you, if it is you they were referring to, might have some connection to something they are interested in. What did you all do when you first arrived at Gabriella's house, Natasha? Did you see anything, or find anything of value on a trip to town? A wallet, perhaps? Maybe they lost a wallet and they think you have it? Or maybe, a camera? Did you go to the river? They mentioned the river. You must think! Please try!"

"Yes we did," Natasha said quietly.

"We have nothing belonging to them, or anyone!" Gabriella was beside herself. "We found nothing! Alex was looking for artefacts along the banks of the Trebbia River when we rented canoes for the day, but he did not find anything, did he Natasha?"

Natasha shook her head.

"Darius, my dog found an old boot by the river, but I hardly think anyone would want that," Gabriella said.

Natasha stared at Gabriella.

"I know what it could be about," she said softly. She looked at Yanni, her mind racing.

"What? Tell me!" Yanni said.

"Well, I don't know for sure, but I think I know what it might be about. We were given a little tin box to look after, a couple of days ago. It contained an ancient coin from Carthage that was found on the banks of the river years ago, and an spearhead, supposedly from the Battle of Trebbia, which could be valuable, since it is museum quality. But there was something else; an old booklet, a sort of identity passport, that belonged to a German soldier from the Second World War. It was in the tin with the other things. The guy at the boathouse, Aldo, gave the tin to us for safekeeping. You see, he was worried, as he said there had been people asking questions, that's why he wanted us to take care of his valuables while his father was away."

Then she remembered.

"Oh Gabriella! He said they were Germans, remember? Aldo told us they were questioning him! Remember he said they had taken a boat out on the river, but they didn't look like tourists... It must be them!"

Gabriella's eyes filled with tears. She nodded.

"Oh, Natasha, you think we are in trouble again?"

CHAPTER TWENTY-SEVEN

I t was late afternoon and Lorenzo had very much enjoyed spending the day with his father at the excavation site. It was the longest time he had spent with him since his mother had died, and they were getting to know each other again. Both Lorenzo and Alex had taken a genuine interest in the excavation, learning about the technical challenges the team faced and some of the inner workings of the dig itself. Although Alex was unaware of the bonding that was taking place between Lorenzo and his father, he was happy just to be with them in his muddy boots his hardhat.

As the team wound up for the day and Alex, Lorenzo and Marcello headed to the office to take off their boots, Yanni approached them. He greeted Marcello warmly, and waited politely for a chance to speak to Lorenzo and Alex alone.

"I think we will have two new volunteers on our next excavation, Yanni!" Marcello said, jokingly. "These two are quick learners and seem not to mind getting dirty at all."

"Great!' Yanni said. "Do you want me to tell them all the boring bits you probably forgot to tell them about, like the hours and hours they have to spend cataloguing everything?"

Marcello laughed. "Very true, very true! Maybe not just yet!" Yanni, is everything OK? The boys told me of a man pushing you into an argument, or something. It was nothing, right?"

"Nothing, nothing. Just a drunk, or something…"

"Great. Lorenzo, Alex, I'll leave you two with Yanni, if you don't mind I will go and see your mother for a while, Alex. Are all going back to town together?"

"Yes, no problem," Yanni said, understanding that he would rather the boys stayed with him.

"Thank you both for a wonderful afternoon. I enjoyed it immensely." Marcello said. He looked at his son. "I really did, Lorenzo."

"Thanks Father, me too. I'll come back tomorrow, if I may…"

"Certainly you may, anytime my boy! I'll look forward to it. See you all later."

He gave Lorenzo a hug, excused himself to Yanni, then left to find Julia.

"Hey guys, could you come back to the hotel with me?" The smile Yanni had for Marcello had disappeared. "I need to talk to you about something. It's important," he said.

"Sure, what's up, Yanni? Can we get a drink first?" Alex asked.

"Actually, it's very important, if you don't mind, I really think you should come back with me to your hotel straight away. The girls are waiting for us at there. We need to talk."

"What is it?" Lorenzo looked concerned.

"Please, just come with me."

He turned and started walking without waiting. The boys looked at each other and shrugged.

"Looks like we have no choice," Alex said.

Yanni walked quickly ahead with Lorenzo and Alex close at his heels. He didn't talk, but glanced over his shoulder several times. He led them swiftly through the back streets of Pisa towards their hotel in the centre of town. After turning into a narrow alley, he suddenly told the boys to run.

"This is so cool," Alex said, sprinting beside Lorenzo. "Are we on the run, or something?"

"Alex, I think this is serious," Lorenzo replied. "Yanni isn't joking."

They followed Yanni until he stopped outside the restaurant door where they'd first had dinner with their parents. Yanni knocked on the door and Massimo let them in.

Yanni quickly ushered the boys in and closed the door behind them.

"Yanni, my man, how are you...?" Massimo started.

"Hello Massimo, we... we are thirsty, may we have a drink; we do not really want to eat as we should leave in a minute."

"Of course my friend, come in, come in."

The two confused boys were invited down the steps into the courtyard, where they were sat at a table in the corner. Massimo brought them a drink, then excused himself to the kitchen.

"Yanni, what on earth is going on?" Lorenzo asked at last, when Massimo was out of earshot. "Please explain!"

"I am not sure, but all I know is that we were being followed just now. It was one of those men from the Leaning Tower this morning. I don't understand what is going on, but something isn't right. Finish your drinks, guys, and I'll go and check if it's clear to leave."

Lorenzo and Alex looked at each other.

"Excellent!" Alex said. "Never a dull moment since our families met!"

Yanni came back down the steps after a couple of minutes, and paid for the drinks.

"I think we can go now."

They walked swiftly back to the hotel without talking. Once in the hotel, Yanni phoned the girl's room from the lobby, and asked them to come down so he could hold a meeting. Once together, they sat in at the far end of the lobby on the sofas, away from any windows or doors where they could be overheard, and Yanni retold the story of what he had overheard the German gentlemen saying in the restaurant at lunchtime.

Alex and Lorenzo were as shocked as the girls had been. They couldn't understand how these men would know the name of the house, let alone what their interest could be in it; Lorenzo's home was almost a hundred and eighty kilometres north of Pisa, and there was no connection that they knew of with these strangers whatsoever. Lorenzo was sure Yanni must have made a mistake, and asked if he had mentioned it to his father.

"No, I haven't mentioned anything to Marcello, yet," Yanni said.

"Good. Let's wait until we are absolutely sure, before we do," Lorenzo said.

"I agree. I wanted to speak to you all about it first, so we can try to work out what's going on. You have to try to remember everything and anything that could be connected to this. Anything at all, anything that was maybe a little strange, or odd, over the last few days, while you were staying in Trebbia."

No one said a word.

"Maybe there is something you have that they want?" Yanni continued. "Perhaps that old *Soldbuch*, you mentioned, Natasha, the spearhead, the coin, anything at all you can think of. I seriously think we should tell your father, Lorenzo."

Lorenzo was a little reluctant about approaching his father on the subject. He was only just beginning to build a relationship with him, and his father was at long last not looking at him as a child anymore. Approaching his father with a suspicion on something Yanni thought he had overheard, could sound really childish and perhaps spoil their developing relationship. But he couldn't really say this to Yanni, or the other three; it was too personal.

"Look," he said, "we can't tell anyone yet. Just what would we tell our parents, anyway, Yanni? Let's think logically for one moment," he reasoned. "The fact that three tourists may have said the word 'Montesonnellino' over lunch, and they may have been looking for 'something', and they may have seen teenagers on some river or another. Teens are everywhere! And which river? They didn't say, Trebbia River, did they?"

Yanni shook his head.

"No, sorry, Yanni, I don't think we have enough to be bothering our parents with," Lorenzo said. "Montesonnellino could have been mistaken for a million words, and it is highly unlikely we have anything of interest to anyone. The spearhead and coin? What of them! My father had a hundred such things in his collection. And the old passport of the German soldier? Who would want that? I am sorry, girls, Yanni. If there were more information, then yes, perhaps, I would tell my father and worry him. But is it worth him possibly halting his busy schedule while he has to investigate something that may be nothing? You know that better than I, Yanni. He has much on his hands this week with interviews, reports and so on, and he is under pressure to get things done before he leaves Pisa on Friday to go back to Trebbia for the party on Saturday. We cannot bother him with these trivial things. I am sorry, Yanni please, don't say anything to him."

Yanni shook his head. He wasn't happy. "Lorenzo, I think we should say something…"

"Yanni, be serious," Lorenzo interrupted, "we can't say anything to my father, as there is really nothing to say!"

Yanni threw his arms up in the air in exaggerated submission.

"As you wish, as you wish. It is up to you. I will say nothing. But I suggest you go back home and look more closely in the container you have from this young man at the boatyard. Talk to him, and see if there is any kind of connection. Ask again what exactly he was being questioned about by these men who worried him so much, that that he had to give you this box to take care of."

He stood up, ready to go.

"And if I were you," he added, "I would go back to Montesonnellino today. Find the connection. Unfortunately I would come myself, but I am not free to leave until we all come up for the party. And I have to pick up Signor Muretti, anyway. Oh boy, there is so much to do here before then."

Natasha's heart pounded at the thought of the party. Everything else she heard was now almost muffled in her ears.

"I am staying here in Pisa," Lorenzo insisted. "I've only just arrived! I want to spend time with my father."

"Well, we've all just arrived and want to stay really," Alex said. "Yanni, you said, find a connection, but find a connection to what? Lorenzo's right. What on earth are we looking for? Aldo said that three Germans were asking him questions. So? That doesn't mean anything. They were asking about his grandfather anyway; nothing to do with us."

Then Alex went quiet for a moment, and put his hands on his head.

"Oh God, remember the story about the bodies on the river? You don't think there is some connection, Lorenzo, do you?"

"What?" Yanni looked at him horrified. "Bodies?" He immediately sat down again. "What bodies, Alex?"

"Aldo told us a story about the Italian partisans shooting three escaping Germans on the river at the end of the war, near Lorenzo's house, you know, when the Allies were pushing the Germans north. Their boots were stuffed with money. Not only that, the I.D. found on the boat they were in didn't match any of the men found..." he paused. Then he looked at Lorenzo.

The boys stared at each other.

"You were saying, Alex?" Gabriella goaded him. "Now will you come back with us?"

"Actually," Natasha intercepted, "you two have got to come back with us... because there's something else."

"What?"

"We, I mean Gabriella and I, forgot to tell you guys."

"What?" both boys asked.

"Well you know your quiet old gardener, who you said doesn't speak much?"

"Yes, Giovanni, Maria's father. What of him?" Lorenzo said.

"Well, he actually does speak when he wants to..."

"Well of course he speaks!" Lorenzo said, frustrated. "No one said he didn't speak! He is just a quiet man who keeps to himself. What is your point? Do you girls actually have one?"

"Our point is, Lorenzo," Natasha said, "Gabriella and I heard him shout quite loudly at Darius, when he thought no one was around."

"And so? The dog was probably annoying him."

Natasha glanced at Gabriella.

"Lorenzo, he shouted at Darius in German."

CHAPTER TWENTY-EIGHT

T he sky was dark, but it was still only early afternoon. The black clouds that had been following the car for the last hour all the way up the motorway from Pisa, threatening to drench the hilly countryside had burst open unable to hold their contents another second, letting the rain fall in an unforgiving, torrential downpour. It came down so hard, relentlessly pounding the car with such force, that any dreamy thoughts Natasha was having of dancing with Yanni in the moonlit garden were flushed from her mind. It was probably a mud bath by now, she thought. She just hoped the marquees that had been erected hadn't been completely washed away.

After the painfully slow journey, with the wipers thudding at full force and the four passengers dozing off for most of the boring journey, they finally arrived outside the gates of Montesonnellino. With the click of the button, the gates opened and the car slowly splashed in and out of the puddles down the tree-lined driveway towards the villa. Natasha thought how sad and miserable the statues looked in the rain, half naked, grey and sodden.

Piero parked as close as he could to the steps at the front door. They all sat waiting for the rain to abate before they opened the car doors. But it didn't. If anything, it was getting worse. Eventually, prompted by a roll of thunder, Natasha and Gabriella made the quick dash up the steps to the house. They stood under the porch, dripping wet and laughing.

"I've never, ever seen rain like this!" Natasha shouted against the tremendous noise. "It's like an old film when they over-do the rain scene, throwing buckets of water at the actors. It's absolutely chucking it down! Unbelievable!"

"I know, look at this!" Gabriella bent over and squeezed her hair out. "I am completely soaked!"

Piero dashed up the steps from the car with their bags, and dropped them in the hallway. The boys followed him into the house and ran straight upstairs. Piero said something to Gabriella in Italian before he ran back to the car again.

"What did he say? I didn't understand," Natasha asked.

"He said that Saturday night may be too wet to party."

"Oh no! I hope they wont have to cancel it!"

"I know. But I think it's too late to cancel now. But even if it stops raining today, it will still be very muddy. All the food was going to be set up in the marquee next to the ballroom; it will be disastrous if it doesn't stop raining. My grandmother will be very upset."

"Me too!" Natasha said.

To Natasha's surprise, the thought of the Contessa being upset didn't seem to bother her like it would have a few days ago. She wasn't scared of her anymore, if anything, she was more curious about her. She had been thinking about her in the car, and the Contessa had begun to intrigue her. That was, of course, when Natasha wasn't thinking about Yanni. Natasha wondered what the connection could be that would cause Giovanni and the Contessa to become so close that she would feel comfortable rubbing his back, even if it were in sympathy. She was pretty sure the Contessa would have known if he were really German; nothing gets past her. Didn't she even say something about the war, when she and Alex had first been introduced to her? Natasha tried to remember what it was. It was something about letting things go. Something about, what's done is done, as it was healthier for the mind. She tried to recall the conversation.

"Gabriella, lets go up and get dry,' she suggested, "then I think the four of us should all sit down together and discuss everything that's been going on, to try to get it all into perspective and in some kind of order. There are a lot of things we need to put straight. So many little odd things that aren't related but could be. We should go over everything and write it all down before we forget something, don't you think?"

"Children! For goodness' sake! Come in the house, away from the rain and close the door!"

It was the Contessa. She was in the hallway waving them in off the porch.

"Why have you all come back so soon? The preparations are still under way you know, we are by no means finished here. It's still going ahead, despite this weather. You do realize Piero had to leave his duties to pick you up at a most inconvenient time, you know. And of course this confounded rain does not help, either. Did Pisa not hold your attention at all, Natasha?" She sounded irritated, and didn't wait for the answer before turning to go upstairs.

"Grandmother," Gabriella said, running up to kiss her. "Pisa was lovely! Natasha bought the prettiest dress…"

"Please, go to your rooms and change out of these wet clothes. Tea will be waiting for you in the drawing room. Tell the boys I need to have a talk with you all. I'd like you all down here in thirty minutes."

A few minutes later Lorenzo rapped on Natasha's door. Unable to wait for the reply, he burst into her room. She screamed, as she had only just put a dry shirt on and was still zipping up her jeans.

"Excuse me Natasha," he panted, "but I have to tell you! It's gone!"

"What's gone?"

Alex's head appeared over Lorenzo's shoulder. Natasha couldn't believe the intrusion.

"Alex! Lorenzo! Excuse me, guys! I'm changing! This is my bedroom! Do you mind?"

"Natasha! The little ID book-thingy! It's gone!" Alex said.

"The coin and the spearhead are still in the tin," Lorenzo explained, "but the *Soldbuch* has been taken. We just went to have a look at it; Alex and I wanted to see the picture of the soldier. We couldn't wait any longer, we were so curious to see the photo. But it's not there! It has been removed from the tin! Stolen! We need to talk. There is definitely something going on. Yanni is absolutely right. We seriously need to work out what's going on here."

CHAPTER TWENTY-NINE

While the rain outside continued to pound the terracotta tiles on the veranda roof, Lorenzo, Alex, Gabriella and Natasha, now changed and dry, sat in silence in the humid drawing room waiting for the Contessa. Subdued and apprehensive, they had put their urgent discussion about the *Soldbuch* and all the other strange events on hold, at least until this inconvenient meeting with the Contessa was over. While they waited, Natasha asked Lorenzo in a low whisper if he knew the reason for the summons, but he shrugged; he had no idea what it was about, either.

They suspected that the vanishing *Soldbuch* must have been an internal job. But why anyone in the house would have taken it, was a mystery. They imagined the reason for this meeting with the Contessa could only be about this, and they hoped she would be able to shed light on what was going on, if indeed she knew. But they all agreed that if this meeting turned out not to be about anything related to all the odd events, they wouldn't mention anything to the Contessa. Not yet, anyway. They needed to talk over every little thing that had happened to try to piece it together.

Just as the air outside, the atmosphere in the drawing room was heavy. The French doors leading to the veranda were all wide open, and an occasional breeze swept through the room making the rain pound and splash loudly on the ceramic floor tiles outside. Maria was on the veranda, dragging the furniture nearer to the wall in an attempt to save it from the splash and spray of the downpour. She had laid towels down on the wettest sections of the tiles to soak up the puddles, which were beginning to form and spread like miniature straight rivers between the tiles along the grout.

Lorenzo, seeing Maria struggling to move one of the large, heavy sofas, jumped up and went out to help her.

"No, no, Lorenzo!" she whispered, almost pleading. "Go back! Go back inside!"

She looked at him, frightened, and then glanced quickly to see if his grandmother was in the room yet. "Please... go back inside, leave me!" she begged him.

Perplexed at the fear in her tone, he hesitated. So he did what she asked, but her red face and puffy eyes hadn't gone unnoticed. He went back into the drawing room and sat down again, wondering what ever could be wrong.

The Contessa's office door opened at the far end of the room, and she swanned in, papers in hand, towards the four confused teens. Lorenzo stood up, and Alex quickly followed suit.

"Please sit," she said, nodding in appreciation. She came straight to the point.

"Well, something inconvenient, and I might add, rather disturbing has happened while you were in Pisa. I won't beat around the bush. Giovanni, Maria's father, my gardener for over sixty years, has completely disappeared."

Her hands flicked the air as if she were a magician doing a magic trick.

"It is really most inconvenient," she continued, sitting down in the chair by the fireplace, "as Maria and Piero have had to neglect their regular duties at this terribly stressful time with everything going on for the party. What, with the opening up of new rooms because of the rain soaked lawns, not to mention the fact that Piero had to waste valuable time going down to Pisa to pick you four up, all this time and energy looking for Giovanni is not something I had accounted for. It's really very silly of him. Very silly indeed."

She made it sound as if the old man were a boy, just playing hide and seek for fun. "However," she continued, "because he has not been found, and it is very obvious that he wants to be left alone, I have instructed Maria and Piero and the rest of the staff helping us this week, to continue on, as before. We are far too busy to search the grounds any longer, especially in this weather. Even the vineyard workers have gone home early this week, as there is nothing for them to do in the rain. So I'm afraid he will just have to come out on his own accord when he realizes we are not playing the game any more. He will, when he is hungry enough. So I just wanted you to know so that you could keep an eye out for him as you go gallivanting around the grounds."

She looked out of the French doors, and added, "not that you will be doing much of that, yet."

Unbelievable, Natasha thought. She was so callous it was almost comical. Was she joking?

"But... when did this happen, Grandmother? When did Giovanni disappear?" Lorenzo asked.

"We believe some time yesterday, or perhaps the evening before. It s neither here nor there when he left."

"But Grandmother," Gabriella said, her voice quivering, "perhaps Giovanni has died somewhere on the estate. Poor Giovanni!"

The Contessa shook her head. "No, no. He took a blanket or two, and food. And there was a note left in the kitchen. He is quite alive, believe me."

"But in this rain!" Gabriella said. "He will catch pneumonia!"

The Contessa ignored the comment, and was about to speak when Lorenzo spoke first.

"What does it say?" he asked, almost demanding of his grandmother. "What did he say in the note?"

The Contessa looked at her grandson as if she didn't quite hear the question.

"...The note, Grandmother, what does it say?" he repeated.

"I do not believe it was addressed to you, Lorenzo."

She stood up. "Now if you will excuse me children, I have some pressing paperwork to attend to, I also have to compile a list on my computer," she glanced at Alex, "of everything taken from the property during the war."

"Why Grandmother?" Gabriella asked. "We should all be searching for Giovanni!"

"The original list is old and almost illegible, and I feel it is time to re-write it. I will have it sent to the various organisations that have sprung up over the world in recent years dealing in wartime art theft. I feel it is my duty to do this now, as there is much interest in recovering these stolen treasures. From legitimate as well as illegitimate sources."

Natasha couldn't believe she was discussing her art, when her old and trusted gardener was missing.

"And although this confounded rain will no doubt deter you from going outside," the Contessa continued, "I would rather you all to stay out of the way until Saturday; the flower people and the piano tuner will be here later today; and the ballroom floor and the ante-room is being polished this afternoon. So that section of the house is out of bounds, too, I'm afraid. You really should have stayed in Pisa."

She walked towards her office door, and Lorenzo stood up. She turned round and looked at him.

"Oh, Lorenzo, a young man came to the house yesterday asking for you, I believe Maria said he was a boatman of some kind. Please, Lorenzo, remember your position; if you must invite these types to the house in the future, at least make sure you are here."

And with that she left the room. They were speechless.

CHAPTER THIRTY

L orenzo immediately ran out to the veranda to find Maria. She was struggling to wring out the heavy, soaking wet towels. He walked straight up to her and gave her a big hug.

"Maria, I am so sorry about your father. What is it all about?"

She covered her face and broke down.

"Sit down, Maria, please! Tell us what happened," he said in Italian.

He sat her down on one of the sofas then sat next to her, holding her hand. She pulled out her handkerchief.

"It all started when Darius found the boot," she spluttered. "My father tried to dispose of it, several times, but Darius kept returning it to him. Somehow the dog knew…"

"Knew what?" Lorenzo asked.

Gabriella, Alex and Natasha had followed Lorenzo out to the veranda, and Gabriella quietly translated what Maria said.

"About the boot," Maria said. "I know nothing of it, but Darius somehow knew."

"…That it belonged to a German officer? A long time ago?" Lorenzo asked, coaxing Maria to continue. Lorenzo and Alex had worked that much out earlier that morning.

"No. A young man who deserted, gave up everything, for the love of a local girl," she sobbed.

Natasha put her hand over her mouth when she heard about the boot. She was horrified. She turned to Maria.

"Maria, don't say that boot belonged to one of those dead German soldiers they found on the river!" she said. The thought of it coming off a dead person was unimaginably disgusting.

"Dead soldiers? No!" Maria looked at Natasha, confused. "I know nothing of dead soldiers. No, the boot, it belonged to my father."

"Your father? It belonged to your father?" Lorenzo said, looking stunned.

"Maria," he continued, "so was he a soldier, here in Italy, during the war? Was he a German soldier?"

She nodded, and replied in Italian as she sobbed.

"I knew you would guess, all of you. I knew it. Secrets never stay hidden. Something always comes to the surface. In this case it happened all at once for some reason, and if my father cannot hide a boot, he cannot hide a mountain... You had the *Soldbuch*... you would have found out... I had to find it, I am so sorry. Forgive me, my father was going crazy until I found it."

"So you took it from the trunk?" Lorenzo asked.

She nodded and held her head low.

"Was it his *Soldbuch*, Maria, was it Giovanni's?" Lorenzo asked softly. "You can trust us, you can tell us. Was your father the German soldier, the owner of the *Soldbuch*?"

She nodded into her handkerchief.

"He had to get it from you, before you realized it was him in the photo."

"But why has he gone away? Why must he hide? What is he afraid of?" Lorenzo asked. "Surely, after all these years, it is over. No one cares now, who was German, who was Italian, who was anything! Europe is united. We are one! It's all in the past, he is Italian to us; He is family."

"I am not exactly sure why he ran, Lorenzo," she sniffed. "The boot that Darius found by the river was the beginning. It put the fear of God into him. It was a fear in my father that I had never seen before. Then when the *Soldbuch* turned up from nowhere, he was in shock. It made him ill. And then this man, coming to the house to ask questions..."

"What man?" Gabriella asked.

"A man who interviewed your grandmother one day. You were still here, it was before you went to Pisa."

"Who was he? What did he want with my grandmother?" Gabriella asked.

"So Yanni was right, then," Alex whispered, "there was a man at the house..."

Maria shrugged. "I think he wanted some information about Montesonnellino, or maybe about paintings or something. They spoke in German, so I didn't understand much, and the door was closed most of the time. It is a thick door... I tried to hear..."

"They spoke in German? Are you sure?" Lorenzo asked.

"Yes, he was from a German magazine, or something. Herr Hoffmann, I think he said his name was. Anyway, when my father heard about this man asking questions to the Contessa, it was unbearable for him. He must have put him under so much stress, and now he has gone into hiding. He said he had to go, in a note. I do not understand why, but it was making him so ill. He could not eat or sleep..."

"But why is he so afraid of this man, Hoffman?" Gabriella asked.

"I don't know, but there must be more to my father's story than he has told me. He thinks these men are after him."

"But why?" Gabriella probed. She was becoming frightened. "What could Giovanni, an old man who has been a gardener here all his life, possibly have done? Or what does he have that they would want?"

"I don't know," she answered in Italian, "but it must be something very important and very frightening to make him run. My father does not scare easily."

Gabriella translated to Alex and Natasha all that Maria had said.

Natasha thought about it.

"Maybe Giovanni had seen something. Something he shouldn't have seen. Maybe years ago," she suggested. It was possible, she thought, he was always snooping; it would make sense.

"I don't know; I have no idea! Now he has disappeared, in weather like this!"

They looked at the rain overflowing the gutters.

"He told me that he could not face the Contessa, ever again," Maria said.

"Face the Contessa? But…" Lorenzo was now totally confused. Why couldn't he face his grandmother? What has she got to do with anything?

A bell on an ornate coiled spring rang on the wall next to them, and Maria jumped up. She blew her nose, took a deep breath, straightened her dress and tried to compose herself.

"Please, you say nothing to nobody?" she pleaded to Natasha and Alex in English.

They shook their heads. "We promise, Maria."

"My father is a so good man," she continued, "quiet, kind, he loved my mother and sacrificing everything for to be with her. It is not right that his life turn to be so, especially that now he is old. If you can to think of some place for hiding, please to tell me, or Piero. The Contessa promise she not to call the police. She understand my father is good man. She help him many ways before. But I think he is now hiding from Contessa same as these men."

The little bell on the wall rang, again.

Maria excused herself, and went inside the house.

The four children sat on the sofas in silence while the rain pelted the terracotta roof above them. They had a lot to digest.

"So now I'm really confused," Natasha said after a while. "So if that was Giovanni's *Soldbuch*, and his boot, does this mean that he was on the boat with the men who were shot?"

Alex shrugged. "I'm totally lost, now."

"I mean," she continued, "you don't think he killed them, do you? Maybe that's his secret, and these guys are after him because of that!"

"But why now, after all those years? And who were those men in the boat? I thought we had the feeling that Aldo's father was involved in their shooting. He was the partisan, remember? They were the ones shooting. Why would a German soldier shoot fellow Germans?" Lorenzo asked.

"I don't know. It's all so confusing," Natasha said.

"And why would anyone leave an ID on the boat?" Alex asked. "Wouldn't you make sure you took it with you? I would, if it were mine. If I wanted to escape being shot like the others."

"Not unless you wanted to give the impression that you were on the boat, or dead, like them." Lorenzo suggested. "If you wanted to disappear…"

"Good point," Alex said.

"Poor Giovanni, he is not a bad man," Gabriella said. "He would not kill anyone! We must not speak of him like this. He must have just fallen in love with Maria's mother; that is all. He has hidden his identity his whole life because of that, not because he is a murderer!"

"Well it just doesn't make sense to me," Natasha said. "The man is terrified, and has risked his life to hide from three of his fellow countrymen. They wouldn't be after him after all these years for nothing! And they're not even military people. Maria said that the man who came here, Hoffmann, was from a magazine or something. Anyone from, say, the army or war office or something, chasing him for desertion, would be long dead by now, wouldn't they? I think there's more to this story than love and desertion; in fact, I think Giovanni believes they are after him for something else."

"They want something. Yanni is right about that," Lorenzo admitted. "We should at least check Aldo is all right, I think we should still pay him another visit."

"Yes, we should find out why he came here yesterday," Natasha said. "It certainly wasn't to have a swim, that's for sure, in this weather. And another thing…" Natasha lowered her voice, "I bet your grandmother knows more than she's saying. I mean, I don't want to be rude or anything, and don't take this the wrong way, you too, but Gabriella, you should tell the boys what you saw, you know, by the chapel."

"What?" Alex asked.

Gabriella said nothing, and shook her head.

"If you don't say, I will!"

"I cant," Gabriella said.

"They were having a bit of a… tender moment, shall we say," Natasha said for her. "He was being comforted by the Contessa, in a very close way."

"Who was?" Lorenzo demanded.

Gabriella hesitated. "Giovanni."

"That is ridiculous!"

Gabriella shrugged. "Forget it, I know. But I'm going to find him. I think I know where he is. You boys see if Piero can take us over to Aldo this afternoon. Coming, Natasha? Let's go for a walk in the rain. It is warm, like a shower. We can take an umbrella."

CHAPTER THIRTY-ONE

"Go on, Artamis, good boy, out you go, it won't hurt you..."

Gabriella gently pushed the two horses out of the shelter, and Natasha quickly stepped in out of the rain.

"See, Natasha, he was here, I was right," Gabriella said, looking at the sodden ground at her feet. She knelt down and felt like crying. A few of Giovanni's belongings had been trampled into the soggy ground by the horse's hooves.

"Look, the horses have ruined all his things, poor Giovanni. His blanket is soaked; and his cup... and look, the bread and cheese he brought with him... oh, Natasha where would he go? He must be desperate; poor man!"

"I don't know, Gabriella. But at least we know he is probably still alive."

"I think it was Giovanni who used to care for me when I came here to sleep at night, I know it! Now I should be caring for him, and I'm too late, he has gone!"

Natasha didn't know what to say. She put an arm around her.

"I fear Natasha, that his frail body could not last a night in this weather without shelter. The horses must have pushed him out."

"Or maybe he knew you would come here looking for him, and he felt he had to move on. Maybe he heard us approaching just now and has only just left," Natasha said. She peered out of the shelter but couldn't see anything in the rain. There were so many trees it would be impossible to find him, even if the visibility was good.

Natasha bent down to pick the cup up, and as she did, she noticed something sticking out from under the sodden blanket. It was the *Soldbuch*! It was wet, smudged with mud and the ink had run on many of the pages. It was ripped apart at the spine where the horses had stood on it.

She wiped the worst of the mud off the pages, and put it back together the best she could. She carefully opened the *Soldbuch* to the first page. Both girls looked at the black and white picture stapled to the first page. It was still a little too muddy too see the face. Natasha wiped it again with the edge of her sleeve, and there he was, a very young, handsome soldier. He had a pale complexion and angular features, and his hair was neatly combed for the photograph, and he was smiling very slightly, but not enough to show his teeth. But it was the nose that looked familiar, and there was something about the eyes, too.

"It's definitely Giovanni," Natasha said. "You can tell; it's him."

They read the name under the photograph. The blue ink was smudged, but it was clearly signed by the soldier. In his own hand it read, Johann Fuchs.

"Johann Fuchs… He is really called Johann!"

Gabriella looked into the eyes of the young man in the photograph.

"Poor Giovanni, so he is really, Johann. He looks so young, doesn't he? He doesn't look much older than Lorenzo."

"I know, and look, it says he was from Berlin," Natasha said. "How sad to think he never went home. This is all so weird."

"Yes, it is. I am wondering if what we are doing is right. We shouldn't have found all this out, I mean, it's really not our business. I feel intrusive. We are changing his life by doing this. Perhaps we should just bury the *Soldbuch* for him and forget it?"

"Gabriella, someone was bound to find out, sooner or later. Better it is us, who he can trust. Remember he is hiding, and it's not because of us."

They waited for the rain to die down a little, and decided to take the *Soldbuch* back to the house for Maria to look after, until her father returned. Natasha put the *Soldbuch* in her pocket. Now she felt for Giovanni, seeing his picture of him as a young man. She saw Giovanni in a different light, not as a weird, old man, but a scared, young man who has grown old with the weight of an old secret on his shoulders. How he must have loved Maria's mother, she thought, to have changed his identity to be able to stay with her.

They shared the umbrella back to the house.

CHAPTER THIRTY-TWO

Natasha and Gabriella kicked off their heavy, muddy boots and belted up the steps of the veranda and into the house through the kitchen. As they ran through the hallway towards the main stairs, they passed the open door of the ballroom where Natasha noticed three people polishing the vast, wooden floor. Her heart jumped at the thought of Yanni coming. She couldn't help smiling to herself; it wouldn't be long, she thought, before she would hopefully be dancing in his arms…

"Girls…. *Ragazze*…!" The Contessa's voice called to them as they ran upstairs.

They stopped in their tracks.

"Girls, would you please come down here?" she called again. "We are waiting, rather patiently, I might add, for you in the drawing room. Please come down now, straight away."

The girls looked at each other and then at their own soaking hair and clothes. They sighed and slowly went down stairs again, trying to tidy their hair and straighten their dirty, wet clothes as best they could.

Upon entering the drawing room, to their surprise, they saw that their brothers and the Contessa had company. Aldo and another gentleman were all seated and politely waiting.

"For heavens sake girls, you are soaking! This is too much, Gabriella; what is it with you and water!" The Contessa looked at their jeans. "Here…" she passed them a couple of magazines from the coffee table.

Natasha looked at the cover of the *Country Life* magazine in her hand, wondering what she was supposed to do with it.

"Well, for goodness sake, girls, open them up and sit on them!"

"Excuse me, Grandmother for the state of our clothes, but we found where Gi…"

The Contessa put her hand up to stop Gabriella in her tracks. She turned to the stocky, middle-aged man. His wide, fleshy face was partially covered by a closely cropped greying beard.

"Signor…?" The Contessa hesitated, struggling to remember his name as she stretched out her hand to introduce the gentleman to the girls.

"Trimarco," the man said.

Natasha noticed, when he had stood up as the girls entered the room that he wasn't looking very happy at all. Natasha glanced at Aldo standing next to the man, and she thought how subdued he looked, too. He had lost his cheeky spark. He actually looked quite pale and worried. She wondered what on earth had happened. What was he here for? She sat down on her magazine next to Alex on the sofa. She saw Aldo's tin was on the coffee table in front of them. The lid had been removed and was lying beside it.

The Contessa sighed, looking at the girls in their drenched clothes, she made it quite clear by her tone and demeanour, that she really didn't need this meeting and would rather be doing something else.

"Signor Trimarco, this is Gabriella, my granddaughter, and Natasha. Signor Trimarco has come to tell us something rather disturbing. Please let us all make this as quick as possible. Signor, if you would, please, in English…?"

She nodded to him to begin.

"*Certo*. So, I come back from my 'oliday," he started, in a very thick accent, "and I find my son distressed from the fact three men broken in my office yesterday. Before I make telephone to police, same men come back to my boatyard early this morning! They smashing my office and they say they looking for information! I say, what information?" He used his arms in a gesture that showed he had no idea what the men had been talking about.

"They demand me information about a man who name is *Fuchs*. I say them, I never hear this name. What, *Fuchs*? I say. I know nothing! And ees the truth! But they looking and looking, and find old jacket of German soldier in the back room, and they saying ees belonging to this man, *Fuchs*! I say, no, ees of collection my father! They say *Fuchs* had *Soldbuch* in this jacket on a boat, and they want very much this *Soldbuch*. This jacket of German soldier was things of my father. I don't know why he keep it. I tell these men exactly this! Why Aldo now keep this jacket and *Soldbuch* of the German soldier, I don't know why! *Stupido!*"

He glanced at his son as if to imply that this was all his fault.

"So," he continued, "they want this *Soldbuch* or they say they coming make more damage. They say they make hole in all my boats! I say, OK, OK, I get *Soldbuch*! I look for book after they gone. But ees not there! Then Aldo say me he, give *Soldbuch* to you!"

He looked at the four teens, then at the tin on the coffee table.

"So. Now I come for *Soldbuch* to give these men. I want no trouble. This book nothing to me, non ees my business. So, book is here, non? My son, Aldo give it you for safety. Now I come for book and to give to men, and 'ave peace. I never before 'ave trouble. I am honest man and all my life 'ave honest business. I leave my son in charge of business one week only, and now coming big trouble! Why ees important, this book? You see picture? You boys see this picture of soldier?"

He looked at Alex and Lorenzo.

"I am sorry, Signor Trimarco, I never looked inside the *Soldbuch*," Lorenzo said truthfully. "It stayed in the tin, and we did not look inside. But the *Soldbuch* is missing."

Natasha watched the Contessa. She thought she noticed a slight smirk as she looked at her grandson.

"No, nor did I see the picture." Alex offered. "We were going to look at it this morning, when we came back from Pisa, but we opened the tin, and it had disappeared... strange really, becau..."

Natasha stepped on her brother's foot so he would shut up. He got the hint. She slowly put her hand to her back pocket and gently pushed the muddy *Soldbuch* in deeper to make sure none of it was showing. This was getting serious, she thought. She wasn't going to hand over Giovanni's identity to Aldo's father so that some bullies could identify the poor old gardener and take him away. She didn't know what the consequences would be for Giovanni. She was concerned though, wondering if she was doing the right thing. She glanced at Gabriella and she gave her a wide-eyed look that said, 'keep it hidden'. So she did.

"So you see," the Contessa said, "I am afraid, Signor, we cannot help you. There is no old man on my property called Fuchs, nor, it seems, is there anything else belonging to him. Perhaps, it would seem, that we have been broken into by these same people who took the soldier's jacket from your office. Now if you would excuse us, Signor, the girls are wet and dirty and need to change, and I have much to do before tomorrow. In case you hadn't heard Signor, ...Tri..." she hesitated, her hand prompting him to repeat his name.

"Marco," he told her, through his teeth.

"Signor Trimarco... I am holding a grand party here tomorrow night, in honour of my son, the Professor Bonamici-Milanese, I am sure you have heard of him, to celebrate his engagement to the mother of these two children. And with over two hundred guests, I am afraid I must get on."

She stood up.

"Signor..."

She offered her hand, and both father and son rose to shake it. It was obvious Signor Trimarco was not ready to leave, but he had received his cue. Natasha felt Aldo's eyes on her as he leant forward to pick up his tin from the coffee table, but she didn't look at him; The mention of the party brought it all back, and the dream of dancing the night away with Yanni. He would be here within twenty-four hours, and she would be in his company the whole evening, and hopefully the following day, too, if he stayed.

No, she thought, she didn't need to give Aldo a second glance.

Chapter Thirty-Three

L orenzo quietly knocked on the Contessa's office door. He listened with his ear almost pressing against it and waited for the response.

"Enter…" came the reply.

He looked at his three accomplices standing behind him, then, opened the door.

"Grandmother, excuse me for disturbing you," he said, peeping around the door, "but we need to talk to you."

"You do indeed, Lorenzo."

"No, I mean about Giovanni, Grandmother."

"You do indeed."

She looked at him over the rim of her reading glasses, then took them off and folded them slowly and thoughtfully. She placed them on her desk in front of her.

"Well come in then, all of you. I am surprised it has taken you so long. I have been expecting you, of course."

The four children gingerly entered her office and stood awkwardly in front of her desk. There was a very large, illustrated art book open in front of her, and as Lorenzo, the nominated spokesperson, stepped forward to talk to her, he noticed newspaper cuttings and various articles neatly spread around the far side of her desk. Some had yellow notes stuck to them and others were even protected in cellophane jackets, indicating that they were perhaps older and she had had them a while. He couldn't help glancing at the clipping nearest him, because it had a black and white photograph of Nazi officers proudly posing in front of large paintings, in what looked like a tunnel, or a cave. He saw the word 'Pisa', but reading upside down was difficult at a glance. He wondered what his grandmother was up to.

"Yes?" she prompted him, distracting him from her desk. "You did come here to talk, did you not, Lorenzo, or are you going to just look at my desk?"

He quickly focused back on Giovanni and the reason they had come to see her. He came straight to the point.

"Grandmother," he said in Italian, "here is the *Soldbuch*. We think you should see it. The girls found it earlier over in the horse's shelter at the paddock."

His grandmother indicated for him to place it on the desk by her glasses. She hardly glanced at it.

"You should look at it, Grandmother," Gabriella said, surprised at her nonchalance. "It is Giovanni's! It is the one that Signor Trimarco was asking for..."

"Oh, I know very well who's *Soldbuch* it is," she replied, "and who was asking for it, thank you, Gabriella. So you have had it since this morning, have you? You had it in your possession even when Signor Trimarco was here asking for it, and you intentionally kept it from him? You did understand that these uncouth men of whom he spoke will be returning to him, to bully him for it, do you not?"

"Err... yes, but we were thinking of Giov..."

"Well, Gabriella, I have to say that I am glad you have come to me with it, anyway," she interrupted, "albeit a little late in the day. And it was a good decision not to hand it over immediately without discussing it with me first, despite the threatening behaviour of these men who seem to be harassing the boatman and his son. And do not worry; they will not be bothering them again. Piero and his friends will, I am sure, help them find their way back to the airport. Now, where were we? Ah yes. The *Soldbuch*."

Natasha and Alex looked at each other, surprised at her positive attitude towards their actions. If anything, they had all been expecting quite the opposite.

"So you knew it was Giovanni's *Soldbuch*, Grandmother?" Gabriella confirmed. "You knew he was the soldier in the photo? You knew about him, all along?"

"Oh *please*, Gabriella, what do you think?" she said with an almost pitiful expression. She leaned back in her chair and looked at them.

"You presume that because I am old, I know nothing? In fact, it is quite the opposite. They would have been in a far worse a mess, years ago, had one been unaware of their situation… "

"Who?" Gabriella asked. "Who would have been in a far worse mess?"

"Why, Gabriella, do I have to spell it out for you?"

"Beatrice Dafiume," Natasha said quietly. "Maria's mother."

The Contessa looked at Natasha. "At least one of you has worked it out."

"But…" Alex started, looking at his sister in surprise, then, back at the Contessa, "I mean Contessa, if you knew all along that Giovanni was a German soldier and had hidden from the authorities all this…"

"Aha! Stop right there, young man! Was he a soldier? Yes, most definitely. And has he been keeping a low profile all his life? Certainly! The fact that he had risked his life and given up his family to stay with my closest friend, said more to me about him than the colour of his ugly uniform he had to wear."

"So you helped him?" Lorenzo asked, astonished, "when our loyal partisans were looking for ways to kill them, you helped him? After all the Nazis had done here, you actually *helped* him?"

"Oh do calm down boy! Life is not always black and white, Lorenzo. There are many shades of grey."

"Well if he wasn't all bad, Grandmother, tell me, why is he hiding from the authorities?" Lorenzo asked defiantly.

"Who says he is hiding from the authorities, Lorenzo? Hiding, maybe, but from the law? This I doubt very much. No, in fact, I am sure of it. Who these men are exactly, I am still in the process of finding out." She taped the laptop in front of her. She thought for a minute.

"But there are two things I do know," she continued. "One, is that these extraordinarily intrusive Germans in the village are not in any way linked to any authority, and two, that they are not even who they are pretending to be. Please, sit down all of you, you look ridiculous hovering around the desk like a flock of lost lambs."

There were two large, leather armchairs in front of her desk. The girls sat in the chairs and the boys perched on an arm of each one.

The Contessa tapped her laptop again.

"This has proven to be very helpful over the last few days. However, until I have found out who these men are, exactly, Giovanni is free to hide or go wherever he chooses. I will not do anything dramatic yet, like call the authorities. He has his reasons for being fearful, though at this point I have to admit I am at a loss to understand what these reasons are. The man is no criminal; there is no crime in having a past that one could not control. He was a German soldier, serving in the German army because he just happened to be born in Germany. During that unfortunate time when war broke out, he was a young teenager called up to fight. He hardly had a choice. Had you boys been born in Germany around the same time, you too would have been in the German army and fought for Hitler too. One cannot choose one's place of birth, Lorenzo. One should always give someone, especially someone you have known and trusted all your life, the benefit of the doubt."

"Yes, of course, Grandmother." Lorenzo said. He couldn't even imagine fighting for Hitler, but she did have a valid point.

"So, did you know Giovanni during the war, when he was a German soldier, Grandmother?" Gabriella asked.

"Know him? No, of course not! No one had contact with the Germans! They were hated Gabriella, they were the enemy! We lived in fear of them!" She paused then, added, "I really don't understand how Bea got to know him. She was at the house, you see, working for the officers, who had taken it over. I had my suspicions; close friends cannot hide much from each other, even when they try. But I knew for a fact later, of course; she had to tell me, the child was beginning to show. It was only a matter of time. And of course, she desperately needed help by then. So she came to me. Bea had to be very, very careful. No one knew. And if one did, there were very harsh consequences to pay. Very harsh."

She looked at the four of them. "What is said in this room, you understand, stays in this room..."

They understood, and nodded. When she was satisfied of their sincerity, the Contessa sat back in her chair again. She turned her head towards the French doors and gazed out, into the distance.

She thought for a minute.

"How did you know Bea, Grandmother?" Gabriella asked, after a while.

The Contessa's thoughts turned to the present.

"Know her? She lived with us here, in the house. My family, as you, Gabriella and Lorenzo probably know, were forced to move down to the village when the Germans took over the house. But Bea had to stay, you see, as a servant girl. She was ordered to live here with her parents throughout the war to work for the officers. Her parents had already been working for us at the house and the Germans needed staff as much as anyone would in a house this size. This is how Bea and I had known each other from childhood. She had lived here in the annex all her life and she was always my closest friend, despite the difference in our statuses. I would have been very lonely without her. Very lonely indeed... "

The Contessa was quiet for another moment, and her eyes seemed to glaze over a little.

After an awkward silence, she cleared her throat.

"She died in her early thirties, after all we had been through. So young, poor girl, so beautiful... and ..." the Contessa stopped.

"I am very sorry, Grandmother," Gabriella said. She had never seen her grandmother looking so vulnerable before. The girls glanced at each other and wondered if they should all leave. Natasha thought it was almost embarrassing to see; she preferred it when the old woman was being nasty. Hating someone who was horrible was easy and justified, but this feeling of pity that came over Natasha for someone who was horrible felt weird. But then the Contessa cleared her throat again and continued in a stronger tone, and Natasha felt better.

"Yes, it was unjust. Bea survived the war and all that it entailed; the hunger, the cruelty, and the terrifying raids. And then to die after having survived all this, when she already had a little girl, was so, so unfair..."

"What did you mean by 'the raids', Grandmother?" Lorenzo asked, trying to divert her a little.

"Well Lorenzo, the raids could happen anytime, day or night, 'out of the blue', as the English say. They were after the men. Young or old, it didn't matter. The soldiers would turn up and hammer on the doors with their rifle-butts. If you didn't open within seconds, the door was knocked in; it was extremely terrifying for children and adults, alike. They would line the whole family up at gunpoint against a wall in the house, and then take just take a son, or the husband, the brother, a grandfather. Sometimes they would take just one or two males, or sometimes they took them all; there was no telling; it all depended on why they had come, you see. It was especially bad towards the end of the war, when we thought it was coming to an end. It was all in response to the partisan activity. The partisans were very active towards the end of the war, and unfortunately there was a heavy price to pay. All of us lost at least one member of the family, if not more."

"Really?" Lorenzo asked. "You and Bea both had family members taken?"

"Of course, Lorenzo. No family was spared this unimaginable terror. My brother was sixteen when they found out where we had hidden him. They found the false wall in the cellar where we hid them. Most houses had hiding places, you see. But they found ours, and I never saw my brother again after that night. The partisans did their best, picking the soldiers off when they could, but the raids were inevitable. It was retaliation, you see, when things didn't go well for the Germans. The men were beaten and thrown into trucks. When there were no more men left to take, they took the boys and the old men. You can imagine the women; mothers, wives, screaming as the trucks drove away with their loved ones. Bea lost her two elder brothers in one night."

"How terrible!" Gabriella said.

"Where did they take them?" Lorenzo asked.

The Contessa just looked at Lorenzo. She shook her head.

"You children have no idea how lucky you are, to be living in peacetime. You know, any person from my generation... *anyone*; male or female, would tell you things that would shock you and move you to tears. Everyone has a story. Everyone."

"Did they take many men and boys from our valley?" Lorenzo asked.

"Hundreds were taken from our area, Lorenzo; Thousands from all over Italy. In Rome, they suffered terribly."

"Wow," Alex said, "they don't tell you that in school, do they."

"It isn't such a long time ago, either," the Contessa continued, "it seems like yesterday to me. Bea, my dear friend, survived all this, and helped her parents through the loss of the two elder brothers. She lived mostly here at the house, forced to work for the officers. The house became their headquarters, you see. Her younger brother lived in town with the Aunt."

"Oh, there was another brother," Gabriella said, almost relieved for Bea and her family. "That would mean that Maria has an uncle. Does he still live in town? I thought she just had her husband, Piero. She never talks about her uncle."

"I haven't finished, Gabriella," the Contessa said dryly. "There is more. One night towards the very end of the war, when the Germans were leaving the area, we had begun to celebrate in the streets. The British and Americans were coming. We were outside, hugging and crying with joy as the last German armoured car drove through the village. But only an hour had passed when we heard the familiar rumble of armoured cars climbing their way up the windy road again; they were back, and in force. The Germans were looking for perpetrators. They were after men and boys, and the boy, who would have been Maria's Uncle, was one of those taken in retaliation, along with dozens of others. They wanted three hundred men, but of course three hundred men were not easy to find, there weren't three hundred men left. So the young boys were taken to make up the numbers."

"Three hundred? In retaliation for what?" Lorenzo fired at her. "That's outrageous!"

"Three hundred for the officers. They found three officers shot dead in the river."

"Oh!" Natasha was shocked.

"Unfortunately, the news travelled fast. Three officers dead in the river was a serious business," the Contessa continued. "The news reached the drones of departing Germans long before they were far enough away not to retaliate. Our joy in the village over their leaving turned into the worst night of terror of the whole war for us. Three dead German officers was the equivalent of three hundred Italian males."

"Three *hundred*? But how could they find three hundred men?" Gabriella asked.

"Well, they didn't, of course. And at this stage in the game, age was irrelevant. As I mentioned, we had already started to celebrate the enemy leaving the area, and the boy, only eight or nine, I believe, along with many others even younger, was playing in the street one moment, then thrown into a truck the next. There were no hugs, no goodbyes, nothing. He was gone with the rest."

"Unbelievable," Lorenzo said under his breath.

"Believe it, Lorenzo. As I said, you are lucky to be living now."

"What happened to Bea's poor mother?" Gabriella asked. "All her boys had been taken."

The Contessa shook her head. She looked down and fiddled with her glasses. "Unfortunately, she was not to recover. She had a complete breakdown, I believe she lost her mind."

"Oh, how terrible, and what about Bea, Maria's mother? What did she do?" Gabriella asked.

"Bea suffered, but she took care of her mother. By then, I believe she and Giovanni had been secretly together for some time, he may have been already in hiding, but I forget exactly the timing of events.

"Oh, the poor lady," Gabriella said.

"But it made things difficult for him, too, you know, Giovanni. He had taken no part in this rounding up. Luckily, he had already decided to stay, and had to lie low while the army left, in order to stay with Bea. Their love for each other was very strong; he had given up everything for her, including his identity. Don't forget, he, too, was now in a very precarious position, having deserted. Had he been found, without a doubt he would have been shot for desertion, and of course it goes without saying what the partisans would have done to him, had they found him."

"So, how did they survive?" Gabriella probed. "What did they do, Bea and Giovanni, when it was safe for him to come out? He would have been hated by everyone!"

The Contessa took her time in answering her question.

"What did he do? Well, a few months later, a young man, suffering from amnesia, or shell shock, secured a job as a gardener here. He stayed, married Bea in the private chapel on the estate, and kept a very, very low profile."

Lorenzo was shocked at what he was hearing.

"Grandmother, you mean you helped him...? You, of all people..." he tried not to sound judgemental but it was hard not to.

"You mean I, of all people have compassion, Lorenzo? Yes, even I have a heart, though you might not want to believe it."

"That's not what I meant, Grandmother... But he was a Nazi! Not only that, wasn't that dangerous for you and your family? You put everyone at risk! Our family!"

She gathered up the papers on her desk and tidied them into a neat pile as if she were summing up the meeting.

"Helped who?" she asked nonchalantly.

"Johann! I mean Giovanni," Lorenzo said.

"Who?" she feigned confusion. "You are surmising too much, be careful with your tongue, my boy."

Lorenzo looked confused.

"What about all the boys and men that were rounded up in retaliation for the officers who were found shot on the river? What happened to them?" Alex asked.

"Two hundred and sixty young men, old men and boys were buried in a valley four miles to the west of here. Now I must get on, if you don't mind. I have work to do."

The children were shocked. She didn't need to elaborate further.

"But did you help him? Johann, I mean," Lorenzo probed. "You did, didn't you, Grandmother? It was you who helped him start a new life, wasn't it?"

"Do you honestly think I would get involved in helping a young German soldier? A young man so in love with my best friend? Do you honestly think, Lorenzo that I would let him hide here in the annex of my home for the rest of his life? You think that I would help him with Italian lessons and provide all his books to study, and help get him false Italian identification papers so he would have a chance, so Bea would have a chance? So the baby could have a father? You honestly think I would do that?"

She looked at Lorenzo. He was silent.

"Surely you are mistaken, Lorenzo" she said. "You must not let your mind get carried away. It's a very delicate subject, even today. If word ever got out of your suspicions…"

She looked at the four of them for a moment. There no one said a word.

"I can see why you wouldn't help him," Lorenzo eventually said dryly, looking her in the eye. "That would be unimaginable, especially after the bodies of the boys in the village were found… how could anyone?"

"War is war, Lorenzo. Terrible, terrible things happen. You can choose to die inside, thinking of it, hating everyone forever, or you can move on and give love and life a chance. It doesn't seem to matter which side you are on; war is war. No country is exempt from committing atrocities. War makes monsters out of men, no matter where they were born or what colour of the uniform on their backs. Look at the British in Africa; the Zulus. Look at America; where are all the Native American tribes now who lived on that land for thousands of years? Gone! War atrocities were not only carried out by Hitler's army, my boy, oh no. Look again at history; Look at the so-called Christian crusaders who came from all over Europe to unite under one mighty killing machine; Slaughtering seems to have been a sport to even the most civilized countries, including the Spanish and Portuguese in South America. And don't forget Alexander the Great; he was only 'Great' if you were on the blunt end of his sword. I doubt the Persians, the founders of democracy, called him 'Great' at all, after he burned down Persepolis and murdered every person in sight before arriving there. I could go on," she looked at him. "No Lorenzo, the generals of every nation have given despicable orders."

Lorenzo was quiet. He didn't know if he admired or despised his grandmother for what she had done.

"So what happened to Bea, Grandmother?" Gabriella eventually asked.

The Contessa sighed.

"...So unfair, so unfair, poor Bea. She was to pass away of complications after the birth of her second child, who also died."

"And Johann, what did he do after Bea died?" Lorenzo asked.

"Who?" She looked at Lorenzo.

"If you mean our gardener, Giovanni, well, he was devastated. But when dear Bea died, he already had little Maria, which must have given him the strength to carry on. I must say there has always been a shadow over him, and he has kept very much to himself. This is why I give him his space now, for whatever reason, he needs it."

"But where do you think he is, Grandmother? Where could he have gone?" Gabriella asked.

"For all we know, he could be on a beach in Saint Tropez. But it is pointless worrying now; he will turn up again, mark my words. No need for any outside help. That would just create more problems and questions. That wouldn't do at all, especially with this party tomorrow. Now, on a lighter note, we have a ball to prepare for, and I must get on with the last minute details. And this little project," she said, looking at the clippings and artwork in the open book on her desk, "must, I am afraid, wait until next week."

She closed the book and pushed her chair back. The meeting was over.

"What project is that, Grandmother?" Lorenzo asked, as he got up.

"Our family heritage; all the artwork that was taken when the house was occupied. It has never surfaced anywhere, in any auction house, museum or gallery; and some canvasses, I might add, were very valuable. There was even a small Canaletto, and it has never come to light anywhere on the open market. One would think that a painting of that quality, surely, would have surfaced in the art world by now. But with it being over sixty years since it disappeared, I must conclude that..."

"They are all still hidden somewhere?" Lorenzo asked.

She smiled at her grandson.

"My dear boy, I believe you and I have a little research project on our hands next week. In the mean time, understand one thing, Lorenzo; if you hold a heavy grudge, the only person pulled down by its weight, is yourself."

CHAPTER THIRTY-FOUR

It was seven o'clock in the evening, and the night of the party. Despite the miserable weather, the preparations had gone to plan. Julia and Marcelo had arrived home the day before, cutting it a little short, as Marcello usually did before every deadline. But the weather had co-operated a little; it had stopped pouring so heavily. The tents were still standing, floors were polished, and the first of the guests were there. The long line of cars and limousines were arriving, albeit at a snail's pace down the long, drenched, potholed, floodlit driveway. The grandeur brought it home to Natasha and Alex as to what a special occasion this was for Marcello and their mother. There was certainly no turning back for her mother now, even if she wanted to.

When Julia and Marcello had arrived back at Montesonnellino the day before, Marcello had been very upset upon hearing about Giovanni's disappearance, and the German visitor who was presumed to be the cause of his fleeing. He had wanted to get the police searching for him straight away. But the Contessa had insisted that Giovanni would be fine, saying she felt that he was alive and well, since he had taken food with him; an indication that he intended to just have some time on his own; certainly not to die. She told Marcello about his *Soldbuch*, and the fact that he had been a German soldier stationed at the house hardly surprised Marcello. If anything, he was a little annoyed with his mother for not letting him know before. But he understood there might be more to the story than she was saying. Marcello decided to get everything straightened out after the party, when there was time to think and discuss everything with the children. The day after the party he would start his search for Giovanni, and get to the bottom of what was going on.

But for now, it was a time for celebration. The four teens stood in line the hallway with their parents, formally welcoming the guests as they arrived at the villa. The ladies looked magnificent in their long evening dresses and the men, both young and old, looked dashing in black tie. Everyone was sparkling and radiant and Marcello was grinning from ear to ear, happier than he had ever been. He proudly welcomed his friends, some of whom he hadn't seen for years, introducing them to his beloved fiancée, his children, and his children-to-be. Julia looked beautiful, and when Natasha looked over at her as she shook hands with Marcello's friends, she realised how happy her mother was with Marcello. Deep down, as much as she didn't really want to admit it, she knew her mother had made the right decision. Considering her mother was going to have to contend with a dragon for a mother-in-law, Natasha thought she was doing very well. Natasha felt proud of her; especially as she hadn't even complained once about the silly tiara the Contessa had given her in an almost ceremonial ritual earlier that morning, before the hairdresser had firmly imbedded in her over-sprayed hair.

Natasha and Alex continued to shake hands, curtsey and bow with Lorenzo and Gabriella at their side, greeting the guests in the few polite Italian sentences Marcello had taught them.

But at the back of her mind, Natasha was looking out for Yanni.

Occasionally, between shaking hands and smiling, she tried to peer beyond the doors outside to see if Yanni was in the line of people on the steps, but unfortunately, there was still no sign of him.

"Your Italian accent is almost perfect, I would have thought you were from Italy, my child," a beautiful, tall woman in a red, sleek dress and a tiara, said to Natasha. She herself spoke English beautifully.

"I expect you are musical, are you not?" she continued, smiling at her. "Most people who have an ear for languages, as we do, sing very beautifully, is it not so, my dear Marcello?"

The woman looked over at him, and he stared at her, wide eyed with a fixed smile on his face.

"Thank you," Natasha replied, breaking the silence. "I do take piano lessons, and I was in the school play last year. But I have a very long way to go yet, before I can converse in Italian."

Natasha saw that the tall, beautiful lady wasn't really listening to her reply. She was still looking at Marcello, and Natasha realised there had been a hidden meaning behind her comment. She flushed at the thought of having been used in that way. She glanced across at Marcello and her mother to see what on earth was going on.

"Dear Isabella," Marcello said at last in English, "I am afraid I wouldn't know a good musical note from a bad one, and I have to admit I have never really cared to."

He stared at her, and continued, still smiling, "I am unfortunately, or perhaps, rather fortunately, tone deaf you see, and I suppose that would account for my thick, Italian accent when speaking English and other languages."

The elegant lady glared at him, and was obviously not amused by Marcello's comment. She smiled at him politely, and she and her escort gracefully moved on into the ballroom without a word.

As she left, Lorenzo let out a snort, doing his best not to burst out laughing.

"What was all that about?" Natasha asked him under her breath.

"Remember I told you about a Princess who came to stay in order to try and get my father to marry her?"

Natasha nodded.

"That was her! Would you believe it, as well as all her luggage, she brought her harp with her! And every evening, after dinner, she would play her harp and sing to Father, in the drawing room!"

"*O Dio*," Marcello said. "Is that what it was? Singing? I always wandered what that terrible noise was coming from her throat!"

The children giggled, and Natasha noticed he smiled at Julia, and kissed her on the cheek before the next couple approached them. Natasha appreciated his trying to put her mother at ease. He was OK, she thought. Marcello was definitely OK.

The relentless line of cars kept dropping guests at the foot of the steps, and they continued to formerly meet and greet the guests for another ten minutes. The sparkling arrivals were ushered into the ballroom, where a glass of Champaign and the diamond-clad Contessa waited to greet them. The quartet in the corner of the ballroom played a lively waltz, and the atmosphere was loud and buzzing.

After half an hour, almost everyone had arrived, and the line of guests had at last trickled to an end. Only the odd car now pulled up to the steps, so Marcello let the children off the hook, saying they were now free to party. The boys immediately announced they were going to the marquee to find the food. But Natasha didn't want to leave the entrance hall, and asked Gabriella if she would stay with her to wait for Yanni.

"He is definitely coming; he is probably just a bit late," she told Gabriella. "Heavy traffic on the motorway from Milan, that's all. I know he is coming because he had said he wanted to discuss those three men we'd seen in Pisa, and he wanted to try to get to the bottom of what ever it was that was going on. Not only that," she added, "he mentioned he would be coming with Signor Muretti."

"Well Signor Muretti is always late, just like my father is!" Gabriella said.

The thought of Yanni skipping up the steps towards her at any moment, with his curls bouncing over his face, gave Natasha heart palpitations. With the volume of the music and voices rising from the ballroom, the party was now in full swing, and she knew she would see him soon.

But she waited. And still, there was no Yanni.

Just as Marcello told the girls that he and Julia were going to join his guests in the ballroom, the headlights of one last car came into view at the top of the driveway. Natasha watched the headlights slowly approach and turn around the fountain. She hoped, like she had never hoped before, that it was Yanni.

It had started to rain heavily again, and as Julia and Marcello were making polite conversation with the last rather elderly, late arrival, the car rolled round to the base of the steps, and stopped in front of the door.

The back door was opened, and Natasha saw him jump out.

He was here!

Her heart thumped as she watched him politely wait in the rain by the open door for Signor Muretti to get out of the back seat. His curls were tied back in a little ponytail, and he looked so handsome in his suit. He leant into the car to offer a helping hand. A valet rushed over and sheltered him from the rain with a large, black umbrella, obscuring Natasha's view of him. Natasha now couldn't see him very well at all, so she focused back to her task of saying 'good evening' in Italian to the penultimate guest, and tried to compose herself. Her heart thumped, but she took some deep breaths and tried to calm down. The anticipation was killing her. She couldn't wait for her evening to begin.

"He's here," she whispered to Gabriella. "Yanni is here at last! Do I look OK?"

"I know. I saw him too. Don't worry, you look beautiful, Natasha. He will gasp at your beauty, and then when he has recovered, he will dance with you the whole evening!" Gabriella reassured her.

Natasha smiled. From the corner of her eye, she knew he had entered the hallway, but she just couldn't look at him yet. She took another deep breath and when she was ready, she finally looked up at him as he approached Marcello and her mother; but what she saw she couldn't believe or take in. She turned white, for standing next to Yanni, with her hand holding his arm, was something Natasha had not been prepared for in a million years. He had at his side, the most graceful, beautiful young girl. She had jet-black hair and the longest eyelashes Natasha had ever seen. Yanni looked over at Natasha and Gabriella and smiled, giving them a little friendly wave with his free hand, as if there were absolutely nothing wrong, and he escorted the young lady towards Marcello and Julia, followed by Signor Muretti and his wife.

She felt numb. She heard the name, 'Stefania Muretti', and everything else was a whirl. She excused herself, and thought she was going to be sick. She walked as gracefully as she could down the hallway, lifting her dress so she didn't trip. It was all she could do not to run. She walked past the ballroom and the awful noise of the orchestra and the happy, chatting voices, towards the veranda at the back of the house.

CHAPTER THIRTY-FIVE

A mixture of music and the voices of two hundred guests could be heard coming from the French doors of the ballroom a few feet outside the food marquee. But as yet, the boys hadn't ventured near the ballroom; they had avoided the party completely by going around the outside of the house so they wouldn't have to talk to anyone, which might divert them from their mission; food. Once in the marquee, they wasted no time in finding a plate each, and checked the buffet tables before they decided what to have. Except for the two caterers talking at the far corner of the tent, it was still void of any guests. The vast 'u' shaped buffet table ran around three sides of the tent, laden with delicious dishes, both hot and cold.

"How come no one's come in here to eat, yet?" Alex asked Lorenzo. "I'd rather eat than talk and dance, wouldn't you?"

"Depends on who you are talking or dancing with! I saw a girl who I wouldn't mind skipping a meal for."

Alex looked at Lorenzo. He personally couldn't think of anything worse.

"Really? Like, who?"

"La *bella* Signorina Stefania Muretti, for a start. She is stunning! Didn't you see her, when she arrived?"

Alex shrugged. He honestly hadn't noticed any girls.

"You know, Signor Muretti's daughter? She was accompanied by Yanni. I saw them arriving just now before we snuck round the side of the house. She is a little older than me, but I don't care, I am going for it. But first, I need some food to give me energy. Sorry Alex, but after I have eaten, you are on your own tonight. There were a couple of younger girls more your age, you could hang out with them, perhaps. You did at least notice them when they arrived, didn't you?"

"I can't remember, I must have since I was at the door, but…"

He shook his head. He really hadn't noticed any young girls.

"Alex! You seriously need to wake up! Aren't your hormones kicking in yet?" Lorenzo laughed.

"Lorenzo! Give me a break!" Alex protested, almost blushing, then quickly got back to the previous subject. "Wouldn't that mean that that girl you liked was Yanni's girlfriend, if he had brought her?"

"The beautiful angel? We'll see! If she is his, she won't be for long!"

Lorenzo looked towards the two caterers, in deep in conversation at the other end of the tent.

"Are they going to serve us, or do we help ourselves? I thought my grandmother said there were going to be at least six servers in here tonight."

He looked towards the ballroom, the music was livening up, he wanted to eat and get to the party.

"Excuse me, do we just help ourselves?" Lorenzo called over to the men in Italian.

There was no response, they looked at him blankly and said nothing. It was almost as if they hadn't understood him.

"We eat?" Alex mimed to them. "It's OK to help ourselves?"

The two men nodded. "Si, si…"

"Well, they understood English, at least," Alex said under his breath.

Lorenzo walked over to the two men, still thinking it odd that no other staff members were around.

"Haven't we met before?" he asked them in Italian.

They looked back blankly at him. Lorenzo looked down at his plate, his mind racing. He smiled, carefully helped himself to some chicken, and thanked them in Italian. He then walked towards Alex, examining the food along the long table to his left.

"Alex, come over this side and see the desserts," he said. "This one looks amazing. Look at the cake!"

Alex walked over with him.

"Alex, don't turn round," he whispered. "Just keep looking at the cake. Don't over-react, but it's *them*! The men from the tower in Pisa! They are standing right there, in my home! I don't know who they are, or what they've done with the other caterers, but these two are not from the catering company, I am sure of it! There's something going on here. I can't believe it. Look, Alex, I am shaking! What on earth do they want? This is serious. What shall we do?"

"Wow, that's an amazing cake!" Alex said, loud enough for the two men to hear. "How on earth did they manage to shape the cake into an Etruscan ship like that?" He lowered his voice, "you're right, Lorenzo, it's them. They're looking at us. I think they know we're suspicious. We don't have time to get your father, do we? Say something else in Italian to them, so they think we don't suspect them."

Lorenzo picked up a strawberry and popped it into his mouth. "So sweet and delicious," he said it Italian and smiled at them. He turned away and lowered his voice, "but there's one missing, remember, Alex? The one that actually confronted Yanni at the top of the tower. These two were the ones who defused the situation. Remember, Alex?"

"Yes but it doesn't make the situation any less threatening. They are imposters! The real catering staff are missing. They've done something with them! It's the same men that smashed up Aldo's place for the *Soldbuch*. God, what's going on? This is crazy! Why are they here? What shall we do? Shall we take them on?" he whispered.

Then he said loudly, "I'm definitely having a piece of that cake later!" He lowered his voice and said through his teeth, "if we don't do something, they may suspect we know who they are, and get away. It will be too late by the time we find my father in the crowd of guests. Look, they're whispering to each other..."

"You're right, we have to do something now. Alex, shall we try? Do you think they're armed? Our only weapon is surprise. Ask them something to distract them while I think," Lorenzo said.

"I would love some ice cream and fruit. Look, is that tiramisu?" he asked one of the men.

He nodded back.

"Let's go back over to where the hot dishes are," Alex whispered. "Do you think we could tip hot food over them, then jump them?"

Lorenzo nodded.

"Looks like tiramisu to me," Lorenzo said, "let's have our main course, then come back for some of that... or maybe, I think I'll try the soup first, coming, Alex?"

"Oh, definitely!"

"So, what do you recommend here?" Lorenzo asked the men in Italian, who had come over to the hot food. The man had his hand inside his jacket. Lorenzo put his plate down and casually held the under edge of the table. "The lamb or the... SOUP..."

He flipped the table up and over towards the men and the contents of the hot, silver terrine, the goulash, soup, salads and vegetable dishes all flew towards them. Alex grabbed a hot chicken dish and threw it over the one man who was staggering to get up again. He screamed as the hot dish covered him, and he fell back against the tent wall and onto boxes of napkins. Lorenzo, meanwhile, had leapt over the table and thumped the first, stunned man in the jaw before he knew what had hit him. He quickly reached into the man's inside trouser pocket and pulled out a gun. Lorenzo stared at it in his hand for a second, and the man struggled and tried to get it off Lorenzo. It fired into the air. The man stopped struggling and tried to calm Lorenzo down so he wouldn't shoot again.

"Don't shoot... don't shoot," he pleaded. He tried to sit up, his hands slipping in the béchamel sauce surrounding him on the wooden floor. Lorenzo squeezed the trigger again and shot into the ceiling of the tent.

"Alex! Check the other man's pockets, quickly!" he shouted.

Alex leapt onto the other man, who was on his back, still stunned and suffering from burns from the hot soup. Alex's knees landed heavily into his stomach, winding him. He reached into the man's jacket, and quickly felt his trouser pockets. There was nothing.

"Where is your gun?" he shouted at him.

"I have not a gun, but I have this...!"

He sprang up and punched Alex so hard in the jaw that he fell back onto the floor. Lorenzo panicked and aimed the gun at him.

"You move and I shoot!" he shouted. "I mean it, I will shoot you!"

His hand trembled and he felt the sensitive trigger cradled in his finger. He felt nauseous with fear.

"Lorenzo!" he heard his father's voice. "Lorenzo! Drop the gun!"

He ran to his son, followed by Yanni and about twenty other male guests.

"Drop it, Son, drop it, it's OK, Son."

Lorenzo dropped the gun onto the wet, slippery mess on the floor, then sat back heavily into the chicken and sauce. He was shaking, and in shock.

His father pulled him away and helped him to his feet. Yanni and several others apprehended the two men, but not without a struggle first. Alex was helped up, and other than his nose bleeding and his aching jaw, he seemed to be OK. A napkin was found for his nose, and he was helped to a chair at the other end of the marquee and attended to by Signor Muretti and Julia.

"Alex, my darling, are you all right? What on earth have you two done? What's going on? Did you two have a fight?" Julia asked. She couldn't believe the scene her son and Lorenzo had created.

"It's them, Mum. They're imposters. They're not the caterers; they were following us in Pisa... I think we stopped them doing whatever they came here to do."

"What do you mean? Oh my goodness!"

The Contessa pushed her way to the front of the guests. For once in her life, she was speechless.

Lorenzo, still stunned at having been so close to shooting a man, broke free from his father. He ran past his grandmother and out of the marquee, past the beautiful Stefania Muretti and the crowd of guests, still gathering by the marquee entrance. He ran towards the back of the tent and vomited.

After a couple of minutes, he recovered. He took some deep breaths. Something in the dim light caught the corner of his eye; he looked up to his left, and at the side of the tent wall a few feet away, lying on the grass, bound and gagged, were the missing caterers.

CHAPTER THIRTY-SIX

E ven outside on the veranda, where she curled up on the sofa, there was no escape from the music. It seemed to penetrate the thick, wet air around the house as much as it did inside. The music echoed in her head, around her head, in the trees and in the gardens beyond. It drove Natasha mad. Even the rain on the tiles was hardly noticeable over the unbearable, happy noise of her mother's party. It was deafening.

She had to think, she had to focus, but she couldn't. She had to get away. She got up from the sofa and walked down the veranda steps and into the rain. It beat down on her, and she was almost immediately wet-through. Her hair that had painstakingly taken the hairdresser over an hour to get just how she dreamed it would be, was already a soggy, matted mess, hanging limply on her shoulders, and the new dress she had bought with Gabriella in Pisa, was drenched.

But Natasha was almost unaware of it; all she could see in her mind's eye was this beautiful young girl with her long, black eyelashes, holding Yanni's arm. And worst of all, what really stabbed at her heart was his cheerful grin, as if nothing was wrong.

It was a nightmare; she had to get away, away from the house, away from everything. She began to walk along the path into the garden, faster and faster, cutting through the manicured hedges, through the rose garden where the thorns pulled at her dress. But she hardly noticed, nor cared. She quickly walked across the grass, her heels sinking in the ground, sucking her shoes from her feet, but still, she walked on barefooted in the dark, not knowing or noticing where she was going. She thought she heard a gunshot in the distance, but she didn't flinch. All she knew was she had to get away from the house, the music and Yanni, with that beautiful girl.

With the manicured gardens behind her, she now found herself on the outer edge of the property where the undergrowth was naturally untamed and the ground began to slope down into the valley. She walked on, stumbling in the darkness, but before she even took note of where she was, she realized she was slipping and sliding down a steep hill. She managed to right herself, take a couple more steps, but then she lost her footing completely, rolling and tumbling over and over. It was the end, she thought, and she felt nothing. She was numb.

She came to a stop, and she lay on her back, with the rain slapping face. She was bruised and should have hurt, but the pain on the outside was nothing compared to what she was feeling inside. She was cold, but at least, she thought, she couldn't hear the orchestra anymore, and that was all that mattered. Now she could cry, and cry she did. She cried and sobbed until every ounce of the energy inside her had been sapped from her core. She had no more tears left, and she lay there, shivering, thinking.

She asked herself why she was so upset. Was it more than the realization that Yanni wasn't in the least bit interested in her? Was she crying over all the hours she had been dreaming and thinking of him since Easter? Or was it more? She tried to think logically. It was the whole Marcello and her mother thing, too. It was her mother being away so much, it was her father being distant; it was the uncertainty of knowing where she would be living, or going to school. Yanni had been her distraction form this upheaval, a glimmer of hope that things would be OK, that someone would take notice of her. She had felt close to him, he was her hope for something stable in her life. But now, she realized, he obviously hadn't felt anything towards her at all.

Her relationship with her father was polite and friendly enough, but it wasn't a particularly close one where she could confide in him. And anyway, he was always with his girlfriend and didn't really stop to listen. It was all a bit superficial, as if everything was all always 'fine'. There was nothing ever read between the lines when Natasha tried to talk to him. He just didn't get it. He was always in too much of a hurry. Natasha didn't even understand where she would be living after this wedding. She certainly wouldn't accept living with the Contessa here, in Italy, she thought. She didn't know what was happening. Her mother had said that it would all sort itself out in the end, but that wasn't really very helpful at all. She felt like she didn't fit in anywhere, and Alex was totally oblivious.

Her mind drifted back to Yanni. Was he handsome? Yes. But was she ready for a full-blown relationship, had he been interested? No. She really wasn't. She was too young. She would wait.

"He can have her!" she said defiantly to herself. "I don't need him or anyone! I'm a survivor."

Shivering and soaking wet, she had had enough crying. She thought she would sneak back to the house, use the back stairs, and go up to her room without anyone knowing, where she could have a lovely hot bath. There, she could be alone, warm up, and think it all through. She knew Gabriella would be there for her. She was glad to have Gabriella, she thought. Having a sister would be a god thing.

In the dark, she started her way back towards the house. But after a couple of paces she became aware that her feet were in cold water.

She was at the river's edge. The river had obviously swollen and risen up the bank. She lifted her dress, and stumbled about in the dark, trying to climb up the slippery bank. Once at the top of the bank, she knew she would hear the distant sound of the party, which she would follow back to the house. Did he love Stefania? Had they kissed? How long had he known her? Did she love him? She didn't even want to know the answers. She tried several times to climb the bank while she went over these questions in her mind, but she slid back down again. Not giving up easily, Natasha decided to try going along the river's edge for a while before climbing up again, but she slipped and stumbled while trying to find a less steep part of the bank climb. She imagined the scene of Yanni dancing with stunning Stefania Muretti. Now Natasha was furious with herself for running away like a child. She should have held her ground and faced it head on. She had to get back, warm up and talk to Gabriella!

She realized the water was now up to her knees, and the flow was beginning to push her in the opposite direction. In fear of being swept into the river, she attempted to climb the slippery bank again, as she worried that her situation was becoming dangerous. She was now aware that no one knew where she was; not even Gabriella. She took some big steps up the slope, digging the sides of her feet into the bank as if she were on skis, but it was so muddy she struggled and slipped. She grabbed at the grass and shrubs at her side. Then it happened; she stepped on her dress, and before she knew it, she had slid down the slope and was in the cold water.

She gasped. It happened so quickly. Before she even realised she was in the river, she was out of her depth.

The water was fast moving. She was stunned. Was this happening?

As hard as she tried to reach the bank, she couldn't. The flow of the water, even at the edge, made it impossible, and she was swept away downriver.

She tried not to panic and instead, tried swimming with the flow, keeping as close to the bank as she could. But it was useless, although the water was flat and calm, it was fast flowing, unrelenting and so, so cold. She tried to think quickly, going into survival mode. She had to concentrate and not panic. She had to focus. Knowing she would never be able to swim against it, she went with the flow, feet first, as she had remembered Aldo telling her before they took the canoes out that day. She had to survive.

It was dark and terrifying, and as she continued to move downriver, further and further away. She began to realize that she was going to die, without anyone even knowing she was missing. She called out into the night for help between gasping with the cold, but it was pointless. She used her arms to keep herself afloat, from rolling over to her side. She only just managed to keep her head above the surface.

She was exhausted, freezing and terrified. If she could see where she was going it would be less frightening. But in the dark, it was terrifying.

Slowly but surely, she drifted away further and further down river.

Consumed with fear, she closed her eyes and waited for whatever was to come.

Then something struck the side of her foot underwater, and it hurt. She was jolted hard against something across her stomach and shoulder. It stopped her flowing down river, and she was pushed hard against it. She grabbed hold of it, gasping for air. She held onto the smooth and cylindrical thing beneath the surface for her life. Thankfully, it was stuck fast, but she hardly cared how or what it was, she just tried to hang on to it. Now she had stopped moving, the force of the water pushing her from behind was so strong it funnelled over the back of her head, forcing her head under. She tried with all her strength to keep her face above the surface so she could gasp for air.

"Help, Mum! Alex!" she yelled, choking. "Lorenzo!" was all she could manage between coughing and spluttering, "Help…"

She screamed and shouted out into the darkness, until at last, she had run out of energy. She knew it was over. She was too cold to hold on any more. She was freezing, scared, and couldn't even feel her hands. Her strength was seeping from her and she couldn't hold herself up any longer. It was pitch black, raining heavily, and nobody was around to hear her cries for help. Her fingers were so cold she couldn't tell if she were holding on or not. She thought of all the Romans who had died in the river, all those hundreds and hundreds of years ago, and she somehow she didn't feel so alone. She felt a closeness to them, and it didn't scare her at all; strangely, they were almost a comfort, as if they were watching out for her and she wasn't dying alone. She thought of the elephants that had marched all the way from Africa to Spain and from Spain to Italy, over the mountains, only to die in this river. Wow, she thought, as the water pounded and pushed the back of her neck, this river has taken so many, and she was going to join them.

With her energy sapping away, freezing and with the weight of the water forcing her under, she was giving up. She became very calm and resolved to her grave situation. She didn't worry about trying to stay above the surface anymore. She couldn't hold on any longer. Nothing mattered. She let go of the cylindrical thing that had saved her life. Exhausted, she took a last breath, and let whatever was to happen, happen.

She felt herself floating away. She closed her eyes. It was over.

She relaxed, and went under.

CHAPTER THIRTY-SEVEN

Natasha lay motionless, wondering if she were dead or alive. She gradually became aware of a gentle rocking motion, almost as if she were on a boat. She presumed, then, that she couldn't be dead; she must be alive. She became aware of the sound of lapping water nearby, and something else; breathing. She wasn't sure if it was her own breathing or someone else's. She tried to move, but couldn't. She tried again, but still couldn't. She felt a restriction around her, as if she were in a tight tunnel. She couldn't quite work it out, and wondered if she were really dead after all, or paralysed.

She tried hard to focus, but she couldn't make sense of anything. She attempted to open her eyes, but she couldn't do that, either. She tried to go over in her confused mind, what had happened.

The last thing she remembered was the force of the river pushing her under. But now, she felt dry, and she had the sensation of being cocooned, squeezed and rocked. She needed to focus and understand where she was, but the rocking motion made her feel so tired. She drifted back in and out of sleep.

When she came round, this time Natasha knew she wasn't dead. She became aware of a disgusting smell of mould, or rotting seaweed. If there really were a heaven, she thought, it would smell lovely, not disgusting.

She panicked; perhaps she was in hell!

She managed to open her eyes, but it was dark and she couldn't see anything at all. She tried desperately to move, but she was still restricted. She knew that she was lying on her back, but still, with the tight feeling constricting her torso. The rocking motion continued. Now panicking, she made another, determined attempt to move, this time with all the effort and will she could muster, using all the strength in her arms and legs. She became completely focused and aware; something, or someone was holding her! Her arms were pressed tightly against her own body; something warm was restricting them! She tried to turn her head, but it seemed to be pressed up against damp fabric, or clothing. She struggled, and the rocking started again, and the grip tightened around her.

But slowly, her eyes adjusted, and the darkness gradually changed to a dim, fuzzy light. She could make out an arched, stone roof directly above her. Then to her horror, only inches away from her own face, staring down at her, was the filthy face of a wrinkly, old man.

Horrified, she shrieked, struggling to sit up, but the man held her down. She was lying cupped across his lap, while he held her tightly against his body, restricting her every attempt to move.

She screamed, trying to escape his grip. She struggled, wriggling desperately, jabbing him repeatedly in his stomach and groin with her elbow. She hurt him, and he winced, let go of her and doubled over onto his side, groaning in pain. She broke away, disgusted and frightened. She scrambled on her hands and knees across the pebbles to a wall, as far away from him as she could to where she thought she saw the vague outline of a door. She desperately tugged and pulled at it, but it wouldn't open; the rotting handle only broke away in her hands. She pulled and pushed at the door again, and again, almost screaming at it to open. But it wouldn't budge.

She looked down at the ground at her feet. It was hopeless even trying to get the door open. The pebbles on the floor had completely blocked it. She would never open it. It was stuck fast.

She crouched down by the door, thinking, trying not to panic. She looked around her. She was in some kind of damp, stinky shelter. It only had three sides to it; the forth side at the far end was a low, arched opening and the only source of the dim, morning light. She had to make a dash for it, but the disgusting old man lay between her and the opening. She glanced at her captor; he was still doubled over on his side, between her and her freedom. She had to get past him! She could see he was recovering from her blows, and she desperately looked around one last time to find another way out; but there wasn't anywhere else to go.

She watched her jailer slowly stagger to his feet, and she knew she had to do it, now, before he recovered completely.

She gradually stood up, watching him, waiting for her moment, then she suddenly dashed past him, taking him by surprise, but she tripped over her long dress before she reached the open end, landing heavily on her hands and knees.

"Please, please," her captor said, reaching out to her with the arm that was not cradling his stomach, "attention, please!"

He staggered towards her, the dark silhouette of his arm reaching out to her, almost like a silly horror movie. But this wasn't a movie, this was real! She glanced at his silhouette, terrified. Was this a murderer who had held her so tightly against him with his arms gripped around her body all the time she had been asleep? She was both horrified and revolted at the thought of it. She had to escape! She lifted her dress so that she didn't trip over it again, scrambled over the pebbles and made another dash for the opening.

She stopped in her tracks.

There was water in front of her. It was the river. She realised that she was in an old, damp boathouse.

Natasha didn't care about getting cold and wet again, or even risking her life. She had to escape; there was no choice.

She lunged over the wet pebbles towards the open river, but his hand grabbed her arm and she was pulled back with a jolt. She screamed, falling heavily against him, and he tightly gripped her with both hands, squeezing her upper arms so hard that he dug into her skin. He pulled her down, forcing her onto her back. He bent over her, demanding her attention. He stared down at her, his eyes wide and angry.

"*Ist* danger now, *vasser ist* much high!" he shouted. "Vait! *Vasser ist* high, please, must you vait!"

"GET YOUR HANDS OFF ME!" she screamed.

Her inner strength had returned. She looked defiantly at the old man. She jerked herself free of his weakening grip.

"Let GO! Get... off... me, you creep!"

He tried to grab her again.

"Get away from me! Don't even think about touching me again, you disgusting man!"

She struggled to get up again; her long evening dress was not helping the situation at all.

"Signorina, Natasha. Please, I am not danger. Vasser ist danger!" He grabbed her again.

She stopped struggling.

"What?" She looked at him. "How do you know my name?"

In the dim light, she looked closer at the old man. She recognised the wrinkled, tired face.

"Oh my God..." she cried.

"Please, not fear," he said, letting go of her arm and putting his hands in the air, as if in surrender, over-emphasizing his intentions not to harm her. He went towards the water.

"I take from vasser you, make varm you, much much time all night."

He embraced himself with a rocking motion, miming his actions from the previous night. "You much danger, much, much cold. *Molto fredo.* Now *morgen kom*, you good. But more, more danger *kom*, Natasha."

He pointed to the entrance of the shelter.

"Now *vasser kom* more up. Please; Now you *kom mit* me, to help."

Natasha was stunned. Giovanni, poor, poor, old Giovanni. She wished she had realized who it was before she'd hurt him. She should have known.

"Oh dear, dear Giovanni... I am so, so sorry I hurt you," she almost sobbed. "I am so, so sorry. What are you doing here?"

"*Si, si*, Giovanni," he said softly. "*Sono io*, Giovanni!" He smiled at her. "Giovanni," he said, patting his chest. "Yes, Giovanni. Not fear. Giovanni."

"Oh Giovanni, I am so sorry..."

She burst into tears.

CHAPTER THIRTY-EIGHT

G iovanni staggered towards the back of the shelter, and sank down exhausted against the wall. He was aching and bruised, and couldn't stand for much longer. Natasha had hammered in to his already frail body, and because he was already so weak, he was suffering quite badly. She felt remorse for the old man and repeatedly told him how sorry she was for hurting him. He had rescued her from the river, kept her warm and alive through the night, and his reward had been a severe beating from her.

She felt terrible, but he seemed to insist that her apologies were not necessary, and because of the language barrier, indicated with his hands that there was a more imminent danger to worry about; the level of the rising river. Natasha understood that they had to get to higher ground, or they'd be in serious trouble.

He asked Natasha to dig down amongst the stones in the corner of the shelter by the old wooden door, where, she understood, she should find something important, but what it was she couldn't quite understand. He was telling her in German, then Italian, pointing to his head, but since she spoke neither language, she wasn't sure what it was she was supposed to be digging for. But she willingly did what he asked. She had a lot of making up to do. And he seemed determined.

After several minutes of scraping away with the tips of her fingers, she had made a dent in the stones and grit and reached the damper level a few inches below the top surface.

Even after she had scooped out an elbow-deep hollow, she still didn't understand what she was digging for. She was about to try to ask him again, when she felt something hard and smooth imbedded in the wet mud beneath her sore fingertips. She felt around the edge of it, and cleared the little stones and grit from its perimeter. She put her fingers under its smooth ridge, and tugged at it. Giovanni's face lit up as he watched her pull it out.

She examined the muddy object in her freezing hands.

It was a helmet. A rusty, old helmet.

She looked at Giovanni.

"*Ist* Giovanni," he said, patting his head with a twinkle in his eye. "*Ist* Giovanni."

He smiled at it for a second. "*Ma tante anni fa.* Long, long time."

He took it from her and almost affectionately wiped the mud and grit from it.

"OK, but what are you going to do with it? Wear it?" Natasha asked, nursing her sore hands in the folds of her dress. There was a hint of irritation in her voice. Her fingers were so cold and grazed from digging the thing out, that she was almost a little annoyed with him for wasting her time and energy. She thought there was a plan. Now she wondered if he had just wanted to recover his old uniform, for memory's sake.

"*So!*" he said, slowly leaning forward. He began to mime a digging motion. It seemed he wanted her to dig again, this time in a different location, using the helmet as a shovel to clear the stones from the base of the wooden door.

"Vasser kom snell! Ve go door!" he said, and coughed. He leant back against the wall. He was very weak and pointed to the door.

"Ve go door," he repeated, and slumped to his side, exhausted, holding his side.

Seeing the condition he was in, she felt terrible for feeling irritated with him and hoped she could get him out of this situation before he deteriorated further. Perhaps there was a step or ledge behind the door that they could stand on, until the water level subsided.

So she now dug away at the stones at the base of the door with much more efficiency, while the river continued to rise into the boathouse. She glanced back towards the boathouse entrance. The morning sunlight reflected on the river and she could tell it was quietly sneaking up on them. She shovelled even faster, scooping copious amounts of pebbles away with the helmet, as quickly as she could.

CHAPTER THIRTY-NINE

M arcello was tired and stressed; neither he nor Julia had slept all night after the dramatic, unbelievable events that had taken place the previous evening with the boys and the imposters. But now, last night's drama at his engagement party was the least of his problems; Natasha was missing and hadn't been seen since the beginning of the party. She hadn't even slept in her bed.

"It's down there, Father," Lorenzo said, pointing towards Aldo's boatshed. Marcello parked the car in the shade, and they walked the rest of the way the early morning sun down the muddy dirt track. It was the first time in three days of torrential downpour that the air was finally clear and the sun was out. There wasn't a cloud in the pale, blue sky. The soaking wet undergrowth smelled fresh and earthy, almost musty. Marcello took a deep breath to clear his head.

"It looks like someone is here," Marcello said, noticing a car parked in the shade, beside the old building.

"I'd like to have a chat with your friend Aldo and his father, before the police arrive asking questions of their own."

He took some more, deep breaths and tried to focus. He needed to think logically and positively, for his son's sake, at least. After the drama of the previous night, he didn't want to stress Lorenzo any more than he already had been.

He looked around the boatyard to see if there were any signs of Natasha. But there was nothing, as far as he could tell, that would indicate she had been here. He called her name a couple of times, as did Lorenzo, but there was no reply. They walked towards the water's edge.

"You know Lorenzo, I haven't been to this boatyard for years. It hasn't changed much, at all, you know."

"I've been here a lot. I love the river, Father. We sometimes come here canoeing."

"So you come here with Gabriella, do you? Can canoe well?"

Marcello felt a twang of guilt as he asked. He realized he didn't know what his children did in their spare time. He promised himself to be more of a father, now that he was back in the fold. He would look forward to it, once they had found Natasha and Giovanni, then life could move forward.

"Yes, Gabriella and I both come here. We used to come with Mother, before she... before..." he hesitated, "well, we used to come here and picnic along the river, when we were younger."

Marcello smiled at his son and affectionately put his hand on his shoulder.

"Yes, yes, of course. The river must hold many memories for you. I am sorry. You've been through a lot, Lorenzo. I am sorry I haven't been here so much..."

"Gabriela is a pretty proficient canoeist," Lorenzo quickly interrupted, "she can do a one-eighty turn, even quicker than I can."

"Can she, indeed? I will have to see her in action. I bet you are not bad, yourself, either! Let's check out the office, and find this friend of yours, shall we?"

The canoes and kayaks were neatly stacked on the higher ground beside the office. But upon closer inspection, despite the parked car, there seemed to be no one around; the office was completely locked up. They walked around the side and to the back of the building, looking for signs of life, but neither Aldo nor his father, were anywhere to be found.

"Where is this friend of yours, then?" he asked Lorenzo. "I was hoping that the boatyard owners might be able to tell us if they had seen Natasha or Giovanni."

"Maybe they're on the river," Lorenzo suggested. "You know, Father, this is where the three men first drew attention to themselves, before Pisa. They had apparently taken a boat out for a couple of hours, the same day we were on the river with Natasha and Alex. They actually caused us to capsize, and Alex was almost knocked out. It could have been nasty!"

"Really? Poor old Alex! I noticed a mark on his forehead. He seems to always get the raw end of the deal, doesn't he? He does seem to get knocked around, I must say."

"He does, father," Lorenzo said, remembering last Easter in the cave, and now this horrible incident last night. "I must do a better job at protecting my step-brother."

Marcello put his arm around his son's shoulders again.

"It will be all right, wont it? Our families, together?"

"Yes, I think so, Father. I am already fond of both Natasha and Alex."

"So glad. So glad. That is good to hear, my boy. And Julia? You like her, don't you?"

Lorenzo nodded.

"We will be fine, we will be fine, my boy. It may be difficult for you at first, but we will be fine."

There was an awkward pause.

"So," Marcello said, changing the subject, "tell me about these men and the little outing they had on the river."

"Well, they questioned Aldo, rather aggressively, I think."

"What kind of questions? Did Aldo mention anything to you about what they wanted to know?"

"Yes. They asked him if he had found anything of interest along the river. I think Aldo thought they were looking for artefacts from Hannibal's battle, like most tourists would. Aldo told us that it didn't cross his mind that they might be asking about the old book he had in the tin. He had no idea at all what they were after. When they later returned, they became aggressive towards him and he knew then that they wanted something more than the old artefacts that he had given to us for safekeeping. That's when Aldo came up to the house with his father and spoke to Grandmother about the *Soldbuch*."

"I see," Marcello said.

"Do you think Giovanni is really involved with these men, Father? Why on earth has he disappeared? What is he afraid of?"

"This is what is worrying me. I really don't know, Lorenzo. I am at a loss as to what's going on. The whole thing is bizarre."

Marcello slowly walked down to the water's edge, deep in thought. Lorenzo followed him. His father stared downstream. The river had flooded most of the lower section of the boatyard, and the jetty was almost submerged. But Marcello hardly noticed. His mind was elsewhere.

"Son, I have no idea what is happening, about Giovanni, or about last night. But I must first say, you and Alex had a terrible experience last night, and I am so proud of you and the way you both handled the situation. You made a decision to take control and you did a fine job."

He looked at Lorenzo. "I am very, very proud of you Son, you know that, don't you?"

"But Father, I nearly shot the man…"

"No, no you didn't Son. No you didn't."

He smiled at him. "I am sorry to have put you in danger like this, truly, I am. You make me very proud, do you understand, Lorenzo?"

"Yes, I suppose so."

"You have always made me proud, my boy. I want you to know that I really will be here for you. I will be, Son. From now on, you can count on me. You believe me, don't you?"

Lorenzo looked at him. "Yes, thanks, Father. That means a lot to me."

"Good. Because it's true."

He sighed and looked back at the swollen river.

"But unfortunately, I fear all this is not over yet, despite the arrest of those two imposters last night. It is obvious that something more is in the air. Whether these events with Giovanni, his old *Soldbuch* and these fake art dealers are somehow connected, I don't know, but I suggest that when the police arrive, we don't mention Giovanni to them."

"But Father..."

"I know he is missing, and there seems to be a link, but let's try and find him on our own first, OK? Let's find Natasha with all the help we can muster, but we'll find Giovanni ourselves. Right? He is obviously terrified. I don't want the police to terrify him any more."

Lorenzo nodded. He guessed his father had his reasons. Perhaps he wanted to protect Giovanni's identity.

"OK, Father."

"You mentioned three men earlier, Lorenzo, who bothered Aldo, but I presume you meant to say two men, right?" Marcello checked. "Two men questioned him here..."

"No, Father, there were three of them; Three in Pisa and three here, we saw them, on the boat. And three came to question Aldo."

Marcello was surprised.

"But there were only two at the house last night! Only two imposters dressed as catering staff! Only those two were arrested! I didn't tell the police last night that there was possibly a third man! I didn't realize..." He looked at his son, worried. "Are you sure, Lorenzo? Are you sure there were three of them in Pisa?"

Lorenzo nodded. "Yes, definitely!"

The fact that there was a third man on the loose, dangerous and possibly armed, with Natasha and Giovanni missing, changed everything.

"Three, Father. Even Grandmother knows this. They were all staying in town. The one who was not there last night at the house was the one who had come to Montesonnellino to interview Grandmother about the war and the artwork stolen from the house. That was also the same man with the big mouth, the one on the tower in Pisa who tried to insult Yanni. I am sorry, perhaps in all the confusion in the marquee last night and the finding of the missing caterers behind the tent, it was not made clear that there was another man..."

"*O Dio*," Marcello said. He tried to make a call on his phone, but of course, because of the surrounding hills, the reception was non-existent.

"I didn't tell the police. I didn't realize. They're not looking for a third man... in fact, they're not looking for anyone!"

Marcello looked worried. He thought for a minute.

"OK," he said, "let's focus on one thing at a time; for now, we must concentrate on finding Natasha. Two of those men, at least, are in custody; this third man is probably on the run. But this business is totally secondary to me until we find Natasha."

"And Giovanni, Father?"

"He will be OK; he is a survivor, Lorenzo. Whatever his reason for hiding, I know he is a good man. Don't worry about that now. Julia, Gabriella and Yanni are going crazy searching the grounds for Natasha up at the house, and until she is found, I cannot think of anything else."

He paused, and checked his phone again for reception, then put it back in his pocket. He looked downriver again.

"I must tell you, Lorenzo, that I fear that Natasha may have become lost in the dark last night, and perhaps come down near the water's edge." He looked at his son. "I think that if she were up by the house, she would have been found by now."

"Father, you think she may have..."

"No, no," he quickly replied, "but I think we should start looking along the riverbank, in case she slipped, do you understand? This is why I called the police here. It was a terrible evening last night; the visibility must have been non existent in that rain; she could have become disorientated."

The thought hadn't even occurred to Lorenzo that Natasha might have had an accident by the river. Their coming to the boatyard, or so he thought, was merely to ask if Aldo had seen Natasha, or just to ask him and his father more questions. It was a shock to Lorenzo hearing his father's fears, and that he had called the police to look for her by the river. He didn't take it well and he turned pale.

"Lorenzo, my boy, we will find her, but we should get going. The fact that there is a third man..." he paused, then continued, "anyway, whatever state she is in, she will probably be wet from the rain last night, and very cold. I do not want these Carabinieri getting side tracked, at all. Our mission is to find Natasha first and foremost. Giovanni and the missing con-man or dealer, whoever he is, will have to wait..."

"Signor! *Professore!*" A voice called from behind them.

Two smartly dresses *Carabinieri* officers closed their car doors, adjusted their caps, then casually meandered down to meet Marcello at the water's edge.

"Well," Marcello said, turning to them, irritated at the policemen for taking their time, "my son and I have already checked the area, Natasha, my step-daughter isn't here. Shall we move on and start the river search, as I had suggested earlier this morning?"

"As you know, *Professore*, it was to kill two birds with one stone. We had intended to interview the boatyard owner and his son about the two impostors..."

"This can wait. These two impostors are really not important to me now, my only concern is my future stepdaughter. My son, here, is just as anxious to start looking. I suggest we take a couple of those boats with an outboard and go downriver. The poor child may be dazed or lost somewhere along the water's edge. The sooner we start looking the better. And by the way, I should inform you, there are three of these imposters, not two. It appears that one man is still missing."

"So, three missing people now! The stepdaughter, the gardener and an imposter! It sounds like the beginning of a good joke!" the police officer said grinning. "Any others missing, while you can think of it? Our resources are apparently all at your disposal, *Professore*."

Marcello swung round and glared at him. He didn't realize they knew about Giovanni.

"This is no joke," he hissed. "My step-daughter is missing."

"Yes, yes course," the police officer corrected himself. "Perhaps I might join you in your boat?" he asked, adjusting the white sash of his smart, black uniform that tightly held his bulky torso in. "And while we travel down the river looking for all these missing persons, perhaps you can explain to me the relationship between your gardener and these three art dealers."

Marcello looked at him. "My gardener?"

"Well, it seems, *Professore*, according to these two gentlemen we are holding in Piacenza, that your mother, the Contessa... and perhaps even you, yourself, have some skeletons in the closets of the 'illustrious' Villa Montesonnellino, regarding a certain gardener...?" he smirked openly, almost gloating.

Marcello looked at him. He took his time in replying.

"With all due respect, I will not discuss the Contessa with you, or anyone else. And as far as skeletons go, in my case, as you are no doubt aware, skeletons are my livelihood, Officer."

Marcello half smiled. He picked his words carefully before he continued.

"You see, an archaeologist without a skeleton, is like a policeman without a crime..."

"Or a job," Lorenzo mumbled under his breath.

The police officer nodded slowly at Marcello. He understood. The annual donations to the police department from Villa Montesonnellino were not to be sniffed at, either. They had paid for his last holiday as well as the new staff kitchen.

"Indeed," he said, eyeing him carefully. "I understand, *Professore*."

"However," Marcello continued, "should I happen upon a skeleton in the closet, as it were, I would always do my utmost to preserve it and treat it with the utmost respect. And before I came to any wild conclusions, I would research and examine it and its past. I wouldn't want to jump to any wrong assumptions, as I am sure you wouldn't, if you were to come across a skeleton, yourself, so to speak."

They looked at each other.

"You see, many skeletons, upon first inspection," Marcello continued, "can appear to be in an unsavoury, blemished state. But closer examination, after all the layers of time are removed, shows the skeleton is actually quite clean. It must be similar in your profession; finding that not everything is as it would first appear on the surface..."

"That is sometimes so, *Professore*. We first have to do some careful examining though," the officer said.

"Actually, first we have to find my step-daughter," Marcello said, putting an end to the banter. I am going in a separate boat with my son, so excuse me. Come on Lorenzo, help me get this boat into the water."

CHAPTER FORTY

O nly after removing a large amount of the gravel that had accumulated at the base of the door, then fruitlessly trying to pull and tug it open, it occurred Natasha that the door might actually open the other way, not towards them as she and Giovanni had presumed.

When she glanced over at him to ask if it were possible that she had been wasting her time and energy pulling at the door when she should have been pushing it, he seemed to have lost all interest in their escape. This worried Natasha. The water was still creeping higher into the boathouse and she realized that it was entirely up to her to get them out.

"Giovanni, listen to me! Have you been through this door before? I mean, do you actually know what's behind there?" she asked, but she received no response at all. He only looked down, staring at the water around his ankles.

"Well, it's not budging this way, so it's got to open the other way!"

Natasha hammered, pushed, kicked and thumped at the door. Because it had been damp for so many years, the door had swollen and almost sealed itself into its frame. But with the water rapidly rising, there was no question in Natasha's mind that either way, she somehow had to get it open. After a few minutes, the cold, rising, river had reached her ankles too, and she began to panic. They had to get out soon or they would drown. Had she been on her own, she probably would have tried swimming out, but she could never manage swimming and supporting Giovanni. She wasn't a lifesaver like Lorenzo was with Alex.

Giovanni seemed to be suffering from the cold even more than she was; she noticed his weak, skinny frame was shivered uncontrollably. She moved him back further and leant him against the wall. Now she began to panic inside. In desperation, Natasha kicked at the stubborn door with her bare feet, shouting at the top of her voice at it. But nothing happened. A deep fear came over her; if she couldn't open the door, Giovanni would drown in front of her. That frightened her more than her own death. The water was now almost up to her knees, and she had a vision of his dead body floating around her, face down, and she really began to panic. Her fingers were now raw; she pushed and thumped with all her might. She grabbed his helmet and pounded the door. Then suddenly, after thumping with the helmet she saw a crack in the wood. She rammed it with her shoulder and the whole centre panel cracked inwards. The whole panel gave way, and water gushed past her legs into the void beyond.

A dank, musty smell greeted them. She quickly pushed and pounded the rest of the panel out, and peered into the darkness behind the door.

Facing her was a flight of stone steps going up the hillside, covered by a damp, flaky, arched stone roof. Natasha looked at Giovanni.

"*Schloss!*" Giovanni said. He pointed upwards and broke into a smile.

"Come on, I'll help you," she said, wading towards him.

"Non, non, Natasha, you only."

He indicated that Natasha should go on ahead, leaving him there.

"Are you crazy, Giovanni? I'm not leaving you here to die! You're coming with me!"

She lifted her evening dress to her knees, and tied a large knot at the side so that her legs were free. It took some time, as her sore fingers were so cold that she could hardly feel them. She put her arm under his shoulders.

"Come on, Giovanni, we're doing this together."

He looked at her and smiled.

"*Danke*," he said, "*Danke*, Natasha. *Molto grazie, molto gentile.*"

She took his weight and they slowly started to climb the steps together, and at last they were out of the immediate danger of the rising river.

The initial flight of ten or so steps was completely enclosed by a stone archway, almost like a short tunnel, which was dark and a little scary, but after a few steps they came out into the open, and they cold breathe the fresh, morning air and see the sky at last. They rested at the top of the first flight to warm up a little.

There was at last the promise of a nice, clear, day ahead. They pressed on up the hill. Several times Natasha sat Giovanni down on the uneven steps to rest, and each time the view of the swollen river below became more dramatic and distant. Natasha skimmed the river for boats, for help, for a search party; anything, but she saw nothing. She tried to hide her disappointment. Looking upriver, with not a boat in sight, Natasha could believe that her mother hadn't sent a search party for her. It then occurred to her that perhaps no one had noticed that she was missing! Perhaps the sheer number of guests at the party disguised the fact that she was missing at all! Surely Gabriella would have noticed? But after a night of dancing and eating, they would probably still be in bed, asleep! Perhaps no one would be looking for her!

She knew she had to do this herself; she couldn't hang around waiting for help. She had to take control and get Giovanni back home.

She wondered how she was ever going to do it. It was quite a distance back to Aldo's boathouse, and even further to where she had fallen in the river by Gabriella's property; that was several bends upriver, at least. Not that she was thinking of swimming back to Montesonnellino, she wasn't sure what to do, but it was obvious he wasn't able to go very far on foot, either. The terrain was impossible; dense undergrowth covered the hills. An overland escape wasn't even worth thinking about. Giovanni was having to rest every fifth step or so, and his breathing seemed laboured. She was hungry, but if she was hungry, she couldn't imagine how starving Giovanni must have been. She had no idea when he had last eaten.

Natasha tried to remember what Gabriella had told her about the old castle at the top of the hill, where the mother of the young girl in the hall portrait had lived. They had seen it in the distance when they had first arrived at Montesonnellino and she remembered Gabriella saying it was dilapidated and very isolated. There was no road to it, and no one ever went there. She now wondered if she was doing the right thing climbing up towards it; perhaps she should have stayed closer to the river where they could be seen by passing boats. She didn't know what to do. Perhaps she would try to light a fire as a signal.

She sighed. They were really stuck. But for now she thought it better to get Giovanni into the sun to warm him up, and that meant climbing a few more steps to get to the top of the hill. She felt protective of him. Perhaps it was because he had saved her life and had kept her warm all through the night. Just thinking about being rocked in his lap brought mixed feelings. She didn't want to remember it, nor that she had really hurt him. She focused on getting him to safety instead.

A lizard ran across the step in front of her.

"Breakfast!" she joked to herself. She imagined making a spear and skewering it over a fire, but the thought really made her sick.

"Fat chance," she said out loud. She didn't really know how to make a fire. She had once tried rubbing two sticks together with Alex when she was eight or nine, playing in the garden, but they hadn't even managed to make smoke. All she got was a blister on the palm of her hand. She wished Alex were with her. She missed him.

She felt helpless; she didn't recognise the berries on the brush beside the path, so as she didn't know which were edible, she didn't want to poison Giovanni. Lorenzo would have known, she thought. She missed them all. Had they even noticed she was missing? If they had, perhaps they were looking in the wrong place. She sighed. She wished she hadn't run away like a baby; she had made a complete fool of herself. She wished she had kept her cool and won Yanni over like an adult would have. But then, she thought had she not run, Giovanni would probably have drowned in the boathouse.

So there was a reason for everything.

She looked at the old man sitting beside her in the morning sun. He seemed to have stopped shivering at last. She was curious about him. She wondered if she should try to ask him what he had been running away from, and what the connection was with those three men. She thought she'd have a go.

"Giovanni," she said. He opened his eyes.

"These men from Germany, are you hiding from them?"

He looked at her, then nodded.

"Why?" she asked.

He said nothing. He thought for a minute, then managed to lift his arm and pointed further up the hill.

"*Die Kunst.*"

"*Kunst?*" Natasha didn't understand.

He nodded. "*Ja, Kunst. Quadri, pitture di olio. Kunst.*"

She shook her head. "I don't understand, sorry."

"*Illustrazione! Kunst!*" he said louder and clearer, as if it was obvious.

The effort to talk exhausted him, and he lent back and closed his eyes again.

She wondered what he knew. She tried to see beyond the scary, wrinkly face of this old, frail man struggling for breath. She tried to look for the young man who had fallen in love with Maria's mother, risking his life for her. Here was a man who had lived his whole life in hiding in fear of being found out. Now, for whatever reason, his dreaded time of truth had arrived and he had been so frightened that he had hidden in a dark, damp boat shelter, rather than face the consequences. She wondered what on earth he was afraid of. She wondered what he knew, or what he was hiding.

"This goes directly up to the old house, Giovanni?" she asked, pointing to the top of the hill.

"*Penso di si*," he said, nodding.

She didn't quite understand, but understood the 'si' part. He sounded exhausted. She worried that he was really going to die.

"And how shall we go home from here, Giovanni?" she continued, trying to keep him awake. "It is a long way, and there are no roads around here. How will we get back to Montesonnellino? What shall we do?"

He leant further back against the prickly undergrowth. He shook his head without opening his eyes. He exhaled deeply.

She looked at him and panic swept over her. He looked dead!

"Don't die on me, don't leave me here alone!" she whispered, shaking him. "Don't die, please, Giovanni!"

CHAPTER FORTY-ONE

J ulia sat down heavily on the steps of the veranda outside the kitchen door. She had finally run out of energy and places to look for he daughter. She was pale, tired and stressed. Natasha wasn't anywhere, and she hoped the police had started looking with Marcello. Yanni came and plonked himself next to her, exhausted too. He put his head in his hands.

Neither of them spoke.

It was only after the guests had finally left the previous night, and the police had finished asking questions and taking care of the two impostors, that Natasha's absence was actually noticed. Julia and Gabriella presumed she had gone to her room. When Julia realized she wasn't in her room, and hadn't been seen all evening by anyone since the guests had arrived, Gabriella told her that Natasha might have been upset about Yanni arriving with Signor Muretti's daughter. They then realized that something was seriously wrong, and she had perhaps gone off somewhere. Only then was the extensive search started with everyone involved. Her shoes were found almost immediately in the grass a few yards from the veranda, but Natasha was nowhere to be found.

Julia and Yanni now sat in silence for a while. It had been a long, fruitless night.

"Julia, I'm so sorry," Yanni said after a while. "I don't know what to say. It's all my fault…"

"You can't blame yourself, Yanni. She is young, and takes things to heart. You weren't to know she had a crush on you."

"Well, I have to admit that I did have an idea, but I didn't know to what extent. I assure you, Julia, I did nothing to encourage it. I decided not to email her for this reason. It wasn't appropriate. It was all so innocent, at the dig last Easter. I really had no idea..."

"Yanni, I know you didn't have anything to do with it, don't worry. I don't blame you at all. I realized she liked you when we all met that morning for breakfast in Pisa. But I didn't realize how much, though."

"But still, I should have been more subtle. I just didn't think..."

Gabriella came and stood in front of Yanni.

"Do you love her?" She demanded, looking directly at him. "Stefania, I mean. Do you love her?" She was annoyed with Yanni. If he had known Natasha liked him, how could he have been so insensitive to arrive with Stefania Muretti?

"No, I don't love her, I've only known her a few days..."

He looked up at Gabriella, almost pleading for redemption.

"Good!"

She sat down next to Julia. "So when we find Natasha, tell her so."

"Gabriella, darling, Yanni owes Natasha nothing, he doesn't need to say anything," Julia said gently. She put her arm around her shoulder.

Gabriella got up and walked away.

"Oh no?" she called back over her shoulder. "He should tell her that then, if it makes him feel better."

She needed to be alone. She needed her Artamis. She needed to think about where she could find Natasha. She headed towards the paddock.

The Contessa came out onto the veranda, followed by Alex, whose face was swollen and bruised. He was holding an ice pack to his cheek. He sat on a chair by the coffee table behind his mother, and the Contessa poured him and herself a glass of lemon juice then settled on the sofa.

She picked up the morning newspaper.

"Oh the incompetence!" she exclaimed out loud, so that Julia and Yanni could hear. "I shall have to contact the editor; you know they spelled the name of the house wrong! You would think they would get their facts right!"

The two art dealers were on the front page, and a photograph of the gun. There was a full-page article about the brawl in the marquee, and the bravery of Lorenzo and Alex. She lowered the paper and looked at Yanni.

"I say, young man, where is your beautiful girlfriend? Has she left already?"

He turned and looked at the Contessa. He couldn't believe her insensitivity at a time like this.

"She left last night with her father. And she is not my... anything!" He got up and started to walk away towards the tennis court.

"She is so lovely," the Contessa continued, picking up the paper again. "Though I think my grandson may have had eyes for her too. I saw him looking before all this drama started."

"He is welcome," Yanni called back. "I'm going to keep looking for Natasha."

"Wrong way," she called nonchalantly from behind the paper.

Yanni stopped.

"What?"

"I said, 'wrong way'. I would go towards the river if I were you, young man!"

"What? You know where Natasha is?" Julia looked at the Contessa. She stood up. "You know where my daughter is, and you haven't told us? After a whole night of searching?"

"Oh, *do* calm down, my dear, I am only being logical. It's the only place you haven't looked, is it not? If I ran down these steps into the dark, in the driving rain, would I turn left or right? Neither! Would anyone be in a position to make the decision if one were upset? One cannot think rationally when one's head is spinning; one just keeps going. So, one would presume that she had gone straight ahead. And straight ahead is that way; and that way, as I said, ends up down by the river."

Julia was stunned at her calm, callous attitude and was about to tell her so, when the Contessa added, "but I do believe my son already drove down there a little while ago; He probably didn't want you to know in case you over reacted, which I can now see that you most probably would have…"

Julia stared at the woman, speechless, and turned on her heels and headed straight for the river, with Yanni at her side.

CHAPTER FORTY-TWO

N atasha stared at the old man. He was breathing; his chest was rising slightly. She thought long and hard how she could keep him alive and realised that, other than sleep, he probably needed water. So she left him sleeping on the steps in the sun, and ran as fast as she could all the way back down to the boathouse. The river had almost risen up to the ceiling now, and had reached the fourth step outside the door. It brought home to Natasha that had she not managed to open that door, they would probably both have drowned by now. She took off her long dress to keep it dry and walked gingerly down the last couple of steps in her underwear. She slid into the cold, dark water, and hoped nothing nasty would grab her from beneath the surface. It was frightening going into water where she couldn't see the bottom. She wanted to get out as quickly as she could. But she needed that helmet.

She remembered she had left it in the corner. She dove down into the blackness, swam along the side of the wall, felt around the bottom and luckily recovered it almost immediately. She surfaced, gasping, and kicked her way out of the creepy boathouse as fast as her legs would go.

She ran up the first flight of steps to the open-air, and put her dress back on. It was filthy, torn and ridiculously long. She ripped over a foot off the bottom of it to make it shorter and easier to walk in. Keeping the long strip she had torn off, she then tied it round her waist a few times. She felt better, neater; less flimsy and vulnerable somehow. Now she was free of the annoying fabric around her legs. With Giovanni's helmet in hand, she went back down to the water, squatted on the first step, and washed it as best she could. As she squatted there, she wondered whether she would turn into one of the characters from 'Lord of the Flies', thrilling in the hunt and the kill, or the poor Rugby team she had read about, who had survived an air crash in the Andes and had been so hungry they had resorted to eating the other passengers in order to survive. It was normal, she thought; our basic instinct for survival. She remembered reading about other incidences of sailors eating their fellow shipmates when lost at sea. It must be the strongest instinct, she thought. As her stomach grumbled, she almost understood how it would happen if one was hungry enough. Then, she wondered if Giovanni would eat her if he survived and she had died of starvation. The thought horrified her, and she quickly decided he wouldn't, even if he were starving.

She thought of something else, and took a long, slow drink of water from the helmet to fill her stomach, before refilling it to take back up the hill to Giovanni. She hoped the water was clean enough so as not to make her or Giovanni ill.

She ran up the steps to the spot where she had left him. But to her surprise, he wasn't there! There was no sign of him at all.

Now she was worried.

She knew he hadn't come down the steps towards her, so he must have continued up the hill. Perhaps he thought something had happened to her and he was looking for her.

She called and yelled, but there was no response. Still carrying the helmet full of water, she ran up the steps towards the top of the hill, trying not to spill any and, hoping to find Giovanni sitting on the steps at every turn, but she didn't. She eventually found herself at the top of the hill in front of a low, overgrown, crumbling, stone wall. She climbed up onto it, hoping to see Giovanni sitting somewhere in the shade on the other side, but she didn't. She called out to him several times, waited, but heard nothing.

She climbed off the wall, and hastily walked through the weeds and overgrowth towards the massive, stone castle. Although was called a '*castello*' in Italian, it was really more like a very large, fortified home, with thick walls, small windows, and a tall tower with crenulations and narrow pointed windows that reminded her of the architecture she had seen in the Middle East last Easter.

She carefully made her way across the courtyard to the front of the building. Although the walls of the imposing home were far from crumbling, it was obvious that the whole property was in a sad state of repair. She tried to avoid stepping on remnants of what had once been wooden shutters to the windows and the terracotta roof tiles that were strewn on the ground. She liked the look of the home; it had a warm feel to it, and she wanted to know its story. She walked around the *castello* with curiosity, wondering why the very last occupants, ancestors of Lorenzo and Gabriella, would have abandoned it. That must have been a hard decision, she thought, to leave one's old ancestral home for good.

She noticed weeds and plants growing in the oddest of places, even managing to cling to crevices and cracks in walls and ledges, creating ideal living quarters for birds and lizards. Trees of all shapes and sizes had now sprung out of the ground where they really shouldn't have. Natasha thought it sad to see such a lovely home deteriorate like this. She wondered why Gabriella family hadn't taken care of it.

She still saw no sign of Giovanni, so she thought it a good idea if she headed towards the tower and climbed to the top, then she could perhaps spot him from up there. Over the tower's arched entrance, was the date, 1067 AD, carved into the keystone. Images on the Bayeux Tapestry sprang to mind, and Natasha imagined what the people living in this house in the eleventh century must have worn, their tunics, their pointed shoes, soldiers in chainmail with their pointed, leaf-shaped shields. She knew that 1066 was the Battle of Hastings, when William the Conquer invaded England with bows and arrows. It had seemed just a date in a history book when she learned about the Battle of Hastings, merely pictures in a school textbook, but here she was, standing outside the home of a family from that time. It made it all seem so real, so human. She touched the sides of the doorway, thinking of all the generations of children who had brushed past it, touched it, lent against it. The mothers who had called their children in for lunch, the father's and sons who had walked in and out of this archway with farming equipment; All gone, long, long ago. It was times like this that she wished she could see ghosts. How she would love to talk to a teenager who had lived here a thousand years ago.

She peered into the tower entrance. A startled bird flew past her face making her jump and she nearly dropped the helmet of water. She recovered, and peered in again. Although it was dark and shaded inside, it was, in places, open to the elements from the narrow windows and a vast gaping hole in the roof, allowing a thin shaft of sunlight to beam down from the top of the tower.

She didn't really want to go in, but she had to. She had to find Giovanni.

"Giovanni? Are you in here? Giovanni, I have some water for you!"

Nothing. She sighed, and ventured in. She gingerly looked around.

"Giovanni…?"

The floor felt almost soft in places, due a thick covering of something over the boards; on closer inspection she realized it was years of bird droppings, probably bat guano too, rotting, decaying bird's nests. There was a wheel-less body of a large, heavy, eighteenth century carriage, damp and rotting sitting on its belly on the floor, its leather seats had been home for generations of mice and other small animals. A broken wheel, probably belonging to the carriage, leant against a wall on the other side of the room, along with old gardening tools and flowerpots. Everything was encrusted in dust, dirt and droppings. The original carved, wooden steps, leading up to the top of the tower were still there for the most part. They clung around the wall in a sad, broken spiral. Natasha's eyes followed the circular steps up the tower, squinting at the dusty shaft of light streaming down from the top. They looked very rickety and dangerous. Several sections of the banisters were missing, and some rungs of the steps had large gaps with nothing but thin air between them and the floor below.

She couldn't help thinking how sad it was that such a beautiful, old building could be left to rot.

Natasha put her foot on the first step to test it. It cracked loudly under her weight, and the noise echoed up to the top of the tower, startling about six birds. They flapped their wings noisily and flew up through the hole in the roof.

There was silence again.

Then she thought she heard something.

"Hello, Giovanni," she called. "Is that you?"

Nothing. She walked back to the doorway, looking out into the bright sunshine. She waited there and listened, but there was nothing except the crickets and the hot sun beating down on the landscape. Then she heard the noise again. It sounded like a distant moan, or a groan. She listened hard. There it was again, a deep, groaning sound coming from the opposite side of the room. But there was nothing there! She slowly and carefully walked over to the far wall. She then noticed, almost beneath a small window, there was a hole in the floor. This had to be where the noise was coming from.

As quietly as she could, she tiptoed towards the hole. Sure enough, she heard the groans again.

"Giovanni?"

She peered down through the gap in the floorboards to the floor below. The old, wooden floorboards had completely rotted and caved in, presumably helped by the recent wet conditions under the glassless window. She held onto the little windowsill, and leant over and peered through the floorboards.

"Giovanni?" she called out. "Are you down there, Giovanni?"

Another groan was heard and in the dim light, Natasha could just make Giovanni out in a heap on the floor below. He was lying in the large chamber below. He was on his back, looking up at her, and obviously in a lot of pain.

"Oh my goodness, Giovanni! Don't move! Giovanni, don't move! I'll get help!"

She ran to the doorway, and ran back again, not knowing what to do or where to go. She needed to do something but she didn't know what! She was desperate! The poor man! She tried to keep calm; she remembered the water, and ran over to the helmet that she had left at the base of the stairs. She untied her improvised waistband and carefully tied it to the straps of the helmet. In her haste, she spilled a little, but it was still three quarters full. She carefully walked over to the hole in the floor, and lowered the helmet down to Giovanni as gently as she could.

"You will have to reach for it, Giovanni, it is full of water; I don't think it can reach you otherwise. It's *aqua* Giovanni, *aqua*!"

She watched him slowly sit up and stretch his arm out towards his helmet. When she thought he had it, she let go, and he caught it in his hands. He drank copiously, then looked up at her, and thanked her.

"OK, now I'll get help... stay there, don't move, Giovanni!"

She backed away from the hole, and wondered what on earth she would do. She knew which direction Montesonnellino was; upriver, but it might take her hours getting there through the woods and undergrowth, she was bound to get lost. But she had to do it, what alternative was there?

Then she had an idea. She looked up towards the shaft of light again coming from the roof of the tower. There was a ledge at the top of the spiral staircase. As far as she could tell, most of it was intact. Could she manage to make it to the top, she wondered? She could then perhaps see where the house was exactly, or where Aldo's boatyard was, then have a better idea about which direction to aim for.

Chapter Forty-Three

G abriella cupped her hands and called Artamis from the bottom of his paddock, then went into the shelter and prepared his saddle while he trotted over to her. She checked around the ground, hoping to find a sign or a secret hint from Natasha to say she had been there since she and her father had checked there the previous night. But unfortunately, there was still nothing to indicate that Natasha had been there at all. Not even Giovanni had been back and slept here. She sighed, worried for them both, but more so for Natasha. Where on earth could she be?

With his head nodding, sensing he was going for a ride, Artamis was already waiting for her outside his shelter. He greeted Gabriella by nudging her in the neck.

"Where's Natasha, Artamis, has she been here to see you, boy?"

The horse snorted, and she stroked his main and nurtured him for a while before lifting the saddle onto his back. She mounted him, and immediately headed for the top of the hill. Galloping and pushing Artamis as hard and as fast as she could, she went over conversations in her mind that she had had with Natasha in case there was any hint as to where she could have gone. But she drew a blank. She stopped on the crest of the hill, and took in the wonderful panorama, where she could breathe and think clearly. She sat there, panting along with Artamis, looking across the beautiful valley. She realized how fond she had become of her sister-to-be. If anything happened to her, she would be devastated.

The river sparkled below, and Gabriella was surprised at how much it had swollen; she couldn't remember it ever being as wide and high before, even after the heaviest snow melt in the Springtime.

It worried her. She felt she should go down to the river to look for Natasha there. She knew it was unlike Natasha to bottle everything up for this long, and she knew Natasha would have been cold and wet all night, wherever she was.

Gabriella couldn't believe that Yanni's arrival with Signor Muretti's daughter on his arm last night would have caused such a drastic reaction from Natasha; she knew Natasha liked him, but certainly not his much! She would have come home to talk to her about it before it ever came to this, surely. She knew something was seriously wrong. This was beyond Natasha just needing 'alone' time.

She looked down the valley again remembering what Natasha had said about the surrounding countryside when they had been up there together; about the river, the hills and castles; that it all had the taste of sadness about it, or bloodshed. She was right, Gabriella thought, she didn't think she was at the time, but now she felt it, too.

Feeling down and lonely, she pulled on the reins to turn around, wondering what could have happened to her new sister. But as she turned Artamis around, something caught her eye a couple of hills away in the distance. Something moved at the top of the tower of the old ruined *castello*. She nudged Artamis to go forward a few paces. She shielded the sun from her eyes and was now absolutely sure; yes, there was someone waving at the top of the tower! It couldn't be... was it?

"NATASHA!" she called, cupping her hands around her mouth. She frantically waved. "NATASHA!"

She was too far away to hear, but it was her, it had to be! She could just make out a tiny figure waving at the top of the tower!

What was she doing all the way over there? More to the point, how on earth did she get there? She waved her hands above her head, shouting her name, and far, far away she thought she heard Natasha calling her back! She had seen her! She had heard her!

"I'll get help!" she shouted! "Stay there! STAY ... THERE!"

She flew back to the paddock as fast as she could, Artamis's hooves hardly touching the ground he galloped so fast. She jumped off and called her mother's horse, Lily, over from the bottom of the field. Lily trotted over, gracefully and obediently, and Gabriella quickly saddled her up, her mind buzzing. She then jumped back onto Artamis, gave Lily a tug to let her know she was coming, too, and galloped with Lily in tow past the perimeter of the paddock and into the woods along the top of the ridge.

CHAPTER FORTY-FOUR

N atasha was elated. She could almost jump for joy, but she didn't, because the wooden floor of the platform she was standing on would probably have given way. But she was sure it was Gabriella! She had seen her!

From her vantage point, she could just see the red roof of Montesonnellino in the distance behind the hill where Gabriella had been, which gave her her bearings; she now knew exactly where she was. She wondered if she should stay in the tower, so that Gabriella could follow her calls and know which way to come. But Natasha surmised that Gabriella probably knew the way to the old estate well enough, so she decided to carefully climb down the staircase again, and tell Giovanni the good news.

Very slowly, sticking to the side of the wall like an insect, using her fingertips to hold the flaking bricks, she gingerly came down, step by step, testing every rung before she put her full weight on it. On two occasions, she was glad she had been cautious, as the steps cracked and began to give way under her weight. The two sections where there was a missing step, she sat down and stretched her leg out until it touched the next rung. She used the wall or wobbly banister to push her weight forward onto it. It was very scary, but she eventually got down the tower steps in one piece. She ran over to the hole in the floor to call down to Giovanni to tell him the good news. She dived onto her stomach and looked through the gap in the floor to call down to him, but as she did so, she screamed as she felt it give way, and before she could scramble to her feet and away from the rotting floorboards, she was falling down into the chamber below.

She landed on her back, and lay there, in a heap of dust and debris.

CHAPTER FORTY-FIVE

S he waited for the air to clear, then, she tried to move her neck and head. She was OK. Nothing broken, she was just sore. She was amazed she wasn't dead. She looked around for Giovanni.

In the dim light, she saw him. He was sitting against the wall opposite her, looking very weak, but he managed a smile.

"*Wilkommen*, Natasha," he said with a grin.

She lay there dazed for a minute.

"Look," he said, turning his head towards one of the walls. "*Die Kunst!*"

She sat up, then, looked in the direction he was pointing and saw what he was referring to. She didn't immediately understand the significance of what she was seeing, but then the penny slowly began to drop. She followed his eyes around the room, and she realised what it was.

"Oh Giovanni! *Kunst* means art, doesn't it!"

All around the perimeter of the room, leaning against the walls, stacked and in neat and dusty piles, were rolled up scrolls of canvasses, boxes of various shapes and sizes and heavy, lumpy, looking bundles carefully tied up in burlap. But mostly, there were paintings.

"Giovanni, is it…?"

He smiled at her.

"Is it the stolen art from the war?" she asked.

"*Si*, Natasha, of *la casa* of Contessa. Is *die Kunst*. Now am to die. Big trouble."

"Oh my God, why? You knew it was all here? All these years? Why didn't you say something? Why couldn't you tell anyone?"

He exhaled heavily. He shook his head in answer to her question.

"This is fantastic, Giovanni, you have found the Contessa's stolen art, she will be so happy with you. Don't give up now!"

"Happy? No." He shook his head very slowly. "Many years Kunst its here, I say nothing to Contessa. Now Contessa know, police know, so I must to go."

He closed his eyes. "*Voglio morire.* Bea, Bea..." he mumbled. "Bea..." he began to cry and Natasha went over to him and held his hand.

He eventually fell asleep. Natasha hoped he would regain some strength and wouldn't cry when he woke up. There was nothing more scary, she realized, than being with someone she didn't know very well, especially a man, who was crying.

She looked around the room. It was an incredible stash; apart from the scrolls of oil paintings, there were other things, too. She opened a couple of the boxes and unwrapped the bundles of burlap inside them, and found heavy, ornate gold chalices, silver candlesticks and silver platters. There was a set of cutlery with coats of arms on the handles, heavy, domed silver serving dishes, and another set of cutlery with bone or ivory handles. On the other side of the room, another box contained engraved napkin rings, and a pair of miniature ivory elephants. There was china, too; a set of dainty teacups and saucers, which were similar to her grandmother's set that she used to play with as a little girl. Each piece had two tiny crossed swords underneath it, just like her grandmothers.

"Oh, Granny, I wish you were here," she said out loud. She noticed one of the pieces rattled in the burlap, and she carefully unwrapped it thinking it was broken, but to her surprise, it wasn't, it was the sugar bowl with some brown, crystallized sugar granules inside it. She took a little piece between her fingers and tasted it. It seemed OK, so she ate it and put a fist full beside Giovanni on a saucer for him, when he woke up.

She looked at him. What confused her was why he had kept the hoard, which he'd known about, a secret. If he hadn't wanted to steal it, why hadn't he just told someone that he knew where it was? Surely living in the house where the paintings and antiques had been stolen from must have made him feel terrible all these years. Perhaps the Contessa would have turned him in had she realized he had known where it was stashed. Natasha presumed it could be because once you've kept something hidden, and then changed your mind about coming clean, there was no way of going back; you were damned if you did and you were damned if you didn't. Perhaps once the police were involved, Giovanni's true identity would eventually be blown, and he probably would have been accused of hiding the hoard himself. Worse still, he could have been accused of killing those officers on the river, all those years ago.

She understood Giovanni's dilemma. Poor old man, she thought. His worst fears were now becoming realized. He must be scared out of his mind.

Two long hours passed, and knowing that Gabriella had seen her, she was able to drift in and out of sleep. Giovanni sometimes make weird, groaning noises, holding his stomach, even in his sleep, which frightened Natasha. Her only escape from it was when she dropped off to sleep again. But then something other than his groaning woke her from her drowsy state; She thought it had come from behind her, but then realized it must have come from the floor above. She looked up through the hole in the ceiling. She heard footsteps, then a man's voice, and Natasha immediately found the strength to jump up. It was Yanni, she was sure of it! He had come for her! Despite her ridiculous behaviour, running away like an idiot, he had come for her!

"Natasha?" she heard him call.

"Yanni, we're down here! Look in the corner of the tower, over by the window, there's a hole in the floor!"

She couldn't believe it! He had come for her! She heard his footsteps above her. "But be careful, Yanni," she added. "The floorboards are absolutely rotten in the corner; we fell right through!"

"Natasha! It's me, Gabriella!" her voice called down from the floor above.

"Gabriella! We are down here!"

"OK! We'll get you out, do not worry!"

She was so pleased to hear her voice.

"Gabriella, I'm with Giovanni, We're both here!" she called back almost crying. "He's not very well at all, please hurry, I'm so glad you're here."

Two heads appeared over the lip of the hole above her.

"Natasha, don't worry," Gabriella said, "we will rescue you! But I am with Aldo, he has come to find you, it is not Yanni. We are going to find some rope. We will be back!"

"Aldo?"

"*Si! Ciao* Natasha! *Si*, Aldo! I helping you. Please, you can to wait one moment, please."

Gabriella and Aldo's heads disappeared again, their footsteps faded away and then there was silence. Natasha sat back heavily against the wall.

"*Aldo?*" she thought out loud. She wasn't expecting that.

CHAPTER FORTY- SIX

N atasha had woken Giovanni to give him the sugar crystals, which he gladly sucked.

Time passed very slowly, and while she waited for Gabriella and Aldo to return, she paced around the room. She tried not to think too much of Yanni and what she would say to him when she did see him again. If she were to presume the worst and he had gone off with Stefania, then she wouldn't have to say anything to him, anyway. That was almost preferable to facing him! But what if he were somewhere out there looking for her? That would be so embarrassing; she couldn't bare thinking about it.

Trying to distract herself from her dilemma, she re-examined in closer detail the hoard of stolen property around her, unwrapping and looking closely at the scrolls of paintings and artwork. She still couldn't believe what they had stumbled across. This was major, she thought; this had implications beyond the local villages. This was newsworthy!

She heard a noise from behind her again, and she turned to Giovanni to see if he had heard it too. But he was slumped against the wall, asleep again. Then she noticed, in the dull light, the wall behind him; there was a dark, oblong shape in it; she realized he was leaning right next to a door! They obviously hadn't noticed it before because of the dim light and the disturbed dust when they fell in. She woke Giovanni.

"It's a door Giovanni! It was here and we hadn't noticed it! Gabriella is coming to get us out!"

She grabbed the rusty, iron latch, lifted it, and to her amazement pulled the heavy door open without any problem.

"I can't believe how stupid I was! We could have got out of here a couple of hours ago!" They heard footsteps beyond the door.

"We're in here, Gabriella! Aldo, we're in here!" she called into the dark passageway. The noise of the footsteps on the stone floor came closer.

"In here! We're in here!" she repeated. But to her shock, it wasn't Gabriella or Aldo who appeared from the dark corridor. It was the man from the Tower of Pisa, the third man of the trio; She recognised him immediately.

"Good day," he said dryly. "I have come to your rescue. I am so sorry, were you expecting somebody else?"

She darted away from him, then, tried to make a run for it towards the open door, but he grabbed her by the arm and pushed her into the wall.

"How rude of me! I haven't introduced myself! My name is Heinrich Streuber... junior, that is. And you're not going anywhere young lady," he said dryly.

He took her by the wrist, and turned her arm behind her back so that she couldn't move. Giovanni groaned and attempted to stand up, but he was pushed to the floor again.

"We have come across each other once before, but you probably don't recall..." he said to Natasha, and then he looked down at Giovanni on the floor.

"And as for you," he hissed at him in German, "you have been more trouble than you know. Get up, you old traitor, you deserter, you despicable coward!"

He kicked Giovanni's foot.

"Get up and explain yourself. Your days of hiding are over, Fuchs. It's payback time."

He kicked him again. "You will pay with interest. You are an embarrassment to the country and you do not deserve to live a minute longer! Now get up!" he ordered, kicking him. "Stand up like a man!"

Natasha had to watch Streuber abuse her new friend. She felt desperate, unable to help him. Streuber's grip was still tight around her wrist and she struggled in vain. Giovanni took the abuse, and was not strong enough to fight, nor, it seemed, was he even strong enough to answer or defend himself verbally. He just looked up at him, almost accepting his fate. It was too horrible to watch.

Natasha glanced up at the hole in the ceiling, hoping Aldo and Gabriella had heard what was going on. But if they had, they didn't respond.

Giovanni was grabbed by the front of his shirt by Streuber, and pulled to his feet.

"Come on you spineless coward, what kind of soldier were you, eh? It was soldiers like you who let us down, you manure heap!" Heinrich shoved him against the wall and spat in his face. "Surely you didn't think you would get away with it forever did you, eh, Fuchs? Did you... eh?"

He pushed him again, and Giovanni took it, without flinching, without even caring.

"Stop it! Stop it!" Natasha screamed. "Leave him alone! How do you know he has done anything wrong?"

She struggled as hard as she could to be free of his grip.

Heinrich looked at her.

"I am going to release you. But if you should be so stupid as to run, he will be hurt. You understand?"

Natasha nodded. She believed he would hurt him.

"OK, I won't run," she said.

He released his grip around her wrist then walked further into the room and stood directly underneath the hole in the ceiling above. He pulled out a crumpled letter from his inside pocket, opened it, and held it out to catch the dim source of light. He looked at Giovanni.

"Remember Otto?" he asked, "Otto was your friend, was he not?"

Giovanni gasped. "...Otto?"

"Yes, I have here, a long letter from your friend Otto. Weren't you wondering at all how we came to find you? I am sure you were. I am sure you were very curious. Well, it was your dear friend who led us to you..."

"Otto?" Giovanni mumbled, "Otto...?"

"Would you like to hear what he said? Your friend, Otto?"

"Otto," Giovanni repeated, slowly sliding down the wall again then, sat heavily on the floor.

"I'll give you the background, my dear," Heinrich said, turning to Natasha. "This was a long, long time ago, when this man here was barely out of his teens, isn't that so Fuchs? But even at that age, he was a fool!"

He kicked Giovanni again, and then said to Natasha, "I'll give you an outline my dear; a little history lesson. You like history don't you? So listen hard. Three bodies were found in the river, you see, not far from here. In fact, one of them, one of the shot men left floating in the river, just happened to be my grandfather," he said bitterly, and glanced back at Giovanni.

"Oh! Your grandfather!" Natasha said; it was all beginning to fit into place.

"This is what your friend here, this heap of dung, sitting on the floor did; I shall read it to you. It is from his friend Otto. Otto, it seems, had some pangs of guilt in his old age, unlike him, and sent this letter to my brothers, almost as a sort of confession, though it should be this man here who had more to confess, right Johann?"

He tapped Giovanni's foot with his own, making sure he had Giovanni's attention. "Surely you remember him, don't you, your old friend Otto? He was picked up by some soldiers, you see, on his way back home to Germany, and this is what he was told about the men found dead in the river. I will translate it into English, so that this young lady knows what a coward you are."

Heinrich then began to read to Giovanni the letter from Otto.

"...they informed me that they had been German, probably high ranking officers, judging by their age, trying to escape by boat, dressed as peasants. I asked how they knew they were German, and they told me that their boots were of the highest quality, and stuffed with more cash than any Italian peasant would see in a lifetime, and identity papers were also found. The word was that they had been shot dead by partisans in the hills overlooking the river. To my surprise, I am told the papers found in the boat were those of my friend Johann Fuchs," Streuber looked down at Johann. "Sound familiar? That's you. Bet you never thought your papers would come back to haunt you, did you?" He read on, *"which perplexed me greatly. His Soldbuch and jacket were apparently tucked in the stern. Johann was, like myself, serving under your grandfather at the house for almost eighteen months, but his body was not found. The picture in the Soldbuch apparently did not match any of those men found in the river. I only hope he made it home, though after many years of unsuccessfully trying to contact him or members of his family after the war, I have to presume he did not make the journey home, and he had been shot."* Heinrich stopped reading and looked at Giovanni in contempt. He was sitting staring at the floor, the tears trickling down his cheeks, his face absolutely emotionless.

"So not only did you desert your country, but your friends also. Tut-tut Johann! Well, there is more! Would you like to hear more, young lady?" he asked turning to Natasha, "it is an interesting read!"

Natasha looked at him defiantly, hating him. How could he be so cruel to such a defenceless, old man?

"I shall continue. Otto asks here, *Why his Soldbuch was in the boat is a mystery to me, I can only presume he met up with your grandfather somewhere along the river. I certainly did not bring him to the river in the car with us'..."* Heinrich stopped reading and looked at Giovanni. "So, you met up with them did you? Perhaps you got a ride in their boat?"

He squatted down next to him, and almost whispered in his ear. "Perhaps you escaped the bullets and swam to shore, knowing their secret, and keeping it to yourself for the right time, eh? Or perhaps you made a deal with the partisans, so as not to be killed yourself. You told them where the officers would be, and had them shoot so you could escape unharmed. Which was it, Johann?" Heinrich was inches from his face. "Which scenario worked better for this lowly coward?"

Johann groaned, and shook his head.

"So how does it feel Johann, to be responsible for all those innocent deaths... for you were, weren't you? Responsible? My grandfather's and his two friends, you let them die while you escaped, and hid, then all those poor, poor Italians..." He gently slapped his cheek repeatedly, mocking him.

"Aldo, help!" Natasha called through the ceiling, finding it unbearable to watch. "Aldo!"

Streuber laughed. "He won't be much use to you, my dear; let us say that he is a little 'tied up' at the moment. The silly man thought he could follow me without me knowing. So he won't be coming to your rescue just yet, I'm afraid. Now young lady, while we leave Johann here to reflect on his past, your job is to help me carry this little lot down to the river. So you can start right now by tying it all up securely to prevent any damage. So come on, take your first armful. The sooner you cooperate and load the boat, the sooner I will be gone and out of your life."

"And if I refuse?" Natasha retorted defiantly. He didn't frighten her, she thought. She had experienced worse; she had been held up at gunpoint and had her hair chopped off by a crazy woman, then tied and left without food or water in a cave. Surely she could take this man on. In fact, he seemed to need her. Perhaps she had the upper hand, she thought.

"And if I refuse to help you steal all this?" she defied him, "you'll never manage to move it all on your own, you'd have to make several trips up and down the hill, and by then help would be ..."

"If you refuse," he shouted, cutting her short, "this old man's death will be on your hands. Understand? And it is not stealing," he shouted in frustration, "it is rightfully mine!"

He pushed Giovanni's head back against the wall and held it there. Giovanni was so weak he hardly blinked.

"Is that what you want young lady? This old man's death on your hands?"

"OK, OK! "Natasha said quickly. "Let go of him! I'll help you! I'll do it!"

CHAPTER FORTY-SEVEN

Earlier, when they had met by the tower, Aldo had explained to Gabriella that he had come up to the old castle because someone had made off in one of his motorboats. When he had arrived for work that morning at the boat yard, he had seen a car parked half way up the lane, but hadn't seen anyone with it. Then, when he saw that one of his boats were missing he had wasted no time in jumping into another one to retrieve it.

After only ten minutes he had seen the stolen boat tethered to the riverbank by the flooded, old boathouse. Hiding his own boat from view in the reeds, he crept up the hill using the undergrowth as cover. It was then that he bumped into Gabriella by the tower, and after their mutual surprise at seeing each other, she explained to him why she was there. He was amazed to hear that Natasha was somewhere around the old tower, and had immediately decided that he would forgo looking for the thief who had taken his boat in order to help Gabriella find Natasha and get her home safely.

But after they'd found Natasha and Giovanni in the basement of the tower, Gabriella had seen it all happen. She had gone to untether the horses, since Aldo had had the brilliant idea of tying rope to them, then using the horses to pull Giovanni and Natasha up through the hole, one by one. So while Aldo was outside making a sling-seat for Giovanni with the rope and some sacks they had found in the tower, she saw him being pounced upon from behind.

Stunned, Gabriella had kept herself hidden from view in the undergrowth.

So now, crouching down by her horses, Gabriella watched this extraordinary scene of someone, whose face she couldn't quite see, tying up a very stunned Aldo. But when the attacker dragged Aldo over to a tree to secure him to it, she was shocked when she recognised the same aggressive tourist from Pisa that had been provoking Yanni on the leaning tower! Now she knew he wasn't a tourist; he was the third man of the trio of impostors in her home. But what on earth was he doing here? And why did he want to prevent Aldo from helping Natasha and Giovanni get out of the basement? She crouched down low, hoping the horses would remain calm and quiet, and she watched him as poor dazed Aldo had his feet tied. The man then disappeared into the main section of the house.

"What's going on here?" she asked Aldo, as he slowly came round rubbing his head.

She wasted no time in untying him.

"It's just too coincidental. We saw him in Pisa, and then he was at our house questioning my grandmother. What's going on, Aldo?" she whispered.

"Strange, I know. And why would anyone climb all the way up to a ruin on top of a hill and tie me to a tree?" he wondered, rubbing his wrists. "It's crazy!"

"He doesn't want anyone to know what he is doing, or to stop him from doing it, that's why," Gabriella said.

"But what *is* he doing? Do you think he knows Natasha and your gardener are in the basement of the tower?"

"I don't know," she whispered, "he must have seen or heard us talking to them. He must have! If not, what else could it be? He must be here for something; he is involved in the art world, this much I know. He was probably part of the 'plot' at my house with the other two men, even though he wasn't with them. There was a horrible scene. It was terrible. They had a gun!"

"I saw that in the paper! Amazing!" Aldo grinned. "Your brother and Alex did well! They have made us all famous! It will bring tourists to the area, to the river, I'm sure!" he almost joked.

Gabriella looked at him, not amused.

"I am only kidding. But it must all be connected somehow. Don't forget, Gabriella, it was he who ransacked my office in search of something, questioning me, pushing me around, remember?"

"Yes, Aldo. It scares me. This man is dangerous. He may have a gun, too. We must be very careful. He is after something important."

Aldo looked worried, and thought for a moment.

"Look," he whispered, "I think I should follow him into the house and see what he is up to. If he is dangerous, I need to stop anything to happening to Natasha and the old man. If he is not armed, all the better, of course. I need to know why he wrecked my office for that *Soldbuch.* We need to find out what on earth he is doing here."

"Aldo, I think I know. A *Soldbuch,* you see, it identifies someone. But why he is interested in it, I have no..." Gabriella stopped in her tracks. "Aldo, did you just say 'basement'?"

"Yes, why?"

"Basements have doors."

Aldo looked at her.

"You're right! Why didn't I think of it? We won't have to haul them up with ropes and the horses; there must be a door! Look, we can probably do the two things together; apprehend this man, and get Natasha and the old gentleman out..." then he turned white. He didn't want to frighten Gabriella, but this man may be a step ahead of them already.

"Gabriella, you run down to the river, find his boat, and let it go. Make sure mine is well hidden from the shore so that he can't use it to escape in. In the meantime, I will apprehend him here in the house, somehow. I'll get the old gentleman and Natasha out."

"OK. It's risky. Are you sure you don't want me to help you up here?"

"It's OK, just get rid of the boat, so he can't get far if he runs. If you can push the boat to drift downriver, all the better; an empty boat on the water is not a good sign, especially one of mine. It will raise a red flag for help. It will not be long before we have help on the way."

"OK. Good point. See you later."

She checked that the coast was clear, then started running across the courtyard towards the wall and the steps down to the river. She stopped in her tracks, turned, and quickly came back.

"Aldo..."

"What?"

"How do I know which one is your boat?"

"They're both mine, silly! But get rid of the smaller of the two."

"OK." She ran swiftly and silently towards the stone wall, leapt over it, and was gone.

CHAPTER FORTY-EIGHT

A ldo quietly slipped through the heavy, doors. He
thought how odd it was that he had never been up to
the old house before, even to explore as a young teenager
with his friends. But then, he reasoned, as the cool air
touched the back of his neck, it probably had something to
do with the stories of the dead soldiers of Hannibal's battle
coming up from the river and haunting the place.

Once in the hallway, he stopped and listened. It was
quiet in the cool hallway, and although he heard no ghostly
moanings or groanings from two thousand-year-old wounded
soldiers, the thought did cross his mind to turn round and
leave. The sheer height and emptiness of the hallway, and
the thickness of the walls made the slightest sound echo
through the building.

At first he heard nothing at all but his own breathing,
which seemed amplify in his head. He tried to control it by
taking long, deep, quiet breaths. Then, when he had his
breathing under control, he listened harder, knowing that the
boat-thief was around somewhere, probably hiding, watching
him, and waiting to ambush.

He jumped when he heard the groan of a door hinge
from the other end of the hallway. Bracing himself, he
waited to see if he could hear any other sound follow it; he
almost expected to hear footsteps creeping up behind him,
but he didn't. He decided to walk slowly in the direction of
the sound, trying his best not to make any noise himself by
stepping on loose floorboards.

He passed several rooms off to his left and right, and past the grand, stone staircase, hoping he wouldn't have to go up it. It reminded him of a horror film, austere and castle-like, with its mahogany panelling and banisters. A gargoyle-type creature at the base of the bannisters looked at him with evil eyes.

He made his way towards the back of the house and stopped outside the old kitchen. He listened hard but couldn't hear anything. He peeped round the door and nearly leapt out of his skin; a mouse scuttled across the floor, then, disappeared under the stone sink. When his heartbeat had settled, Aldo listened again. He heard something. Determined that it was coming from a room off the kitchen to the right, he walked towards it, carefully avoiding stepping on anything loose or broken on the floor. He turned sideways with his back to the wall so he couldn't be pounced upon from behind.

Cautiously, he checked around the room, then relaxed a little when he found no one there. He surmised that this ante-room had probably been the parlour, or the laundry room in the old days, as in the centre of the room was a stone well, its dusty, wooden cover lying in two halves on the floor. He cautiously peered down into it. He picked up a piece of broken china off the floor, and flicked it into the void. There was no splash; the well was dry. It hit the bottom almost immediately. As he peered down the well, he was suddenly distracted by a noise and nearly jumped out of his skin. He looked up and from the corner of his eye, saw the door leading down to the cellars move.

He quietly crept towards it, stood behind it and waited. Not quite sure what to expect, he peered round; no one was there. He could see steps leading down to the cellars. Aldo cautiously opened the door a little more so he could see further down the steps. A cold draft greeted him. Although dark and uninviting, he had a feeling the steps would lead to Gabriella's missing gardener and Natasha, and probably the boat-thief, too. He felt a little apprehensive at the thought of going down into the dark basement, but he had to.

He took five slow, very cautious steps down the steps, and stopped. He heard distant voices; they were a way off down the corridor coming from one of the cellars at the far end of the passageway. His heart thumped. He slowly continued to creep down the worn, dusty steps, letting his eyes adjust to the dim light as he went.

Each cellar he passed on his right had a shaft of sunlight shining through a little barred window, and he was able to peep into each one to make sure no one was hiding, waiting to leap out at him. He could hear a distinct voice coming from further down the corridor; someone was calling, and he froze.

"Aldo! Gabriella! Help!" he heard Natasha call quite clearly.

Aldo ran towards the cellar, stopped outside, and listened. There was a lot of shuffling and commotion. His heart raced. He peered round the door and saw an old man being knocked around by the boat-thief, and Natasha was trying to stop him, hanging on to his shoulders, thumping him. Aldo leapt into the room and tackled the man to the floor. He pinned him face down, but struggled to keep him down; the man was strong and very determined.

"Wow! Aldo! Where did you come from?" Natasha exclaimed, absolutely shocked to see him flying to the rescue.

"Help me Natasha, help me…" Aldo pleaded. "Come, help… Natasha!"

Natasha grabbed Heinrich Streuber's struggling, kicking legs and sat on them. Aldo sat on his back. Together, they had him pinned.

Chapter Forty-Nine

"*A*rrivaderci, Signor," Aldo gave him a shove, and Streuber fell feet first down the well, his hands tied securely behind his back.

"He non get out easy," he said to Natasha grinning with a nod. He brushed his hands theatrically to show his job was complete.

"Come, now we to Gabriella!"

Aldo put his arms under Giovanni's shoulders and helped him out of the house and into the sunlight. They walked him far enough from the house so as not to hear the angry, echoing cries of Streuber, then settled Giovanni in the shade by the horses across the courtyard. Aldo then went over to the little stone wall and peered down the hill.

"I have them!" he called in Italian, "Gabriella, Natasha is safe now."

"Aldo you are a star!" Gabriella's voice replied, followed by her head appearing from behind the wall. "But where is that man?" she puffed.

"In the well! I put him down the well," he said in Italian, laughing. "He can stay there until the police arrive."

Gabriella ran over to Natasha and gave her a big hug.

"Natasha! You frightened us; you know everyone is looking for you! How did you get here? Are you all right?"

Natasha nodded.

"Oh, I'm so sorry Gabriella. I fell into the river, and Giovanni saved me from drowning. He really saved me, Gabriella. I would have been swept away. He kept me warm

318

and alive, poor man. He's not well, Gabriella, he is so weak, I don't know when he last ate…"

Gabriella hugged Giovanni, then quickly went over to Artamis, and opened the saddlebag. She came back with an apple and a chocolate bar, and handed it to Giovanni. He could hardly lift his hand to take them, and Aldo realized he needed to get to a hospital.

"I take Giovanni in boat to my office and get help," he said, opening the wrapper for him. He broke off a piece of chocolate. Giovanni managed to put it in his mouth.

"Yes, yes, go, Aldo! Take him back," Gabriella said, looking at Giovanni. "I'll get Natasha back home, I've got the horses, don't worry about us. We'll sound the alarm as soon as we're home and let my father know about Giovanni and the man in the well. But hurry…"

The girls helped Aldo lift Giovanni over Aldo's shoulders, and he carried him towards the steps.

"I see you later Natasha? Gabriella?" he called, turning to them before he disappeared over the wall.

"Definitely!" Natasha said. "And Aldo, thank you for everything!"

"*Da niente*," his voice called back from behind the wall.

The girls were left alone, and Natasha thanked Gabriella profusely for coming to her rescue.

"I feel so stupid. I don't know what I would have done if Giovanni hadn't rescued me. I think I would have drowned, Gabriella. It was so frightening. I blacked out and thought I had died. I don't know how he saved me. The last thing I remember was this thing that was tuck in the bank and it stopped me flowing on down river. I don't know what it was."

"That was so lucky!"

"Yes, and then you and Aldo coming to my rescue here! Thank you so, so much Gabriella! Poor Giovanni, he is so weak. You saved us both. "

"It was all Aldo, you know, I did nothing!"

"I know, but you came to my rescue too, Gabriella. You are here, and that's what matters!"

Gabriella shrugged. "Sisters," she said, handing Natasha the apple.

Natasha took a bite and passed it back to Gabriella to share.

"So how was the party after I left?"

"Oh Natasha! Of course! You do not know!"

"What? What don't I know?"

"There was a terrible fight between the two men..."

"What two men?"

"Natasha you missed everything! Alex and Lorenzo are heroes! It is even in the morning paper! Our brothers fought like warriors and apprehended these two imposters! Remember those men we saw at the top of the tower in Pisa?"

"Yes, this is one of them, isn't it?"

"Yes, the other two were impostors at the party, dressed as catering staff. They had managed to get into the grounds, and had tied the real caterers behind the marquee!"

"I don't believe it! I knew there was something. Remember our worries in Pisa? Remember I thought I saw someone watching us? And remember Yanni's fears? He was right!"

"I know. My grandmother thinks they are art thieves, and there even seems to be a link between them and Giovanni, though my grandmother hasn't mentioned that. Can you believe it? They were armed with a gun and our brothers jumped them and stopped their plot to steal paintings, or information, or Giovanni... I am not quite sure. Anyway, this man that Aldo caught here, is the third one of the three."

"Oh my God. It is all beginning to make sense. Listen to this! He had a letter, and he read it out to Giovanni before Aldo came to our rescue. It is apparently from Giovanni's old friend from ages ago, when they were both here during the war. A man called Otto. It was all about those men in the boat; remember the story? The ones who were shot with their boots stuffed with money?"

"I don't quite understand. So what is the connection, exactly?"

"Well, one of the men found by the boat in the river was apparently the grandfather to these three men. Their grandfather, who was based at your house during the war, was in the process of hiding your family's art and other valuables when he was killed on the river. Now it seems that these three brothers have returned to find the hoard, and this one, is really determined to get it. And he almost did, until Aldo stopped him! Gabriella, I have to tell you, the basement is stuffed with all the missing art and valuables that I presume are from your house!"

"Oh Goodness!"

"And I think Giovanni knew about it! It's all kind of creepy, isn't it?"

"Really. How odd. To think this was all going on in and around my house. I don't like to think of it. So that's why these men wanted the *Soldbuch*. Whoever it was in the *Soldbuch* would know where the valuables were hidden. Natasha, you don't think Giovanni had anything to do with those deaths on the river, do you?"

"No. Of course not. Well, I hope not. But who knows, it was wartime. People sometimes do anything to save their own lives."

"But if Giovanni knew about the art and where it was hidden, why wouldn't he say something, instead of keeping quiet all these years? My grandmother would have understood, she would have loved him for letting her know."

Natasha thought about it.

"Are you sure? I mean, look at it through his eyes. Wouldn't it look as if he had been involved? And your grandmother as well! Perhaps he was protecting her! Remember, Gabriella how she hinted to us that she helped him change his identity to help him have a new start in life?

She was still a bit cagey about telling us, wasn't she? Perhaps Giovanni had to keep quiet about the stolen artwork in order to protect your grandmother! Ever thought of that? She would have been shot, wouldn't she, for helping the enemy? He was a German soldier, remember, so your family, too, would most likely have been rounded up and shot. Wow, Gabriella, you wouldn't even be here today! Oh my God, I think Giovanni saved your whole family by keeping quiet!"

Gabriella looked at Natasha.

"Poor, dear Giovanni. The weight he has carried on his shoulders all these years, and for it to all come to a head now, as an old man. We have to help him, and reassure him. We have to tell Grandmother!"

"Gabriella, so… where was Yanni all that time, I mean, when this fight was going on at the party last night. Did he fight those two men with Lorenzo and Alex, or was he dancing?"

"Natasha, I'm sorry, I didn't see him, that's not to say he wasn't there, but I wasn't really checking on him."

"It's OK, the fact that he's not here, and Aldo was, says heaps about him. I guess I am just a stupid teenager, too young to know the 'leave me alone' signs. Maybe because I liked him I presumed he liked me. I can never face him again. I'm so embarrassed."

She stood up, sighing at the thought of what she had done.

"Come on, let's make a move. Are you sure you know how to get back? I suppose I have to face the music sooner or later."

"Of course I do," Gabriella said. "It wont take too long."

The girls untied the horses, and Natasha put her foot in the stirrup and effortlessly swung her leg over Lily, resolved to facing humiliation and embarrassment upon her return to the house. She would have to face Alex, her mother the Contessa; everyone. And she hoped she wouldn't ever have to face Yanni again.

"Ready? Lead the way home, Gabriella, let's get it over with."

"Don't worry about it Natasha. You are only human! I just want to get out of here before that man gets out of the well!" Gabriella laughed.

"He's not going anywhere until they come for him, his hands are tied tight." Natasha said.

"Natasha," Gabriella said as they set off across the courtyard, "Aldo is nice too, he likes you..."

Natasha shook her head dismissively.

"Na, sorry, Gabriella; he's Italian. He likes every girl."

CHAPTER FIFTY

G abriella led the way a couple of paces in front of Natasha. As they rode past the vast front doors of the old house, Natasha was glad that Streuber was finally out of the way in the dry well and unable to do anything. None the less, she quickened Lily's pace to be closer to Gabriella and Artamis.

"You don't think he'll get out, do you, before the police get here, Gabriella?"

Before Gabriella could answer, she saw Streuber run from the shadows of the house. He grabbed both horses' reins, taking both girls completely by surprise. He was red faced, hot and very angry.

"And don't you dare think of running, young lady!" he shouted at Gabriella as she instinctively slid off the saddle the opposite side of him.

"I have Natasha!" he shouted, grabbing Natasha's leg and trying to pull her down from the saddle.

"This is better than before; two girls, two horses!" he said. "This time, there will be no escape, my dear. Now get down off that horse or I will drag you off!" he shouted at Natasha. "You will now both help me load up the boat, and fast!"

Before Gabriella could inform him that his boat was gone, as if from nowhere, Streuber was pounced upon from behind and pinned to the ground with a heavy thud. It was Yanni. Streuber, winded and hurt, lay pinned to the ground in a daze with Yanni saddled on top of him.

"Find some rope, hurry!" Yanni shouted out to the girls, who stood there, utterly stunned. "Come on! Quickly! Rope!"

They ran to the tower, and came back with rope and a sack. Yanni tied Streuber tight, covered the sack over his head and tied it round his shoulders. He then with help from the girls, threw the man over Natasha's horse, and tied him securely to the saddle, just like they did in cowboy films.

"Yanni! Where did you come from?" Gabriella laughed.

"Ha! The river, and then, well, over there!" he said, rubbing his knee. "I saw the empty boat when I was searching for Natasha along the riverbank, it was stuck further down river on a sandbank. An empty motorboat, stuck in a bank means only one thing; trouble upstream! So I pulled it free, took it back upstream, and on my way I saw another boat in the reeds tied to the bank, near a boathouse. It looked as if someone had attempted to hide it, so I parked the boat, climbed up the hill and found steps leading to this house. I then saw you sitting in the shade; I was about to come over, when I saw him from the corner of my eye. He was hiding in the doorway."

He checked the ropes around Streuber's legs as he spoke.

"Ha! It is the man from the tower, I thought to myself! The same man who was with the other two men at the restaurant in Pisa, discussing your house! Ha! I thought. He is up to no good. So I crept round the side of the house and came in the back door... well, the door is not there anymore, but after this and that, here we are!"

Natasha said nothing, and looked away. An overwhelming feeling of love and admiration for him came over her, combined with total embarrassment. She wanted so much to hug him, and at the same time she wanted to run. She turned red.

"I would say," Yanni continued, "if it hadn't been for Natasha leading us here, we might never have prevented this man from taking these wonderful family treasures. There is quite a hoard, you know, have you seen what is stacked in there?"

They were about to answer him, when a voice called from the steps.

"Gabriella! Natasha!"

It was Lorenzo and Marcello.

"Father!" Gabriella called. She rushed over to greet him as he jumped over the little wall by the steps.

"Are you both all right? My darling girl, you found Natasha before we did, Gabriella! We just passed Aldo on the river, with dear Giovanni. I am so glad he is found. Aldo briefly told us what happened here. Unbelievable!"

He looked at the lump straddled across Lily's back.

"*O Dio.* Are you both OK? This is he? According to Aldo, he was supposed to be down a well."

"Well he was," Gabriella said, "but he got out. Yes, we are fine, Father. Natasha is OK, too. But in the short time since Aldo left, things just changed a little! Thank goodness for Yanni!"

"Ah! Well, the *Carabinieri* are here, too. They were just tying their boat up, after we arrived. They will take care of him form now on."

"Is my mother here?" Natasha asked, seeing Gabriella getting a hug from Marcello and Lorenzo.

"She is at home, by the phone, going crazy, waiting. I will try to call her from up here and tell her the good news. *O Dio*, Natasha, thank God you are safe. Are you all right?"

Marcello walked over to Natasha and threw his arms around her, hugging her as he had his own daughter.

She felt safe, and she hugged him back.

Chapter Fifty-One

"We're back, we're back!" Gabriella called. "I have her! I have Natasha!"

Gabriella slid off Artamis and ran up the steps into the villa. She was greeted by Maria, and Julia, running towards her in the hallway. Darius came bounding out of the bushes and pulled at her shirt in excitement.

"Girls! Darlings! You're back safely! Thank goodness!"

Julia helped Natasha off Lily and hugged her daughter tight. She stepped back to look at her, and was shocked to see the state she was in. Apart form the torn, unrecognisable evening gown, she was filthy, her hair was a matted mess, and she looked very weak and tired.

"Darling, are you all right? I've been beside myself with worry!"

"Yes, a little tired and very hungry. I'm so sorry, Mummy for all the trouble. I slipped into the river in the dark. I didn't mean to. I was trying to come back to the house. I was swept downstream, then Giovanni saved me, then Gabriella saw me up in the tower! It's a long, long story."

"I know, I know, I'm just so glad you are back safe and sound! Marcello and Yanni told us how you found Giovanni, and how he found you! Plus all the missing art and valuables from the villa! You are a heroine, darling! You really are!"

"I'm not, it was Giovanni; he saved me. I didn't do anything."

"Oh *Dio*, but you are both safe," Maria said, "and this is the only important thing. Come now into the kitchen and eat some of my delicious soup. Piero will take care of the horses."

"It sounds to me that perhaps you and Giovanni saved each other's lives." Julia said.

"Kind of," Natasha said. "I hope Giovanni will be OK. Where's Alex?" she asked.

"He went to Piacenza with the Contessa to see her doctor. He has a bit of a black eye, but he's doing fine. The Contessa is taking care of him. The boys were in the papers this morning because of their bravery! I can't believe it. When you four get together, something always seems to happen! Come on, let's get some food into you and then you can have a shower and rest. You must be exhausted. Come on Gabriella, you must be hungry too. Rescuing people on horseback is a hungry business!"

"Poor Alex. Hope he is OK. I missed him," Natasha said.

"He has had a rough time so far on the whole, with the bump on his forehead and now the black eye. He was worried about you."

"Is Lorenzo with Father?" Gabriella asked.

"Yes, Marcello and Lorenzo took Giovanni to the hospital by ambulance. They'll be little while. Now that you two are safely home, I must phone him to let him know."

"Where's Yanni?" Natasha asked, hoping he had gone, too.

"You've just missed him. He came back with them in the boat, a while ago. He waited for the ambulance then, walked into the village for something. He wants to see you, Natasha, in private, when you have rested and eaten. I told him maybe this evening would be a good time."

Natasha looked at her mother, horrified.

"Mum! I really can't face him!"

"Come on, yes you can. It's all right. Lets get you fed and rested."

Marcello closed the ambulance door behind him, and settled himself next to Giovanni for the journey to the hospital. He looked at the thin, frail man lying there, and as the paramedic inserted the intravenous drip into his hand, he couldn't help remembering how, as a young boy, without siblings to play with, he had always had Giovanni to fall back on for company. Giovanni had always tried to make his childhood interesting when he was alone and needed something to do. As an only child, living on a vast estate outside a small village, he was sometimes lonely, and left to his own devices. He remembered how Giovanni had always been there for him, often creating exciting games for him, often playing along with him. Marcello remembered how he had set up trails for him to follow, with clues, maps, and arrows made of broken twigs on the ground, pointing the way to find the next clues. Sometimes, he had tied pieces of cotton to branches, just like the Victorian explorers did so they didn't get lost in the thick jungles of Africa. The memories all came flooding back to him. Marcello had loved these trail games. He imagined himself as an explorer, or treasure hunter, and he often found ancient coins and artefacts along the river, having been led down there by Giovanni's clues. Giovanni had even built the tree house for him, where Marcello had spent days on end reading books on ancient battles and warriors and kings.

Now, as the old man lay there looking like he was on his deathbed, Marcello didn't think he had ever thanked him for all his time and the fun he had given him during his childhood. He reflected how the gardener had always been there for him, even when his own parents had not.

Marcello's eyes became moist, and Lorenzo noticed.

"Are you OK, Father?"

"He is a good man, Lorenzo," he said quietly. "A good man. He has always been loyal and at my side, even when I didn't realize it."

He held the old gardener's hand as he slept, feeling terrible that Giovanni had had to live with this internal torment, this secret that he couldn't divulge to anyone. Marcello felt a tremendous guilt for not realizing what he must have been going through. He just never imagined the valuables taken from his home at the end of the war would be so close at hand, let alone have any connection with Giovanni.

As the steep road wound its way down the other side of the valley towards Piacenza, Giovanni half opened his eyes, and gently squeezed Marcello's hand.

"Signor..." he whispered, looking up at him. "Many things I must say to you..."

"Shh, Giovanni, don't speak. It's all right, it's all right old friend, you must rest," Marcello pleaded.

"Many times I made a you a map, to lead you to the paintings, to the Montesonnellino treasures... but you never found them... I left a trail to the boathouse, to the steps, many times when you were thirteen, fourteen, but you never came home with the news that you had found the paintings..."

Marcello looked at him stunned, then at his son.

"You did? Yes! I do remember going down there, following a couple of your trails. Yes, I did, but I was so excited to find an spearhead or a coin or an old belt buckle, I didn't think of looking further. It hadn't crossed my mind to look for the stolen art... I didn't think... you mean you tried to show me?"

"I tried for many, many years for you to find these things. I did not know how else to do this... I once cleared the doorway in the old boathouse for you to go up to old house on the hill, but you didn't follow the clues... I drew a map, with steps, with the house, you remember?"

"I'm sorry, I don't..."

"Yes, yes, is still in your trunk in your old room... you remember!" he interrupted.

Giovanni's breathing became very strained, and the paramedic took his pulse and indicated to Marcello that he should let him rest. Marcello sat back against and watched as the old, tormented man drifted off to sleep.

"Poor Giovanni, it must have been always on his mind, always," Marcello said. "He must have never been able to rest with this burden he carried throughout his life, yet he wasn't ever able to say anything, lest it would damage your grandmother's reputation."

"Really?" Lorenzo was surprised.

"Yes! Who knows how people would have reacted for helping the enemy. Even after the war."

"Not well, I am sure," Lorenzo said. "What happens next, Father?"

"Well, I have to think. Now that the family paintings and valuables are recovered, and the art thieves taken care of, and most importantly, Natasha is home safely, all thanks to Giovanni, I'm not sure. But I will take care of this man, Lorenzo. I need to make sure Giovanni knows how much I appreciate everything he has done, how much I appreciate him carrying this weight on his shoulders to protect our family name. I want to make it up to him somehow."

CHAPTER FIFTY-TWO

It was early evening, and Natasha, showered, fed and rested, waited on the veranda for Yanni and the dreaded meeting. She heard his approaching footsteps on the tiles, but couldn't look up.

"Natasha, thank you for coming down," he said, as he sat next to her on the sofa. "I hope you are rested after your terrible ordeal. But I need to talk to you. Thank you for meeting with me this evening."

He placed a bunch of white flowers across her lap.

She was shocked, looked down at them. She thanked him, but still couldn't look at him. She was too nervous. She didn't know what was coming. Both Gabriella and her mother said that having a chat with him about the whole thing that had caused her to run, would be the more mature thing to do, to clear the air, rather than simply hide from him in her room, which she wanted to do. So here she was, alone on the sofa with Yanni, the love of her life, but for the most horrible reasons.

"I went into the village to get them. They are to say sorry, Natasha. Because I am, very sorry."

"Thank you, they're pretty," she managed to mumble. "But there's nothing to apologise for."

She noticed he was a little nervous too, which was unlike him. She wasn't sure what more he had to say. She cringed at the thought of it.

"You've been through hell and it is my fault, entirely," he said, after a long pause in a rather soft, gentle tone.

"Natasha, I am so sorry if I gave you the wrong impression by befriending you last Easter on the dig."

She shook her head. She wanted to be swallowed up whole right there and then on the veranda.

He shuffled on the sofa and leant forward, leaning on his knees, his dark brown, wavy hair falling forward hiding part of his face. He stared at the iced water on the coffee table, then grabbed it and poured a glass for himself. He took a gulp.

"I understand that you are fond of me Natasha. I am aware of your feelings towards me; well, I certainly am now, anyway. I am flattered. You know I am very fond of you too. But not in that way, you understand. You know the age gap is too great, don't you?"

She nodded.

"You are very pretty, and there will be boys more your age lining up to go out with you in a year or two."

Natasha groaned inwardly.

"Who knows, when you are old enough, perhaps I might be one of them!

"Really?"

She looked up at him, surprised.

He shrugged. "Maybe. As we get older, the age gap narrows. Four or five years' difference is nothing when you are older. I like you a lot, Natasha. We have much in common."

"Oh. We do?"

She wasn't expecting that, either.

"But I am not saying we must wait for each other," he quickly clarified. "I am starting my degree in London in September and I will meet many people, and make friends, you know."

"Girlfriends, you mean."

"Well, yes, probably. Hopefully, girlfriends. Just as you will meet boys, too, and go out with them. I'm just saying Natasha, that I like you, and had you been older, sure, we could have been... you know, there might have been a chance of something. But you mustn't wait in vein for me. We must continue our lives. If something happens in the future, it is meant to be. If not, it wasn't meant to be. Do you know what I am saying?"

She wasn't sure, in fact she was confused, but she nodded.

"Great!" He slapped his knees, finished his glass of water and stood up.

"Now, I have to get packing. I am off to Pisa again to continue the excavation. I hope you come down again to see the ships before you go back to London. I would love you to be there when we uncover the next hull. We already know where it is! It is perpendicular to the one with the sailor and the dog, but six feet deeper! Ha! Remember that one with the sailor? I am excavating the rest of the hull next week. I can't wait to get started on the next one. It's got to be older than the one on top! Exciting, no?"

She nodded and forced a smile.

"Great!" he said. "So I will see you in Pisa next week then?"

He raised his hand to high five her. She obliged and smiled.

"OK," she said. "I'd like to see the new hull. I'd like to see Pisa without being afaraid of being followed."

"Thanks to you, Natasha, there will definitely be no art thieves following us or provoking a fight on the tower! Ha! See you later!"

He left the veranda through the French doors, and she sat there trying to work out what had just happened. As soon as he had gone, Gabriella appeared from around the corner.

"Well? What did he say?"

"To be honest, Gabriella, I'm not entirely sure."

CHAPTER FIFTY-THREE

Three months later, Marcello was standing in front of an audience of five hundred in the lecture hall of the Museum of Natural History in Milan. In the audience, there was a delegation of international art restorers; men and women from all over the world who had spent their lives dedicated to preserving and saving wonderful works of art that had been lost, neglected and damaged. There were also art historians, a representative from the fraud squad from Scotland Yard in London, and the directors of all the major auction houses of the world. In addition to these professionals, there was, as always on occasions such as these, the press, and major international media coverage.

Giving seminars was nothing out of the ordinary for Marcello. Public speaking was a part of his life. In fact, he had only two weeks earlier returned from London and Philadelphia, where he was updating the world on the on going Pisan sunken ships project.

But this gathering was different. This one was very personal to him; it was a subject very close to his heart. Because of this, there were some very special people in the audience, including his close family and friends, Maria and Piero, Aldo and his father, and another very special person, his trusted and beloved gardener, Giovanni.

As briefly as he could, Marcello started to tell the story of a young German soldier who had been stationed in the Trebbia Valley. At the end of the war he had risked everything to stay behind for the love of a local Italian girl.

"At the end of the war, he had hidden himself at the back of an old boathouse on the banks of the Trebbia River for weeks on end, half freezing to death at night, and living in fear during the day, having given up his past life and his true identity. Our younger generation today perhaps does not quite understand the implications of his situation. Were he to be found by his fellow German officers, they would have shot him for desertion. Were he to be found by our loyal Italian partisans, they would have shot him for being the enemy. But he was saved from his hopeless predicament with the help of a benefactor, who shall remain anonymous. He was given safe refuge and the chance of a new a beginning. He was able to come out of hiding with a new identity and to be with the young Italian girl for whom he had risked everything. He was now able to marry her in a private chapel, away from of the eyes of the world.

"He lived a simple life, very much under the radar, so to speak, but always with the constant worry of his past catching up with him. His past was not altogether bad; he was simply a boy who was born on the 'wrong' side of a line of the map, which dictated that he fight on the 'wrong' side in the war. But there was another layer of weight on his shoulders that even his benefactor could not know, for while in hiding in the damp, smelly boathouse, he had inadvertently stumbled across a secret hoard of valuable art, ironically stolen by the same officers from the same, private home, where he had been serving during the Nazi occupation. The hoard of stolen art was stashed away under his nose, for the purpose of being collected and transported back to Germany after the war.

"But he could never divulge this, lest he betrayed his kind benefactor who had risked her life by offering him a safe haven. Police interviews and investigation would surely have exposed both him and his benefactor. Exposing his Nazi identity would have had terrible consequences for them both, despite him being a young boy not even out of his teens. So this young man, from the age of nineteen, had had to carry this burden of knowing where the art was hidden, all his life."

Marcello took a sip of water.

"Before we judge our enemy, we must remember one thing; a child cannot help which side of a border he is born, any more than he has a choice as to which uniform he wears in war. We are all human. We are all the same flesh and blood. I am very happy to say that after so many years after the war, it is safe for this humble man to come out of hiding without fearing any consequences.

"So this new wing of the gallery is dedicated to this gentle man. His story is not so much of bravery, but of self-sacrifice. He paid the consequences of falling in love and acting upon his youthful impulse. I have the honour of dedicating this new wing of the National Art Gallery to this man."

There was a hush from the audience, then, slowly, one by one, people started to clap, until there was a standing ovation.

"Please, please," Marcello tried to quieten the audience. He indicated to Julia to help Giovanni up onto the stage.

"I have a surprise for you all," he continued. "The man to whom I am so grateful, who saved my family's art collection, and the life of my daughter-to-be, I might add, which is another story, is here tonight. Please, Giovanni, please come and stand with me."

Marcello leant forward and helped the frail, old man onto the stage.

"Ladies and gentlemen, the unsung hero, Giovanni, or more correctly, Johann Fuchs."

The applause was tremendous, and it led to a standing ovation. Marcello struggled to hold back the tears, and he looked at Julia and smiled. He had honoured his old gardener in the most lasting, fitting way he could think of.

A very bewildered Giovanni smiled and bowed a few times at the audience, and then Marcello led him a few feet to the back of the stage, where the mayors of Piacenza and Milan were waiting to shake his hand. The director of the Chamber of Commerce put a pair of scissors in his hand, and Giovanni cut the red cord. The heavy curtains behind them separated with a swoosh, revealing the grand entrance to the new wing of the building, *The Johann Fuchs Gallery*, which contained a fantastic collection of recovered, stolen art from all around the world.

The audience clapped and the cameras flashed, and for the first time since Maria had known her father, Giovanni looked proud and confident. He smiled and looked on in awe at the gallery named after him.

Marcello went on to explain the origin of the collection. It was a compilation of recovered art and antiquities stolen by the Nazis form all over Europe that had now been donated or leant by private collections or galleries. Some pieces in the collection had been found stashed away in tunnels beneath the Alps, while other pieces from Zurich, New York and London had been identified in art galleries, whose art experts had been unaware of the shady provenance of their pieces. Marcello's new wing included his own sixteen paintings stolen from his own home, including the Canaletto, which would remain in situ as a permanent exhibit.

Gabriella, who was sitting between her grandmother and Natasha, whispered to Natasha. "My grandmother wants me to say, thank you!"

"What for?"

Natasha leant forward and looked at the Contessa, wondering what she had meant.

"For being so young at heart," the Contessa whispered to her. "For having feelings for the young Pole, and therefore for saving Giovanni, and my family paintings. Why else, my dear? You are very a large part of why we are here today, and one must not forget it."

"Oh... you're welcome," Natasha said, hesitantly. So are you, she thought, a very large part of why we are all here today.

"And that young Pole," The Contessa continued, leaning across Gabriella towards Natasha again, "the person who I believe was the cause of all this commotion on the river, is apparently coming back to stay at the villa for a week. I believe he is coming with a special guest. He is coming with ...what is her name?" the Contessa wondered out loud.

She stopped and waited a minute while her son spoke a little more on the stage.

Meanwhile, Natasha's heart had sunk to new depths. How could he? She had that old feeling return in her the pit of her stomach, the one that felt like she had been kicked in the gut. She felt like running again.

"He is bringing his girlfriend?" Gabriella prompted her grandmother to contunue, incredulous at Yanni's tact, or lack of it.

"Oh no, my dear, I don't believe that girl and he have anything in common at all, except their beauty, of course. No, no, his mother... I forget his mother's name... Mrs. Janowski, or something like that, I believe, is coming from Krakow. Marcello invited them both to stay. And she is bringing a friend of hers, an old gentleman who used to be a friend of her husband, would you believe. Very odd, I might say. Anyway, I will be leaving next week for Capri for a month, just as they arrive, so I will miss them all. However, I have instructed Piero and Maria to look after everyone. Their stay will be a comfortable one."

Natasha was dumbfounded. Yanni, his mother and the old man who tried to court her were coming to stay?

"They're coming here? Next week?" Natasha asked Gabriella.

She shrugged. She had no idea either.

"My father is talking, shh... listen!" Lorenzo hissed at them. They turned their attention back to the stage, but Natasha's mind was far away.

"...And what ultimately saved her from being swept away down the river," Marcello was saying, "was this..."

He looked at Alex and Lorenzo in the audience.

"Boys, would you do me the honours of coming up here for a minute to help?"

Alex and Lorenzo looked at each other, not knowing what was coming next. They made their way up onto the stage. Marcello whispered for them to go behind the curtain to fetch something...

"And don't drop it!" he called backstage to them, pulling a face anticipating hearing a crash. The audience laughed.

They returned carrying something very heavy in a long, padded, wooden box. The audience stirred. They placed it at Marcello's feet.

"Thank you boys. This is just incredible," Marcello beamed. He separated the tissue and protective wrapping from the object inside. He then lifted a long, heavy discoloured tusk out of the box.

"All those beautiful, summer evenings I spent walking the banks of the river as a boy, looking for one of these, finding nothing. For years I searched! Then presto! Buried for centuries in the silt and mud below the Trebbia River, this elephant tusk was finally dislodged during the heavy rains we had a few months ago. It was an absolute miracle! To think that Hannibal himself would have touched this tusk and patted the sweet animal it belonged to."

The audience clapped and the cameras flashed.

"It was a miracle. It was lodged in the riverbed in such a position that it stopped Natasha, my soon-to-be stepdaughter, from being swept down river. We could say we owe this amazing evening to this poor elephant, who, centuries ago had made the long, now historical journey with

Hannibal all the way from Spain, through rivers and over mountain ranges, to lose its life, here, in our river in 218 BC at the Battle of Trebbia."

The audience applauded and Marcello waved Natasha up onto the stage to join him. She groaned, then, reluctantly did what was requested of her. She stood next to the boys, and stared for the first time at the long, heavy elephant tusk in their arms.

Gradually, a strong a wave of emotion began to engulf her.

A week after the commotion and drama of the events on the river had died down, a curious Marcello had a hunch one morning. Setting off on a quiet search on his own, he discovered what it was that had lodged itself in the mud below the surface of the river which had stopped Natasha from being swept away. Flabbergasted at the importance of the find, he later managed to pull it out with the help of a very excited Lorenzo and Alex.

However, the whole family was surprised that Natasha didn't want to see the tusk. She couldn't explain it, but she had been shocked and moved when she had heard what it was that had saved her. She just didn't want to see it or have anything to do with it. It was too sad. She wondered if she really had the guts for archaeology, as she always seemed to too become emotionally involved with what was discovered. And this tusk was a prime example.

But now, having listened to Marcello's speech, she looked at it. For the first time she imagined the elephant's immense size and weight as Alex and Lorenzo held its tusk. She owed her life to Giovanni, yes, she thought, but even more so to a poor elephant, an animal that had made that terrible journey 2,000 years ago across the South of France, over rivers and icy mountains, it's padded feet probably bleeding, frostbitten and cut, only to die there on the banks of the River Trebbia in a brutal battle. She felt so sorry for it. Standing next to Lorenzo, she gently reached out and put her hand on the tusk. She felt it, almost connecting with the animal, and thanked the poor elephant from the depths of her heart.

"Sweet, dear elephant," she whispered, "I'm so, so sorry you died. But I thank you for saving me. I think I will forever be in your debt."

She looked at her mother beaming up from the audience at them. Then Natasha looked at her soon to be stepfather. Archaeology was fantastic, and he made it accessible for everyone, with his emotional and amusing speeches; she too loved the ancient history, the discoveries and bringing ancient people back to life, as it were, by putting the pieces together. But, she thought, she wanted to give back somehow, as Marcello was doing to Giovanni. Alex could be the archaeologist, she decided, looking at him as he pretended to almost drop the tusk, making the audience laugh. He would look cool in a floppy, leather hat. But she was going to do something else in life. She decided at that very moment, that she would, if possible, dedicate her future to helping elephants.

She looked at Gabriella and Lorenzo. She grinned.

She felt very lucky to be alive. Things were turning out just fine.

CPSIA information can be obtained at www.ICGtesting.com
Printed in the USA
BVOW03s0100040515

398066BV00001B/1/P